The Murderer's Daughters

The
Murderer's
Daughters

R. S. MEYERS

SPHERE

Published in the United States of America in 2010 by St. Martin's Press
First published in Great Britain in 2010 by Sphere

A CIP catalogue record for this book
is available from the British Library.

ISBN 978-1-84744-317-5

Printed and bound in Australia by Griffin Press

FSC
Mixed Sources
Product group from well-managed
forests and other controlled sources
Cert no. SGS-COC-005088
www.fsc.org
© 1996 Forest Stewardship Council

Sphere
An imprint of
Little, Brown Book Group
100 Victoria Embankment
London EC4Y 0DY

An Hachette UK Company
www.hachette.co.uk

www.littlebrown.co.uk

To my husband, Jeff, who made my dreams come true
To my sister, Jill, who is my other half
And to my daughters, Becca and Sara, who own my heart

Part 1

1

Lulu

July 1971

I wasn't surprised when Mama asked me to save her life. By my first week in kindergarten, I knew she was no macaroni-necklace-wearing kind of mother. Essentially, Mama regarded me as a miniature hand servant:

Grab me a Pepsi, Lulu.

Get the milk for your sister's cereal.

Go to the store and buy me a pack of Winstons.

Then one day she upped the stakes:

Don't let Daddy in the apartment.

The July our family fell apart, my sister was five going on six, and I was turning ten, which in my mother's eyes made me about fifty. Daddy didn't offer much help, even before he left. He had problems of his own. My father wanted things he couldn't have, and he hungered for my mother above all else. Perhaps growing up in the shadow of Coney Island, Brooklyn's fantasy world, explained his weakness for Mama's pinup façade, but I never understood how he missed the rest. Her sugary packaging must have kept him from noticing how much she resented any moment that didn't completely belong to her.

Mama and Daddy's battles were the heartbeat of our house. Still, until the day my mother kicked him out, my father was the perfect example of hope against knowledge. He'd return from work each night looking for supper, a welcome-home kiss, and a cold beer, while Mama considered his homecoming her signal to rail against life.

"How many hours a day do you think I can be alone with them, Joey?" Mama had asked just days before he moved out. She'd pointed at my sister, Merry, and me playing Chutes and Ladders on the tiny Formica table stuck in the corner of our undersize kitchen. We were the best-behaved girls in Brooklyn, girls who knew that disobeying Mama brought a quick smack and hours spent staring at our toes.

"Alone?" Beer fumed off Daddy's lips. "For God's sake, you spend half the day yakking with Teenie and the other half painting your nails. You know we got a stove, right? With knobs and everything?"

Mama's friend Teenie lived downstairs on the first floor with five sons and an evil husband whose giant head resembled an anvil. Teenie's apartment smelled like bleach and freshly ironed cotton. Ironing was Teenie's Valium. Her husband's explosions left her so anxious that she begged Mama for our family's wrinkled laundry. Thanks to Teenie's husband, we slept on crisp sheets and satin-smooth pillowcases.

I dreamed of deliverance from my so-called family, convinced I was the secret child of our handsome mayor, John V. Lindsay, who seemed so smart, and his sweet and refined wife, who I knew would be the sort of mother who'd buy me books instead of Grade B faux Barbie dolls from Woolworth's junky toy section. The Lindsay family had put me in this ugly apartment with peeling paint and Grade C parents to test my worth, and I wouldn't disappoint. Even when Mama screamed right in my face, I kept my voice modulated to a tone meant to please Mrs. Lindsay.

Mama sent us to take a nap that afternoon. The little coffin of a bedroom Merry and I shared steamed hot, hot, hot. Our only relief came when Mama wiped our grimy arms and chests with a washcloth she'd soaked with alcohol and cold water.

Lying in the afternoon heat, impatient for my birthday to arrive the next day, I prayed that Mama had bought the chemistry set I'd been hinting about all month. Last year I'd asked for a set of Britannica encyclopedias and received a Tiny Tears doll. I never wanted a doll, and even if I did, who wanted one that peed on you?

I hoped Mama's recently improved mood might help my cause. Since throwing Daddy out, Mama hardly yelled at us anymore. She barely noticed we existed. When I reminded her it was suppertime, she'd glance away from her movie magazine and say, "Take some money from my purse, and go to Harry's."

We'd walk three blocks to Harry's Coffee Shop and order tuna sandwiches and malteds, vanilla for Merry and chocolate for me. Usually I'd finish first, wrapping my legs around the cold chrome pole under the leather stool and twirling impatiently while I waited. Merry sipped at her malted and nibbled itsy-bitsy bites from her sandwich. I yelled at her to hurry, imitating Grandma Zelda, Daddy's mother. "Move it, Princess Hoo-ha. Who do you think you are, the Queen of England?"

Maybe she did. Maybe Merry's secret mother was Queen Elizabeth.

After Daddy moved out, Mama instituted inexplicable new rules. *Don't open the door for your father and when you visit him at Grandma Zelda's, don't say a word about me. That old bag is just using you for information. And never tell anyone about my friends.*

Men friends visited Mama all the time. I didn't know exactly how to keep from saying anything about them. Not talking about Mama meant being outright rude and disobedient, since seconds after he'd kissed us hello, Daddy's questions started:

How's your mother?

Who comes over to the house?

Does she have new clothes? New records? New color hair?

Even a kid could see Daddy was starving for Mama-news.

I felt a little guilty at how relieved I was by Daddy's absence. Before he left, when he wasn't demanding or, later, outright begging Mama for attention, he'd be staring at her with a big, moony face.

I sometimes wondered why my mother had married Daddy. Because I was too young to do the math and figure out the time between their wedding and my birth, it had never entered my mind that I was the reason, and Mama didn't invite girlie mother-daughter conversation. Mama didn't cotton to anything smacking of introspection. That's probably why she was so close to Teenie. Teenie didn't dip into the deeper meanings of life. She'd spend hours and hours judging Mama's fingernail polish, glancing away from her ironing long enough to pick the tone most flattering to Mama's pale skin as my mother painted one nail after another.

I flipped the page of *The Scarlet Slipper Mystery*, sweat dripping from my arms. Since I could take only six books per visit from the library, I had to time it right, or I'd be stuck on Sundays rereading the five Reader's Digest Condensed Books sitting on our red lacquered living room shelf. Green-bronze statues of fierce-looking Chinese dragons with long, sharp tails bookended the volumes. Symbols of luck, Mama said.

Black onyx boxes in various shapes and sizes with mother-of-pearl inlay covers decorated the living room shelves. They were smooth and cool to the touch. Mama's father brought them back from the war in Japan. Mama's mother, who we called Mimi Rubee, gave Mama the boxes after our grandfather died because Mama demanded them enough to drive Mimi Rubee crazy.

Mama was used to getting what she wanted.

Sun snuck over the walls enclosing our gloomy courtyard and blazed into the bedroom. I flipped and rotated my pillow, squashing it into semi-comfortable lumps, seeking a bit of cool cotton to tuck under my head. Merry, cross-legged on her bed, moved her paper dolls into various constellations. She propped them against the wall, folding down the tabs on first one outfit and then another, moving her lips for the silent plays they acted out for her alone.

Merry was supposed to be taking a nap, and I was supposed to be making sure she did. Merry looked all proud and happy wearing her apple green sunsuit, the one that tied on the top with little yellow ribbons. I hated it because I had to help her pull it all the way down, then tie it back up every time she had to go to the bathroom. Merry loved it because it came from Daddy. Grandma Zelda really picked it out, not Daddy, but I didn't say anything. I didn't want to ruin Merry's good times.

Merry was unusually cute, and I was unusually plain. People stopped us every day, bending down to gush over Merry's black curls or her

Tootsie Pop eyes—the chocolate ones—or to stroke her rosy cheek as though her skin were a fabric they couldn't resist fingering. I felt as though I toted around the Princess of Brooklyn.

Daddy doted on Merry. Aunt Cilla had said that while watching Daddy pop M&M's into Merry's mouth one by one. "Does it ever make you jealous?" she asked my mother. Aunt Cilla, Mama's sister, looked like a puffy blowfish version of my mother.

"Yeah, right. He's a big shot with the five-year-olds," Mama had responded to Aunt Cilla, but really for Daddy's ears.

Merry made Daddy happy. I never did. He'd make a joke or something, and I'd narrow my eyes, wondering if the riddle or knock-knock joke was funny enough to merit a laugh. Then he'd get mad and say, "Jesus, Lulu, do you have to analyze every single thing a person says?"

I switched position on my bed, leaning on the windowsill with my elbows halfway out, trying to catch some breeze. Music from Mrs. Schwartz's stereo blasted through the courtyard. Someone had probably told her to shut it off, which usually made Mrs. Schwartz turn it up. "Raindrops Keep Falling on My Head" played so loud that I missed hearing the first quiet taps on our front door.

"Someone's knocking," Merry said. "I'll get it."

"Stop." I swung my legs to the floor. "Are you nuts? Do you want Mama to kill us? Let me. You're supposed to be sleeping."

Merry jumped back on her bed, landing with her feet tucked under her butt. She was skinny and small for her age. In her green sunsuit, she looked like a grasshopper leaping up.

I tiptoed to the door. Mama used our nap time to take her own nap, her beauty sleep, she called it, and she hated waking before her time. I held a finger to my mouth, letting Merry know to keep quiet. She opened her eyes wide, her Tootsie Pops asking, *Do you think I'm stupid?*

Our bedroom and the front door practically touched. I opened our bedroom door inch by inch, trying to be quiet. The knocking got louder. "Who is it?" I murmured, practically pressing my lips to the edge of the door.

"Open up, Lulu."

I heard my father breathing.

"Come on, Lu. Open it now."

"I'm not supposed to let you in," I whispered, praying Mama wouldn't hear.

"Don't worry, Cocoa Puff. Mama won't get mad. I promise."

My eyes filled a little hearing my pet name. When things had been better, I'd been Cocoa Puff and Merry had been Sugar Pop. He'd call Mama Sugar Smack Pie, because he said that was the sweetest thing of all. Then he'd smack his lips and my mother would throw whatever she was holding at him.

But she'd smile.

"I know you're scared of Mama, but you have to let me in. I'm your father." Daddy lowered his voice to a conspiratorial tone. "It's my name on the lease."

I didn't know what a lease was, but maybe he was right. I opened the door a pinch, leaving the tarnished chain on, and saw a sliver of my father.

He pulled up real close and smiled. His teeth looked cruddy, as if he'd eaten crackers or something without brushing after. He smelled like cigarettes, beer, and something else. Something scary. Something I'd never smelled before.

He put a hand up against the door and leaned in. The chain tightened. "Unbolt it, Lulu."

I backed away, wondering if I should get Mama. I felt Merry behind me. I didn't know if Daddy saw her. I didn't think so. He would have said hello.

"I'll get Mama," I said.

"You don't need your *mama*. Just open the damn door. I have something to give her."

"I'll get her for you."

"Stop being stubborn. Let me in now!"

He rattled the knob, and my heart shook.

"Get back into bed," I whispered to Merry. When she disappeared, I reached up for the latch and chain. He let up on the door so I'd have the slack I needed.

"Thanks, Lu." He touched the mezuzah nailed to the doorjamb, then kissed his fingers. He called it Jewish luck, *the only kind us Jews get*, he'd say.

8

Then he chucked me on the chin. I pulled back from his acrid tobacco touch, wanting to wash my face.

"You're my peach." Daddy walked down the short hall, turning left at the tiny alcove where he'd wedged in a desk for me.

I hung behind, hovering halfway down the hall, and then slipped into the bathroom, cracking the door enough to hear, though I couldn't see.

"Jesus, Joey, you scared me half to death!" My mother sounded nervous. I pictured her holding up the thin sheet she used for her summer naps.

"Miss me, sweetheart?" my father asked.

"Louise, get in here now," Mama yelled.

I didn't move. I didn't say a thing.

"We need to talk." Daddy sounded slurry.

"Get out; you're drunk. I have nothing to say to you." I heard her get up and my father stomp after her. The refrigerator door opened with a sucking sound. A can popped. They were in the kitchen.

"You had plenty to say when you talked my paycheck out of my boss, didn't you, Miss America?" Daddy shouted. "Did you wiggle your ass real hard?"

Something thumped back in my room. Merry scampered down the hall, her bare feet sounding soft and sticky on the linoleum. I wanted to reach out and yank her into the bathroom.

I heard her stop at the couch, the springs squeaking as she jumped. I pictured her balled up, holding her knees and trembling. You could see into the kitchen easy from the couch.

"Someone's got to feed these kids. What am I supposed to do? Manufacture money?" Mama asked.

"I need that money back, Celeste. Now."

My mother mumbled something too low to hear. I opened the bathroom door wider.

"I'm serious; give it, Celeste. Give it."

Daddy's low voice thrummed like a machine. *Give it. Give it. Give it.*

"Get out before I call the cops."

Something scraped.

"Get out!"

"I need it. I need the money, damn it!"

Something slammed.

My sister whimpered. Had she gone in the kitchen? I should get her.

"Shush, quiet, Sugar Pop. It's okay." My father's words blurred together. I pictured him bending down, kissing the top of Merry's head as he always did, wrapping one of her curls around his finger and letting it spring out and back.

"Go to Mama's room, Merry," Mama ordered.

"Yeah, go to Mama's room," my father repeated. Something clattered, as though a whole bunch of stuff fell to the floor. "Bourbon, Celeste? You buying them booze on my money?"

He sounded like he was crying. I slid against the wall and inched toward them.

"Go to your mother's." Mama sounded more mad than scared now. "Get sober."

"You think I give you money to buy liquor for your boyfriends?"

Daddy's voice had changed again. The teary voice had disappeared. Now he sounded big. Like a wolf. A bear. Heavy banging started. I pictured him slamming and slamming and slamming cabinet doors. Metal screeched, cracking like hinges ripping out of their sockets.

GIVE THE MONEY, MAMA!

"Lulu," Mama screamed. "He's got a knife. He's going to kill me. Get Teenie!"

What if Teenie wasn't home?

No, Teenie never went out.

What should I say?

I stayed frozen in the hall for what felt like my whole life listening to Mama and Daddy yell. Then I ran down the pitted stairs to Teenie's apartment. I pounded my fists on her door over the sound of her television. I banged so loud I expected the entire building to come down. Finally, her youngest son opened the door. I flew inside and found Teenie in the living room watching *Let's Make a Deal* and ironing her husband's boxer shorts.

"My father has a knife," I said.

"Watch the boys," Teenie called to her oldest son as she unplugged the iron without even turning it off.

As we ran out of the apartment, Teenie yelled, "Stay here, boys. Don't move an inch!"

We raced up the stairs. I wondered if I should get someone else to go with Teenie and me. Mr. Ford, maybe. He lived alone. He was a bachelor. Old. However, he was a man, even though my father called him a fruit.

No, we didn't need anybody else. My father liked Teenie. He'd listen to her. She'd make him calm down.

We ran into our apartment, me right behind Teenie as she skidded through the living room and into the kitchen. Wide-open cabinets from where my father had slammed the doors open and shut showed our turquoise and white dishes. A broken door swayed back and forth in the strong, humid breeze blowing the curtains.

Mama lay on the floor. Blood dripped on the green and brown linoleum. Teenie fell to her knees, grabbed the edge of her wide cotton apron, and held it over the place on my mother's chest where the blood pumped out the fastest.

Teenie looked up at me. "Call the operator." Her voice cracked. "Tell them to send an ambulance. Police."

I stared down at Mama. *Don't die.*

"Go, Lulu!"

I ran into my mother's room. The phone was next to the bed. Pink. A Princess phone. Merry lay on top of my mother's pink and gray bedspread. Mama would scream her head off when she saw how blood had spread everywhere. The cute green sunsuit that made Merry into a little grasshopper was slashed down the middle, but the bows I liked to make with the yellow ties had stayed perfectly in place.

My father was beside Merry. Blood leaked from his wrists.

"Did you call?" Teenie yelled from the kitchen.

I picked the phone up from the night table, careful not to jar Mama's bed, knowing she wouldn't like it if I did.

2

Lulu

My grandmother Mimi Rubee sat at the table sipping black coffee and eating melba toast with cottage cheese. This was her breakfast and lunch. She was in charge of us now. Mama's funeral had been over a week ago, on my birthday, though no one said anything at all about that.

I'd made myself a butter and orange marmalade sandwich, the only food in the house that I understood what to do with.

Every day since the funeral, I'd asked Mimi Rubee to take me to the hospital to see Merry, and every day she'd said no. I couldn't breathe right, picturing my tiny sister all alone in some giant white building.

"Can we go today? To the hospital?" I asked between bites of my sandwich.

"Please, I can't take any more heartache today." She took a loud sip of coffee as if this proved her point. "I promise you, the nurses take good care of her. I saw."

"When then?"

"Soon. Maybe Aunt Cilla can take you tomorrow."

"Aunt Cilla won't go," I said. Besides, I didn't want to go with Aunt Cilla. Difficult things became unbearable with my mother's sister.

"She'll go, she'll go." Mimi Rubee gave a long, wet sigh.

"But Merry's alone," I pleaded. "She's scared."

"She spends most of the day sleeping."

"Please, Mimi Rubee, please take me to see her."

"Enough already!" Mimi Rubee wet a paper napkin in her water glass and dabbed at the crumbs around my plate. "Your sister's fine. I told you a million times. Now stop. Can't you see you've given me a migraine?" She rubbed small circles on her temples.

I ignored the warning signs of what was to come—my grandmother's rising voice, the compulsive crumb catching, the temple rubbing. Her savage scrubbing of the table. "Merry shouldn't be alone," I said.

"*Enough! He* did this to her!" Mimi Rubee clutched her dyed red hair as though she was going to start yanking strands right out. "A monster, that's what he is, your father. A monster!" She banged the table so hard that my bread jumped, and her coffee sloshed over.

Mimi Rubee hadn't let me go to my mother's funeral. I'd stayed with Grandma Zelda, Daddy's mother. We'd watched hours of television, one show melting into another, neither Grandma Zelda nor I bothering to change channels. We just stared at whatever shows came on while Merry lay all alone in Coney Island Hospital, my father rotted in jail just like everyone kept saying, and Mimi Rubee buried my mother in the ground. I imagined Mimi Rubee screaming so hard at the funeral she could almost have woken up Mama.

Mama used to call Mimi Rubee a real Sarah Bernhardt, who was apparently some old-time actress. Some afternoons, Mama would sip a cup of Sanka with brandy and reminisce about the fits Mimi Rubee threw when she and Daddy started dating. Mama did a great job mimicking Mimi Rubee's phony cultured accent, enunciating each word as she did her imitation: "You're too young, too beautiful, and too thin, for God's sake. Don't throw yourself away. You'll never be this slender again."

Mama always finished the story by grabbing at the nonexistent fat on her thighs, giving a sad chuckle, and saying, "Remember, Lulu, in the end, mothers are always right. No one else tells you the truth."

After her crying fit, Mimi Rubee headed for one of her headache-driven afternoon naps. She went into her room, closed the blinds, and climbed into bed. She called out for me to bring the special white enamel bowl with the chips all around the edge. The bowl was in case she vomited. Then I brought her a cold washcloth for her forehead, making sure it wasn't drippy.

Once I'd done this and cool air blew from the metal fan I'd dragged to her bed, she sighed and gave me a weak half smile. With a few tears wetting her lashes, Mimi Rubee declared me her little soldier. "You're always so good. That's why your mother loved you."

Mimi Rubee's migraine pill took hold, her breathing got heavier, and she fell into a noisy sleep. I tiptoed out and closed the door behind me. I grabbed my shoes from under the sofa, a plank of teak similar to the rest of the furnishings in the apartment. After Grandpa died, Mimi Rubee had stripped away the dark Victorian furniture and dense Oriental rugs he'd loved and, declaring her desire to be up-to-date, bought Danish Modern and fluffy rugs with sunsets woven in them. I slept on the knuckle-hard sofa and woke up most mornings cramped in a knot. Mimi Rubee promised me she'd buy a Castro Convertible when Merry got out of the hospital.

As Mimi Rubee napped, I got out the phone book and copied the address for Coney Island Hospital. The hospital was on Ocean Parkway, the same street as our apartment, but Ocean Parkway went all the way from one side of Brooklyn to the other. The hospital was way down near the boardwalk where Grandma Zelda and Daddy lived before in a tiny bungalow near the water. Someone tore the bungalow down years ago, but I had seen it in pictures.

I wrote "Went for a walk" on a note for Mimi Rubee and left it on the kitchen table. After slipping a dollar from Mimi's wallet, I put on my sneakers and left.

Unsure of which bus to take, I walked up McDonald Avenue to Ocean Parkway. I looked around for a bus stop. I wanted to get away fast, before Mimi Rubee woke up and came looking for me. Finally, I turned in the direction of Coney Island and the ocean and began walking.

Hazy white sun heated my bare shoulders. My wrinkled shirt felt sweaty

14

and bunched up where the shirttails tucked into my too-short jeans. Who-ever had gone into our apartment to put together my clothes and other stuff had chosen random things that made no sense at all. Instead of the locket my mother had given me when I turned eight, stray Monopoly pieces were crammed into my ballerina jewelry box. Galoshes rested on top of my bathing suit. Each day I rummaged through the strangely packed paper bags crowding Mimi Rubee's closet.

Today, I'd searched for something to take to Merry—the tiny stuffed moose we'd named Bullwinkle, the frog puppet she slept with—but only crumpled clothes and jigsaw puzzles we never played with were stuffed in the bags.

Even with my hair pulled up into a ponytail, a sticky dampness envel-oped me as I walked block after never-ending block. Merry and I got red rashes in the heat. My mother called it prickly heat and dusted our necks with Cashmere Bouquet. She'd shake the powder from the pink can and rub it on us until the sweet-scented dust filled our nostrils.

I finally saw the huge white hospital rising in the distance and sighed with relief. I felt like I'd been walking an entire day. Before going on, I stopped at a familiar-seeming corner candy store. Like at Greenburg's—where I'd bought Mama's cigarettes—newspapers, school supplies, and magazines crowded the shelves, but this place looked a lot more run-down than Greenburg's.

In the back, I found a shelf of dusty toys. I picked through the selec-tion, looking for something that might comfort Merry. A stuffed tiger was cheap, but his mouth was mean, his filling seemed made of crumpled pa-per, and he looked hungry enough to eat a little girl. An old-fashioned doll with brown ringlets had eyelids that clicked as they blinked. She wore a pink dotted dress. Merry would love her. She'd name her something like Mitzi or Suzi. Merry loved names with z and i, but Mitzi-Suzi was marked one dollar.

I picked through water guns, paddleballs, and packages of jacks. Finally, behind some old Halloween masks, I found a tiny wooden cradle no bigger than a fat man's thumb. Inside was a minute pink baby doll covered by a miniature yellow blanket. After searching for a price sticker, I picked it up and carried it to the old woman at the cash register. "How much?" I asked.

She squinted at the doll lying in the cradle, then at me. I closed my hand around the worn bill in my pocket. Despite the heat, the woman wore an old gray cardigan. It looked like a sweater a grandpa would wear, all pilled and stretched.

"Fifty cents."

I nodded and put a Zagnut bar, a pack of Juicy Fruit gum, and a roll of cherry Life Savers, Merry's favorites, next to the doll. I put my dollar beside it. The lady snatched it, handed me back a dime, and returned to her *Daily News.*

"Could I please have a bag?"

"A bag?" she asked as though I'd requested free candy for life.

A vibrating thrum ran through my throat. I wanted to throw the doll and candy at her. "A bag," I said. "I need a bag."

The woman drew a thin brown bag from underneath the counter. She stuffed everything in, and the bag tore along one side. She thrust it at me.

My throat hurt from wanting to scream. "I need another bag, a bigger bag."

She poked the bag toward me with a swollen finger. "This fits fine."

"No, it doesn't."

"Listen, girlie, this isn't Sears, Roebuck."

"I need another bag." I banged the wooden counter. "It's for my sister."

She shoved a larger bag toward me. "Here. Get out." She backed away, shaking her head and whispering under her breath, *"Meshuganah."*

If she thought I was crazy, she should meet the rest of the family.

I crept into the hospital, hoping nobody would notice me. Mimi Rubee had written 602, Merry's room number, on the kitchen notepad. Figuring out how to get upstairs was my challenge.

With a plan in mind, I took a seat in the lobby. If somebody asked, I'd say my parents were parking the car or something. The worn benches felt cool and smooth under my hands. How many millions of nervous behinds had polished the wood? For about fifteen minutes, things were quiet. I counted the speckled green floor tiles, watched the receptionist flirt with the security guard, and tried to be invisible until visiting hours began at three, as posted on a large sign.

At a quarter of three, clumps of people started gathering in the lobby, waiting by elevators and watching the clock. One family knotted so close together, they looked like a six-legged animal.

"Three o'clock. Visiting hours have begun," the security guard announced.

Everyone shuffled toward the elevator, pushing buttons, clearing throats, and brushing away invisible dust. Women wormed their hands into the waiting palms of husbands and fathers. One person in each group held a bag, flowers, or a stack of magazines. I let the first wave of families go, watching the lights on top of the elevator doors.

Visitors poured through the hospital entrance. Some stopped at the information desk where the flirty woman sat. Others marched right to the bank of elevators. Finally, gathering my courage and making myself as small as possible, I slipped up next to a large family who spoke to each other in nonstop Italian. We all squeezed into the elevator, no one seeming to notice me. I watched the controls, praying, scratching 6, 6, 6 into my palm, until I saw someone press the button for the sixth floor.

Three people got out with me. Large signs with arrows pointing in opposite directions read ROOMS 600–605 and ROOMS 606–610. I turned left, holding my breath. Children rolled down the hall in wheelchairs. Children on crutches thumped past. Nurses hurried down the halls on rubber-soled shoes.

Room 602 was quiet and empty except for Merry, who barely made a dent in her iron bed by the window. I crept into the room, past three beds with folded white blankets on bare mattresses. Merry turned at the sound of my footsteps. Her usually creamy pink cheeks looked the color of cooked oatmeal.

"Lulu." Merry's voice sounded rusty. "You're here." She sat up, moving like Grandma Zelda.

"I'm here, Merry." I took her hand in mine.

"Are you mad at me?"

"Mad at you?" I asked. "Why would I be mad at you?"

"You didn't come. And Mimi Rubee looked mad."

"I promise; no one's mad at you." I sat on her bed.

Merry inched toward me, wincing as the bandages over her chest moved. She wore a thin pink cotton hospital gown that left her backside open to the world. Her underpants looked grayish white, as though she'd worn them for days. "I want to go home."

"Soon," I promised.

"Now. I want to go home now. Please?" Merry grabbed my hand and kissed it.

"You just can't. It's not time yet."

Merry began crying. "Daddy's mad at me. He hurt me. Mimi Rubee said."

"Daddy didn't hurt you because he was mad at you."

"Because I was bad?"

"You weren't bad."

"I was." Merry curled down her lower lip. "Now no one wants to be with me."

"I couldn't come before because I'm not a grown-up. I snuck in today."

"Where's Daddy? Where's Mama?" Merry's leg shook up and down. "Are they mad at me?"

"Some bad things happened, Merry," I said and fingered the top of the brown bag. "Daddy got mad at Mama."

"Was she bad?"

The orange marmalade turned over in my stomach. "No. Daddy was drunk." I tried to push away the memory of Mama lying in all that blood under the stark kitchen light, no one with her, Mama all alone on the floor. Dead.

"Bad drunk?" We'd seen Daddy drunk before.

"Really bad drunk." Daddy's bloody hands, bloody from Mama, bloody from Merry, bloody from where he cut himself.

"And he hurt me?"

I nodded, trying to talk without crying. "And he hurt Mama." Would he have hurt me if I'd stayed in the apartment? Probably. But maybe I could have stopped him from hurting Merry and killing Mama. If I hadn't hid.

This was my fault, anyway. I let him in the house.

"Is Daddy in trouble?"

I scratched the word STOP on my arm in big capital letters and sucked back snotty tears. "Bad trouble. He's in jail." We'd seen jail on television. On *Gunsmoke* and *Mighty Mouse*.

"Is Mama in jail with him?" she whispered.

Telling my little sister the truth seemed as mean as hitting her, but I couldn't imagine what lie to tell. I shook my head. "No. Mama got hurt. Bad. Mama's dead." Merry knew dead from *The Wizard of Oz*. The Wicked Witch had died.

Why had I thought such mean things about Mama?

Merry touched the tips of her fingers to her chest, to the bandages, where Daddy had stabbed her, right to where I thought her heart might be. "I want Mama," Merry wailed. She started to shake so bad I thought she might die. I wanted to call the nurses, but was afraid they'd throw me out.

"I want Mama," Merry repeated, tears drowning her words. "Who's going to watch us?"

"I'll watch you." I took the brown bag and put it on the bed. "Here. I bought you something." I unrolled the top of the bag where it had gotten all shredded and wet from my sweaty hands. I reached in, took out the little doll and crib, and put it in her hand. "You take care of this baby and I'll take care of you."

I climbed up on the bed and lay next to Merry. She couldn't roll over to be spooned as we usually did when we were scared, so she put her head on my shoulder just like she used to do with Daddy.

3

Lulu

1972

A faint fuzz of grass grew on top of Mama's grave. Mama's unveiling would begin any minute. Even though Mimi Rubee had explained that Jewish people covered the headstones for a year, and then came back and took the covering off, I still didn't understand what any of it meant.

Merry and I stood at the foot of Mama's burial plot. Everyone else huddled by the cloth-covered headstone. No one seemed to notice us. I tried not to picture Mama's feet beneath us. She painted her toes with the brightest red nail polish of any mother in Brooklyn. Had chips of it stayed on her bones?

"Mama is under the grass?" Merry whispered.

"Her body is," I said.

"She's probably scared," Merry said. "It must be so dark."

"It's like she's sleeping."

"Are you sure?"

"Positive."

Mimi Rubee shrieked as the dour-looking rabbi pulled the white cloth off the headstone. Merry and I jumped back. Aunt Cilla clutched Mimi Rubee's elbow. "It's okay, Mom. She's in a better place."

Mimi Rubee's mouth got that pursed-lips look that made my stomach clench. "Better place? She's not in any better place." She pointed a bony finger at the grave. "She's in the black hole where that bastard sent her."

Merry twined her sticky arm all around mine and I let her, even though it was so hot that when I rubbed my arm little balls of dirt came off with the sweat. I craved something cool. I itched all over but didn't dare scratch.

I wanted to lay my head against the cool granite of Mama's headstone and trace the flowers twined around her name: CELESTE ANASTASIA SILVER. BELOVED MOTHER. DEVOTED DAUGHTER. LOVING SISTER. They'd erased my father and his last name, Zachariah, our name, from my mother's life.

Everything in the world hurt.

Back home, I leaned in the doorway, watching Merry snuggle into Mimi Rubee. They were on the new sleeper sofa. Mimi Rubee had looked stricken the day the movers carried it in, her face puckered as she stared at the bulky tweed couch hulking against the wall, waiting as they took away her beloved Danish Modern—the one that tortured Merry and me. The thin Danish mattress barely covered the metal rods threaded below. Before Mimi Rubee had gotten rid of it, Merry and I had learned which sleep positions avoided the pinching steel, training ourselves to tuck our arms under our stomachs and curve into unnatural shapes to adjust to the bed.

The crowd of people at Mimi Rubee's house overheated the already warm room. Aunt Cilla's husband, Hal, squeezed against her. She held my cousin Arnie in her lap. Cousin Arnie disgusted me. Nine years old and sitting in his mother's lap like a little baby.

People slobbered kisses on Merry, practically begging her to hug them. Then they'd grasp my elbow and squeeze it, look into my eyes, and ask,

"How are you doing, darling?" as though we were the closest of friends, when in fact I'd bet they wouldn't recognize me if they saw me again on the street.

No one was anywhere near my age except Cousin Arnie, and I'd rather hang out with a leper. Gaggy old-lady-perfume smells mixed with the food odors coming from Mimi Rubee's kitchen. Everyone had brought too much of something, like food was the cure for sadness. Mimi Rubee's sister, our aunt Vivvy, brought a platter with lox, cream cheese, bagels, sliced cold cuts, and chopped liver.

I edged into the living room and picked up a thick chocolate chip cookie from a pile heaped on a gold-rimmed plate. Trying to be invisible, I sat on a hassock, working my cookie like a puzzle, trying to have a chip come out in the final bite.

"So, how's school, Lulu?" Uncle Hal asked.

"Okay."

Mama always said that Aunt Cilla had Uncle Hal so squashed down we might as well call him Uncle Aunt Cilla, though he was always nice to me. Of the two of them, I liked him better.

"Still getting all A's?"

"Uh-huh." The only thing in this world I could count on was getting good grades and having teachers like me. All I had to do was be smart, do my homework, and keep my mouth shut. Now I'd begun worrying if junior high would be as easy.

"Lulu never has to work hard for her marks." Only Aunt Cilla would make getting good grades sound evil.

"She's a smart girl," Uncle Hal said. "I wish Arnie did half as well as Lulu." For Uncle Hal, who always hugged the middle road, this was like cursing in Aunt Cilla's face.

"That won't be a problem." Aunt Cilla tightened her arms around my cousin. Bug-eyes Arnie felt like chicken bones when you hugged him. If she squeezed much harder, Cousin Arnie's guts would come out his mouth.

"Cilla, did you check on the food?" my grandmother asked.

"Here," Aunt Cilla said, turning Cousin Arnie toward Uncle Hal. "Watch him."

22

What did Aunt Cilla think could happen to Arnie, except maybe my cousin might kill himself from boredom? The only toys we had were those Merry had brought home from the hospital a year ago. I missed the collection of books I'd built up at home. Daddy used to buy new ones for me on his payday. Daddy liked to read. Mama only read magazines.

Sometimes, just for a minute or two, I couldn't help wondering things about Daddy in jail. Did he get to read? Did he have to eat soup with nothing but scraps of potato peels floating in it? Then I'd look at Mimi Rubee staring at Mama's picture and I'd remember him shaking, shaking, shaking the door, and I'd feel like throwing up.

I didn't care about Daddy one bit, not for one red cent minute.

Merry kept asking to see him, which drove Mimi Rubee crazy. According to Mimi Rubee, we'd see him over her dead body, and when Hell froze over. I traced a silent THANK YOU, GOD on my arm every time she said that. I never wanted to see him again. As long as my bloody-killing-knife-shaking-door father stayed in jail, I was safe. I wouldn't have to see him or smell him or touch him, and he could never touch me.

"Are we still going to Grandma Zelda's house tomorrow?" Merry asked.

"You're going, you're going. Stop asking," Mimi Rubee said.

Aunt Cilla returned, still holding the cup of coffee I'd earlier spied her lacing with Crown Royal whiskey. "I can't believe you let them go to that woman's house week after week," she said.

Merry curled into a ball on the floor by me, leaning on my knees.

"How was kindergarten?" Uncle Hal asked my sister.

"Okay." Merry frowned, probably because school had become torture for my sister. Ever since she'd had two wetting accidents, the kids called her Pee-pee Pants. At recess, they teased her for not being able to throw a ball, which was because of the scars on her chest. Even though we'd changed schools, everyone knew about us, the girls whose father had murdered their mother. Plus, poor Merry also held the title of the girl whose father had stabbed her.

Neither of us had any friends since we'd moved in with Mimi Rubee.

"I bet you were the prettiest one in the class," Uncle Hal told Merry.

"Pretty is as pretty does," Aunt Cilla said. "Look at Joey, so gorgeous when Celeste met him. Handsome as a movie star. And where is he now?"

"Celeste was the real beauty. Joey looked cheap compared to her." Aunt Vivvy shook her head. "She never should have married him. You should have stopped it," she told Mimi Rubee.

"You think we didn't try?" Mimi Rubee said. "I think he got her pregnant on purpose just to make sure he had her. She could have been the movie star if she hadn't married him. He knew that."

"He's a monster. An animal," Aunt Cilla said.

Did she think Merry and I were deaf? Stupid?

"Stop, Cilla," Mimi Rubee said. "Little pitchers."

"We can't close our eyes, Mama," Aunt Cilla said. "Do you want them to stay blind? You think it's smart, sending them to his mother's house? Sorry, but I have to say it."

Everyone's peering, peeking eyes made me want to run out of the house and do something amazing, like throw a ball far enough to reach Coney Island or memorize the encyclopedia.

Nothing made sense. Grandma Zelda had said, "Don't forget why your father didn't go to trial, girls. He wanted to preserve your mother's name, that's the reason he pled guilty." Hearing those words made me silently scream, *Nothing will make what Daddy did any better.* Yet when Mimi Rubee called him a monster, my heart curled in on itself, and I didn't know why.

"After all," Aunt Cilla continued, her voice becoming slow motion, "who knows? Maybe the poison came from Zelda. And who knows where it'll go next?"

My aunt's mouth looked wet and ugly. Her orange lipstick reminded me of a slab of Velveeta cheese. "They should have given him the death penalty. He should burn for what he did."

Merry's shoulder blades dug into my knees as she backed away from Aunt Cilla.

"The children," Uncle Hal cautioned.

"The children should know. What, are we making it a secret?" Aunt

Cilla bent over and shook her finger at us. "You girls have to watch every single thing you do for the rest of your life."

Mimi Rubee's tears started up again. She cried so hard all her makeup wore off and she looked old and ruined, but Aunt Cilla kept harping until Uncle Hal said, "Enough."

"I miss Celeste," Aunt Cilla sobbed.

"I know, but still, you can't talk like this," he said as he rubbed her back. "You're upsetting everyone."

"Why are you defending him?"

Uncle Hal sighed and took away his hand. "At least he kept us from having to go through a trial."

"For that I should be grateful? I'll be grateful when he's dead. I want him gassed; I want him sent to the electric chair."

"No! *Don't kill my father.*" Merry jumped up and turned to Mimi Rubee. "I want Grandma Zelda. I want to see Daddy." She ran over and kicked Aunt Cilla. "Grandma will take me and you can't make her not."

Everyone stared at Merry as though the chair had spoken and the rug risen up and danced, but I knew this was coming. My sister's nice-nice package fooled people into thinking that was all she was, but wasn't it Merry who'd crept closer and closer as my parents fought their last fight? When pushed, Merry eventually always pushed back.

"*Stop that, Merry,*" Aunt Cilla yelled. "*Stop that right now.*"

Merry made two little fists and beat them against her small thighs. "You stop. You stop! *You stop!*" Her voice got louder with each word. "I want to see Daddy. I want to see him. I hate you. And I hate it here!"

"Stop her, Lulu." Mimi Rubee held her head and rocked. "Make your sister stop."

I shook my head and held out my palms to indicate helplessness. They had no idea. Merry didn't go crazy like this too often, but when she did, only Daddy could reach her. *Good luck, Aunt Cilla.*

Merry collapsed into a kneeling position, locking her hands in prayer. "Please, please. Take me to Daddy."

My throat constricted. A need to comfort my sister fought with urges to kill her for doing this, for bringing Daddy into the room. Every night Merry whispered his name to me, wrapping him over us like a blanket

25

before we went to sleep. I could make her do almost anything except stop needing Daddy.

Uncle Hal scooped Merry up, rubbing her back. She kicked out her feet and sobbed. I watched jealously as he crooned to her. "Don't worry, sweetheart. We'll get you to see your Daddy. I promise."

Three months later, Merry's hand trembled in mine as we walked up the steps to the Duffy-Parkman Home for Girls. I tried to act strong and unconcerned as we climbed the endless granite staircase, listening to our feet thudding. Uncle Hal opened a scarred wooden door, and we stepped into a large hallway surrounded by frosted-glass doors. Scuffed marble lay under our feet. The building seemed so old I thought princesses might once upon a time have roamed the halls.

"This will be okay, girls," Uncle Hal said.

Sure thing, Uncle Hal.

Not only would it not be okay, it was going to be hideous. I expected zombie schoolgirls in long gray dresses to shuffle out from behind a door any moment, but the hall remained empty and silent. It was a Monday, and I supposed all the girls were in school. Uncle Hal had taken a day off from work, canceling all his dental patients, to bring us here. Aunt Cilla stayed in bed with a wet cloth on her head, pretending we were as dead as Mama and Mimi Rubee, who'd had a stroke and died four weeks ago. We'd lived with Aunt Cilla and Uncle Hal since then.

"Please, can't we go to Grandma Zelda's?" Merry whispered as Uncle Hal steered us toward a door marked ADMINISTRATION in thick, sinister letters.

"She can't take care of us and you know it, so stop asking," I whispered back when Uncle Hal didn't answer.

"When will she take me to see Daddy again?" Merry asked.

Grandma Zelda had taken Merry to see Daddy once before Mimi Rubee died, and now it had become Merry's mantra. *Take me to see Daddy, take me to see Daddy.* Each time she said it I hated it more, and I wanted to pinch her until I pinched the desire to see Daddy right out of her soul.

"She'll take you when she takes you," I said. "Now shut up or they won't let us live here. You know what will happen then?"

Merry shook her head.

"We'll end up living in the gutter, stealing food and clothes," I said. "That's what."

I waited for Uncle Hal to shush me, but he just stared at the dusty paintings of Indians hanging on the wall, between a clock and a series of framed quotations stitched in blue thread on yellowed muslin.

Maybe we would end up living in the gutter. Maybe they wouldn't keep us here if we weren't good enough. Maybe Aunt Cilla would open up the *Daily News* and see that the police had found our frozen bodies lying in the street.

I won't have Joey's girls living here. Not in my house. That's what I'd heard Aunt Cilla say after the funeral. "They're black marks on my sister's memory, a dark shadow on my mother's name. Having them here is ripping out my *kishkes*," she'd hissed at a collection of relatives we'd never met. "My mother's dead, my sister's dead, all because of that man. And now I have to look at the two of them every day?"

Merry and I had listened to Aunt Cilla from the doorway of her spotless kitchen, the best-behaved girls in Brooklyn, ready to go in and offer our assistance in bringing out the platters of cold cuts and sliced brisket, the baskets of bagels, the lox spread out in an oily orange pinwheel. Could we take the cookies out from the many white bakery boxes tied with string and arrange them on Aunt Cilla's silver trays? we'd planned to ask politely, proving what good girls we were. With Mimi Rubee dead, and Grandma Zelda too sick to care for us because she had the sugar, we weren't sure where we'd live.

Maybe if we were very, very good, Aunt Cilla would change her mind about us.

I looked Merry over, making sure she'd stayed clean between leaving Aunt Cilla's and arriving here at the Duffy Home. Then I avoided looking at Uncle Hal by turning to the stitched warnings admonishing me from the wall. I only had time to read "A Joyful And Pleasant Thing It Is To Be Thankful, Bible: Psalm 147" before a woman stepped out from behind the frosted administration door.

The midgety-short woman appeared childish until you saw the scowl embedded in her face. She placed her hands on her thick waist and asked, "Yes?"

Uncle Hal coughed before speaking. "Mrs. Parker?" The woman nodded as though she were a hundred feet taller. "Hal Soloman. We spoke last week?"

She gave another royal nod and crossed her arms over her pigeony chest. "You have Louise and Meredith with you?" she asked.

"Here they are." Uncle Hal pushed us forward, a hand behind each of our backs.

"Louise is the older one, right?" Mrs. Parker tipped her head to the side. "You are eleven?"

"Yes, ma'am," I said. I'd never called anyone ma'am before, but this woman was most definitely a ma'am.

Merry sniffled.

"Merry and Lulu. That's what we call them." Uncle Hal kept a hand on Merry's shoulder.

"Yes. You're not Meredith's and Louise's legal guardian, correct?" she asked. "That would be their grandmother? Zelda Zachariah?"

"I have the papers from her, as you requested." Uncle Hal drew an envelope from the inside pocket of his suit jacket.

Mrs. Parker took the glasses hanging from a chain around her neck and balanced them on her fat nose. She made clucking noises as she looked over the long sheets of paper covered with black type, stopping only when Merry's choking sounds were too loud for any person to ignore. Mrs. Parker took off her glasses, tipped her head, and took Merry's chin in her hand.

"Meredith, correct? And you'll be seven in December?"

Merry nodded.

Mrs. Parker bent down and patted my sister's shoulder. "You'll be in the Bluebird dorm, dear. You'll have blue blankets and blue nightgowns." She offered this as though Merry would find it comforting. "You'll have a set of drawers and a shelf for books, if you have any."

My sister nodded again.

"Most of the time, we have no one here to hold you when you cry. Sad, but true. The best thing you can do is find ways to comfort yourselves. I advise new girls to take up a hobby as soon as possible. You can pick either cross-stitching or crocheting. The East Side Women's Group donates kits. Your floor mother will show them to you."

4

Merry

1974

I scuffed through dried leaves, hoping I looked like a normal almost-nine-year-old girl shopping with her grandmother instead of what I was, a motherless girl with a father in prison, who lived in a home for girls, which was just a name for orphanage.

"Again your sister's not coming?" Grandma took my hand, waiting for the Flatbush Avenue traffic to slow down.

"She has to study." Every other Saturday, Grandma asked the same question, and I gave the same answer, sidestepping Lulu's refusal to see Daddy.

"So how is everything at that place?" Grandma always called the Duffy-Parkman Home for Girls *that place*.

"Everything's fine." I gave her hand a little tug.

"Fine. Never mind with the fine. You live in an orphanage. So tell me, how is that fine? It's all because of that Cilla. *Ptoi.* I spit on her and her use-less husband." Grandma repeated some version of a spit or curse on Aunt Cilla every Saturday. "It's okay to cross now?" she asked.

I checked the road left to right. "It's safe."

We wove around the fruit seller wrapped in two ragged sweaters, Grandma sidestepping his stack of pumpkins.

"You're doing great, Grandma. I think your eyes are getting better."

Grandma shook her head. "Dream on, *tatelah*. These eyes are shot."

"Think good energy, Grandma. Send good karma to your eyes like Susannah said. Maybe they'll get better. Then Lulu and I can come live with you." I squeezed her hand to show her how much I loved her and what a help I could be. *See how strong and dependable I am!*

"Enough. Every week it's the same story," Grandma said. "They won't let me take you in. And by the way, your new friend Susannah might look like a Breck girl, but she's still a crazy hippie."

Grandma had been calling anyone she didn't approve of a hippie for as long as I could remember. Anyway, Grandma might not appreciate Susannah, but I thought she was practically the nicest person I'd ever met. I'd met her at prison, where she visited her husband every week, and she didn't once ask me about Daddy's reason for being there. That's how nice she was.

I wondered what Mama would have thought of Susannah, who never wore makeup. Mama had worn apple red Snow White lipstick, and she'd drawn perfect black lines around her eyes. A plain Jane, Mama would have called Susannah. I remembered Mama using that expression a lot. Lulu says I've imagined all my memories, but she's wrong. I remember being little.

Most mothers who didn't wear lipstick looked sick, but Susannah without makeup seemed just right, like a character in a Little House on the Prairie book. Susannah gave me advice about life while we waited for visiting hours in the prison to start, especially when Grandma went to the bathroom and Susannah and I were alone.

"You could take an eye test," I said, as Susannah had suggested. "We take them at school. I could memorize it and teach you, and then you'd pass the test. Then we could come and live with you."

Grandma laughed. "Sweetheart, I can't take care of myself, much less you and Lulu. Any day now, I'll have to go to a home. Between my sugar and my eyes, I can't even walk without my cane anymore. Promise me you'll come visit me when I'm in a home."

I almost hit bone digging my fingernails into the palms of my hands, a trick Lulu had taught me to keep from crying. How would we ever get out of Duffy-Parkman if Grandma went to a home?

"If Lulu and I moved in with you, we'd take care of you, and you'd never have to go to a home."

"Take my advice, Merry." My grandmother gave another of her bottomless sighs. "Don't get old."

We entered Woolworth's, where the saleswomen were setting up their registers and straightening the long counters. The candy counter clerk, who wore a gold kitten pin with diamond eyes like always, gave us a smile as sweet as jelly beans. I loved that she really seemed to look forward to seeing us week after week. Every Saturday, Grandma bought me a bag of candy.

I reached out for a multicolored candy necklace, my hand hovering over the pastel disks strung on rubbery string, pleading silently for Grandma's approval.

"Fine. Pick out your *chozzerai*. I don't pay the dentist bills. Get something Lulu would want, also." Grandma laced her bony fingers and sniffed at the candy she'd called garbage. "You know, I understand more than both of you think."

"Maybe Lulu will come with us next time," I lied. Lulu had vowed she'd never see Daddy again, and anytime I tried to change her mind she'd remind me that he *killed our mother,* practically spitting in my face as she said it. *How can you even look at him? How can you stand to breathe the same air? Look what he did to you.*

Then she'd run her hand along my scar. *What's wrong with you, anyway? Why do you go?*

Because Grandma wants me to.

Because he needs me.

Because what will he do if I don't, Lulu?

I didn't know how to tell her that I was scared that if I didn't go and keep him happy, things could get even worse. Lulu didn't seem to worry about stuff like that.

Grandma shook her head and bent to the candy bins. "Is this the kind Daddy likes?" She pointed to the mound of sugarcoated gumdrops. I smelled the mothballs in which she packed her sweaters. Cherry scents of the Smith Brothers cough drops she constantly sucked puffed around us, mixed with the tang of the Dippity-Do goo she used to set her thinning hair into tight waves.

On the Saturdays we didn't visit Daddy, I smelled like Dippity-Do when I went back to Duffy-Parkman. On those Saturdays, Grandma set me on the bathtub lip and combed the pink, jellylike liquid through my hair while I tried not to squirm. Then she rolled my hair into spongy pink rollers. I'd go back to Duffy-Parkman with hanging sausage curls, the butt of all the girls' jokes, since everyone was trying so hard to get their hair straight, straight, straight, but I could never hurt Grandma's feelings. Anyway, feeling Grandma's fingers fussing through my hair made the jokes worth it.

"Circus peanuts are his favorite." I ran my fingers along the wooden bins, looking for the orange marshmallow candies Daddy liked. "I wish we could bring him some."

"Never mind the peanuts. He'll buy candy from the canteen. I have to put money in. I think he needs Right Guard—he wrote me. But he writes too small." Grandma handed me a folded paper. "Here. Read."

I unfolded the cheap white stationery, hating the blurry blue stamp informing the world that this paper came from the Richmond County Prison. Because of that stamp, I folded Daddy's letters into the tiniest of squares and hid them inside a toothbrush holder to keep them from Enid and scaly-faced Reetha. My enemies. They called me Prison Girl.

Enid and Reetha were the ickiest girls at Duffy, with twisted teeth, burn marks, and scabs from I didn't know what. They tortured me. My few friends and I were the cute ones. We stuck together in the upside-down world of Duffy-Parkman, where ugly reigned.

I unfolded the paper and read my father's words in a whisper.

Ma, here's what I need. Toothpaste. Candy. Deodorant. Put as much as you can afford in my account, but don't leave yourself short! Books—Ian Fleming or Len Deighton if you find any I don't already have. Whatever you find is good, Ma. Thanks. I sure hope you and my little Sugar Pop can come next Saturday. Are your legs okay? Have you gone to the doctor to get pills for the pain? Maybe if you went to Florida for a week or two, the heat would help. The ocean water would be good for your arthritis, right? Love, Joey

"Florida. Hah!" Grandma snorted. Then she smiled. "Joey has a good heart."

"Did you get the books?" I asked.

"I went in and out of every store in Brooklyn."

"Did they have them?" I snuck a finger to my scar; Grandma swatted my hand away from my chest.

"I got them, I got them. Don't be such a worrywart!" Grandma leaned on my shoulder as she straightened up from inspecting a candy bin. "Let's go or we'll be late."

A cool wind blew across the crowded Staten Island Ferry deck. The water was choppy, and I hoped I wouldn't get sick. Every time we rode the ferry, Grandma called it the cheapest date in town.

"See, just like I say, for a nickel, they get a place to kiss." Grandma pointed her chin toward a couple kissing. "Cheaper than a movie and a restaurant, huh? The cheapest date in town. Though maybe he should save up for a barber to take care of all that hoo-ha hippie hair."

I stared at the man and woman in question. His hair fell down his back in thick, curly ropes. He wrapped his delicate-looking companion's black velvet cape tighter as he hugged her.

"Why did people start being hippies?" I asked Grandma. Lulu says I couldn't remember because I was too little, but I know Mama talked about maybe she missed her chance. If she hadn't married Daddy, she'd said, she could be free also. She'd have gone to Woodstock. I knew this was true, even if Lulu didn't think I understood anything.

"To be able to do whatever they want and not have to pay attention to what anyone thinks." Grandma sniffed as she said this, as though she feared I'd run off and become a hippie. Well, if I did, then maybe I wouldn't care when people called me Prison Girl. I'd swirl my cape around and make them disappear.

The ferry reached the dock. The scraping and squealing noises it made as it parked forced my shoulders around my ears. Now we'd take a long cab ride, with Grandma watching the clicking cab fare numbers every second. Grandma refused to take the bus. "I'm not riding with that *dreck* going to the prison," she'd say each time, as though we were better than the rest of the sad people we saw every other Saturday.

Once we were safely sealed into the cab, I leaned my forehead on the dirty window and watched Staten Island silently roll by. These visits were the only times I rode in a car. Single-family homes lined the street; small, skinny trees dotted the square patches of lawn. More sun shone on Staten Island than on Brooklyn. I was positive.

As we got closer to the prison, the neighborhood changed. Ranch houses became big, crumbling homes, trailers, and then stores. Diners and shoe stores butted up to sad-looking buildings with signs announcing LAWYER/*ABOGADO*. The world became grayer.

Richmond County Prison loomed like Dracula's castle. Each visit I expected the wide wooden door to fall open like a drawbridge. Wire wrapped the building like a spider's web. The cab stopped outside the fence by the main entrance, the barbed enclosure keeping us a long distance from the door.

Grandma counted the fare out carefully, peering at the meter as though fearing the bill might rise even as she gathered her quarters. I got out first, offering my hand to help her from the cab. I held her cane. She grunted and rubbed her back before taking it. She stumbled a bit as she closed the cab door. I gasped, picturing her tumbling into the street.

"Are you okay?" I asked. A frantic breathlessness grabbed me. If anything happened to Grandma, what would I do all alone on Staten Island? If anything happened to Grandma or Lulu, I'd be alone in the world.

Grandma held up a hand and waved at me. "Don't worry. Today's not the day I'm dying."

"Grandma, please don't talk like that."

"Fine. I promise I won't die when we're together. Okay?"

Could Grandma read my mind? Did she know that I went from worrying about her dying in front of me, to crying as silently as I could in my bed at Duffy, imagining her dying alone, her corpse rotting away through the week until Saturday, when I came with my key and opened the apartment?

Please, God, let it be one of the Saturdays when Lulu is with me, not a visiting-Daddy Saturday.

Grandma brushed dust off her dotted navy dress and stood straight. "Come. Your father's waiting."

We walked through the gates holding hands. Once again, I patted my jumper pockets, checking for the hundredth time that I didn't have any forbidden items. Grandma kept a list of rules on top of her coffee table. I'd memorized them the way my teacher said to remember history dates: *Say it in your head, say it aloud, and repeat it five times.*

Rule: Children under eighteen must have a birth certificate. A parent or legal guardian must accompany children.

Prison was the reason Grandma Zelda had ended up as our legal guardian, even before Mimi Rubee died. Mimi Rubee wouldn't take me to visit Daddy, but after I begged and begged, she finally agreed to let Grandma Zelda take me, making Grandma the guardian, even though Aunt Cilla screamed at her for it. Now there was no way for me to stop. Grandma expected it, and Daddy, well, I didn't know what Daddy would do if he didn't see me anymore.

Rule: No hats, food, jackets, drinks, gum, or candy. No provocative clothing. Nothing in your pockets.

The skinny lockers where we had to place everything smelled like dirty coats and rotten food, probably stuff people tried to smuggle past the guards.

Rule: You may embrace the inmate briefly at the beginning and end of each visit.

I dreaded and waited for those hugs.

Rule: Inmates may receive, in total, five small soft-covered books, except for those deemed inappropriate by the Officer in Charge.

As we walked down the long, dingy hall toward the check-in place, I prayed for Officer McNulty to be the officer in charge. He'd smile and barely glance at whatever books we'd bring. The worst one, Officer Rogers, always threw away at least one book a visit for being what he called racy. When I asked Grandma what *racy* meant, she shook her head and said, "None of your beeswax." Susannah said it meant sex. I knew about sex. Nothing was secret at Duffy.

Rule: Inmates may receive, in total, five family photos. No portrait photos may be larger than 4 × 6.

I had two dollars saved toward a camera from the quarters Grandma sometimes slipped me. Lulu, knowing about my plan to give Daddy pictures, warned me not to ever take her picture. Not to give to *him,* she'd say.

Grandma touched my jumper pockets. "Empty?"

I nodded and followed Grandma down the hall. Women, children, and a few men lined up in front of the guards. I stretched up on my toes to check the guard on duty. McNulty! Still, even with him in charge, little bubbles of dread filled my throat. I clenched and unclenched my fists. I didn't see Susannah.

A pale, mushy woman stood in front of me, her scalp showing through thin red hair. Behind Grandma, a short woman wearing giant silver hoop earrings muttered "damn" every other second. Her Afro looked even bigger than her head.

"Think they'll let Angela Davis through with those cockamamie earrings?" Grandma whispered, tilting her head back.

"Shush." I wasn't sure who Angela Davis was, but I didn't think Grandma meant it as a compliment. I tried not to peek to see if the woman had heard. My stomach growled. I wished I'd eaten more candy on the ferry.

When we got to the front of the line, Officer McNulty smiled at me. He was tall and straight, like the soldiers guarding the palace in England. "Back again?"

I grinned back big and lifted my arm, waiting for him to pat me. He did it fast, not like some of the others. I hated them.

"Your dad's waiting impatiently." Officer McNulty's kind face made it seem as if he really wanted me to have a good visit. I tried to think of things to say which would make me sound good.

"You have a nice day, Officer," I said. Afro-Hair-Woman smacked her teeth as though sending me a message.

Officer McNulty squeezed my shoulder. "You're a good girl, Merry. Go see your daddy."

5

Merry

Grandma and I stepped into the visiting room. Beige tiles were dotted with spots that I imagined impossible to scrub out in a million years. Probably blood and bits of brain left from prison fights.

Metal tables with rubber edges and attached benches lined the room. Visitors and families sat across from each other, men always seated facing away from the windows. Weak sunlight washed over the backs of their denim shirts. We sat as far apart from anyone as possible, pretending we were anywhere but here.

My father sat at the end of the room in his usual spot. I barely remembered before-prison-Daddy anymore, the Daddy who'd lived with us and then the Daddy who Mama threw out. That Daddy was bloated, and had dirt under his fingernails and thick hair falling in his eyes. Prison-Daddy had muscles and a crew cut and looked handsome as the pictures from when he first married Mama, the photographs on top of Grandma's dresser. I'd tried to show Lulu, but she'd pushed the pictures away just like anything about Daddy.

I studied the photographs every time I visited Grandma, tracing the lines of Mama's beautiful face, the veil like a magic cloud around her head. In black and white, Mama's lipstick appeared dark as blood.

My stomach lurched when I saw Daddy, followed by a hollow hunger.

"Baby girl!" he said. We embraced briefly, as allowed by the guards, me trying to tug away the moment we touched. I hated when Daddy held on for even one second longer than the rules permitted, certain a guard would yell at me or, worse, at Daddy. I'd seen a prisoner dragged away for yelling at his so-fat-it-hung-over-her-pants wife. Everything on the man had seemed shriveled, but his fat wife had shrunk away as though he were Charles Atlas. The guard had come over with his heavy brown stick and just banged him right across the shoulders and hauled him off.

"Oh, my God, look," Grandma had said. "He *klopped* him right across the back!" I was afraid to ask Daddy if he ever got *klopped*, but I'd thought about the brown stick ever since.

Daddy inspected me just as he did each visit. "How do you grow so much in two weeks?"

"Not from the garbage they feed her at that place," Grandma said.

"At least she gets a good meal from you once a week, huh, Ma?"

"Oh, please." Grandma slapped the air with a dismissive hand. "I can barely see the pots anymore, let alone cook."

I slid closer to Grandma and placed my hand over hers. Her skin felt like paper you'd kept for a long time, paper you'd folded and unfolded until it became limp and cottony. Daddy's earliest letters were like that now, those I kept at Grandma's house.

"So how's school?" he asked.

I shrugged. "Okay."

He wrinkled his face. "Just okay? Is someone bothering you?"

"No. Everything's fine."

"I better see some good grades on your report card, miss. Getting-into-college grades. You don't want to end up like your old man, do you?"

I stared across the table at him, puzzled. College would have kept him out of prison? Did he know something about me? Did he know that sometimes I hated people so much it burned? Like Reetha. How did I know I wouldn't kill someone? Maybe Aunt Cilla was right; it could be in my blood. That was probably why she never wanted us in her house. Maybe I'd go to prison one day.

"Don't be a fool, Joey." Grandma shook her head. "You sound crazy when you talk like that."

Grandma hated my father saying anything about why they'd locked him up. She wouldn't talk to me about it either. No one would, except Lulu, and she only talked about how much she hated Daddy and how seeing him was so stupid.

"What do you want from me, Ma?" Daddy asked. "How many fascinating topics do you think I can come up with in here? Should I talk about how the Black Power guys want to kill the guards?"

"Shush," Grandma said. "They could be listening!"

I looked around to see if anyone had heard him.

"Should I talk about how I'm becoming an old man in here?"

"Stop. You're only thirty-one. You're a young man. You'll get parole. You'll be out before you know it."

Would we live with him if he got out? Would Lulu let us?

"Who's talking crazy now?" Daddy asked. "I'll be a hundred before they let me out. I got life. You think they'll let me go with ten years? Twenty years?"

"You'll get parole hearings." Grandma twisted a white handkerchief with black diamonds around the edges. I peeked to see if the guards had noticed. Prison families never looked at other families; we kept our fights low and quiet, leaking out a little at a time.

Daddy shook his head and pressed his lips together as though blaming Grandma for something.

"All the girls made pumpkin pies last night," I lied. "For fall."

"At that place?" Grandma didn't look like she believed me one bit.

"Yes." I stared right at her. "We carved pumpkins and cooked the insides down to make pies." I'd read that in a book, about how long pumpkin took to cook, and about the stringy, raw stuff inside.

"That sounds good," Daddy said. "Too bad you couldn't bring me a piece, huh?"

"Yeah, too bad." I avoided looking at Grandma.

"Boy, it's been a long time since I had pumpkin pie. Did you put a lot of cinnamon in? And ginger? I always liked spicy pie."

"It tasted exactly like cinnamon hots," I said.

Grandma pinched my thigh under the table. *Enough*, her sharp fingers said.

Daddy leaned back, putting his muscular arms behind his head. A dreamy expression came over him. "Pumpkin pie. What I wouldn't give."

"Right," Grandma said. "And if wishes were horses, beggars would fly. So, what about that program you wrote about to me?"

"The optical program?" he asked.

"So it's true? You might be able to learn a trade at least?"

"Ma, I had a job before."

Before meant when Mama was alive. Lulu said it also—except she'd say, *Don't talk about before. I don't care.* I tapped the top of my scar before I could stop myself.

"A widget-wadget job, that's what you had. Shussh. I'm talking about a trade, a profession," Grandma said.

"Making brass fittings for ships isn't exactly widgets, Ma. It's probably that job, the fact that I had to work to tolerance, that's made them consider putting me on the list."

"What's tolerance?" I asked.

"Ask your grandmother, who's so smart, she knows everything."

"Stop with the feeling sorry for yourself. Sorry I insulted you. Answer your daughter." .

Daddy rolled back his shoulders. "*Tolerance* means working to exact measurements; having anything off, even a tiny bit, can ruin what you're building."

"So you can build things in here?" What he did inside the prison bewildered me. Every time I tried to ask, he'd change the subject by saying, *Never mind this place; I'd rather talk about you.*

"A program's starting here, an optical shop, where they'll make lenses. I want to get in, so when I get out I can get a job."

"When are you getting out, Daddy?" He never wanted to talk about that, usually saying, *Only time will tell,* which told me nothing.

"Maybe in twenty or thirty years I can get parole for good behavior."

Twenty or thirty years! I'd be almost twenty-nine or thirty-nine by then. My father would be an old man. He'd be fifty-one or sixty-one. Could he even work?

How could I keep him cheery all those years? Grandma had said that my job was to keep Daddy cheery. "God knows your mother never did it." Grandma shook her head when she said this. "She made him the opposite of cheery. That's why what happened, happened. Believe me. She drove him to it with all her hoo-ha with the hair and the nails and then the men. I don't like to speak ill of the dead," Grandma would say, "but your mother considered herself some kind of beauty queen. She thought she didn't have to do the same work as the rest of the world."

I didn't understand what Grandma Zelda meant. Daddy killed Mama because she was a beauty queen?

Lulu said Daddy did it because Mama dated bad men. Mimi Rubee said the booze and pills made Daddy do it. Aunt Cilla said Daddy killed Mama because of him being an animal. I didn't know what to believe.

Anyway, what about me? That's what I wanted to know. *Why did Daddy stab me?* No one ever talked about that, except once, when out of nowhere Daddy said, "I'm sorry, Merry. I know you probably don't remember what happened. You were so little. But I'm sorry."

Grandma got up. "Time for the torture." Grandma always said that when she left for the bathroom, because she had to wait for a guard to take her down a long, long hall that she said was like a walk of shame. They patted her when she went, and then again when she came out, as though she'd maybe found a gun in the toilet. I never drank water before visits. I didn't ever want to have to pee at the prison.

The air got heavier when Grandma left, as though she fanned it around with her constant chatter and kept us from the extreme edges that made up our lives.

"So, how's Lulu?" Daddy asked. "Still a bookworm?"

I nodded. "Daddy ..." I trailed off, unable to say the words drumming in my head like mechanical monkeys. *Why'd you stab me, why'd you stab me, why'd you stab me, Daddy?*

"What's wrong, baby girl?" His eyes got all swimmy with love and concern behind his glasses. "You sure everything's okay at school? Any-one bothering you?"

I shook my head. "School is fine."

"So what is it, cookie?"

Like Grandma, I blinked and blinked.

"Uh-oh. Here come the banana splits," he said.

Daddy used to say that whenever I cried. Before. Then he'd take out his handkerchief, wipe my eyes and say, *Let's mop it up, honey.* I'd forgotten. I'd never cried here.

Grandma would be back soon. The question pressed harder against my throat.

"Cat got your tongue?" Daddy smiled and tipped his head down, look-ing all wise and kind, as though we were in an episode of *The Brady Bunch.*

"Why'd you stab me, Daddy?" I whispered. Words rushed out like throw-up. "Why'd you try to kill me?" Daddy backed away as though my soft words were little knives. Now I was the stabber.

"You remember?" His voice sounded thin, like it came from high up in his throat.

Daddy pushing me away from the kitchen. Mama lying on the floor. *Lie down, Merry. Lie down on Mama and Daddy's bed. Be a good girl.*

"I remember some stuff."

Daddy holding the knife all covered in Mama's blood. *This will only hurt for a second, baby.* No, Daddy, it hurt for a long time.

"I couldn't do it." He shook his head. "I started to, but I couldn't. It didn't go very deep."

I opened my hand wide and covered the cotton shirt hiding my scar, as if Daddy might see through the fabric. I knew every bump of the ridge. It was purple-pink and straight. It was on my left side and the length of the memo pad in which I wrote my school assignments.

"Why did you want to hurt me?" *Answer my question, Daddy.*

"Oh, baby girl. Booze had me dead-drunk mixed with stupid. Jealousy screwed me up bad. You're too young to understand." He put his head in his hands. I wanted to rip them away, pound his stupid dead-drunk jealous head.

"That's why you did it to me?" I whispered, wondering how anyone ever drank.

"I didn't want to leave you." Daddy crossed his arms as though he were hugging himself. "I didn't want to leave you all alone."

"What about Lulu? Didn't you care about her?"

"Booze knocked the sense from my head," Daddy said. "And I was scared, baby."

"But you were going to leave Lulu all alone? Afraid?" I felt the walls of the room closing in on me.

"Lulu could always take care of herself. You, you're more like me."

I'm not like you. I'm not.

"Oh, Jesus, Merry. I love you so much. All I have left in the world is you and Grandma. No one else cares if I live or die." Daddy took off his glasses and wiped his eyes with his knuckles. Now the guards would come. Now Grandma would be sad.

"I can't stand the thought of you in that place," Daddy said. "Damn Cilla and Hal putting you there. Damn cowards. Cilla, who expected anything from her? But Hal? I thought he was a stand-up guy. If I had just one minute alone with that guy, I swear."

"I'm okay, Daddy. Everything's fine." I had to calm him down. Make him happy. Or maybe he'd hurt Aunt Cilla and Uncle Hal, even from in here.

"You shouldn't be there." He buried his head in his hands. It looked like maybe he swatted a tear away with his thumb. I couldn't stand it if he cried. He didn't have a handkerchief or tissues, or anything. Prisoners couldn't bring anything into the visiting room. I wondered if Daddy could carry things around when he left his cell. Maybe they kept him locked up every minute. Did he ever get to watch TV? Did he have to shower and go to the bathroom in front of people?

Grandma and I visiting him was probably the most important thing in the world for my father, and I was ruining it.

"It's okay, Daddy," I repeated. "I'm all right."

My father's face got hopeful as the puppies in the pet store window on Flatbush Avenue.

"Oh, I forgot to tell you." Under the table, I twisted the skin on my arms. "After the pumpkin pie, we made pancakes." I clasped my hands in my lap and gave him a big, happy smile. "With real maple syrup. We celebrated autumn. It was fun, Daddy. Really, really fun."

45

6

Merry

I raced up the steps of Duffy-Parkman, skidded down the hall, and then flew into my dormitory room. Olive was propped up on one elbow, lying on her cot and staring at the wall. I counted myself lucky it was Olive. She never bothered anyone, she just read, and read and read as though she was holding her breath until her parents came back, which they never would, since they'd died in a car crash. Olive didn't have a single family-person in the world, unless you counted an ancient aunt locked up in an old-person place.

All the Duffy dorms were the same, three cots lined up on one wall, three on the other. A tiny night table separated each bed. My lucky break was having an end bed so I could lean against the wall.

Seeing me, Olive retrieved her library book from where she'd hidden it behind her pillow. Only Lulu read more than Olive, but Lulu didn't have to pretend she didn't. Lulu scared most of the girls, except for the super-tough ones, like Kelli.

I stripped off my jumper and white blouse. After hesitating, I peeled off my sweaty kneesocks, too, which were disgusting from an entire day wearing the plasticky Mary Jane shoes Grandma had bought me back in September. I reached for my last clean socks, knowing they were the only ones left before laundry day, which wasn't for two more days. I'd have to wear them again tomorrow and Monday, but I wanted something clean right now. I sniffed my two pairs of pants to find the cleanest ones.

Lulu yelled at me for not planning things better, but sometimes I needed something that felt good so much, I couldn't stop myself.

I peeked over at Olive, who held *Trixie Belden and the Mystery of the Missing Heiress* about an inch from her nose. "Hey, Olive, want to come hang out with us?"

Us was Janine, Crystal, and me. Janine, whose parents took her home every few months until they started drinking again, looked like a miniature Diana Ross. She had huge eyes and was superskinny-beautiful. Crystal's blond hair made me crazy jealous. It went down past her waist, and the counselors at Duffy liked to brush it and braid and twist it into fancy styles. Crystal's parents died in a fire.

We'd been together for over two years. When we were Bluebirds, the youngest and littlest, the floor mothers and counselors picked us to sit on their laps during TV hour. Now that we were Redbirds, nobody cuddled us much anymore, but we passed out the popcorn, and sometimes we leaned against a counselor during Saturday-night TV time.

"I think I'll just read," Olive said.

"Okay," I said. I didn't have to watch out for anyone teasing Olive. No group claimed her, but no one teased her either.

I looked both ways and ran to the art room. Mrs. Parker-Peckerhead only allowed us to hang out in three places besides our dorms. One was the game room, an old classroom with holes where desks had been unbolted. None of the games had all the pieces. Second was the lounge, which had a television and a radio. Everyone hung out in the lounge, but that's where the worst fights happened, too.

Third was the art room, where my friends and I went. An old pickle tub filled with crayons and colored pencils, outdated magazines, and stacks of used paper donated by some company made up our art supplies. We drew princesses and puppies on the backs of insurance reports and order forms.

Janine and Crystal bent over their pictures. Janine traced the outlines of the paper dolls we'd made from magazine ads, making the dolls new outfits. Crystal, the best artist of all the Redbirds, labored over the mountains she'd drawn coming up from behind a castle.

"How's your grandma?" Janine asked.

"Okay." I never complained about Grandma; at least I had someone to visit. Janine's parents only came when they took her home two or three times a year. We always believed Janine was leaving Duffy for good, and cried and hugged until a housemother pulled us apart. Then, when Janine came back two weeks later, Crystal and I pretended it never even happened, just as Crystal and Janine pretended that I didn't visit my father in prison, and Janine and I pretended we didn't notice the burn marks covering Crystal's legs from top to bottom.

"Here, I brought this from the room for you." Janine handed me the picture I'd started the day before. Part of my puppy series, gold, black, and red ones. Janine and Crystal kept all our drawings and any other special things. Duffy had two Redbird rooms, and they were lucky enough to be in the one without Enid and Reetha.

"We only have about fifteen minutes," Crystal warned. Crystal obeyed the Duffy rules as if she'd die if she even accidentally broke one.

I began slivering a little silver along the edges of a puppy. Not too much, since gold and silver crayons rarely appeared in the pickle jar, and I knew Crystal needed them for her castles.

The art door opened. We looked up, dreading company.

"Oh, look. Prison Girl's back." Reetha flounced in clutching a half-crayoned brown box.

Crystal put a protective arm over her paper. I nudged my puppies over to cover her castles.

"Why don't you crawl back under your rock?" Janine said.

I sucked in my breath at her words. Reetha did remind me of a slug, all sweaty with a face like the goop around gefilte fish. Jagged pink lines on her forehead showed where her mother had scraped her against a wire fence.

"Why don't you go eat shit?" Reetha reached over and grabbed the silver and gold crayons.

"Hey, we're using those," I said, trying unsuccessfully to snatch them out of her hand.

"Why don't you have your grandma buy you some?" Reetha put her wormy face up to mine. "Look, Prison Girl! I found some new drawing paper. Maybe I'll use it to line my box."

I recognized the paper Reetha held, my father's handwriting, the blurry Richmond County Correctional stamp.

"Dear Merry," Reetha read aloud before I could grab the letter. "Grandma wrote me you got an A on your spelling test. Congratulations, Sugar Pop!"

Crystal tore the paper from Reetha, leaving Reetha with a scrap corner of the letter.

"Oh, it's torn," Reetha said. "Don't cry, Sugar Pop! So, how bad was your mother that your father had to kill her? Was she a whore?"

Janine got between us. "How ugly were you that your mother named you Urethra?"

"My name is *Reetha*."

I grabbed at the crayons she'd snatched. She screwed up her face to bite my hand, but I held on to the waxy tips anyway, tired of losing stuff to her. She clamped down on the tip of my thumb.

"Ow!" I screamed, letting go of the crayons.

"Retard," Janine said.

"Wino," Reetha screamed back as she grabbed the violet and red crayons next to Crystal. I hated her. I hated her so much I could have grabbed the scissors from the pickle container and shoved them in her throat.

"Ugly scar-face," I yelled. "Everyone hates you."

The next day I woke up with the kind of bad feeling you get when something is wrong, but you don't know what. It was seven-thirty on Sunday morning, and breakfast was in half an hour. Sunday's breakfast was the best meal of the entire week. Pancakes, three each.

I ran my finger along my chest. The smell of shampoo from my previous night's shower hung in the air. I reached up to fluff out my hair from the ponytail in which I'd slept.

My ponytail was gone. A short, bristly stump stuck out from the rubber band.

I tried not to cry, not to show anything, because crying only made things worse at Duffy. I tasted the tears in my throat. I touched my head again, patting the stump where my long ponytail had been.

Reetha smiled from her bed. I dug my nails deep into my palms. Enid sat cross-legged on the floor—probably looking for crumbs to eat, the porky pig.

Everyone in the room stayed silent.

"What's the matter?" Reetha asked. "Crybaby doesn't look so cute today?"

Curls from my ponytail lay scattered on my pillow. My hands twitched. I wanted to run to the mirror, but I wouldn't give Reetha that satisfaction. Instead, I snatched a thick hardcover book, the largest I could find, from Olive's shelf and ran over to Reetha's bed. Her pajamas looked like a boy's, and she smelled like she never washed down there.

I grabbed the book with both hands, lifted it over my head as high as possible, and slammed it down on Reetha's head.

"Ugly skank." I hit her again, aiming straight at her forehead scars.

Reetha rolled over and kicked me in the stomach. "Stuck-up Jew-girl."

"Stop it," Olive warned. "Someone's coming."

I ran back to my bed and leapt in, clutching Olive's book in my trembling arms.

Our housemother walked in. "What's going on?" She inspected us bed by bed. "Merry, what happened to your hair?"

I bit down on my lip. "I cut it," I said.

I faced the wall, tracing a doggy face on the dirty beige paint with my finger. Circle, circle, circle, tongue. Floppy ears. Everyone was in church. I pulled the stretchy headband Janine had lent me tighter, lower around my ears, pretending no one could notice how ugly I looked. Strings of long hair mixed with short curls sticking out like loose wires. The housemother said I'd have to get a pixie cut, which made you look like a boy. When the weekday housemother for the older girls, the one who took care of haircuts, came tomorrow she'd finish Reetha's job. I kicked the wall.

As soon as all the girls had left for church, I'd torn up my father's letters and flushed them down the toilet. My hiding place had turned out to be useless. I walked my feet up and down the wall. Quietly. Because if Mrs. Parker-Peckerhead came in and found me doing it, she'd make me wash the wall down with the brown disinfectant that practically left holes in your hands.

You think people want to see your footprints on the wall, Meredith? Mrs. Peckerhead would say as she handed me the scrub brush stuck in a pail of soapy water. When she made me move my bed from the wall and saw the real mess, she'd really punish me. *Look at this,* she'd yell. *Candy wrappers. Where did you get those from?*

I'd be in big trouble for having my own candy stash. We were supposed to give any treats we got to Mrs. Peckerhead for the community box, but I tried to keep all Grandma's treats, except, of course, I gave half to Lulu. Anything you handed over to Mrs. Peckerhead, you'd never see again, except for horrible things she didn't want, like the dried apricots one girl got from her grandfather.

The empty room reeked of poison brown disinfectant and talcum powder that smelled like flowered feet. Duffy girls got it from John's Bargain Store on Flatbush Avenue—those who managed to beg money from relatives if they had them, or steal it from the girls who did, if they didn't—and sprinkled it under the cheap, scratchy dresses they wore to church.

Lulu walked in as I bicycled my feet in the air with my hands holding up my hips.

"Where are you going?" Lulu asked.

"Ha ha. Very funny."

Lulu sat next to me. "Are you okay?"

"Reetha will kill you if you sit on her bed," I said.

"I'm truly scared." As if to prove her point, Lulu lay down, even daring to put her shoes on the bed. Lulu had become tough since she'd turned thirteen. Grandma called her a juvenile delinquent in training.

"Really, get off," I begged.

"Okay, okay. Stop being a baby." She switched to my bed. "So, are you okay?"

She pointed her chin at my head, and I tried not to cry, instead air-bicycling faster and faster.

"I'll make sure they never do it again," she said.

"No," I screamed. "Don't. It'll just get worse. I know it. Unless you kill them. Ha ha." I reached up and felt where hairs popped out of the headband. "Why does she hate me?"

"Because of Daddy," Lulu said.

"You blame everything on him."

"How's Grandma?" Lulu always changed the subject the minute Daddy came up.

"She's okay." I banged my feet against the railing on the end of the bed. "Daddy said to say hello."

"Did I ask?" Lulu turned on her side, facing me, cradling her head in her hand.

I sat up and crossed my legs. "Lulu, do you think Daddy will be alive in twenty or thirty years?"

Lulu frowned. "Why?"

"Because he said maybe he'd get out then—in twenty or thirty years." I studied my sister's face.

"He'll probably be alive. Unless somebody kills him in prison."

"Don't say that." I drew up my knees and put my chin down, tucking in my face. "Don't you miss having parents, Lu?" I said to a scab on my knee.

"I just don't think about it." Lulu poked me with her foot. "Neither should you. Forget it. It's over. Come on down to the rec room. We'll play Clue."

"Do you think I might die here?" I asked.

Lulu grabbed my shoulders and pulled me up. "Why are you asking that?"

"What if someone here kills me?"

That wasn't what I really meant. What I really meant was, What if I killed someone? Then I really would be Prison Girl.

"I hate it here. I don't want to grow up here." I pushed Lulu away and fell back on my bed. "I'd rather be dead than live here."

7

Lulu

Merry drove me nuts as we walked toward Grandma's house. Every step I took, she insisted that I move faster. I couldn't rush enough for her, and she refused to copy my snail pace. I lifted my boots through the slush covering Caton Avenue as though I had bricks glued to my soles; that's how much I wanted to go to Grandma's house.

"Come on," urged Merry. She grabbed my arm. "We have to be there by twelve. For lunch."

"Quit it." I pulled away from her. "We'll get there when we get there."

Merry frowned from under the floppy hat hiding her pitiful haircut. Three weeks' growth hadn't helped her raggedy look, but more than her hair, I worried about her dying talk. She needed to leave Duffy. I could handle the place, but Merry wasn't tough enough.

"She's going to be looking out the window!" Merry hopped around me like a baby bird, her need to please Grandma making me insane. "Hurry."

Grandma usually glued herself to the window, her chair angled so she could swivel her head between focusing on the television screen and watching for us coming up the street. Saturdays were tough TV days for Grandma—no game shows, none of her stories—but she watched anyway. She said TV kept her company while she waited to die. Even when she read the oversize, large-print *Reader's Digest* magazines she borrowed from the library, the television stayed on.

As we approached the redbrick entrance to Grandma's apartment building, Merry waved wildly toward Grandma's window. "She can't even see you," I said.

"You don't know for sure." Merry yanked open the door, still rushing even though we'd arrived. The worn-out lobby smelled like an old mop. A messy stack of unclaimed mail almost blocked the mailboxes.

"Grandma can barely see." I tugged at the hem of my short skirt as Merry pressed the doorbell next to Grandma's name. I'd reprinted "Mrs. Harold Zachariah" last month when the ink on the old slip faded to un-readable. Grandma insisted I write "Mrs." because she thought being married seemed more respectable. As I'd slipped the fresh paper rectan-gle into the brass slot, she'd said, "If they know a man wanted you once, they treat you better."

Grandma went on for hours about old people never getting respect anymore. *Just look at these hippies with their hair hanging down to their pupiks, they look like ragamuffins. Do they even stop to say, "Hello, Mrs. Zachariah"?*

College kids crammed four, five, and six into the thimble-size one- and two-bedroom apartments in Grandma's building. She complained they were making the place into a beatnik building. Hippies were old hat to everyone in the world except Grandma, who hated them. When I turned thirteen in July, she'd given me her only real jewelry, a pair of pearl ear-rings and a pearl necklace, scolding me all the while that a young lady wore something like this, not those crazy fruit seeds the hippie girls had hanging around their necks, and reminding me to give Merry the ear-rings when she got older.

Naturally, two days later someone at Duffy stole the earrings and the necklace.

Grandma buzzed us in. Merry raced up to the third floor while I forced myself up the scuffed stairs one by one. Odor of cabbage and onions fried in chicken fat mingled with the smells of patchouli and pot. I recognized the pot because girls at Duffy-Parkman snuck into the bathroom at night and smoked it. Then they'd drench everything with White Rain hair spray to cover the odor. I totally expected the bathroom to blow up one day when some girl blasted White Rain while another lit a match.

The patchouli I'd sniffed on the college girls who volunteered to be so-called special friends to the older girls at Duffy-Parkman. Hillary Sachs was my special friend. I didn't know if they'd assigned me a Jewish special friend on purpose or if it had been a coincidence. Hillary gave me cow-eyed, meaningful looks while we played Scrabble or went on little trips. I hadn't yet deciphered what she offered in those looks. Last week she'd told me to get ready for something great the next time we met, which would be tomorrow.

When I got all the way upstairs, Grandma stood in the doorway, arms crossed over her bony chest. I still remembered Grandma as soft and round, and my heart folded in on itself when I noticed her clothes hanging so loose they looked like I could stuff in another Grandma.

"So, where were you? I was worried sick."

"It's only ten minutes after twelve." I pointed to the cheap Timex that Grandma wore.

"I worry after two minutes." As Grandma gave me a rough hug, Merry stuck her tongue out at me.

"For lunch I made hot borscht. Of course, I forgot the sour cream. Your grandmother is now officially an idiot. Proven this week, by the way."

"By who?" Merry grabbed a hard candy from the bowl Grandma kept filled for us.

"By who? By everyone. Mrs. Edelstein downstairs asked me to take in her mail while she visited her son in New Jersey, and guess who forgot?"

"That's not a big deal," I said.

"Believe me, it's only the tip of the iceberg." Grandma took her purse from the secretary filling most of the postage stamp hall. "Here, Merry. Go down the street and get Grandma some sour cream. Also, I need a quart of milk and three apples, but not the mealy ones they stick in front. Make sure you take the sour cream and milk from the back also."

"Lulu should have to go. She doesn't even come every week, so I end up doing everything," Merry said. "I want to stay here with you."

55

"I'll go." I'd happily go. Grandma's three-room apartment suffocated me. I couldn't believe my father lived here when he was a teenager. He would have filled the place up. The tiny kitchen had a miniature table covered with an overscrubbed piece of red oilcloth, an ancient fridge, and a stove that looked like it should be in the Brooklyn Museum. A maroon velvet sofa and chair overfilled the living room, but even so, Grandma crammed in wobbly little tables smothered with tea-colored doilies. Grandma cleaned the apartment every hour, but everything still had a thick old-lady smell.

"No. You'll stay." Grandma handed the money to Merry. "Remember, take from the back."

Merry left, and I curled up on the old sofa, trying not to let my face touch the scratchy fabric, picking up the only available reading material, a large-print *Reader's Digest*.

"Stop with the bookworm routine. I need to talk to you." Grandma sat next to me on the couch and pulled the magazine from my hands.

I gave her a closemouthed smile. "What is it?"

"You need to hear a few things." Grandma grabbed my hand. Despite her fragile appearance, she held me with a powerful grip. "I'm not going to be around forever, Lulu."

"I hate when you talk like that."

"Shush. By *forever*, I mean not very long at all. The doctor says my heart is getting bad, and the sugar makes it worse and worse. And my eyes, I can hardly get around. Forgive me for saying so, *tatelah*, but dying will be a blessing. Except, who will take care of your father? Who will watch over Merry?"

"I have to go to the bathroom, Grandma."

"You can hold it a minute. Listen to me—when I'm gone, you watch your sister. Understand?"

"I watch her now."

"Don't be fresh." Grandma squashed my fingers as she gave my hand a painful squeeze.

"Ouch!" I tried to pull away, but Grandma held on with her iron gangster grip.

"You watch her like a hawk, do you hear me?" Grandma still wouldn't let go of me. "Merry's your responsibility when I'm gone. I know, I know, you think you do everything already—but believe me, you don't. When I'm gone, you'll be all she has. You can take care of yourself, you'll always be okay, but she's not tough like you."

"Okay, fine." Grandma's words piled on me. Why did everyone think I could take care of stuff? I hadn't done it for Mama, had I?

"And remember, your sister will need to see Daddy," Grandma said. I ignored her, staring down at my knees, and she gave me a tiny smack on the side of my head. "Look at me."

I looked up. "I said I'd take care of Merry, but how do you expect me to take her to prison? I'm only thirteen, Grandma."

"What a character you are. When I try to tell you what to do you say you're not a kid, you're thirteen. Now suddenly thirteen is a baby?" Grandma shook her knobbed finger in my face, still holding on to my hand with her other hand. "We need to talk about your father."

I ran my free hand over the worn velvet nap, pushing it one way and then the other. Merry might be my responsibility, but I wasn't taking him on.

"You haven't seen your father once," Grandma said. "Not once. When I die, you go see him. Do you hear? He'll be all alone in this world except for you and Merry."

"Wasn't that his choice?" I squeezed my thigh. Grandma and I never spoke of how Mama died, that my father killed her, that he ran a knife wet with Mama's blood into Merry's chest.

"Your father did a terrible thing. It's not for me to defend. However, he's my son and he's your father. When I die, you take care of Merry and you see your father. Do you promise?"

"Just how am I supposed to get there?" I pictured the prison as a fortress with rats jumping from everywhere and moving brown patches of cockroaches covering the walls.

"You're smart. You'll figure it out. Call your uncle Hal."

Was she kidding? Aunt Cilla and Uncle Hal hadn't come to see us since Mimi Rubee died.

"It will kill me if you don't promise," Grandma said.

I shrugged.

Grandma squeezed my hand one more time. "Promise!"

I crossed my fingers. I wound my legs together. I'd never go to Richmond Prison. Never.

"I promise," I said. "I promise."

"That's a good girl." Grandma unwound her fingers and patted me. "Remember, a promise is sacred. God listens. Disobey a promise and God knows what can happen. But never mind, I know you'll keep your word." She tilted her head and gave me an approving smile. "I see your father in your face. It comforts me. I'll die easier knowing I can count on you."

The next morning I dressed with particular care. I tried not to get excited as I waited for Hillary to pick me up for our "something great." So far, we'd gone to the movies, gone to the Brooklyn Museum, where she couldn't get enough of the costume rooms and I thought I might fall asleep, and stayed here to play Scrabble. Once she'd dragged me around the Brooklyn Botanic Garden, which actually soothed me. I'd like a life as peaceful as the Japanese section there.

I made my cot up as tight as possible, using the hospital corners Mrs. Parker insisted upon, tucking in the wool blanket, working carefully to avoid the iron ribbing on which the mattress rested. They'd given me enough scrapes over the years. I didn't feel like running to the housemother to beg for Neosporin. However, I would, and did every time my skin broke, because germs loved Duffy-Parkman. No matter how hard Mrs. Parker made us scrub, you'd always find some Duffy girl puking or wiping her snot on a chair. Blood poisoning lived a scratch away here, and before they brought you to a doctor, you had to lose your leg or have a temperature of 105.

I'd debated between being a doctor and being an anthropologist for a long time. As a doctor, you were always doing the right thing, saving and healing people. Doctors knew what to do no matter what happened. You had to take care of disgusting things, but almost nothing made me sick to my stomach. When Olive was afraid to tell Mrs. Parker she thought she had lice, I checked her. I even got Grandma to buy the stuff to get rid of the bugs, and I took care of Olive secretly in the bathroom, with Merry posted as the lookout. I combed out every single nit.

Anthropologists made sense of people. I read *Coming of Age in Samoa* when someone threw it in a bag with other donated stuff for Duffy. It made me think that where you live can make all the difference. I'd have liked to be an anthropologist like Margaret Mead, but I didn't know how I could ever travel that far from Merry.

I beat my flat pillow in an attempt to bring it to life, but the dead feathers had their own dead mind. I dusted and lined up my books in size order, positioning my crayoned "Do Not Borrow Without Permission" sign smack in the middle. No one here read much, but stealing was the Duffy sport of choice. Luckily, no one cared enough about books to want mine, except Olive, and although she was spooky, she was a rare spot of Duffy honesty.

I put my brush and comb into my small and only drawer. Leaving my room without neatening my three shelves until they were perfect, with everything lined up and all the fold sides of my clothes facing out, could ruin my day. I had the neatest shitty stuff in Brooklyn.

I checked myself in the mirror through slitted eyes, trying to imagine what the college girls thought of me. Most Duffy girls dressed like whores, but I rummaged through every bag of donated clothes searching for shirts, pants, and skirts as not-Duffy as possible.

When people dropped off old clothes, the housemothers dumped the bags in the middle of the family room, and we'd eye the bulging sacks as if we couldn't be less interested. The moment someone made the first move, we all pounced.

The toughest and meanest girls wore the best clothes. That's why Merry looked scruffy. I tried to pull out decent clothes for her, but try looking for two sizes while girls knee you in the chest. I had one advantage, though. While the idiots here searched for hot pants that showed their butts, I fought for Levi's and oxford shirts.

Today I wore a blue button-down shirt. I thought my complexion looked almost pretty in that color. Not that anyone cared, but at least I didn't have pimples. Most Duffy girls' skin oozed so bad you wanted to close your eyes. Maybe it was our greasy meals, so I tried to eat the best stuff Duffy served. Of course, I couldn't do that every meal, otherwise I'd have been limited to bread and water. My good skin was probably just luck. Tall and no pimples; these were my big blessings.

Merry burst into the room, her mouth turned down and lonely. Sunday mornings it was as though we were the only people left in the world. "When are you coming back?" she asked.

"I have no idea."

"Where's she taking you?"

"I don't know. It's a surprise."

Merry hopped up on my neat bed, folding her legs Indian style. I wanted to chase her off and smooth it down, but she seemed so pathetic. Poor Grandma tried to make Merry's chopped-off hair look good, twirling it in Dippity-Do for hours, and only succeeded in making her look like a crazy poodle.

"I hate it here." Merry dug her heels back and forth along my blanket.

"Stop messing up my bed. I know you hate it here. I hate it also."

"Everyone hates me."

"No one hates you."

"Reetha and Enid hate me. They cut up my shirt while I was gone. The one Grandma got me. With the tiny flowers." Resignation colored Merry's voice. "Or maybe someone else did it. Someone else who hates me."

"Grandma will get you another one."

"I can't tell her," Merry said. "It would scare her."

"I have some money saved. I'll buy you a new shirt."

Merry lay on her belly, her cheek against my pillow. "Forget it," she said in a muffled voice. "It doesn't even matter. Everything turns ugly here. We're just going to have an ugly-ugly life."

Hillary's something great turned out to be having lunch with her parents. She kept it all a big secret, taking me on the subway, transferring a thousand times, and bouncing around as though we were going to see the president. I tried not to look disappointed. I'd allowed myself to get all excited, imagining all sorts of things: Shopping trips! A Broadway play! Carnegie Hall! Places I'd read and dreamed about, like the top of the Empire State Building and the ice-skating rink in Rockefeller Plaza.

"This is my parents' place." Hillary acted casual as she pointed to a pearly white building guarded by a line of dwarf evergreens. The brass door shone as though keeping it bright was someone's only job. "They're having us to lunch."

Hillary's house seemed out of my imagination. I didn't know homes like this existed in real life. My shirt, which had seemed fine in the Duffy mirror, now looked worn thin. At least the unusually warm November weather meant I could carry my pea jacket and not have to show off the torn pocket.

I touched my hair, feeling for pieces that might have come loose from where I'd clipped it back. Four stories of faceted windows shot off sparks, black lines separating the panes into diamonds. "Which floor do you live on?"

Hillary laughed. "All of them. This is our house."

"Wow," I couldn't help saying. Over on the left, water sparkled. "What's that?"

"The East River." She smiled and tilted her head. "Haven't you ever been to Manhattan?"

I didn't know how to tell her I wasn't sure what Manhattan meant. I thought we were in New York City. "I guess so. Probably."

"This is Sutton Place." Hillary took my hand.

Hillary's parents greeted me as though I were Anne of Green Gables. I had no plans to take the shine off their impression by telling the truth about me. Mr. and Mrs. Sachs wore the clothes I'd use if I designed a mother and father, he in a tweedy brown suit and tie, she in a sun-colored dress that flowed around her like a hug.

They reminded me of Mayor Lindsay and his wife. Hillary's parents were perfect people with perfect teeth and perfect hair.

In the dining room, a world of glass shimmered. Impressions of white and blue flew at me, all soothing and wonderful. In my world, rooms were dingy beige. I sat at the table, ready to imitate Hillary. She shook out a cloth napkin, so perfectly smooth it looked like our neighbor Teenie might have snuck in and ironed it, and laid it across her lap. I did the same, pressing the cloth to my shaking thighs.

Mrs. Sachs tinkled a silver bell. A maid appeared by my shoulder. "Miss?" she asked.

Mrs. Sachs nodded at me. "Lulu, Mary is asking if you'd like a roll."

I looked up. Mary held out a fluffy white roll in a silver holder. I cleared my throat, hoping my voice still worked. "Yes, thank you."

Mary dropped a roll on a small plate next to my dinner plate. Plates filled the table, tiny plates where Mary placed pats of butter, plates for rolls, plates under other plates, on top of which sat bowls. Three forks. Two spoons. Two knives. Ten meals' worth of silverware waited. What were we supposed to do with it all?

Mr. Sachs smiled at me, nodding with a delight I didn't understand. "So, how's my girl doing as your big sister?"

Hillary shook her head. "Daddy, I told you. They call us special friends at Duffy-Parkman."

"Special friend. Indeed. Sounds rather *Well of Loneliness*," Mr. Sachs said.

"Daddy's a literature professor," Hillary said, as though that explained her father's words. "Lulu loves to read, Daddy."

I nodded, wanting to appear as a book lover. "Hillary's been a wonderful friend," I finally squeaked.

"Excellent," Mr. Sachs said. "We should give her some of your old books, Hil."

Mary dipped a ladle into a large silver tureen and poured soup into Mrs. Sachs's bowl, then Hillary's, then mine. Mr. Sachs was last. No one chose a spoon. At Duffy, the first girl who grabbed food from the platter usually finished before the last girl picked up her fork. Finally, when Mrs. Sachs dipped a large spoon in her soup, everyone followed suit. I ate the soup cautiously, calling upon extra vigilance by imagining a bomb would detonate if I spilled even one drop.

"What sorts of books do you favor?" Mr. Sachs asked.

"I like biographies." Biographies sounded smart.

"And your recent favorite?"

I froze, unable to remember anything I'd ever read except *Are You There*

God? It's Me, Margaret, and that sounded as ordinary as dirt. The Sachses watched me, Lulu the lunch star.

"Marie Curie. Her book," I said.

"Ah. Actually, I think you'd say 'a book about Marie Curie,' unless she wrote it herself. Did she?"

"No. That would be an autobiography," I said. "Right?"

Mr. Sachs smiled as though I'd invented radium. "Yes. That's correct. I guess the schools in Brooklyn aren't all that bad, huh, Lulu?"

As I tried to figure out if I should say yes or no, Hillary rescued me. "Stop teasing, Daddy."

"Indeed. I'm pleased to see how well our tax dollars are being spent."

Mrs. Sachs tried to pretend otherwise, but I knew she watched me as I ate. I noticed the delicate way she used her spoon as she tipped her bowl away from her and realized I was doing the opposite. I laid down my spoon. I'd had enough soup.

"Lulu. Unusual name." Mr. Sachs crossed his arms and leaned back. "Where did you get it?"

Hillary looked uncomfortable. She'd never asked me about my background, but from her expression, I figured she knew my story.

"My real name is Louise. Lulu is a nickname."

"Ah. I call my girl Hil." He laced his fingers and brought them to his chin. "Did it have meaning? Lulu?"

I shifted in my seat, wishing I knew how to change the subject. "My parents said when I was a baby my eyes reminded them of Little Lulu. Like in the comics."

I didn't tell him what Mama really said, how I listened from the hall while she and Teenie drank coffee in the living room. *She was the creepiest baby. So quiet. Her eyes were so damn round and dark. Like black holes. Like Little Lulu.*

No one spoke. Maybe they remembered why I was at an orphanage. Mrs. Sachs patted my hand. "You have lovely eyes, dear."

I let out my breath and smiled larger than normal. I tried to look cute like Merry, cute and endearing. Hillary was an only child. She'd said her mother couldn't have any children after her. Hillary had told me she'd always wanted a sister.

"I wish you could meet Merry," I said. "My sister. She's adorable. Everyone says so."

"I'm sure she is." Mrs. Sachs nodded at Mary, which I realized meant bring on the next course. Catching on fast was important.

"Everyone loves Merry," I said

"Perhaps we'll meet her sometime." Rays of goodness and cleanliness beamed from Mrs. Sachs.

I nodded. Merry would charm them as long as she didn't pull one of her crazies, which hardly happened anymore, maybe once a year, but she wouldn't dare do it here. Not if I told her how the Sachses could get us out of Duffy.

"Hillary tells us you're quite a Scrabble player," Mr. Sachs said. "Can we interest you in a game?"

"I'd be quite interested in that." I found myself parroting the Sachses' manner of speaking because I wanted to sound like a Sachs until I became a Sachs.

Unlike the stained tiles and the board marked with scribbles from countless careless girls that I played with at Duffy, the Sachses' Scrabble set matched everything they owned. The tiles were the color of wine, and the sleek plastic board spun in a circle, cradling each letter in an individual holder.

We sat in the living room, though they called it a sitting room. I wondered if that was just another name, a better name, for a living room, or if it meant a different room. Chairs were everywhere, kept company by little tables. In the corner, four chairs surrounded a high square table, where we sat like a family.

I tried to play better than I ever had in my life. I had little practice, since Duffy girls were more interested in television. Mostly I played by myself, pretending to be two people.

I stared at my letters, knowing a seven-letter word was hiding in this batch if I just uncovered it.

GMRAFNI.
ARMGINF.
MARFING.

I was taking too long. They'd get annoyed. They were just trying to be nice to me. They couldn't wait for me to leave. *But I'm smart,* I wanted to say. *Look!*

FARMING.

Where could I put it? Sweat gathered on the back of my neck. A grandfather clock ticked in the hall. Mrs. Sachs sat with her hands neatly folded. Hillary's letters clicked as she switched them around on her tile holder. Mr. Sachs seemed amused watching me. Studying me fondly. Like a daughter. He reminded me of Carson Drew, Nancy Drew's father. Calm and wise.

Oh. I saw it! I put *farming* over *angle,* making *mangle* and *farming* at the same time.

"Splendid, Lulu. Simply splendid," Mr. Sachs said. "Look, she used all her letters. Fifty extra points!"

"And look how she did it. Count it up, dear." Mrs. Sachs seemed so proud. Hillary was right. This was something great.

I won the game, and I didn't think my victory came because they tried to make it easier for me. Everyone acted so happy, so pleased. I pictured cozy winter nights with the fireplace blazing. Maybe Mr. Sachs smoked a pipe. Merry could learn how to play Scrabble. She was smart. Everyone loved her. Everyone always loved the cute girls.

I stayed still, wondering what we might do next. I willed Mrs. Sachs to say, *Why don't you stay for dinner, dear?* and Mr. Sachs to add, *I could drive you back to your place.*

"Good game! Time for us to call it a day," Mr. Sachs said. "We certainly enjoyed meeting you, Lulu."

Say that. Please say that.

"Before you leave," Mrs. Sachs said.

Before you leave, let's make a date for our next visit.

"Go see Mary in the kitchen. I told her to make up a bag of sweaters, some of Hillary's we'd kept. Lovely sweaters. Ones I couldn't bear to throw out." Mrs. Sachs bestowed a radiant smile on me. "Rather than just sending them in a bundle with everything else we give away, I wanted to make sure they got a good home."

8

Lulu

The Sachses sent me home in a taxi. Mr. Sachs put ten dollars in my hand, much too much. Not that it made a bit of difference to him. He could probably give away a hundred dollars without blinking.

I got back to Duffy at six, not wanting to see anyone. When I went to the basement, planning on hiding in the ancient library that no one used, I found Kelli and her crew smoking in the bathroom.

"Oh, look who's come home!" Kelli said. "Did Miss College take you to blow frat boys?"

"Shut your mouth, Kelli."

Kelli blocked my entry to the stall. "Who's going to make me? You? You going to use your book?" She looked around for appreciation. Goony April grinned so wide her black-rimmed eyes disappeared into her fat cheeks. Maureen gave a closemouthed smirk. Their skeevy little mascot, Reetha, hovered in the background.

"Move, Kelli."

Kelli flicked a finger at my chest. "You going braless these days? Maybe you're a women's libber now, huh?"

My flat chest amused Kelli, inordinately proud as she was of her disgusting, floppy boobs. "Fuck off," I said, smacking away her flicky finger.

April pointed at me. "I bet she doesn't have enough to fill an A cup."

"Do you even have a bra?" Maureen asked. Makeup coated her acne-covered face.

"Do you even have a brain?" I asked.

"Maybe you should ask your *father* to send you a bra from jail, huh?" April stuck her face close. I gagged from the smell of too much Jean Naté mixed with sour frankfurter breath.

"What's the story, Murder Girl? Do you have tits?" Kelli leaned back against the stall door. "Why don't you make her show us, Maureen?"

Reetha got closer. "And then we'll get your sister."

"You ever touch my sister again, I'll kill you, you ugly piece of shit." I put the promise in my eyes, and Reetha pulled back.

"Go on. No one's going to hear. Everyone's upstairs watching TV." Kelli pushed Maureen closer to me.

Maureen grabbed the neck of my shirt, tugging it hard enough to pull the fabric down to the edge of my white bra, tearing off two buttons. I kicked out, hitting her in the shin.

"Bitch," Maureen said as I struggled to get loose.

"She's probably wearing her virgin bra." April brayed her donkey laugh.

"Yeah, Murder Girl's definitely a virgin," Kelli said. "Who'd want a tiny tit like her?"

"Keep pulling, Maureen." April sounded excited. "Pull it down all the way."

"Skanky lez." I aimed my foot higher, but Maureen arched away and grabbed me from the back. April went for my shirt.

"Get the fuck away, Maureen, or I'll murder you." I elbowed her hard, connecting with her shoulder, since she was about three inches shorter than I was.

"Shit!" Maureen yelled. "Hold her."

Kelli took a small, vicious-looking switchblade from her jeans pocket and popped the knife open. She held the tiny killer blade up to my neck, pressing the point into my flesh. "Don't move."

"You're dead," I grunted, twisting away from the knifepoint, from Maureen's hands, from Kelli's wet eyes.

Maureen's cold, skinny fingers snaked around my arms. Everything looked sharp and clear. The chipped beige paint. The brown pipes. The overflowing trash bucket. The stupid blackboard they'd put up to stop graffiti. *Fucking bitch damn hate you hate you hate you all.*

The sharp knife tip poked the soft flesh of my throat. I lifted my leg, my foot, and shoved it into her slutty stomach. She fell back. I jumped on Kelli and put my hands around her throat, squeezing, feeling the cords underneath my fingers. I put my knee deep into her chest.

"Get the fuck off her," Maureen yelled, kicking me from behind.

April shouted, "Use the knife, Kelli!"

"Get up, Lulu," Maureen said, "or I'll fucking kill you."

Tears streamed from Kelli's eyes as she gagged.

"Stop it," April yelled, grabbing at me.

The door slammed open with an echoing thud. Mrs. Cohen, the weekend social worker, walked in. "Lulu, get off Kelli right now." Mrs. Cohen held me by my shoulder. Kelli lay on the floor coughing. April and Maureen put on their blankest faces.

"Don't bother hiding the knife, Kelli; I already saw it." Mrs. Cohen looked at me, seeming to notice my torn shirt.

"She was choking me." Kelli touched the finger-mark necklace ringing her reddened neck. She struggled into a sitting position.

"Are you okay?" Mrs. Cohen didn't sound sympathetic.

Kelli only glared.

"We were just fooling around," April insisted.

Reetha huddled in the corner.

"It looked like plenty of fun." Mrs. Cohen gave me a steady stare. "Lulu, what happened?"

I shrugged. "Like April said, we were just fooling around."

Mrs. Cohen loosened her grip on me, then let go. She crossed her arms and shook her head. The other social workers were younger than Mrs.

Cohen, who seemed more like one of the rich ladies who dropped off clothes and books.

"You're all lying. Kelli, Maureen, April, wait for me in the conference room." Mrs. Cohen glared at them. "You, too, Reetha."

Conference room was the polite term for a dirty little punishment of a room without windows. There were no pictures, no lamps, and no rug, just a limp-cushioned sofa and three scratched plastic chairs.

Mrs. Cohen waited until they left, then narrowed her eyes at me.

I couldn't figure out if she was angry or upset.

"Why are you protecting them?" she asked.

"Because I live here."

"They could have hurt you."

"I could have hurt them. At least one of them."

"That bothers me just as much. Maybe more."

Was I supposed to bare my soul in the basement bathroom?

"I'm worried about you, Lulu. You can't afford to lose what you have."

"What do I have?"

Mrs. Cohen ran a hand over my forehead.

"Possibility."

The word hit me more like a demand than a compliment. Her eyes got all soft, as though I was some sort of prize. I saw that she wanted to save me. "I'm worried about my sister," I said. "I'm scared she's going to kill herself."

"Remember," I told Merry a few days later. "You need to be extra-good today. Do that cute thing you do."

"What cute thing?" Merry pulled away when I tucked her shirt in. "Stop it. I'm not a baby. I'll be nine this month."

I rolled my eyes. "Just be yourself."

"Why is Mrs. Cohen taking us out?"

I debated how much to tell her. Everything my sister thought floated to the surface and then she blurted it out. Who knew what she'd repeat. "Because she thinks I'm extra-smart and you're extra-cute."

"Really?" Merry cocked her head, proving how extra-cute she could look. Did she know? Did my sister know she could charm the world just by showing her face?

"I got her to take us out." I didn't plan to tell Merry about my sad little conversations with Mrs. Cohen concerning Merry's depression. About how frightened I was that Merry would kill herself. About the fact that some days I couldn't eat because my throat closed up. I'd spread the baloney so thick that I didn't know how the words made it through the layers of lies. "Maybe she can find us a foster home."

"*No!*" Merry said. "Crystal told me about them. She was in a foster home once. She said it was worse, much worse than here. They made her into a slave." Merry kicked out at me. "I'm not going. You can't make me."

"You're going wherever I say," I said. Before she went crazy, I added, "Mrs. Cohen is taking us for ice cream. At Jahn's."

Merry stopped midscream. Desserts were rare treats for us, and Jahn's practically served ice cream in boats. Grandma had taken us there on Merry's eighth birthday last December.

"What if they send us to two different houses?" Merry said.

For one mean minute, I thought about what life would be like without my sister leaning on me, the end of constant responsibility for her body and soul, but before the idea could settle in, I slapped the thought out of my head.

We were here because I'd let my father into our house. Merry had her scar because I'd opened the door. That's why we were at Duffy. Visions of my mother's body floated up from where I'd buried them. I'd let my father into our house. I'd let him hurt everyone.

"Mrs. Cohen would never let that happen. I'll never let that happen. We'll always be together," I said.

"Promise?"

Merry thought I ruled the world. "I promise, but you have to be perfect today. Perfect. Mrs. Cohen has to really, really like us. She might be the one who can get us out of Duffy before something terrible happens."

"Like what?" Merry looked frightened. Good. If that was what it took.

"Like hurting me or you really bad. Or separating us."

"But you promised," she whispered.

"I know, but you have to help me keep the promise. By making Mrs. Cohen like you. Make her like you a lot."

Jahn's ice cream parlor felt cool and smooth as the ice cream they served. Everything was glossy marble and wood worn to a mirrored finish. Sugar scented the air.

"Does anyone ever get one of those?" Merry pointed at a picture of a giant dish filled with three scoops of ice cream—chocolate, strawberry, and vanilla—topped with bananas and whipped cream.

"Maybe teenage boys," Mrs. Cohen said. "I think a Kitchen Sink would be a little too much for you."

Merry's eyes widened. "I wasn't going to order one, Mrs. Cohen."

"I wasn't implying you would, honey." Mrs. Cohen put an arm around Merry and squeezed. "Get whatever you want."

Merry put her chin up as she grinned at Mrs. Cohen. "Thank you so, so, so much. Are you allowed to take us out like this?"

"We're here, aren't we?" Afraid I'd sounded sour, I quickly smiled, knowing I'd never look as appealing as Merry. "We really appreciate this, Mrs. Cohen."

"No thanks needed," she said. She led us to a table by the window, where Merry and I practically drooled looking over the menu.

The waiter was back soon after we gave our orders. He placed three silver dishes in front of us: a small dish of coffee ice cream for Mrs. Cohen, a vanilla ice cream–butterscotch sundae for Merry with marshmallow goop instead of whipped cream, and a double scoop of chocolate ice cream with sprinkles for me.

My spoon reflected the mirrors all around us. I dipped into the rich ice cream and ate a tiny bite, wanting it to last forever. Once a month we got spumoni at Duffy. The tiny brick of so-called ice cream, multilayered pink and green, wrapped in waxy paper, tasted like freezer burn and tin.

"Good?" Mrs. Cohen asked.

"Delicious." I rested my spoon in my dish. "Mrs. Cohen, can I ask you a question?"

"Of course, dear, what is it?"

"What's Chanukah? What are Jewish people supposed to do?"

Merry looked up from swirling her sundae into a soupy mess. "Grandma says—"

I kicked her hard. "I know, Merry, I know. Grandma says not to worry about it. That's because she feels sad."

I studied Mrs. Cohen's concerned eyes for her reaction. Instead of wearing her usual shapeless, jumper-type dress, she had on a black and white sweater and black pants. She'd swept her graying brown hair into a French knot and appeared younger and less plump.

"You're not familiar with Chanukah?" Mrs. Cohen asked.

"When they talk about Chanukah in school, I really don't know what it is." I exhaled a long, sad breath. "Grandma doesn't have any money for Christmas or Chanukah presents, or even for our birthdays. We try not to ask her upsetting questions."

My sister looked at me as though I were insane. *Keep your mouth shut, Merry,* I telegraphed by opening my eyes wide for one bit of a second.

"I think we're almost the only Jewish kids at Duffy. I suppose that shouldn't matter, but I don't have anyone to ask about my heritage." I cleaned the bottom of my spoon with my tongue. "Is that the right word? Heritage? I could look it up when I get back."

"It's the right word, sweetheart." Mrs. Cohen's face softened, and she looked almost teary. "Chanukah is the festival of lights. It marks the victory, more than two thousand years ago, of Jewish people who recaptured their temple. *Chanukah,* by definition, means dedication. We celebrate by lighting special candles each day at sundown."

"And presents, right?" Merry's voice rose.

"Yes, and presents." Mrs. Cohen smiled and ran her fingers through Merry's curls. "My children loved Chanukah when they were your age. We probably fussed more than we should have in trying to compete with Christmas. Christmas is difficult for Jewish kids."

"We have to wear special Christmas clothes when those women come," Merry said.

I nodded, letting Mrs. Cohen know how tough it was to be a Jewish kid wearing crinoline and singing "Ave Maria" for the rich women who sponsored Duffy's extras, like jigsaw puzzles for the older girls and Colorforms for the little kids. Sometimes we got Prell shampoo so we didn't have to use the brown castile soap to wash our hair. Oh yeah, the rich women changed our lives.

"It's okay, though," I said, laying it on thick, but hopefully not too thick. "We get fruitcake."

"Fruitcake." Mrs. Cohen rolled her eyes. "You girls need to taste potato latkes and rugelah."

"What are latkes?" I asked, kicking Merry again. *Don't tell her about Grandma's latkes.*

"That's it. You girls are coming to celebrate Chanukah with my family."

9

Lulu

1975

Grandma's funeral felt like being in *The Addams Family*, except instead of Cousin Itt and Thing, Grandma's friends were the creepy ones. *The murderer's daughters. Joey's girls.* That's what I heard whispered by the old ladies. *Do you remember her son? The murderer? Those are his girls.* They'd sneak glances at us, and then lower their voices as though I wouldn't know exactly what they were saying. I wished I had the guts to walk over and tap one of them on the shoulder. *Excuse me. Are you talking about me? Joey's daughter? It's not catching, you know. Oh, and I got straight A's on my last report card; thanks for asking. By the way, there isn't a murder gene. I know. I studied biology.*

Except I didn't really know.

Grandma had died five months after she tore her death promises from me.

She'd died in her sleep.

Her brother, our uncle Irving, had found her, called the police, and then driven straight over to Duffy to tell us. I could barely handle knowing that Grandma was dead and I wanted Uncle Irving to go away, but he just kept talking, saying all kinds of things I didn't care to know, like how he got to Grandma just in time, just before she went bad.

I hoped people's brains stopped when they died and that they couldn't think. I hoped life after death was a myth. Grandma shouldn't know she'd waited so long for someone to find her that she was practically rotting.

Everyone ignored Merry and me as we sat in the small chapel waiting for the funeral service. We were in the corner of the overheated room. The carpet looked so worn it might as well have been linoleum. Too-bright lighting emphasized the too few people in attendance.

Merry held my hand so tight you'd have thought she breathed right through my fingers.

After endless minutes of watching old people watch us, Uncle Irving came over. He placed a hand behind each of our backs and pressed us toward the little room off to the side where I knew they had the casket.

"Say good-bye to your grandma," he said. "Before they close the box. Jewish people don't have open caskets at the service, so once they get her ready, she's locked in and you'll never see her again."

Merry opened her Tootsie Pop eyes so wide that I thought she might fall down and die of fright. Could nine-year-olds have heart attacks?

"I'll say good-bye for both of us, Uncle Irving." I pointed Merry to one of the dirty ivory-colored chairs lined up against the wall. "Stay there."

Everyone watched as I walked to the casket room. Uncle Irving opened the door, pushed me in, and then he closed the door except for a little crack, leaving me all alone. It was cold and so bright I wanted to shut my eyes for the rest of my life. My arms and legs felt numb.

Nothing will happen, nothing will happen, I chanted. *It's okay.* I thought of how brave Anne Frank had to be.

Grandma lay on top of shiny white satin lining the coffin. Thick makeup covered her face. Could her closed eyes pop open?

Looking at her so close seemed like stealing secrets. Did people know they were being stared at when they were dead?

"She looks good," Uncle Irving had said as we walked over, as though assuring me. "Pretty."

75

Was he nuts? She looked like the wax apples and bananas she'd kept in a bowl. Grandma would say they'd made her into a hootchy-kootchy dancer. *Imagine schmearing all this on me,* she'd say. The only makeup Grandma ever wore was China Rose lipstick. She kept the old tubes, so at the end of the month, while waiting for her check, she could scrape out a sliver of color.

Too broke for beauty, she'd say to us as she poked out the last bit of lipstick. *Your grandma is too broke to look pretty.*

You always look pretty! Merry would say, hugging Grandma tight. I'd roll my eyes, but Grandma'd seemed pleased. I should have been nicer. Like Merry.

I barely moved my lips as I whispered over the casket, "Uncle Irving is right, Grandma, you look really pretty."

Merry's feet dangled over the deep seat of the funeral limousine. The car smelled of wet carpet and the pinecone-shaped air freshener swinging from the rearview mirror. Merry crossed her ankles in an effort to cover the hole in her pilled black tights. I'd wanted to find decent mourning clothes for her, for both of us, dresses that Grandma wouldn't have called *a shandeh un a charpeh,* but I couldn't, and what we wore was a shame and a disgrace.

Dingy clouds followed us down the highway. I wanted to rip off Merry's gray dress, which exactly matched the depressing March chill and made her look like a tiny prison matron. Oily-looking stains marked where food had probably dripped from the previous owner's mouth.

"Who'll take care of us now?" Merry whispered.

"Grandma didn't take care of us." I stared out the window, watching the road wind farther and farther out of Brooklyn. "We only saw her every other week."

"I saw her every week," Merry said. "Because I went to visit Daddy with her. You didn't go with her even once."

"Be quiet, Merry." I didn't want Uncle Irving and Cousin Budgie, sitting up front, to hear me, so I covered Merry's ear with my mouth as I warned her, once again, to stop mentioning Daddy's name.

Merry twisted the edge of her skirt, ignoring what I said. "Who's going to take me to see him now?"

"Just shut up about it, okay? Be respectful; it's Grandma's funeral." I wanted to smack her. "Do you want Uncle Irving to think we don't care about her?"

Merry pursed her mouth the way I hated. "Seeing Daddy would have been *respectful* to Grandma."

I squeezed my own hand until I couldn't anymore, then I pinched her arm.

"Ouch!"

Uncle Irving turned around. "You girls okay?" Mama would've said his black suit looked older and uglier than dirt. When Uncle Irving had come to tell us Grandma was dead, I didn't even remember he was Grandma's brother until he told me. I'd hardly ever seen him or his daughter, Cousin Budgie, who wasn't a cousin age but more of an aunt age.

Cousin Budgie's shoulders tightened, but she kept quiet. When they'd come to pick us up, she'd barely kissed us, just offered her stupid cheek like some sort of fat prize. I didn't want to put my lips on her slimy, makeup-covered skin. Cousin Budgie smelled like the inside of Grandma's pocketbook.

"We're fine, Uncle Irving." I gave my most responsible girl smile.

"Just be careful." He turned back to staring at the trees lining the highway. We were going to a cemetery in Long Island where Uncle Irving said we had a family plot.

"We don't need any trouble from you girls," Cousin Budgie added, not even bothering to look at us. She glanced at the limousine driver as though worried what he thought. I stuck my tongue out at her back, not caring if the driver saw.

Merry and I were the murderer's girls to them. Just like we were to the old ladies at the funeral home.

The limousine pulled into the cemetery. There were even fewer people here than at the funeral home. Grandma's old-lady friends had made a million excuses as to why they weren't coming. *It's too cold. My feet are killing me. The worst dampness is in March.*

I hoped Grandma couldn't look down and see that hardly anyone would watch her get buried. Five counting the rabbi, but he didn't have much choice. It was his job.

The limousine slowed beside a greenish iron gate woven with Jewish stars and scrolls. We turned in to the cemetery and bounced slowly down a narrow road lined with headstones, some clustered together, some all alone.

"You wouldn't know it," Uncle Irving said as we drove, "but when we bought the family plot, everyone was closer than a box of crackers."

We turned left on Jerusalem Road, driving until the path stopped. The hearse parked, and then we parked. Next, we had to bury Grandma.

"Put on your gloves," I ordered Merry. I pulled on my own clumsy wool mittens, shivering as Uncle Irving opened the heavy limousine door and let the cold cemetery air creep in.

Merry took out her stretchy red and pink striped gloves. They were too small for her, a real bottom-of-the-bag pair of gloves, but they were all she had. We wore ballerina flats Mrs. Cohen had dug up from somewhere. She'd been the one to help us get dressed, coming in special just because we were going to the funeral.

"Look," Merry whispered. "Someone else is here."

"You don't have to whisper. We're allowed to talk." I spoke loud enough for Cousin Budgie to hear, consumed by hatred of my too-good-for-us, old-lady cousin. Merry pointed at a big car, not as big as our limousine but long and dark blue. A man leaned against the hood, his arms crossed over his chest, while another stood ruler-straight next to him.

"I think it's the rabbi."

"Isn't *he* the rabbi?" Merry pointed to a lumpy man wearing a yarmulke and a shawl draped over his suit. He waited by an open hole, watching, nodding, as two men carried Grandma's casket. They lowered her into the hole using some sort of ropy thing.

Uncle Irving and Cousin Budgie walked toward the open grave, leaving us by the car, expecting, I supposed, that we'd follow.

"Should we go with them?" Merry's voice was soft and worried.

"I guess." I fumbled for the pocket pack of tissues given us by Mrs. Cohen.

I guided Merry slowly and carefully over the winter brown grass. A body might be anywhere. The family plot had few headstones. Empty spots waited for us. Uncle Irving had said that Merry and I, and our children and husbands, we all had future graves here. Just what I wanted, to be lying for all eternity next to stupid Cousin Budgie. We crept closer to the open grave.

"Merry? Lulu?"

I jumped at the voice.

"Daddy!" Merry dropped my hand and pulled away. She threw herself at our father. His handcuffed wrists prevented him from hugging her back, and Merry ended up slamming into his chest. He twisted into an awkward curve, resting his cheek on her wool hat, an apple red hat that Mrs. Cohen had insisted Merry wear. Even a kid could see it was inappropriate at a funeral, but I wouldn't argue with Mrs. Cohen.

"Daddy," Merry cried. "I didn't know you'd be here."

"They didn't give me time to write you." He watched me as Merry pressed close to him, staring until I kicked at the frozen ground. "Come here, Lu. Come say hello. It's been a long time."

Yeah. Sure has been a long time since you killed Mama.

The man with my father, his keeper or guard, whatever you'd call him, stood close behind.

"Come on," my father urged.

My teeth chattered hard enough to shake out of their sockets. I pressed my lips together so he couldn't see.

"Lulu, we don't have much time," he said, his voice as ordinary as if we were going to the movies and he was afraid we'd be late.

Merry looked at me, her eyes pleading, begging me to come over. I shuffled the short distance to where they stood, stopping just out of reach. He seemed so different. Not thin, not fat. Thicker. His body appeared hard, even in his baggy suit. His glasses made him look like Clark Kent.

"How old are you?" I asked.

"Thirty-two."

Mama would have been thirty-one.

He cocked his head and inspected me. Merry leaned against him, her head buried in his suit. "And you're thirteen," he said. "You'll be fourteen in July. Wow."

Wow. My throat filled up at the word, and I didn't know why.

I squirmed as he studied me.

"You're tall, like my father."

I tried to remember the photographs Grandma kept on top of the television.

"Your hair is nice," he said. "I like the color."

I touched a mittened hand to my hair.

"I dream of Jeannie with the light brown hair," he sang. I'd forgotten what a nice voice our father had. He'd sung to me when I was little. Never children's songs. He liked to croon, not recite, he'd explain. *Don't expect any "Hickory Dickory Dock" crap from me,* he'd say. At bedtime, he'd sing "Only the Lonely." When Merry was born, "Oh, Pretty Woman" had just come out, and he would go around the house singing that. Hearing Roy Orbison sing always made me think of my father. I turned off the radio whenever one of his songs came on.

"Lulu's lost her voice, huh?" my father said to Merry. Then his face changed. "Come on, girls. Let's go say good-bye."

We walked together, the cold wind stinging my nose, my father swaying a bit, maybe having a hard time keeping his balance since he was handcuffed. How did he walk with his hands locked in front of him? My hands twitched. I wanted to try it.

Cousin Budgie moved as far from us as she could, as though Daddy might reach out and stab her or something. I moved closer to my father, so close the edge of my coat touched his sleeve, and I shivered.

The rabbi chanted in a language I guessed was Hebrew. My father and Uncle Irving swayed with the words. As I listened to the foreign sounds, I wondered if I'd be allowed to lean on my father, if it was legal. Not that I wanted to.

The rabbi switched to English, and I tried hard to pay attention, but too many thoughts fought in my head.

"May you, who are the source of mercy, shelter them beneath your wings eternally, and bind their souls among the living, that they may rest in peace, and let us say: Amen."

"Amen," my father said, his head bowed.

Uncle Irving and Cousin Budgie murmured "Amen," though Budgie might have been whispering, *This is so sick* for all I knew.

"Amen," Merry whispered.

I wanted to say it. I wanted to be a source of mercy. I wanted Grandma to rest in peace, and maybe saying "Amen" was some special way of helping her, but I couldn't speak in front of my father. Finally, I used my right hand to scratch the word on my left arm, repeating each letter in my head.

The rabbi picked up a shovel and lifted a small piece of cold, crumbling earth. He overturned the spade and dropped the soil in Grandma's grave. Merry inhaled as the dirt hit the coffin. The rabbi passed the shovel to Uncle Irving, who repeated the ritual and then handed the shovel off to his daughter. She dug a spoonful of dirt, and then stood holding it, looking caught and angry.

"Why are they doing that?" Merry asked my father. She rubbed her striped gloves over her chapped, wet cheeks.

The rabbi placed a bare hand on Merry's shoulder. "We do this to assist the journey of our loved one."

Merry sobbed, holding our father's arm; he could do nothing but rest his head on Merry's red hat. I grabbed the shovel from my stinking old cousin and placed the thin handle between my father's shackled hands. Side by side, we walked to the edge of Grandma's grave, Merry following. My father and I bent together, lifting up a clod of dirt and, clumsily with our four hands, guided the earth over the grave. Grandma's casket sat dark and lonely at the bottom of the hole.

As one, we overturned the shovel and watched the dirt fall on the center of the coffin.

I handed the shovel to Merry. She dug in too far and came up with an oversize shovelful. I helped her lift it, and together we covered another piece of Grandma's casket.

I'm sorry, Grandma.

"Time to go, Joey," said my father's keeper. The man had a surprisingly kind face, or maybe it was his thick-rimmed glasses. I confused glasses with kindness.

"Can't I visit with the girls a little more, Mac?" My father looked like he'd start crying any minute, making me want to pound my fist right into his chest. Merry clutched his jacket.

"Please," Merry begged. "Stay longer."

My father looked over at the guard, his eyes pleading like Merry's.

"Sorry, Joey," he said. "Time to go, buddy. Say good-bye to your dad, girls."

My father tried to lift his arms to hug us, but his handcuffs held his hands prisoner.

"I love you a million, Daddy." Merry wrapped her arms around his waist. He rested his locked hands on her head.

"I love you a trillion, sweetheart." My father caught my eye. "I love you, Lulu."

I shrugged.

"Look," he said. "Just so you know and don't feel bad later, I know you love me, too."

I stared right into his stabbing, killing eyes. "You don't know that."

"Yes, he does," Merry said, her head still buried in my father's chest.

"Lulu, I'm your father," he said. "You'll never get another one."

"I don't have a father."

"Yes, you do," Merry said. "Daddy is our father." She wouldn't let go of him, locking her arms around him.

"Come on, Joey." The guard tried to pull Merry away from our father, which made her hold on tighter.

"Don't go, Daddy," she said.

Daddy pushed Merry gently away, the fabric of his jacket stretching as she hung on. I had to end this. I put a hand on each of her arms.

"Let go," I said. "Let go, or he'll be in even worse trouble."

Merry released her grip and fell back on me.

"Sorry, baby," Daddy said to Merry. "I'm sorry."

I grabbed Merry and forced her to turn around and start walking.

"You'll be okay, baby," Daddy yelled. The guard touched my father's head as he helped him into the car.

Mama had died almost four years ago, and I didn't even remember where she was buried.

A shandeh un a charpeh.

Uncle Irving and Cousin Budgie were heading back to our limousine. We trailed behind them, ready for the drive back to Brooklyn. I turned around, stretching to see where Grandma was.

I'm sorry, Grandma.

10

Merry

December 1975

I still thought about Grandma every day, even though she'd died nine months ago.

December was almost over; in a few days it would be 1976.

Lulu and I were leaving Duffy, and I was scared.

I'd never packed before. I folded my shirt exactly as Grandma had taught me when I helped her do the laundry, crossing each sleeve across the chest and making a tidy shirt package. Then I placed it in Grandma's beat-up brown suitcase. Why Grandma had a suitcase, I had no idea. She never went anywhere until she died.

I smoothed down my bright blue poncho. The poncho had become my most treasured item of clothing the minute Mrs. Cohen gave it to me for Chanukah.

Nobody had bothered me since they found out about Mrs. Cohen and us. It was as if we were magic all of a sudden. Even Reetha left me alone. Sometimes she even gave me this scary, sugary smile that showed all her yellow teeth, like she thought maybe I'd take her with me.

As if.

I wished I could take Janine and Crystal. We promised each other that we'd always be friends, but Lulu said don't bet on it. *They're not going to take you back here after you leave,* she told me. *Especially since Mrs. Cohen won't be working at Duffy anymore.*

I wondered how soon they would be here, Mrs. Cohen and her husband. Lulu and I didn't know what to call them, so we usually ended up referring to them as "they." Now that we'd be living with them, we needed to figure out better names.

Thinking about moving into their house made me feel like I had to pee. Questions looped through my head. *How could I be good every minute? What would we do in their house? How long would the Cohens like me?*

Lulu stuck her head into my room. "You ready? They'll be here soon." She marched over to my side of the dorm, dropped the paper bag she carried, and immediately began checking the stripped bed for anything I might have forgotten and inspecting each of the rickety dresser drawers.

"I'm scared," I said.

"You sure you have everything?" Lulu knelt, looked under the bed, then got up and dusted off her jeans, which were so long the fashionably shredded bottoms swept the floor. Visible iron springs squeaked as Lulu sat on the thin, bare mattress, bringing her knees to her chin and circling them with her long arms. Lulu got taller, cooler, and smarter each month, while I stayed shrimpy. I needed to grow up. I wanted to rise to the occasion of this most important moment of my life. Mrs. Cohen had to be happy that she took me. The Cohens needed to like me, to love me.

"How long do you think they'll let us stay?" I asked.

Lulu scowled. "I don't know and I'm not asking. You just have to be good. If they let us stay for three years, then I'll be over eighteen, and I can take care of you." Lulu removed my hand from my chest, where I'd been tracing my scar. "*Really* good," she emphasized. "We can't make any trouble for them."

"Aren't they taking us so they can take care of us?"

"They're old. Mrs. Cohen is even retiring."

"She's not that old."

85

"God, Merry, she's like sixty. Sixty! If she were our real mother, she would have given birth to you at like fifty."

Lulu stuffed my collection of Nancy Drew books—her old ones—into Grandma's suitcase. "Mrs. Cohen feels bad for us—but she won't keep us if we cause them trouble. Doctor Cohen won't let her." She gave me the same slit-eyed look I swore I remembered getting from Mama. "They're not adopting us; we're just foster children."

Lulu pushed the bag of framed photos she'd brought into my room on top of everything else in Grandma's suitcase. I'd taken them from Grandma's house when Uncle Irving took us there and said, *Whatever you want is yours.* I didn't know what else to take. The heavy chopper with the worn wooden handle that Grandma always used to make egg salad? The thick maroon blanket on her bed? Lulu saw me examining everything and said, "The Cohens will think you're crazy if you walk in with a bag of Grandma's old stuff," so I just took some pictures, and Lulu kept them safe from Reetha for me.

I wished I'd taken something Grandma had held, though. Something I could touch and feel her.

The biggest photograph showed Daddy on their wedding day. Mama wasn't in the picture. Daddy's teeth were perfect Chiclets, his hair slicked back. He was the handsomest man I'd ever seen.

Daddy held me high on his shoulders as Coney Island wind whipped our hair. I looked like a miniature teenager in a tiny bikini. That was the summer before Mama died. Daddy used to sing the itsy-bitsy bikini song, substituting red polka dot for yellow, because my bathing suit had red dots. Grandma had laughed when I said that. "How could you remember that?" she'd said. "You were just a little *pishkelah.*"

I didn't care if no one believed me. It was one of my favorite memories, and I hardly had any memories of Mama, even though I missed her every single day.

"Do me a favor, Merry," Lulu said. "Don't put the pictures all over your room at the Cohens', okay? Put them away."

Living with the Cohens never felt easy. After almost a year, I knew how to be good, almost perfect, but I kept worrying that, at some point, I'd forget. Lulu kept reminding me how one minute of forgetting could mean disaster.

I walked home from school kicking the blowing October leaves around. Central Park leaves, Manhattan leaves, were prettier than Brooklyn's.

I usually walked the five blocks home from school with my best friend, Katie, but she had a cold and had missed school. Walking alone was okay; just knowing I had a friend kept me company. Plus, I needed to figure stuff out, like how I was ever going to see Daddy again.

I ran my hand down the brand-new coat Mrs. Cohen had bought me at Bloomingdale's, where it felt as though I were in a museum, with everything under glass, sparkling in bright white light. The day we bought the coat, Mrs. Cohen kept hugging me as we walked around the store, both of us touching silky shirts, admiring gold lockets and watches.

Anne.

Mom.

Mrs. Cohen.

I still didn't have a clue what to call her.

The night Lulu and I moved in, Mrs. Cohen had said, "Call me Anne," and a few weeks later, she'd said, "You can call me Mom if you like," in a wishing kind of voice, but when I tried it out, it sounded stupid. The Cohens' real children, who were grown-ups with little kids of their own, looked sour and angry when they heard me call her Mom. Most of all, I couldn't do it because I thought Mama would be mad.

Even if I'd wanted to call Mrs. Cohen Mom, which sometimes I sort of did, then I'd have to call Doctor Cohen Dad, but he hadn't asked, and anyway, I still had a real father. So now, I didn't call either of them anything, which made conversations hard. Grandma would have said this should be the worst thing that ever happened. She'd've told me to stop thinking so much.

I tugged my coat closer, shielding out the wind.

Thinking about my father made everything feel swimmy. Even with Katie, I had to pretend Daddy was dead. Lulu had given me orders, before we started at our new school.

"I have something to tell you," Lulu had begun, acting as though I might throw a fit, which I never did anymore. "When we start school, you're not allowed to say anything about our father or jail or our mother or anything." This had all come out in one fast breath of a sentence.

"Who said? Them?" "Them," of course, was the Cohens.

"I say." Lulu had held her hand out when I squawked. "I'm not going to be Murder Girl anymore and neither are you. Understand?"

I'd started crying, quietly though, so Mrs. Cohen didn't come in all upset and wanting to know what was happening.

Lulu had poked me in the shoulder. "Quit it."

"Ouch."

"Listen to me." She'd put her hands on my shoulders. "This is our story: Our parents died in a car crash. That's it. They crashed upstate. Driving to the Catskills. We lived with Mimi Rubee until she died. We went to Duffy because we had no other relatives. Now we're here. That's that."

Lulu was all I had. I obeyed her no matter what.

Sooner than I'd wanted, I reached the Cohens' large white apartment building on West Eighty-seventh Street. The doorman, Dominic, nodded and smiled just as he always did when opening the door. I usually thought about Dominic in the last few steps before turning down our block. How I had to smile and make sure he didn't think I was spoiled or taking him for granted or anything. I hated having a doorman.

After grinning and thanking him, I ran to the waiting elevator and pressed the button for six, feeling the familiar whoosh as it went up. I put my key in the door, praying no one was home. By myself, I could snoop around and not worry if I was being good or bad.

"Merry?" Mrs. Cohen walked out from the kitchen, wiping her hands on a blue-checked dish towel. "Guess who's here!"

I tried not to show my feelings. "Eleanor?" I asked. Mrs. Cohen's daughter acted like something stunk whenever she saw me. At least Mrs. Cohen's son just pretended I didn't exist.

"Come join us. We have brownies and ice cream."

I put my book bag down in the foyer and shuffled to the kitchen. "Hi," I said to Eleanor, trying not to sound disappointed.

Eleanor nodded as she tried to disentangle herself from her five-year-old, Rachel, who tugged at Eleanor's long skirt. Ugly, as were all her clothes.

Her skirt resembled a burlap bag, and her velvet shirt had stiff spots where breast milk had leaked. A scarf tied on the back of her head held back her frizzy blond hair. Lulu said that Eleanor dressed as if she thought she was still a hippie teenager. I'd heard Doctor Cohen ask Mrs. Cohen why Eleanor had to dress like a peasant. Her brother, Saul, dressed the opposite, with everything perfectly tucked. He was a surgeon, like Doctor Cohen, and kept his life precise and clean.

"Mom, please, can you get her while I nurse the baby?" Eleanor nudged Rachel toward Mrs. Cohen with her knee.

"Merry, why don't you hold Rachel?" Mrs. Cohen turned her nervous sunshine smile on Rachel. "Don't you want Cousin Merry to read to you, darling?"

Rachel raced to the pile of books and toys Mrs. Cohen kept in a wicker basket. Eleanor rolled her eyes. I rubbed my thumb against my lower lip.

"Stop confusing her," Eleanor said. "If you keep calling everyone her cousin, Rachel won't have a clue what it means."

Mrs. Cohen looked apologetically first at Eleanor, then at me. "Hardly everyone." She squeezed my shoulder and handed me a dish of ice cream topped with a fat, walnut-studded brownie, which I'd throw up if I tried to force it past my closed throat.

"Read this." Rachel dropped a Dr. Seuss book in my lap. I grabbed the book and carried her to the living room before Mrs. Cohen or Eleanor said any more.

"The sun did not shine. It was too wet to play," I read. Rachel snuggled in close, slipping a thumb in her rosebud of a mouth.

Across from the couch stood the Cohens' satiny baby grand piano, which seemed not a baby but enormous. Since it was Monday, when the cleaning lady came, the black top gleamed. Pictures and pictures and more pictures cluttered the top, the gilded frames outlining the Cohens' lives.

A lone picture of Lulu and me perched on edge of the piano, taken at the home of relatives of Doctor Cohen's who lived in Long Island. We both wore tiny, flat smiles. I'd clung to Lulu the entire day. Nobody had talked to us except to comment on how beautiful I was—*Look at those curls and dimples!*—ignoring Lulu as though she were my babysitter.

"So we sat in the house/All that cold, cold, wet day."

When we first came to live with the Cohens, I hadn't wanted to be anywhere without Lulu. I'd even waited outside the bathroom for her. The apartment seemed enormous, even though I'd visited before. The prospect of living with a man seemed impossibly strange. My breath had come in short, little bursts as Lulu and I walked around the apartment. Mrs. Cohen had said it was our home now, except we should never go into Doctor Cohen's study; entering that room was forbidden. A month later, I saw Doctor Cohen bring Rachel in to draw and play with her dolls while he worked.

I bet Daddy wouldn't keep me out of his study. Lulu said Mama usually let us play in her room, that we used to make her big bed into our circus grounds, propping a broomstick under the covers to create the big top. Lulu only talked about these things late at night when I had a nightmare that made my head hurt so bad I thought I might smash it open just to make the pain stop and I ran into Lulu's room.

Rachel grew heavy as she slurped on her thumb and settled in deeper. If I lived with Daddy and he had a study, I didn't think he'd forbid me to enter.

As I read the last line of the book, I saw Rachel had drifted off to sleep. I covered her with the patchwork afghan Mrs. Cohen kept on the couch and tiptoed to my room.

Having a space just for me still surprised me. Where everything at Duffy had been limp and worn, here new, shiny things filled my room. Silky yellow ropes tied back billowing orange curtains. Rainbow pillows covered my bed. The only thing I didn't like was the framed poster of a tree in winter, stripped bare with dark limbs hanging against a bleak gray background. I found the picture depressing, but the Cohens liked it so much I pretended to like it also.

I noticed two new envelopes on my bed and rushed over. They had to be from my father. No one else mailed me anything. One was for me, and one would be for Lulu. Lulu wouldn't open Daddy's letters, so he addressed them to me, then I had the job of trying to get Lulu to listen to what he'd written, a task I usually failed.

I slit open my envelope.

Dear Merry, I miss you like you wouldn't believe. Like walls miss paint! Like Abbott missed Costello! Like baseballs miss bats! It's sure been a long sad time since Grandma died and I got to see both you and Lulu.

All Daddy's letters started with this: how he missed me, and how long it had been since he'd seen me. Last week's letters had included skies missing stars and soap missing washcloths.

Nothing new here (ha ha!). Well, that's not true. I got a roommate. Not exactly a good thing in prison. It gets more crowded here every day. I knew that eventually my time would come. At least this guy (his name is Hank) doesn't seem out to do me dirty.

Sometimes the stuff my father wrote made me wish I were blind.

I finished my optician program. Can you believe it? I really did learn a new trade in here. Grandma would be happy. I make lenses for glasses now. I'm a grinder. I'll tell you all about it when I see you. And when will that be? I wrote to your new foster parents, but I'm still waiting for a reply. By the way, Cookie, I told them not to think about adopting you. I don't have any intention of giving up my only family.

Was Daddy mad at me? I thought of him throwing things. Banging things. Hurting the Cohens. Everything tightened, and I tapped my chest until the feeling passed.

Did the Cohens want to adopt Lulu and me? Was that why Daddy had double-underlined? I didn't dare ask my father when I wrote back, because if the Cohens saw the letters, maybe they'd think I didn't want them to adopt me. Or that I did.

Merry, keep telling them you want to come. Ask them a lot! I need you soooooo much!
So, how is school? Are you still best friends with Katie? I look forward to

meeting her when I get out of here. My lawyer is working on another appeal.
He says they should have treated a crime of passion different.

  Anyway, remember how much I love you. I miss you like cars miss wheels.
Love, Daddy

I dropped the prison paper and tried to figure out how I could visit my father. I couldn't imagine Mrs. Cohen, wearing her gold bracelets and scarves, going with me into a prison.

I had to hide this letter. I had to get the Cohens to take me to Daddy before he got us all in trouble. What if they realized we were too hard to have around? What if they gave us back before Lulu turned eighteen?

11

Merry

November 1977

I hope I didn't take advantage of your sister." Mrs. Cohen pushed a handful of stuffing into the turkey as I steadied it. "Do you think buying the turkey for me put her out?"

Lulu worked at a supermarket after school, which Mrs. Cohen thought gave Lulu the inside track to the best bird.

"It's fine." Even after two years, I avoided directly addressing Mrs. Cohen. I'd turn twelve in December, and I still didn't know how to handle the problem. Working with her in the kitchen was torture. I tilted my head down and caught her eye each time I needed to ask or answer her. "All the kids at the A & P try to get the best turkey for their parents. Lulu told me."

I cringed hearing myself say *parent* but used it anyway, knowing it made Mrs. Cohen happy. I didn't care about lying, not when my lies made people feel special. That's why people liked me. Anyway, did Mrs. Cohen actually believe Lulu cared about which turkey we served for Thanksgiving? Not that Lulu would deny any request Mrs. Cohen made, but after she'd go on and on about how annoying Mrs. Cohen was.

"Lulu is so sensitive to breaking rules." Mrs. Cohen patted the turkey. "I just wanted to have a big enough bird. You're sure she's not angry at me?"

Mrs. Cohen mined me for information as though I had some magic bead on my sister. As if. You'd have as much luck breaking into Fort Knox as you would trying to pry something personal from Lulu. Mrs. Cohen was desperate to understand my sister. If I wanted, I could have told her Lulu cared only about applying to colleges outside New York and getting away from the Cohens.

When I'd recently asked Lulu why she hated the Cohens so much, she'd snapped her fingers in my face and said, "Wake up, Merry. We're just their project. You don't really believe they think we're family, do you?" She'd gotten a sort of twisted look on her face, which I almost thought meant she was going to cry. "The only family we have is each other."

I would have mentioned Daddy, but that would only make Lulu mad.

"She's not angry," I assured Mrs. Cohen. "Just tired."

Lulu had practically thrown the turkey on the table when she came home last night. Mrs. Cohen often fretted about the hours Lulu worked, but Doctor Cohen insisted that as long as Lulu stayed on the honor roll—*and for goodness' sake, Anne, she has the third-highest grades in the school*—he approved of her long hours. Working built character. It would help her attain a scholarship.

Doctor Cohen used words like *attain* instead of *get*. My grades, good or bad, never worked him up, even though I was in seventh grade now. He left me to Mrs. Cohen. Most of the time it was Mrs. Cohen and me hanging out alone at home, just the two of us. Lulu was hardly ever around. If she wasn't working at the supermarket, she was serving food at a homeless shelter or volunteering at a hospital in Harlem. *The savior*, Eleanor called her, but she didn't sound like she was complimenting Lulu. *That girl has a savior complex*, she'd say to Mrs. Cohen, shaking her head and pursing her lips.

"Would you start slicing the potatoes?" Mrs. Cohen asked.

I dropped the now fully stuffed turkey, which weighed a ton, and reached for the cutting board. I rinsed and rerinsed the potatoes the way

Mrs. Cohen had taught me, then cut each of them in quarters for boiling and mashing, trying to make all the pieces as equal as possible.

"Is everyone coming?" I smiled to show how excited I was at the prospect of the Cohen family overrunning the apartment.

Mrs. Cohen seemed pleased by my question. "Everyone will be here."

"Do you want me to shine the good glasses?" I hoped not. We'd been in the kitchen for hours, and spending so much time trapped with her exhausted me.

"What would I do without you?" Mrs. Cohen asked.

I turned my back on her and made a face in the toaster. Then I reached for the glasses.

The roasted turkey looked like an advertisement from the *Ladies' Home Journal*. Doctor Cohen placed the silver platter on the dining room table. The table, opened to its fullest extension and covered with a heavy white tablecloth, ironed by the cleaning woman that morning, looked like a television show. Lulu had rolled her eyes when Mrs. Cohen explained how the woman didn't mind coming in on a holiday because they paid her triple time.

"As though that makes a difference," Lulu had muttered. "They should give her extra money for slaving for them all year. A day's salary for not working would be a nice Thanksgiving gesture, wouldn't it? Instead of tearing her away from her family?"

I'd agreed, but been afraid Mrs. Cohen would hear us and get all upset and hurt. Lulu, who'd wanted so much for the Cohens to take us into their home, seemed to hate them more with each passing year.

"Before we slice the turkey, let us give thanks." Doctor Cohen placed his hands lightly on each side of the platter, as though presenting it for thought. He looked to either side of the table, the left, where Eleanor sat with her family, then the right, gazing proudly at Saul-the-other-surgeon and his wife and baby.

Mrs. Cohen sunshined her grin around the room. "Who wants to start?"

I was sure they were all waiting for Lulu and me to give thanks for the Cohens taking us in, as though we were puppies rescued from the pound and certain death, who should roll over and expose our bellies for petting.

Last year I'd mumbled something about being grateful for everyone being healthy. Lulu had said we should give thanks that nobody at the table had family who'd died in Vietnam. Mrs. Cohen had nodded as if Lulu had said the wisest thing in the world, though I knew Lulu had been digging at them for being so entitled. All I'd wanted was for Lulu to shut up before the Cohens got mad.

Lulu thought the Cohens were the worst sort of liberals, stuffed with money and pretending to be regular people. Soon after we'd enrolled in our new schools in Manhattan, Lulu became what Doctor Cohen called *our in-house protester.*

Mrs. Cohen worried when Lulu covered her bedroom walls with slogans like "Boycott Lettuce and Grapes" and "Sisterhood Is Powerful."

"Not that I don't sympathize with Lulu's beliefs," Mrs. Cohen had told me recently, "and of course women should have equal rights, but I don't want her becoming obsessed."

I thought Lulu's save-the-world act was actually a make-the-Cohens-feel-bad thing. Mrs. Cohen desperately wanted to buy Lulu cute outfits and take her for a good haircut. Instead, Lulu hung frayed overalls on her bony body and let her light brown hair hang longer and longer and longer down her back—tying it up with a blue bandanna when the weather got hot. When Mrs. Cohen told Lulu that *the right haircut would complement her simply gorgeous bone structure,* Lulu said college applications wouldn't ask for pictures, but thanks for the idea. Later, when we were alone, Lulu accused Mrs. Cohen of really meaning Lulu was plain as soup and needed help.

"Come on, we're waiting," Saul said.

"I'll start," his wife, Amy, said.

Doctor Cohen nodded and smiled. Anyone could see Amy was his favorite. "Go ahead, dear."

"I'm thankful for so much." Amy looked around the table. "I'm thankful Mom and Dad watch out for everyone."

Amy smiled meaningfully at Lulu and me. My smile felt like it should be on one of those Day of the Dead dolls that we'd studied at school. Lulu laced her fingers together and leaned her chin on the bridge she'd made.

"In this time of racial strife, countries at war, cultural wars, I'm grateful for this safe haven." Amy smiled shyly as she turned to Saul, who held their baby. "And, most of all, for my husband and beautiful baby."

Approving smiles lit up all around the table, except of course for Eleanor. I'd heard her call Amy a simpering suck-up, too good to be true. Eleanor was just too evil to recognize good existed. Amy and Mrs. Cohen were both good, even if I couldn't stand Amy either. Lulu called them liberal Lady Bountifuls.

Defending Mrs. Cohen had become my job.

Rachel pressed herself against Eleanor's chest and whispered.

"Rachel has something to say," Eleanor said.

"What is it, sweetheart?" Mrs. Cohen leaned forward as though she were about to get a million dollars.

"I'm grateful I have a mommy and daddy. And that I don't have to be fostered."

I clenched and unclenched the edge of the stiff white tablecloth.

The room became silent. Finally, Doctor Cohen cleared his throat and said, "We're grateful to be able to provide a home for Lulu and Merry. It gives us great pleasure. Being a father to them adds a new dimension at this time in my life."

Lulu made see-what-I-mean eyes at me.

"What are you girls grateful for?" Amy asked.

I pressed my lips together, praying for Lulu to talk so they'd leave me alone. I opened my eyes wide at my sister, pleading. Lulu's shoulders fell in disgust. *Fine.* She clasped her hands in front of her and gave me a tight little smile indicating, *Okay, you asked for it.*

"I'm grateful the war is over and that we never had napalm raining down on us. I'm grateful I'm not starving in Ethiopia. I'm grateful I'm not in Appalachia with legs bowed from rickets." She stopped and smiled. "Oh, and I'm glad I was taken in here. Thank you, Cohen family."

Doctor Cohen sucked in a deep breath. "While your social conscience is a blessing, Lulu, I hope you someday learn why ethics and principles are best served with respect."

Lulu made a low rumbling sound.

"Do you have a comment, Lulu?" Doctor Cohen asked.

Mrs. Cohen interrupted. "Paul, please, cut the turkey."

"Let me explore this a moment, Anne." Doctor Cohen leaned forward. "Are you uncomfortable with our values, Lulu?"

Why did Mr. Cohen have to embarrass her? Lulu stared at the tablecloth and put her arms under the table, probably spelling words like *screw you* on her arm. I felt as though my skin would pop from all the hot words running through me.

"I'm certain we have something here for which you could be thankful. Or at the very least, grateful," Mr. Cohen said. "Is there nothing about our values you can stomach?"

"Paul," Mrs. Cohen warned.

"Sorry, Anne, I've had enough ingratitude. We've done everything possible for these girls. Didn't we take them from that place and from their virtual gutter of a family?"

I jumped up. "Leave Lulu alone. You're being mean. Why should I be thankful that you won't let me see my father? Wouldn't it be respectful to let me see him? He's not a gutter. He's my family. He's all by himself. *Why are you punishing me?*"

"Merry." Lulu reached out. "Don't."

I pushed away Lulu's hand. "Why can't I say anything? Why do I have to pretend he's dead? It's not fair." I banged my fist on the white tablecloth. Each time I asked to visit Daddy, they shushed me and said *Someday,* and *When the time is right,* and once more I knew nobody wanted to talk to me.

"Sweetheart. Calm down. Where is this coming from?" Mrs. Cohen rose.

"I told you. I want to see my father." I wrapped my arms around myself and rocked back and forth. "Please. Please. Please. Let me see my father."

Amy put an arm over my shoulders and held her hand up to stop Mrs. Cohen from coming over. "Why in the world does she have to pretend that her father is dead?"

12

Merry

February 1978

Going to prison by car felt entirely different from taking the Staten Island Ferry. I missed the kissing couples and the choppy waves and seeing the World Trade Center grow before my eyes. The car ride was boring in comparison, but I was grateful to be going at all, whether by boat, car, or flying in over the prison walls. Mrs. Cohen had worked a hard three months to convince Doctor Cohen to let me visit Daddy. When he finally came around to the idea, he decided he'd be the one to take me.

Did he think the prisoners would attack Mrs. Cohen? Dr. Cohen always said Mrs. Cohen wasn't strict enough; maybe he thought she'd let me hang out with the prisoners, and I'd learn how to rob banks.

I peeked at Doctor Cohen, his hands steady on the wheel. I'd never been alone with him, not since we'd moved in, over two years ago now. He was a quiet man, but not the kind of quiet that made you feel comfortable. I felt stuck in a car silence where I knew I was boring him the entire time, and no matter how much I tried to think of stuff to talk about, I couldn't imagine what in my life could interest him.

"Will we see the World Trade Center towers?" I asked. "My grandmother and I always saw it when we took the ferry. They're six years old now, right?" I asked the question, despite knowing the answer, because Doctor Cohen enjoyed knowing things.

"That's right. Seven years this July. If it weren't for the fog, we'd see the Towers at some point." Doctor Cohen shot me a quick glance, then put his eyes back on the road. "Is engineering an interest of yours? Architecture?"

I couldn't tell Doctor Cohen that the Towers had become a visible marking of my mother's death. "My father told me about them being built," I said. "He read about the celebrations when they opened." I didn't mention that was right after my mother died. When they put him in jail.

"Oh, really? Where?"

"In the newspaper. Grandma sent him a subscription."

"The *Daily News*?"

I knew what Doctor Cohen thought of the *Daily News*. Did Doctor Cohen think my father was stupid?

"No, the *Times*," I lied. Actually, it had been the *Post*.

"Really." Doctor Cohen nodded a few times. He did that whenever he learned something new, as though he were nodding it into a mental filing cabinet.

"My father's a big reader. His cell is probably overflowing with books." I squished my face in embarrassment. Despite the fact that Doctor Cohen was driving me to the prison, I felt weird mentioning anything to do with it.

"Perhaps for Chanukah we can pick out some books for you and Lulu to send him," Doctor Cohen said, turning for a moment and giving me a kind smile. "Or if he can't get presents, perhaps we can make a donation to the prison library."

"That would be nice." My voice warbled in shame. I hated the entire discussion.

"You know," said Doctor Cohen, "helping people out of bad situations is a blessing. I'd be happy to help your father in his quest for learning and growth. Perhaps he and I can become friends."

Doctor Cohen always tried to rise to the occasion and do the right thing. I tried to picture him and my father as friends. Despite Daddy being the friendliest person in the world, Doctor Cohen would make him uncomfortable. Doctor Cohen made me uncomfortable every day—he was too much the kind of man you never imagined messing up.

"That would be nice," I repeated. I couldn't think of one other thing to say, so I leaned on the window and closed my eyes.

It seemed like only moments later I was jarred awake as we pulled up to the prison and parked. I didn't know a parking lot existed at prison. Doctor Cohen's Chrysler New Yorker was sleek and black and stuck out from the rusty, faded cars filling the lot.

Going through what Grandma and I had taken to calling the searching party felt humiliating without Grandma's funny comments. *Look, Merry. Mrs. Feingold's dyed her hair again. She's a chemist's rainbow.* Grandma had worked so hard to make the prison an interesting little world.

Doctor Cohen stuck out standing in the visitors' waiting line, dressed in his suit and tie, surrounded by the worn-out women, their screeching children, and a smattering of lost-looking men who wore stretchy shirts with bright designs or faded work clothes.

I adjusted my valentine red jumpsuit. It was brand-new, and I hoped my father would think I looked pretty. Mrs. Cohen had bought it for me after Thanksgiving. The red denim had a black zipper running past my waist.

"Oh, Merry! You're so perfect and tiny, you look like a little doll," Mrs. Cohen had exclaimed. She'd bought me half of Bloomingdale's trying to erase Thanksgiving. Then she'd let me get my ears pierced and bought me gold balls, then gold hoops for when my ears healed. Lulu said I looked ridiculous, but I didn't care. I thought I looked good. Mrs. Cohen said so, too.

I took shallow, little breaths as we moved up to first in line, holding my hands together in front of me to keep from tapping my chest.

"Why, Miss Merry!" Officer McNulty said. "I barely recognized you. You've grown into a young lady. We haven't seen you for quite some time."

I jumped in front of Doctor Cohen to show him what he was supposed to do for the guard. I lifted my arms, saying as I did, "My grandma died."

"Oh, I'm sorry. Your grandma was a lovely one, a true lady."

I wanted to hug Officer McNulty.

"So who is this bringing you today?" he asked.

"I'm Doctor Cohen." He put out his hand, which Officer McNulty took with a look of surprise. "Merry lives with my wife and me."

"Isn't that nice? Aren't you lucky, Merry?" Officer McNulty patted down Doctor Cohen quickly and with an air of deference.

"It's been wonderful," I said, looking through the crowded room for Daddy. There he was, sitting at their regular table, at the opposite end from Pete and his so-fat-you-couldn't-help-but-stare wife, Annette. People tended to stick to the same tables each week; still, I hadn't expected things to look so much the same. Didn't they ever paint the walls or anything?

"Merry!" Daddy cried as I ran to him. I fell into his arms, ignoring the rules. He hugged me hard, so hard it made up for the fact he had to let go a moment later. I wanted to crawl into his lap and feel him hug me—I didn't care if I was twelve.

"Oh, Jesus, you look so beautiful. Stand up. Spin around. Let me see you."

I twirled for him, glad I'd worn clothes that made me look special.

"You look like a million bucks. You're as gorgeous as your mother, and that is some bit of gorgeous, sweetheart."

Doctor Cohen looked startled. No Cohen ever referred to Mama, acting as though saying her name would be a mortal sin.

"You must be Doctor Cohen," my father said. "A pleasure to meet you."

"Call me Paul, please." He took my father's offered hand.

"How was the trip out?" my father asked as he slid into his seat at the picnic-style table. I sat across from him, gesturing at Doctor Cohen to sit next to me.

"Fine, fine," Doctor Cohen said. "We took the Verrazano. Not much traffic."

"Any trouble finding the place?"

Doctor Cohen's shoulders softened from the locked position they'd been in since entering the prison as Daddy put him at ease. "Easy as could be. The *place* gives good directions." He said "the place" as though saying "Richmond Prison" would embarrass my father.

"So how's my girl been?"

Doctor Cohen shocked me by putting an arm around my shoulders; he'd never touched me before. "Good as gold. I'd have brought her report card, but—"

"How'd she do?" Daddy interrupted, probably not wanting Doctor Cohen to remind him *the place* didn't let you carry in anything.

"Great. We're proud of her. She's a model girl."

I wanted to reach over and pat my father's hand, his cheek. He looked older. His mouth hung looser in a sad way. I counted on my fingers. He was thirty-five years old.

"How's Lulu?" he asked me. "Does she read my letters?"

"Um, most of them," I said. "I got an A on my history and spelling tests last week. And did you remember that I wrote you about getting into the SP class?"

"That's the special progress," Doctor Cohen cut in. "It means she'll be doing the more difficult work."

"I know what *SP* means." Daddy sounded less friendly now. "So how about Lulu? How's my older girl doing in school?"

Doctor Cohen hesitated a moment; then he spoke slowly and without inflection. "Very well. She's in advanced classes for science and math. Lulu has a flair for the technical."

"Probably gets it from me." Now my father sounded plain argumentative. "I made fittings for ships to exacting standards, you know. Did Merry tell you I'm almost a licensed optician now?"

"I don't think I heard that." Doctor Cohen nodded. "But good for you."

"You don't need to patronize me, buddy." Daddy's chest puffed up. Just a little, but enough that I could see it.

Doctor Cohen leaned an elbow on the table and spoke softly. "Mr. Zachariah, you have no argument with me. My wife and I are happy to care for Lulu and Merry." He twisted his gold cuff link. "My wife quite fell in love with them at Duffy-Parkman. They're like family now. I'm not your enemy. Nevertheless, I'll brook no insults from you."

I folded my hands and stared down at the table, twisting my ankles around each other, and pressing them together where no one could see. My hands twitched toward my chest again, but Lulu's invisible hand held me back. I looked sideways at the guards lurking in every corner.

"Now, then," Doctor Cohen continued when my father said nothing. "Merry tells me you like books. Shall we see what we can do about getting you some reading material?"

Daddy gave me a look that frightened and saddened me at the same time. "Merry knows what I like." He sounded deflated. "She can take care of me."

"Don't you think that's a bit more responsibility than a young girl needs?"

"Family takes care of family." Daddy crossed his arms.

Doctor Cohen looked as though he'd just licked a lemon slice. I knew what he was thinking. Daddy knew what he was thinking.

"You think I'm a monster, Doc. Maybe I was." Daddy paused. "Yeah, I guess I was the worst kind of monster. But I was drunk and heartbroken. You think that doesn't excuse me, but I'm paying my dues."

Doctor Cohen leaned in and spoke quietly. "It seems your girls are paying those dues as much as you."

"I guess it looks that way to someone like you, but from where I'm sitting, it looks like they're doing okay. They have you, right? From what Merry writes, your wife is a real doll." My father took off his glasses. His eyes reminded me of Grandma's. "The girls are getting good marks in school. Lulu is going to college."

"But they don't have parents, do they?" Doctor Cohen said. "Nothing makes up for losing a mother."

I couldn't think of what to do to stop this.

"My girls have me. Their father."

"Hardly," Doctor Cohen said.

"I love my girls." Daddy's eyes narrowed. "And Merry looks out for me. She always will. Right, Merry?"

I held my breath and closed my eyes, wishing I were far away. Then I opened them. "Right, Daddy."

Part 2

13

Lulu

1982

Anatomy class began today. In half an hour, I'd be facing a room of draped cadavers. I couldn't get down more than a cup of coffee for breakfast that morning.

Despite autumn being just weeks away, Boston still looked like summer. This city seemed positively bucolic. Even the crummiest neighborhoods had breathing space compared to New York City.

I walked down Commonwealth Avenue, reveling in the wide sidewalks and the grassy mall parting the road like a green river. In a few months, magical white Christmas lights strung up for blocks and blocks would decorate the trees. Even when Comm Ave—as the locals called the street—became ordinary, turning from Back Bay brownstones to student-ridden Kenmore Square lined with dorms, cheap delis, and Burger Kings, I loved it, because no matter what, I wasn't in New York City.

This was my first year at Cabot Medical School, the only place I'd applied. Cabot was in Boston, my birthplace of freedom, where I'd gone to college. In Boston, I'd started over. In Boston, no one knew me. In Boston, I'd killed Murder Girl.

During college, no one thought of me as anyone but the quiet girl who spent all her time studying. As far as everyone but my roommate could tell, I lived in the library, and for as much as I talked to her, I might as well have slept in a library carrel. By my second year, I'd rented an apartment so small and unwanted that between a dribble of Cohen money and what I earned working part-time in the State Medical Lab, I could afford it.

The only way I'd felt safe in college was by keeping my own counsel. Only solitude gave me peace. Loneliness had seemed a small price for four years of relaxed obscurity after my life at Duffy and at the Cohens'. I supposed it would be a long time before the enforced mean togetherness I'd endured at Duffy and the impenetrable guard I'd worn at the Cohens' wore off. The cover story I'd invented during high school had come at the price of constant vigilance.

Sometimes I remembered my brief flush of excitement at thinking I could become part of the Sachs family, when I'd dreamed myself into becoming Hillary's adopted sister. I'd wonder if they'd felt my hunger for their lives and if it had scared them away. Maybe that's why Hillary had disappeared after she'd brought me to her house. I imagined her mother and father warning her away from me. *Find another place to volunteer, dear,* they'd said in my scenario. *That girl is too needy.* My humiliating visit with the Sachses taught me to give nothing away.

Now, when I joined the line of young men and women walking up the steps of Cabot, I didn't recognize anyone, not one person to whom I could say hello or give a friendly nod. Since beginning my medical school studies, just as in college, and high school, I'd concentrated on books and made no real friends; today I wished I'd been friendlier. You wanted someone to have your back when you met a roomful of dead people.

Inside, I ran down the flight of steps to the basement and entered the anatomy lab. Formaldehyde, fresh paint, and the smell of fear surrounded me. Everyone stood frozen, waiting for our professor to speak.

"Ladies and gentlemen, I'm Doctor Eli Haslett. Welcome to death." His gentle smile showed he wasn't out to hurt us, but his words made me shiver. His white coat was stiff and clean. His clear, pink complexion belied his graying hair. He had the face of a guilt-free man, a man with no reason to fear the dead.

"Please approach your tables," he said. "Take note that the table number correlates to your group number."

Doctor Haslett's fatherly voice seemed designed to help scared students slice a corpse. He nodded with approval as we made our way down the line of blue-sheeted bodies lying on surgically clean metal tables.

Most of us clutched yellow papers, our introductory instructions from Doctor Haslett to Gross Anatomy, Section 1. Mine read: "Group Five: Ronald Young, Henry Yee, Marta Zayas, and Louise Zachariah."

"Personal Suggestions" were underneath. Doctor Haslett's wisdom included what to wear: clothes suitable for trashing later; and the best way to remove the stink of formaldehyde: lemon Joy dishwashing soap. He gave hints for emotions and feelings: Nauseated? Use Vicks. Feeling faint? Put your head between your knees. Horrified? Time heals. For emotional or spiritual crises, he suggested we speak to our clergy, our friends, our family, all of which left me swinging in the breeze.

When I reached table five, my shoulders stiffened.

A sheet hinted at the faint outline of a human body. My donor seemed tiny. Good God, they didn't give out children, did they? Henry Yee—we all had small name tags pinned to our short white coats—claimed the place by the cadaver's right shoulder. Did the body offer better and worse places to stand? I took our donor's left shoulder, sure that Henry, Chinese, wearing a crisp blue shirt and standing at attention, knew something I didn't.

Marta Zayas and Ronald Young joined us. Ronald put out his hand. "Ron."

"Lulu," I said without thinking.

"Family nickname?" Ron asked. LOUISE was printed on my badge.

I shook my head and claimed Lulu as one of those affected Muffy, Kiki, Puffy prep names. "School name."

Ron nodded knowingly and exchanged a quick glance with Marta, bonding, black man and Latina woman against the entitled European woman. Table five was the United Nations of anatomy class, and I was going to represent privilege. Marta gave me a warm smile, and I let a tiny chip of ice drop off my shoulder.

I shivered. The room was chilly and windowless. Pungent particles of formaldehyde seeped into my skin, lined my nostrils. I briefly brought my arm up to my nose, sniffing the Vicks VapoRub I'd dotted on my wrist like perfume that morning.

Ron, Marta, Henry, and I looked at each other.

After you, after you.

Steeling myself, I reached out and took hold of the edge of the cold sheet. Slowly, I uncovered the facedown body. I reminded myself to breathe. Thin white gauze wrapped our cadaver's head. My knuckles brushed against cold skin that reminded me of a plastic doll. The bumps of her spine—I could see now the body was female—were visible as strung pearls.

How had this woman died? Had she died alone? Like Mama? I bit my tongue to chase away the stab of pain in my gut. My mother's blood had been Crayola red. No blood ran from this body. I pushed away memories of Mama, refusing to think she might have lived if I'd run faster, gotten Teenie quicker. I refused to think of her as ashy bones.

"Take turns marching your fingers up the spine," Dr. Haslett told us. "Don't forget to include your thumbs."

Henry threw his arm on the body, blocking me. His turn. I'd already drawn down the drape. He walked his thumb up and down the spine three times.

"Hey, Henry, give a brother a chance," Ron finally said.

Henry drew back, and Ron's long, articulated fingers replaced Henry's chunky ones. Ron had surgeon hands. I looked down at mine. A washer-woman's fingers. Short, blunt nails. Broad hands, like Grandma Zelda's.

Marta's nails were shell pink. She had a nun's hands, a saint's fingers. Marta gently ran her fingers up and down our woman's spine, feeling each vertebra. Marta's hands were those I'd want touching me if I were dead.

My mother had had delicate hands. Her rings would be too small for me.

Had Aunt Cilla taken Mama's sliver of diamond engagement ring? Her thick, gold wedding band, the amethyst Mimi Rubee gave Mama on Mama's sixteenth birthday—did Aunt Cilla have everything?

"Lulu?" Marta said. "Your turn again."

My hand shook as I touched the dead skin. I flexed my fingers. If I'd been quicker, smarter, if I'd never opened the door, Mama would be alive. I knew that much was true.

"You okay?" Henry asked.

"Fine." I put my hand flat on her back. Had she been religious? Jewish? Christian? Buddhist? Fast, so no one could notice, I traced a tiny cross on her back, then a Star of David, wishing I knew more symbols.

Four months later, Anne Cohen died.

I was on my way to sit shivah, having missed the funeral. Observant Jews bury their dead fast, and then mourn them for seven days. Doctor Cohen insisted on following the letter of Jewish law and buried Anne the day after she died, giving me permission not to attend. He said he didn't want me to miss any classes. That was the day we were to be dissecting human hearts. Doctor Cohen said he knew how important the heart was.

Anne had died early Monday morning. Today was Sunday, the last day the family would sit shivah. I'd get to New York City in time to catch the final hours of official mourning, and then tomorrow I'd take the bus back to Boston.

The Greyhound bus sped down the highway. December slush covered the grass at the side of the road. I'd dreaded this ride, but resigned myself to it. Bus rides I didn't need, but sleep I could use, desperately.

Hours of brain-numbing classes followed by hours of studying, day after day, month after month, had left me exhausted. Weekends were spent in the library with my study group. Henry, Ron, Marta, and I were now close as family, if one considered *family* synonymous with *close.*

Awake despite my profound fatigue, I numbly watched the passing view. We rode along a stretch of Connecticut road bordering the ocean, and I pictured myself drifting off to someplace new and free.

Mrs. Cohen had died just after Merry's seventeenth birthday. I'd meant to go home for the celebration dinner. The Cohens had been planning to take Merry and me to Windows on the World, where Merry had always wanted to go. Apparently, our father had described it from some magazine he read. *Gourmet? New York?* What magazines did they carry in a prison library?

Merry wanted to watch the world light up just as our father had described. Doctor Cohen planned for us to eat at sunset, but I ended up having too much schoolwork and didn't go. Three days after Merry's birthday dinner, a stroke killed Anne.

I closed my eyes, trying to drag sleep to me. I wanted to be sadder. Mrs. Cohen had been good to us. She'd tried to mother me, but each time she hugged me, I became anesthetized. Hugging her back took all my willpower.

I remember Merry asking why I hated Mrs. Cohen. *They think God patted them on the head the day they took us in,* I'd said. I'd told her how phony Mrs. Cohen was, a real Lady Bountiful all puffed up with noblesse oblige. It was as though I resented Mrs. Cohen for helping us after I'd spent so much time plotting to get her help. Jesus, I'd practically pimped out poor Merry to be cute enough to engender Mrs. Cohen's care.

Once I got us there, and Merry was taken care of, I think I took a breath for the first time since Daddy killed Mama. I off-loaded Merry to Anne. I off-loaded our father by making us orphans. And when Anne tried to be my mother, I off-loaded her.

Maybe Anne's incredibly patient niceness brought out my meanness toward her. Maybe she made me feel safe enough to act angry, but how horrible that I chose to lash out at her. I counted headlights to calm down. I scratched out a silent apology to Anne.

Maybe I owed myself an apology also. Anne had been my last and only chance to be mothered, and I'd thrown it away.

Doctor Cohen, Saul, Amy, and Eleanor sat on wooden boxes sunk into the deep Cohen carpet. Vague memories surfaced from Mama's unveiling.

Doctor Cohen rose and took my hands. "Lulu. Thank you for coming."

"I'm so sorry I wasn't here for the funeral."

He dismissed my concern with a wave. "This place was filled until yesterday. Be happy you're here when it's peaceful, just family."

I looked around for Merry.

"Your sister's in her room watching the children," he said as if he'd read my mind. "She's been a godsend."

I nodded, kissed him perfunctorily on the cheek. Saul-the-surgeon-son rose from his seat and hugged me. Had we ever touched before? "I'm sorry about your mother. She was a good woman," I said.

"She was an angel." Eleanor struggled to her feet. The Cohens' daughter looked to be in the fourth or fifth month of another pregnancy. "Who'd know that as well as you and your sister?" She shook her head. "An angel."

Saul's wife Amy's tears wet my cheek as she put her face to mine. "We missed you at the funeral."

"Lulu couldn't leave school." Eleanor's tone left no doubt that I'd shown my true colors.

The apartment seemed devoid of oxygen, a vacuumlike warren of rooms overstuffed with expensive furniture. The same couches and chairs from when we'd moved in. I'd been shocked when my childish plan to get Mrs. Cohen to take us had worked. Of course, I was grateful. I'd have been insane not to want to escape the misery of the Duffy-Parkman Home for Girls. Another wave of shame, even stronger than on the bus, overcame me. I wished my gratitude had morphed into the love for which Anne Cohen had seemed so hungry. I wished I'd told her how much I loved the room she'd set up for me. I wished I'd shaken the feeling of being Project Lulu—an identity I hated as much as that of the murderer's daughter.

Merry and I had little privacy until we took a walk the next morning. People raced down Broadway with copies of the Sunday *New York Times* tucked under their arms, rushing to get home before the arctic air froze the fresh, warm bagels they carried like edible treasures.

"You left me alone. It was horrible being at the funeral without you," Merry said.

"Doctor Cohen said it was important I stay for classes." I turned my head, daring Merry to challenge me. She stared back, her purple-and-black-lined eyes saying *bullshit*. She shook her hair off her face. Merry looked shockingly different from the last time I'd been home, back in August. Silky, dark waves had been replaced by blond-streaked, ironed-straight hair. A shredded satin blouse fell off her shoulder. She looked like she'd stolen the outfit from the GoGo's last concert. Had Mrs. Cohen let Merry out of the house like this on a regular basis? Was slutty now the look for high school seniors?

"Right," Merry said. "You couldn't leave school for your foster mother's funeral."

"You don't know what medical school is like, Merry."

"You don't know what it's like for me here." She grabbed my arm. "What am I going to do? What will I do this summer? What about college? Where will I go on breaks?"

"Calm down, Mer. Do you think he's going to throw you out? Not pay for your college?"

"Do you think I can live alone with him? God, how creepy can you get?"

Despite her ratty hair, Merry looked like a kid. Tears clung to her lashes, and mascara dirtied her pink cheeks.

"Why? What's wrong?" I asked.

"Can you imagine being in that house without Anne? He never wanted us in the first place, you know that."

"It'll only be a few months. After that, I'll come back for the summer. You'll have me with you, I promise." Even as I spoke, the world darkened.

"You need to come home every weekend," Merry said. "Otherwise, I swear, I'll go crazy. I could barely stand one week alone with him. At night, when people left after sitting shivah, it was like living in a monastery with vows of silence. I'll run away. I'll find someone to live with. I met some guys from Columbia and NYU at a party last month."

"Hold it right there." I held up a hand. I hurried ahead and walked into a coffee shop, Merry following. I fell hard on a stool at the counter. I grabbed Merry's arm and pulled her down next to me.

"Stop pushing me around," she said. Hail hit the coffee shop windows with icy pops.

"You're not moving in with anyone." I held her arm. "Are you seeing someone?"

"I see lots of guys."

"You know what I mean. Are you sleeping with anyone?"

Merry picked up a sugar packet from the metal rectangle holding a neat pile. The counterman came over and wiped the area next to Merry's elbow with a dirty rag. "Hey, you girls ordering anything or just using this for your coffee klatch?" he asked. "This isn't a living room."

"Two coffees." The place reminded me of Harry's back in Brooklyn. Two malteds, I wanted to say, one vanilla, one chocolate.

Merry rested her head on her arms, her hair spilling on the counter. She turned toward me, looking like a sleepy five-year-old smeared with her mother's makeup. "I'm seeing one of the guys from Columbia. I could stay in his room."

"Right. You're going to live in some guy's dorm."

Merry sat up and walked her fingers up and down her chest. My fingers itched to pull them away.

"Listen," I said. "We'll work this out, I promise. Leave everything to me. You only have a few months till you graduate."

Merry shook her head. "I don't know if I can make it that long."

I took her hand away from her chest. "You'll make it. When you need to, you can come up to Boston." As I spoke, Boston's freedom shrank away.

Henry Yee gave me a quiet smile as I punched one of his pillows into a more comfortable shape. His room had become my salvation since Anne Cohen died. I didn't know if I'd started seeing Henry out of attraction or because I needed a peaceful place to study on the weekends that Merry visited. My dorm room had become her escape, and when she was there, the walls closed in on me.

Henry stroked my arm as though touching a present.

"You have lovely skin." He touched his chunky fingers to the tops of my meager breasts and smiled. "Perfect."

Henry deemed perfect those things most men found wanting. My girlish breasts, the almost-black eyes that most men found spooky, my boyish, straight hips—perfect, perfect, perfect according to Henry. What one guy had called my *friggin' inability to express anything that's not a goddamned fact* seemed catnip to Henry. We both valued having a significant someone who didn't care that we spent ninety-nine percent of our waking moments buried in a stack of books. We were simply grateful to share sex and watching *Saturday Night Live*.

I laid my head on Henry's fleshy chest. He talked about going to the gym, swimming, lifting weights, but we both knew his words were hollow. It didn't matter to me—his endomorphic body comforted my ectomorphic build.

He nibbled his way down my body in his usual fashion. Henry and I made love as I imagined middle-aged married people might. Nothing outlandish. No surprises. We were satisfied.

"I'll rub your back, and then you do me," Henry said. He rolled me over and massaged my back the way I liked, long, deep strokes. I groaned. We took turns erasing the week's tension from each other's muscles. I hoped I could stay awake long enough to give Henry a compensatory massage.

We'd been together four months, since January. So far, we'd gone to one movie and eaten out twice, and on both our so-called dates we'd doubled with Ron and Marta, who'd also connected in a medical school quasi romance. Like ours, their relationship consisted of sex, studying, and watching television while eating cheap takeout.

Henry and I had the advantage of having meals sent over by Henry's mother. I loved Mrs. Yee. She could barely speak English, but she'd smile and say *Nice girl* each time I came over. Then she'd feed me. My ideal situation might be living with a deaf or non-English-speaking family.

After I stroked Henry's back for a few minutes, we had our meat loaf sex, kissed, and snuggled into our separate sides of the bed. As usual, we fell instantly asleep. Seven hours later, when the alarm went off, I surprised Henry by climbing on top of him.

"We only have half an hour before we have to leave," he said.

I didn't insult him by mentioning this wouldn't take but a few minutes. "Think of how much more relaxed we'll be during the test," I said as I slipped him inside. We had an exam, organic chemistry, that morning. I didn't worry about using sex as a study aid; we often used each other that way. I'd bet half our class had paired off because the orgasmic endorphins helped us memorize how the pneumogastric nerve was distributed.

It was after nine on Monday night when I finally dragged myself back to my dorm room. I'd meant to call Merry the night before and make sure she'd gotten back to New York safely, but I'd forgotten, and then one class had followed another in an unceasing round, ending with study group.

My life chased itself in a circle. Stultifying words and pictures piled up in my brain and my notebooks, jamming my circuits until I released the facts and images during tests and in anatomy lab. That day Henry, Ron, Marta, and I had labored over the tangled mass of nerves in our cadaver's neck. Twiggy, we'd named her. She'd died of anorexia, or so we'd surmised using the scant differential diagnostic tools available in our circumstance. Twiggy's body became an Erector set in our hands.

I took the elevator up to the fourth floor. Cabot's medical student dorms were worn and seedy. Scruffy carpeting the color of vacuumed dirt lined the hallway. Doors and halls were devoid of decorations. Female medical students had a series of single-occupancy cells where we lived like nuns who screwed. I'd wake at odd times to hear Irene next door humping and thumping away, the thin walls pounding rhythmically, until upon reaching orgasm, she'd shriek theatrically. I was glad the feral Irene only occasionally attracted partners willing to visit her room.

Incense, marijuana odors, and the vision of Merry stoned on my bed assaulted me when I opened my door. "What the hell are you still doing here?" I asked.

Merry turned her head from where she lay on the bed, her pot-red eyes barely focusing on me. Rick Springfield crooned from the tinny speakers of my tape player. Red sweatpants—my favorites—and Henry's gray University of Michigan sweatshirt, which he kept in my room, engulfed my sister. She'd propped the dirty soles of her little feet on the wall, tapping to the beat.

"I couldn't face it," Merry said.

"Face what?" I wanted her out of my room.

"Everything. Doctor Cohen. Eleanor coming over to look daggers at me and making me babysit for her kids. Daddy's letters begging me to come because I haven't visited in three weeks."

"I doubt that happens all in one day." I picked up the empty tub of ready-made onion dip and a half-empty bag of Doritos and slammed them in the trash. "And you're not responsible for our father."

I didn't look forward to spending precious sleep hours cleaning up Merry's mess. "Have you been alone in here all weekend?"

"Daddy doesn't have one other person in the world, except me. In addition, for your information, no, I wasn't alone all weekend. I met someone nice from the floor below."

"That's the guys' floor."

"Isn't that the point?" Merry laughed and reached into a king-size bag of M&M's, coming up with a handful so large she had to jam it into her mouth.

"Does this guy know that you're still in high school?"

She rolled over on her side. Her deceptively innocent look and dirty-girl attitude made a perfect odalisque. Compared to Merry, I was an Amish schoolmarm crossed with Grandma Zelda.

"I don't think he'd care either way."

"How about some self-respect?" I waved my arms around the room, indicating everything—the pot, her skankiness, the crappy food she'd been living on. "Not to mention showing some respect for me, for my space, my stuff."

"Your space? I need to show more respect for your stuff? You don't realize how lucky you are; at least you have this fricking room. What have I got?" Merry's voice got louder and shriller. "Nothing. I come to see you, and I get about fifteen minutes of Madame Medical Student's attention before you leave."

"I'm studying. I'm working."

"You're screwing Henry. Can't you give it up one night?" Merry tucked her knees under Henry's sweatshirt, her voice turning plaintive. "Will you stay here tonight?"

"No, I can't. Not when you make my place look like this. This has to stop. I never know what I'm going to find here, who I'm going to find here, and I'm not planning to wake you up from some weed haze before I can get into my own bed."

My words seemed to melt Merry. She fell on her back, letting the bag of M&M's drop to the floor. "All I have is you, Lu. Sometimes, I can't even breathe unless I get high or have someone with me."

I scowled but held my tongue, sighing and then stretching out on the bed beside her. She rolled over and put her arms around me.

"It's okay. You'll be okay." I felt her heart beating.

"Daddy's going to be upset; this is my third weekend not seeing him."

"Is that what's bothering you?"

"You don't have to say it like that. That's just a part, and anyway, isn't that plenty? I have to worry about him being all alone and sad waiting for me, and then him getting mad."

"Just forget about him. Stop going."

"You make it sound so simple." Merry pulled away. "I can't do it like you. I can't just shut him out."

"Learn how." I got up and began gathering empty food wrappers. "For your own self-preservation."

"You just wish I'd stop seeing Daddy, so you could stop thinking about him."

"There's not much chance of that." I savagely folded a pizza box and stuffed it in the trash can. "Not with you always talking about him and bringing him in the room whenever you come."

Merry swung her feet off the side of my bed. "Daddy's always in the room, Lu. You forget that saying he's dead is just a frickin' story. Not talking about him isn't going to make him any less alive."

"Seeing him isn't going to bring back Mama." I bent down and picked up another dirty sock.

'If that's why you think I see him, you're clueless," Merry said. "Don't you want to know why I see Daddy?"

I shook out a crumpled towel and shoved it into the hamper. "No."

14

Lulu

December 1986

I swore I could still feel the cheap prison paper crackling in my hand even though I'd washed my hands surgeon-style after crumpling my father's letter and throwing it in the trash, then washed them again the moment I'd arrived at the ER. With harsh hospital soap. However, my father's letter kept worming into my head and sliming my skin, his words ricocheting like bullets.

Why don't you come visit me?

You're not afraid of me, are you, Lulu?

We can talk, we need to talk, Cocoa Puff.

It's making me crazy not seeing you, sugar.

I'm your father for god's sake.

I rode a wave of nausea as I smiled at my young patient. I tensed my neck muscles for a moment, determined to squeeze my father from my head. I didn't know why I'd opened the letter instead of throwing it still sealed deep into an outside trash barrel as I usually did.

No matter how hard I pretended he wasn't there, sometimes his hand clawed out and he caught me unawares. I'd chalk today's mistake of opening his letter up to overwork.

Thus far, my ER rotation had been a trial by nuclear war. Diagnoses flew from me as I spun from patient to patient. Thank God, I hadn't begun my internship with the ER like Marta, who'd started here, had turned into an ER zombie within weeks. She had taken to lighting candles in church, chanting, *Blessed God, let me have more patients live than die.*

"Melissa, I'm Doctor Zachariah," I introduced myself to my patient.

She nodded, barely looking at me. Plump and December-pale, with limp brown hair hanging over her face, she seemed ready to disappear.

"And this is"—I peered at the student's name tag again—"this is Doug Keller. He's a third-year medical student who'll be working with me today."

"I'll be assisting Doctor Zachariah," Doug said. He moved toward the exam table.

Melissa pressed her knees close together.

"Where exactly is the pain?" I asked.

Her cheeks turned hot red, and she shrugged.

Doug picked up the chart from the cracked counter. Each time I looked at the crumbling hospital surfaces—the counters, the cabinet knobs, the examining table—I imagined microbes jitterbugging along the jagged fissures and wanted to soak the whole place in Clorox.

Doug read the nurse's notes aloud; Melissa twisted her drape tighter with each word. "Abdominal pain, left side, upon intercourse. No localized vaginal pain. How about when you urinate?" he asked.

"Huh?" she asked.

"Does it hurt when you pee?" I asked.

She gave an infinitesimal nod.

"Let's make you feel better." I squeezed her knee. "Are you in pain now?"

A few tears spilled down Melissa's cheeks. I was afraid sympathy could induce a crying jag faster than cruelty, so I dialed back the compassion.

Learn one. Do one. Teach one.

*

I sent off Melissa's lab tests, betting she had pelvic inflammatory disease. Stopping only to wash my hands, I headed to the next patient, giving a perfunctory knock before entering. The odor of alcohol, unwashed flesh, and something indefinable but familiar overwhelmed me. Doug, following along, hesitated at the door.

A fiercely dirty man perched on the exam table. Blood flecked the crumpled paper lining under him. The patient looked to be in his forties but might have been anywhere from twenty-five upward. My time in the ER had showed me how alcohol acts as a fast-forward on the face.

"Mr. Hammond, I'm Doctor Zachariah." I studied his face from a distance, trying to determine if he were still drunk or if the smell of cheap wine came from yesterday's binge. "This is my medical student, Doug Keller."

Per the chart, my patient had been in a bar fight and suffered superficial knife wounds to one of his shoulders and his back. Judging by the amount and color of blood soaking his shirt, that sounded right.

"You need to take off your shirt, Mr. Hammond. We'll leave while you disrobe." Why hadn't the nurses better prepped this patient?

He ignored my instructions and said, "You should see the other guy."

"Right," I said. "But let's take care of you. Tell me, are you in much pain?"

"I'm not in any pain at all, girlie." Bravado filled his voice. "Instead of you taking care of me, how about I take care of you?" He cackled, almost falling off the table as he reached for me. "I'll make you happy, sugar."

"Mr. Hammond, we're going to leave the room. When we come back, please have your shirt off."

"Yeah? How about you don't tell me what to do? Last one who talked to me like that got a lot worse than this." He stripped off his shirt, revealing a long gash from shoulder to elbow. "What's the matter, cat got your tongue, sugar?"

A tight stabbing knifed through my chest. A lump stuck in my throat felt as though I'd swallowed my stethoscope.

"You okay?" Doug asked.

I shook my head, not knowing what I was trying to convey besides the sensation that I might die. I thought he must hear my heart thumping.

"What the hell's going on?" Mr. Hammond slurred. "What's wrong with her?"

Shut up. Go away. Go away.

His opened wound gaped at me, begging for closure. Blood matted his thick brown hair. Clumps of it stood straight up.

"She going to take care of me or not?" he demanded.

"Doctor Zachariah?" Doug took my arm. "Should I get someone?"

"What kind of place is this?" The patient advanced toward me. "Fuck this shit."

I ran.

The women's room seemed miles away. I needed to pee so bad I didn't know if I could make it. People lining the hall backed away as I raced past them, their concerned faces barely registering.

"Doctor Zachariah," Doug yelled as I turned the corner, closing in on the bathroom. I felt like I was running in slow motion, as if I'd never get anywhere.

I could barely lock the stall door with my shaking hands. Voices, too loud, assaulted me. Doug's and others.

Are you okay?

Louise, do you need anything?

What's wrong?

Their words were miles away. I flushed the toilet and sat back down, lowering my head to my knees. *It's just a panic attack,* I told myself, mentally listing as many symptoms as I could remember: palpitations, sweating, shaking, choking sensations, smothering sensations, derealization, depersonalization, paresthesia, urgently needing to urinate or defecate.

Feeling as though someone would die.

Smelling anger.

My father's hot metal smell flicked out at me from that hot July day. If I'd stayed, would Mama be alive? Would I be dead?

Why had I gone so slowly to Teenie? Why hadn't I flown to her apartment?

"Security's going to take off the door if you don't come out, Louise."

The determined voice brought me back. She sounded familiar.

"No," I croaked. "Okay. I'm okay. Just got sick." I slowly stood and

125

unlocked the stall door. The harried-looking charge nurse watched me with arms folded.

I ran my hand over my mouth, pretending I'd been sick, and went to the sink. I splashed water on my face. My heart beat too fast. My breathing remained ragged. Too bad knowing what these symptoms represented didn't make them go away. I reached down as far as I thought I could and pulled out a few words. "Flu. Sudden. Can barely stand."

"Do you need help?" The charge nurse seemed suspicious.

I shook my head. "I'll phone a cab."

"I can drive you," Doug said. He stood in the doorway, unwilling to breach the entry to the women's bathroom.

"Stay. They need you." I wrapped my arms around myself.

"I'll get you that taxi," the nurse said.

My messy studio offered comfort. For once, I didn't care that it had been weeks since I'd had time to clean. I was safe here. I threw off my coat and collapsed on the unmade bed, burrowing my face deep into the pillow. Long-buried emotions rose, and I bit down on my hand to keep from screaming, from seeing my mother's bones in the dusty ground.

I'd hated her for yelling, for sending me to the store, for not making supper, for not being soft and understanding. For not knowing that I existed until she needed something.

Play with your sister.

Bring the ironing to Teenie.

Save my life.

I hated myself for having hated her.

Maybe my hate had helped Daddy kill Mama. Why hadn't I jumped on Daddy's back? Thrown myself in front of him? Screamed at him? Why hadn't I opened my mouth instead of hiding in the bathroom? Merry ran out to them. I didn't go in even when Mama screeched. *He has a knife. Get Teenie! He's going to kill me.*

Had Mama said that? Did I remember it right, or was I imagining the words? Had Mama said he was going to kill her? Why hadn't I gotten between them?

What if he'd killed Merry?

Why hadn't he killed himself?

Why hadn't I saved anyone?

The next morning when I returned to work, I explained away the disappearing flu by renaming it food poisoning. At least I'd gotten a decent night's sleep, although it took NyQuil—the closest thing I had to a narcotic—to put me out.

After shift, I'd allotted my first night off in two weeks to seeing Merry, now a senior at Northeastern in Boston. She'd asked me to meet her because she needed money, and, naturally, she was twenty minutes late. I stared at the restaurant door, checking my watch every three minutes. Cold fear took over after half an hour. By the time she walked into Rubin's deli, I wanted to scream my head off.

"Where have you been? Why are you late this time?" I asked, though Merry's bloodshot eyes and unwashed hair told me exactly why she was late.

"The trolley's on Sunday schedule. I had to wait forever." She fell into the wooden chair across from me. "I need coffee."

"You need a keeper," I said. "You look like shit."

"Thanks. It's always a comfort to get your support. I've been studying for finals all week." She dug into her bag, rummaging around until she pulled out a pack of cigarettes.

"Could you wait until I'm finished eating?" I pulled the pack of Marlboros from Merry's hand. "Did you study in a bar last night?" I picked up my thick corned beef sandwich and took a large and deliberate bite.

"Blech," Merry said. "That looks disgusting."

"Staring at your ratty hair while I eat isn't exactly a treat."

"Why do you have to be so mean?"

"Why can't you treat yourself better?"

Merry took a pack of matches off the table and began ripping them out one by one. "Sorry everyone can't be a saint like you." She grabbed my thick white coffee mug and took a sip. "Ick, you put sugar in. When did you start that?"

I leaned over the table and snatched back my cup. "When I started having to wait for my sister after I've been working insane shifts for weeks and my sister doesn't show up on time and my blood sugar drops so low that I'm forced to load three sugars in my coffee. Does that answer your question?"

Merry slumped. "The trolley really was running slow."

"You should leave more time on a Sunday, knowing it's a slower schedule." Pent-up anger made me want to shake her until she listened, really listened to me. Terrible things happened in this world. She should remember that, instead of pretending everything was just fine. I hated her reeking of cigarettes, and I hated her clothes holding the memory of beer.

"I'm twenty-one now. When are you going to stop criticizing me?"

"When will you stop coming to me to be rescued?" I reached down and grabbed the old suede bag I'd been carrying since Anne gave it to me for my eighteenth birthday. Anne had said the bittersweet chocolate color matched my eyes. I remembered being surprised by her poetic turn of phrase and, even more, by her knowing the color of my eyes.

The familiar feeling of not being nice enough to Anne rushed in. She'd tried so hard, and I'd been a bitch. I poked at the thought, wiggling the pain like a nagging toothache. Merry stared down at her hands, as if waiting for more of my criticisms. Instead, I reached into my bag and took out my wallet, grabbing five twenties fresh from the bank.

"Take it," I said when she didn't reach for the bills. "I gave you a hundred."

"I only asked for fifty." Merry sipped at the steaming black coffee the waiter had slid to her, swiftly and smiling, far different from the attitude with which he'd carried over my sandwich and cooled-off coffee. All Merry had to do was glance at a man and the shower of nourishment began.

I placed the bills down on the gritty tabletop and pushed them toward her. The old couple at the next table glanced over. "Take it," I repeated. "I can't stand the idea of you going around without money."

"Don't worry. When I graduate in May, you'll never have to worry about me again."

I took my sister's hand, folding the bills in and squeezing. Feeling guilty. When I'd graduated from college, the Cohens had sent me touring from Italy to France to the Greek islands. Even as I made fun of the tour guide and my fellow travelers from some Upper West Side young adult synagogue group, I'd lived in the moment for the first time in my life. Nobody knew me. I could be anyone. That's probably why I finally lost my virginity, which by then I wore like a giant scarlet *V*.

David Stern, one of the temple's tour team leaders, with his thick, dark hair and a wide-open smile, looked like a classic handsome bar mitzvah boy, despite it having been ten years since he'd stood at the bimah—the synagogue prayer altar—and read the haftarah. Even though we all lived out of backpacks the entire trip, his blue shirts and tan chinos seemed freshly pressed. He opened doors and made sure everyone had returned to the bus before we left each stop.

When Mindy Grossman drank absinthe and started puking, David brought her chamomile tea and found French saltines for her hangover. Like me, he was about to start medical school. Unlike me, David had been raised clean and adored, swaddled in love and high expectations.

The first time David and I made love, a golden Jewish star dangled from his neck, swinging above me, and all I could think of was headstones being unveiled—my mother's, my grandmother's. I wished he would have taken the star off, but I didn't know how to ask. We broke up, and Mindy Grossman enjoyed his vigorous lovemaking through the Greek islands.

David had been a great graduation present. What would my Merry get? Doctor Cohen had barely stayed in touch with us after Merry began college, other than paying the bills. Any semblance of our so-called family relationship with the Cohens had ended when he started dating. Merry's present would come from me, and she wouldn't be going on any trips to Europe. If I were lucky, I'd be able to buy her a Timex.

Merry pushed the money back at me. "You can't afford this much, and anyway, I don't deserve it. I'm a brat. I'm late, I'm rude, I smoke, and I drink." She stuck her chin out. "Don't you just want to cut me loose? Don't you ever think maybe you could just get on with your life like a normal person?"

"We're normal." I started scratching lines on my arm. "Nothing can make us separate, Merry. Don't ever talk like that."

"You can't guarantee anything."

"Yes," I said. "I can. We have control of our lives, Merry. Don't forget that."

15

Lulu

May 1987

By spring, I feared my control was slipping. I finally understood how people fell asleep at the wheel. I was terrified of nodding off while putting in an IV. Marta kept reminding me about Ron's party that night, but I'd have been satisfied spending the night watching *Dynasty*. Our internship ended in five hours, and I'd be happy spending every hour in the Neuro Step-down Unit, sitting in Mr. Vincent's room, enjoying the food his wife brought to the hospital.

The Vincents had been married for fifty-five years, and Mrs. Vincent was determined to keep her husband alive. Hour after hour, she held his hand, craned her neck to watch the mounted television, and fed the staff. She and her son arrived at the hospital each day by ten, her son carrying a cardboard box stuffed with newspaper for insulation. Inside the box were Tupperware containers filled with warm comfort food, daily variations of ravioli, lasagna, and roasted eggplant. The list seemed endless. In addition, her son carried a plastic bag slung over his shoulder crammed with cannoli and cookies from her cousin's bakery.

"Hello, Mrs. Vincent," I said, walking into the room. "Hi, Mr. Vincent. How are you feeling today?"

"Look, Joe, it's Doctor Zachariah." Mrs. Vincent tenderly wiped a line of drool off her husband's mouth. "We're watching the news. Joe loves the news. Right, Joe?"

Mr. Vincent smiled and nodded, as he did at everything. Mrs. Vincent took his happy expressions as signs that he'd recover from his stroke despite the gloomy reports from his neurologist.

"Hungry, sweetheart?" She reached into a wrinkled Jordan Marsh shopping bag.

I dropped into the chair next to her. "Starved." I'd been seeing patients since arriving Saturday morning. It was now past seven Sunday evening.

Mrs. Vincent made up a paper plate with lasagna. The food was cold, but I didn't care. She handed me a plastic fork and a folded napkin. I rolled my eyes in deep pleasure as I took a mouthful of the sweet-spicy-meaty dish.

Somewhere during my internship, food had replaced sex as my source of tension release. Having time for bouts of aerobic sex seemed part of another life, in the relatively easier world of medical school, *relatively* meaning, of course, how in the land of the blind, the one-eyed man is king.

A strand of pasta fell on my white coat, blending with the blood just spit up by my patient down the hall. I picked up the noodle and, for a moment, almost considered eating it. I dabbed my jacket with a napkin, succeeding in making the small blood spot into a saucer-size red smear that would no doubt be visible from Mars.

"Here, here, take this." Mrs. Vincent held out a moist towelette. "Are you trying to terrify your patients?"

"They should be scared," I said. "Do you know how long I've been here?"

Mrs. Vincent snorted. "Big deal, look at Joe. You get to go home. He never leaves. You'll be fine. Be happy you're young and healthy. Strong girl like you, you can handle everything. Just make sure to have a cannoli, you need the sugar."

Mrs. Vincent was one smart cookie. Didn't her husband get the best care in the place? Who'd be crass enough to leave without doing a little something for Mr. Vincent—listen to his heart, do a little eye check, a squeeze test—after eating Mrs. Vincent's lasagna? I struggled not to fall asleep as I ate and watched the national news, keeping my eyes open by playing the FQ game, fuckability quotient, deciding if Peter Jennings was fuckable. This had recently become the new craze for Cabot interns, determining who was worth bedding. We judged movie stars, hospital staff, presidents, everyone but patients. Ethics still played a role in our lives.

FQ got us through. If we couldn't have sex, we'd pretend. During our fifteen-minute cafeteria meals, we'd throw out names for the FQ, though never obvious choices, like Richard Gere or Demi Moore. We'd offer people like Gorbachev or Nancy Reagan, forcing decisions among each other.

Peter Jennings was too easy; they'd laugh me out. Obviously, Jennings was eminently screwable. How rude would it be to ask Mrs. Vincent to change the channel? I needed to find someone different, someone under the radar.

"Coffee? My son brought in a thermos." Mrs. Vincent held up an empty cardboard cup. I salivated at the idea of her not-hospital coffee, especially as I considered going to the end-of-internship party instead of my usual postshift sleep.

"Thank you. I'd love coffee."

"Wonderful. By the way, I think Joe's pulse is a little high."

Ron Young, my former anatomy and study group partner, hosted the party in the two-family in Dorchester he'd inherited from his folks. His father had been a carpenter and had rebuilt the home from the basement up. Every corner had another inviting specialty—built-in bookcases, cherry wainscoting, intricately bricked fireplaces—and lilacs from the garden filled cut-glass vases. Ron's home looked like family and history all twined together.

Ron invited everyone from our original medical school class who was still in Boston along with what seemed like five thousand others who could have been anything from fellow Red Sox fans to performance artists, knowing Ron's eclectic taste.

"See anyone you like?" Marta appeared at my side bearing two glasses of wine.

I nodded noncommittally.

"Take the red," Marta told me. "Too bad Henry's left for L.A. You guys could have one for old times' sake—a springtime 'Auld Lang Syne.' He could slip you a cup of kindness. How long has it been?"

Marta's delicate features belied her dirty mouth. I tipped my chin toward a man in the corner, listening and nodding patiently to a too-cute redhead. "Who's that?"

Marta smiled. "Nebraska."

"That's his name?" I sipped at my wine, planning to make it last.

"That's where he's from."

Nebraska looked ruggedly appealing in his jeans and navy corduroy shirt, shirtsleeves folded back to reveal thick arm fuzz matching his dirty blond hair. "You spoke to him?"

Marta nodded. "For a bit. Too white-bread for me." Marta's taste ran to olive-skinned men—Italian, Greek, Jewish, or Puerto Rican, like her—with big paychecks. "He's not a doctor."

"What is he?"

She shrugged. "An artist."

"You say that as though it's boring."

"He does commercial art. Hallmark cards, maybe. I forget." She waved away my frown. "You'll love the artist. He'll float your boat. Next to Henry, he's a wild man. He actually seems to have a bit of personality. I don't know if you can take it." Marta had long ago pegged me as prissy.

I studied Marta's clothes. Her spiky heels were over three inches high, giving her an edge, and her teal dress hugged her tight in ways no dress of mine ever would. Comparing myself to Marta made me want to race to Saks Fifth Avenue. I threw back the cup of wine, dousing my emotions before they flared up. "I'm getting a refill, want one?"

Marta shook her head. "I'm checking him out." She pointed her glass in the direction of a rather dumpy man. "Number one in his class at Harvard, intern of note, and top surgical resident at Mass General." She ran her tongue over her upper lip. "Slated for big dollars. He'll be the perfect husband—Jewish, surgeon, and plain enough to worship me." She brushed her perfect nun fingers over her Virgin Mary face.

"Don't be so sure of the Jewish-men-make-the-best-husbands theory." I couldn't tell her how I'd disproved this hypothesis. Like everyone, Marta knew me as a car crash orphan. "Personally, I think Jewish men invented the line themselves. Self-promotion."

I headed to the wine. Marta headed toward her husband-to-be.

As I drank my second glass of wine, I concluded that Nebraska emanated a high FQ. The question was how to get rid of his Chatty Cathy companion. The more I studied him, the more I liked his clean, natural look. In a room full of moussed-up men, it was a turn-on to see someone whose hair moved. I wanted to pull off his shirt, lay my head on his broad chest, and rest there for hours.

I drained my glass, tousled my hair, and headed over to Nebraska. When the redhead's attention drifted, I caught his eye and tried for a Marta-like smile.

"So, what kind of doctor are you?" I felt superior knowing the answers to the questions I asked.

"I'm not a doctor." He had a soothing voice, slow and measured, not New York, not Eastern.

"If you're not a doctor, what brings you here?" I asked by way of greeting.

"I'm hoping to meet a doctor." Behind a pair of wire-rim glasses, Nebraska's eyes knew more than I'd expected, including kindness.

"Lucky you," I said. "I'm a doctor."

"Lucky me," he said. "And what kind of doctor are you?"

"Right now, a tired, tired one. A finishing-her-internship-exhausted one."

"They overwork you, don't they?" His tone had a level of concern I was used to giving, not getting. "Your eyes, though quite beautiful, look like the before picture of a sleeping pill ad. It makes no sense putting folks through the wringer of deprivation to teach them to help sick and vulnerable people. Why ill-equip those who'll care for the neediest?"

"I think the theory has to do with training us to manage well even under the worst of conditions." I put my hand to my throat, wishing I'd worn something prettier, something sparkly, something Merry would have worn.

"Maybe that's what they say to get long hours of cheap labor." He put a light finger under my chin, tipped it up, and looked into my eyes. Then he swept away my too-long bangs, which, as always, threatened to block my vision. "I see a need for deep sleep, nutritious food, and nonmedical conversation."

"I see someone who can provide at least number three." It was either the wine or his voice; whatever the reason, this man had engendered my first case of flirting.

"I can. And I will. But only if you let me buy you a decent meal."

The next morning I woke up next to Nebraska. How much had I drunk? I staggered out of bed, hoping not to wake him, too hungover to walk on tiptoes.

I made it to the toilet just in time to heave up red wine and the remains of a roast chicken dinner—Nebraska's idea of a decent meal. Revolting. Then I collapsed on the floor. The linoleum looked disgustingly grimy and germy. I kept meaning to clean the apartment, but sleep always won my what-to-do-with-my six-free-hours-a-week conundrum.

Alcohol and I had never been well suited. I pulled a towel from the rod above for a blanket and made myself as small as possible. Between bouts of vomiting, I slept on the cold, dank linoleum, wedged between the toilet and the tub.

I woke to a dog's-eye view of bare male legs covered with golden brown fuzz. Fighting vertigo, I struggled to rise.

Nebraska squatted beside me, wearing boxers. My gorge rose again.

Even sick to my stomach, I wanted to touch him.

"Hey, hey, it's okay," he said when I finished throwing up what little remained in my aching stomach. He held a wet washcloth, and I wondered where in my apartment he'd found a clean one. He took my hands and wiped away the sweaty grime, starting with my fingers. I watched in silent appreciation as he worked the soft, hot cloth over my skin. Afterward, he stood, rinsed the cloth carefully, and ran it gently over my face and the back of my neck.

"Thanks," I said. He had a sure touch. I couldn't remember the previous night, but my body remembered him. It must have been good, because I wanted him so bad.

He handed me my white terry robe, which he'd somehow unearthed from the pile of clothes in my bedroom. "Not that used to drinking or too used to it?"

I started to shake my head, but the motion made me dizzy. My hollowed-out stomach protested any unnecessary movement. My head pounded. "Not." I couldn't eke out more than one word.

"Good," he said. "My mother's a drinker. Not a good quality." He motioned around my tiny bathroom. "As you can see."

Moving my head with as little motion as possible, I saw and cringed at the heaps of dirty towels I'd made into a nest and the mound of toilet paper I'd used to blow my nose and wipe my mouth. If I'd been less nauseated and my headache hadn't grown to nuclear proportions, I'd have felt more shame. Later, I probably would.

"Let's get you out of here. I'm not the doctor, but I don't think this is the most healing environment."

He led me back to bed, where I quickly fell asleep. Fortunately. When I woke, the first thing I saw was Nebraska reading the paper. I was surprised he hadn't taken the opportunity to leave. I would have. He brought me a cup of tea and a plate of Uneeda biscuits. He must have gone to the store for both the tea bags and the crackers, as neither were part of my sad larder.

I was beginning to wonder if Nebraska was real or part of some alcohol-induced dream. A good dream, with men as knights, protectors, and healers.

"Secret family recipe." He placed my battered television tray next to the bed. The bed sagged as he sat. He held out a steaming mug. I took a hesitant sip of the strong sugared tea, unsure of my reaction.

Nebraska handed me a Uneeda, and I nibbled. "Any better?"

"Marginally. Thank God I don't have to go to the hospital today."

"Your patients should be thanking God. Imagine the soaring mortality rate if you went."

Nebraska had a sense of humor. Good.

"I don't even know your name," I said. "Did I not ask? Jesus. I slept with a man whose name I can't remember." I brought my knees up and rested the mug between them. "I've never had a one-night stand. Do you believe me?"

"My name is Drew. Short for Andrew. Andrew Winterson. And yes, I believe you." He took my chin between two fingers and tipped it up. "Although I think you'd lie if necessary. I'd like it if you never lied to me, though."

"I've been calling you Nebraska in my head."

"How did you know where I came from?"

"My friend Marta told me. You told her. And she told me."

"You asked about me?"

"I did."

"What else did she say?"

"That you were boring. Marta's attracted to dangerous guys, although she wants to marry a rich, stable guy. I suppose she'll have affairs."

"Good she didn't know that I'm rich. However, she's right. I am boring."

"Are you?"

"Boring?" he asked.

"No. Rich."

"Not really, but my family is more comfortable than most. My father owns a chain of tire stores."

"That's boring."

"True, but it allows my mother to drink without the ladies of the town judging her. Instead, they put her on all the boards. And she gets to spend winters in North Carolina and indulge in Diet Sun Drop and gin."

"I'm not an orphan," I blurted out.

"I didn't say you were."

"I tell everyone that I'm an orphan. That my parents died in a car crash when I was ten. But it's a lie."

"So why do you say it?"

"Because my father killed my mother. He's in prison. I've never told anyone, at least not since a foster family took my sister and me out of the orphanage. I don't want a soul in this world to know."

"Then I won't tell anyone." Drew lifted the covers. "Move over."

"I smell awful," I said, even as I made room for him.

"Not awful. Though not great." When he put an arm around me, I felt it from my shoulders to my thighs and in a spiraling elevator ride to my stomach. "But I'm from Nebraska. We have an awful lot of fortitude."

Drew felt like a rare species. A trustworthy man who gave me the shivers.

Three weeks later, I confessed that I'd revealed the family secret. I sat at my kitchen table, crumpling my napkin as I waited for Merry's reaction. I wished I were with Drew.

"Seriously, how could you tell him just like that?" Merry rummaged in my refrigerator. "Don't you have any orange juice?"

"Be happy that I have any food or drink at all," I said. "It came out naturally; it wasn't even a decision."

I didn't know if Merry could understand how different Drew was from the rest of the world. Saying it sounded hokey, but he'd keep me safe. He'd keep us safe. He could be trusted, even with things like secrets.

He was the sort of man who'd bring you presents you wanted, not ones he thought you should have.

Drew was an honorable man. Maybe I'd never find one again, especially one who, after making me tremble in the dark, held me in the sun.

"So we can stop lying?" Merry bit into an apple that had seen better days.

Could it just be about me and not her? Where was my credit for inviting Merry over the first free moment that I wasn't at work or wrapped in Drew? I wanted to be with Drew every minute. I wanted to drink him, sleep him, and inhabit his body. I wanted to spend the day in his pocket.

"Nothing's changed," I said. "You can't tell anyone. Not until you've met the one." When would that be? At least Merry looked decent today. Her tucked-in white blouse revealed less than her usual torn T-shirt emblazoned with a band's name. Since going to work, she'd calmed down, though I imagined the Freudian horror of working with crime victims slapped her in the face daily.

"Stop inspecting me." Merry took another giant bite of her apple. Merry and I raced through life hungry. We ate fast, often, and a lot. God save us the day our metabolisms slowed down, and without any genetic material to judge by, who knew when that might be? Merry described our father as getting a little doughy—but honestly, did I want to think that his current physical condition was any portent of my future body?

"Did you really sleep with him the night you met him?" Merry said, grabbing an Oreo from the open sleeve. "Where's Miss Perfect gone?"

"Falling in love is different than falling into someone's bed." I looked at my sister's kohl-rimmed eyes and cherry-popped lips and felt like some crabby old maid lecturing a student.

Merry ignored my nasty words. "What does this miracle man do?"

I smiled. "Art."

"He's an artist? Like a painter?"

"Commercial art. Like greeting cards and stuff. He's planning to illustrate children's books."

"He draws kittens for birthday cards?" Merry said. "Hallmark puppies?"

I didn't care what Merry said about him. I let her chatter while I leaned into my memory of being in bed every minute that I wasn't at the hospital. With Drew. Exploring Drew's FQ and mine. They meshed damn fine.

After meshing, we'd watch whatever movie happened to be playing when we flicked on the TV. Themes, reviews, actors, genres—none of it mattered. We never made it to the credits.

For the first time in my life, I lived somewhere other than alone in my head.

I leaned forward and put a hand on my sister's arm. "You're going to like him, Mer," I promised. "He'll be good to us."

She drew back. "Why didn't you talk to me before you just told him? You'd kill me if I did that. Why is it always up to you?"

I didn't want to be honest and tell her I had better judgment. "He's family. I know it. You'll love him."

"I want to meet the right man also, you know, but how am I supposed to when I visit Daddy all the time? It's not easy having to hide going to prison from every man I meet."

"Going there's your choice, not mine," I said.

"Why are you getting mad? Because I don't want to lie about my life anymore either?"

"Telling is the most dangerous thing we can do. I'm looking out for both of us. Someday we'll have children, and they don't need a goddamned murderer for a grandfather."

16

Merry

September 1989

Summer was over, as were the salted-sex ocean weekends spent with Quinn, drinking Bacardi and Cokes, hidden away on desolate Maine beaches known only by locals. The rum and the sun had let me push away reality for two months. Push away Quinn's wife. September brought the serious side of life. My job, my so-called relationship, and, of course, my father weighed down on me as I climbed off the bus and faced the court-house.

Iona was my first client today, and I dreaded seeing her, positive she'd whimper and cry her way through our meeting. She'd take the dozens of tissues I offered while resisting any suggestions I made, giving me the poor Iona reasons why they wouldn't work. In the parlance that I'd learned during my psych classes at Northeastern, Iona was a help-rejecting com-plainer. In my vernacular, I'd grown to detest her, which made me feel like pure shit.

Iona's ex-boyfriend had battered, raped, and nearly killed her, so my re-actions to her, though outwardly sympathetic, were hideous. Everything drooped on Iona—her hair, her shoulders, her damn fingernails. In my heart, I wanted to push her away. What kind of victim witness advocate—my official title—thought that way? My title should have been fraud.

I lit a cigarette on the courthouse steps, one last stall before going into work. Funny, I'd been so keen on this job. Working with victims seemed perfect for me. Victims' programs were the new thing when I'd graduated with my degree in criminal justice, offerings designed to appease the activists who'd lobbied for the recently enacted Victims' Bill of Rights. I hadn't known they were stingy, undercooked offerings.

Despite knowing from my college psych courses that I'd be working out some of my own issues on the job, I was aware that my reactions seemed extreme. I backed away from all my clients, wanting to yell at them to shut up, stop crying. Buck up, for Christ's sake.

Even as I offered kindness and support, Iona's tears of rage and self-pity made me want to slap her. I murmured comfort, nodded, and handed over tissues while internally screaming, *Shut the fuck up.*

Sometime after Anne died, between my finishing high school and starting college, a seismic shift had taken place inside me. Living alone in that deadly quiet apartment with Doctor Cohen had stolen my hope. He'd hired a housekeeper who managed everything from food to correspondence with my school. If it were possible, Doctor Cohen would have hired someone to talk to me.

Doctor Cohen's sole manner of caring for me had lain in driving me to Richmond County Prison. He'd upped the visits from monthly to once every two weeks to weekly, and I hadn't known how to tell him it was too much. In some grotesque way, I think he'd believed he could off-load his fatherly responsibilities on Daddy.

Without Anne, Doctor Cohen hadn't known what to do with me. I became the vestigial limb of his life. When he'd begun dating a woman closer to my age than to Anne's, he couldn't get me out of his home fast enough.

I took one last drag on my cigarette, then snuffed it out in the concrete planter guarding the courthouse before opening the heavy glass door. The door groaned as I entered the darkly wooded and hushed space; I felt I should genuflect. Criminals and victims alike walked around with their eyes downcast. Lawyers and courthouse personnel scurried through the halls puffed up with self-importance, as I imagined Roman cardinals strutted around the Vatican.

I rode the elevator to the fifth floor. Dirt obscured the brass panels, testimony to the carelessness of the Commonwealth of Massachusetts. Victim Services Office, the afterthought of the judicial system, was stuck in the no-man's-land of the courthouse along with unused office furniture, a typewriter cemetery, and softening cardboard boxes filled with evidence of forgotten crimes.

Just like our clients, we, their advocates, were not, nor would we ever be, the attractions of the legal show. The starring roles belonged to the judges, the criminals, and the lawyers. Even the probation officers, though only supporting players, were still in the main cast. Victims and their advocates were merely extras.

I stepped out of the elevator. Air conditioners belched out barely cooled air. Being on the top floor, we were last to get the chill. The advocates' desks spread out over a too-large area without dividers, preventing even a pretense of privacy. Iona drooped over my desk eating a bagel, spreading sesame seeds and crumbs across my scattered files.

"Take this." By way of greeting, I handed her the napkin that had wrapped my hot coffee. "Sorry about being late." Actually, I wasn't late. I was a few minutes early. Other than the unit secretary studying her pores in a magnifying mirror, I was the only one who'd made it in yet.

Iona mumbled her thanks.

"Are you okay?" I cleared a pile of memos off my chair. Each night I piled them there so they'd get my attention first thing in the morning. Then, first thing in the morning, something more pressing rose up, and I relegated these memos, like so many before them, to the floor.

Iona raised her narrow shoulders in an attempt to communicate. She looked ready to collapse. Everything about her seemed depressed, including her lank blond hair. "He's stalking me again."

According to Iona, her former boyfriend stalked her twenty-four hours a day. I had no reason not to believe her; I just didn't know what my options were besides the same blah, blah, blah I'd offered so many times. She already had a restraining order.

Nothing scared me more than knowing that she or some other client might die on my watch.

I leaned across the desk and handed her a tissue. "What makes you think so?"

"How could they have given him bail? It's not fair. Why do I have to be the one looking over my shoulder every second?"

"It's so hard, isn't it?" I took her hand and squeezed. As with most of my clients, I never knew what to do besides petting and comforting. I pitied them for having me as their advocate. "What has he done?"

"I feel his eyes on me," she said. "All the time. I'm sure he's watching me."

"Where?" I picked up a pen. "Give me specifics, something I can tell his probation officer."

Iona slumped forward, catching her head in her hands. "It's not like he makes himself visible. Jesus."

"How do you know he's there?"

Iona's eyes reminded me I was useless. "Trust me, when you've been with someone like Larry, you know when he's been around."

"I understand." Did I? "I don't doubt you, but we need something to show the judge that Larry's breaking his restraining order."

"Why doesn't he have to prove he's innocent, instead of me having to prove he's guilty?"

I skimmed through my years at Northeastern, sifting for words of comfort. I peeked at the inventory of miracles that the court instructed my clients to expect from me, a list given to them at intake, which I kept under the glass top of my desk.

YOUR VICTIM WITNESS ADVOCATE WILL PROVIDE:

1. Crisis intervention and emotional support
2. Planning and assistance for protection and restraining orders application
3. Explanation of the court process and information regarding the status of cases
4. Assistance in offering Victim Impact Statements to the court

5. Assistance with applying for notification of an inmate's status
6. Assistance with transportation to court

Numbers two through six were no problem; we had protocols for those tasks. Providing number one seemed over my head. For training, I'd received spiral-bound books of protocols and forms and heard lectures about the various ways men abused women and why. No one explained how we did the saving-victims part of the job.

Iona banged my desk with her fist. "I'm all alone. I had nobody except Larry. Now I only have you."

Nicotine urges assaulted me. I glanced down at my list and offered the pat answers I'd come up with since beginning this job. "Iona, you have to think of seeing a mental health counselor. Trauma becomes more manageable when it's verbalized." I tried to personalize the words so I didn't sound as though I were reading. "Maybe if you share your feelings about Larry with someone you trust, you'll feel better."

"You're the only one I trust," she said. "I don't want to see a shrink. At least you don't try to mess around inside my head."

"Keeping a journal helps many women in your situation." My cigarette itch got stronger.

"I can't concentrate." Iona grabbed another tissue from the box, shredding the used one into little, mucusy bits.

I turned back to my sheet. "That's natural. One's thinking is compromised after trauma." I couldn't do this.

"I'm always crying. I can't stop."

"You will," I said. "You will."

"I miss Larry."

"No. You don't. You're missing the idea of him, not the real him," I said, parroting words I'd read, concepts I'd learned.

"I miss *him*. I can't stop crying for the life of me. What if no one ever loves me again?"

"Tears are a tribute to our pain. They remove the toxins from our body." I pushed the box of tissues closer to Iona. "But you can't return to the source of your pain to heal the wounds."

That was it, I'd read my entire list. Maybe Iona wanted a cigarette.

That evening, I couldn't get to Burke's Bar fast enough; there I'd find loud music, cheap drinks, and a place to pretend I wasn't lonely. Burke's was clean enough to ward off disease, and dirty enough for me to believe drinking there tagged me as young and hip. Layers of nicotine baked into the dark wood stools, the worn bar, and the scuffed linoleum floor tinged everything a jaundiced yellow.

It was Thursday night. Customers jammed the place, but not elbow to elbow like Friday, when everybody seemed frantic. By Saturday, you could smell the desperation. Smart people knew to avoid the poison of Saturday nights at all costs, unless they were so friendless they might otherwise blow their brains out.

Thursday was my night.

The bathroom smelled of perfume and pot. I washed my hands, checked my makeup, and then made my way carefully down the steep steps leading back to the bar. Only in a boys' bar like Burke's would the women's room be at the same level as the tiny stage. Walking down from the restroom meant being on display, but I didn't care. I felt good. I felt fine. My hair flew wild, my red shirt wrapped me tight and low, and my crystal earrings threw off sex sparks.

I elbowed through the clumps of overgrown frat boys. The so-called band had taken a break, so instead of off-key wanna-be-a-rock-star music, I moved to Chaka Khan as I headed to the bar. "Ain't Nobody (Loves Me Better)" drummed in my ears.

Wasn't nobody loving me at all, at least nobody good for me. "Another one, Mickey," I called, taking my barstool and finishing my remaining quarter inch of Jack Daniel's and Coke.

Mickey gave his Little League smile and picked up a glass. Sweet Mickey would never pressure you to go home with him, but, of course, he never had to. Mickey had his pick, as bartenders usually did. We'd gotten together a few times, both of us aware we were simply passing the night in safe harbor. Mickey wasn't my dream man, but he kissed sexy, nibbling without gorging, and always brought me a hot cup of coffee before leaving the next morning. When I told Lulu why I considered

Mickey a gentleman, she asked if my standards could possibly get any lower.

Sorry we can't all have the love of our lives dropped into our laps, Lu.

"You have to work tomorrow?" Mickey placed my drink on a Heineken coaster gone soft and blurry.

Pat Benatar blared. "Tomorrow's Friday. I can slide."

"Nevertheless, I made you a mild one." Mickey gave me a fresh napkin.

"Am I supposed to thank you for that?"

"You will. Tomorrow." He tapped my forehead. "Trust me."

Mickey had witnessed my hangovers.

I swept my hair from my face and looked around. The band started to warm up, making me wonder from which musical sludge pond the owner had dredged up this group. Burke's was famous for off-key Police cover bands.

"Hey, beautiful."

Someone put his hands on my shoulders from behind and squeezed. I leaned back a millimeter. Someone felt tall and smelled married. "Hey," I said.

Someone removed the Red Sox hat marking the stool beside me. Someone tossed the hat on the bar so he could sit. "Haven't seen you for a long time," he said.

"I've been here." I wanted to wind my words back so he didn't think I hung out waiting for him.

He moved a curl from my eyebrow. "Then I should have been here."

My stomach shot down. Quinn's touch inverted me. I picked up my glass and tried not to drain it. Quinn motioned Mickey with two fingers. Mickey nodded to acknowledge Quinn, nobody ever ignored Quinn, but he took his sweet time making our drinks, doing little more than wave the Jack bottle over mine. It didn't matter. My previous drinks already had me halfway to drunk, and being next to Quinn did the rest of the job.

There wasn't a worse choice than Quinn. He wasn't just married; he was five-kids-Irish-Catholic-guilt married. Tough luck for me that Quinn melted the skin off my body.

Quinn had played for the Patriots years before. Unlike the other former football players who hung around Burke's, Quinn hadn't gone soft or bitter. Muscles covered his chest and arms, and he wore the same ironic grin I'd seen in his old game tapes.

Quinn never told me what a bitch his wife was or that she didn't sleep with him. He just told me he wanted me. His beautiful wife probably slept with him upon command.

Quinn pressed me against the wall outside my apartment. He jammed his mouth to mine. He smelled like ocean and leather, like the health club he owned in South Boston.

"Come inside," I said, barely able to talk from wanting him.

"I can't wait," he whispered. "Let's just do it here."

I wasn't that drunk. I pulled away and jammed my key in the door.

Quinn loved taking chances—with sex, on the field, with love, with me. Resisting him seemed hopeless. Each time I managed it, he dragged me back. Lulu called me naïve and stupid, but Quinn was a ride I couldn't get off. He had almost twenty years on me. He took me to candlelit restaurants on the water while guys my own age took me to the International House of Pancakes. He gave me a tiny gold locket that held a tiny picture of him in his Patriots uniform.

Once inside my apartment, Quinn lit cigarettes for both of us. I took mine to the kitchen, where I made us drinks, uncapping his bottle of Jameson for the first time in a month. He came up behind me while I popped ice out of the tray, pushing against me. I leaned back and let him outline my body.

"I missed you," he said, his voice dark and gritty.

"You shouldn't be here."

"Yet I am. Why is that, do you think?" He nudged his leg between mine.

I shook my head, unable to come up with a tart answer, unable to admit I'd let him in because he'd asked. Did he know it rarely took more than that?

Quinn and I had been going on since December, almost a year. Every now and then, I found my emotional muscle and threw him out of my life, and he'd respect my wishes for a week or a month.

"You need me to take care of you." He answered his own question. "I want to make you happy, baby. My poor little orphan."

Poor little orphan.

Quinn didn't have a clue about my real life, but I liked the person he imagined me to be. Better his darling orphaned girl than daughter of a man who'd murdered his wife. My mother.

I handed him his drink. I'd already finished half of mine, strong, unlike the watered-down versions Mickey fed me.

The room spun as I emptied my glass. It didn't matter how drunk I got. I'd slept with dozens of men without being tempted to break Lulu's rules of engagement; the secrets she'd made for us so long ago, even though she'd slept with Drew one time and given away all our stories. However, I'd understood once I met him. I wondered if I'd ever be with a man like Drew, if I'd even allow myself to date a Drew. In truth, I didn't think a Drew would want me.

Quinn and I made our way to my bedroom. I hadn't planned on his visit, and the apartment looked it. Dishes filled the sink. Clothes hung over chairs, the ratty couch, the end of the unmade bed. Coffee-stained cups covered my Salvation Army coffee table. I pictured Quinn's mysterious wife as a marriage of Cleopatra and a *Good Housekeeping* fairy, and I hated her. Sometimes I imagined her looking like my mother, the most beautiful woman I'd known in real life.

I tried straightening the sheets, a difficult task as I could barely stand without weaving.

"Leave it." Quinn unwrapped me from my shiny red shirt as though I were a Christmas present. After getting me down to bare skin and lowering me to the bed, he knocked away a pile of books, fumbled around for my tape player, and hit Play, ready to accept any sounds that came on. Marvin Gaye poured out, and I didn't give a damn how obvious the choice sounded. Quinn seeped through my pores and up into my brain, and once again he owned me.

He covered me, rocking us, welding us together, and then pressing me down hard to finish. I thought maybe I'd never come back. Then I fell into a deep sleep.

*

At four A.M., I woke to find Quinn standing over me. When he saw my eyes open, he sat at the edge of the bed and tried to cover me.

"Don't," I said. I struggled up and rested my head on his shoulder, smelling bar, soap, and cigarettes.

He ran his hand over my tangled curls. I nuzzled my chin into his large, warm hand. "Got to go, kid."

"Where does she think you are this time of night?"

"Who?"

"You know who." My hand crept to my chest.

"She thinks I'm exactly where I am, hanging out with a friend." His voice closed the topic. Don't broach the holy wife, whore. Don't name the sainted children. Quinn's scowl slammed my words down my throat. I backed away and locked my arms around my knees.

"I'll call you tomorrow," he said.

"Don't."

"Are we starting this again?"

I picked up my wrinkled cotton robe. Quinn had taught me to go to bed naked. No man before Quinn had seen my scar. He'd accepted my lies about a knife fight at Duffy without comment or judgment. At first, I'd loved that. Now I knew the truth; he simply wasn't that curious. Thus, I realized, he didn't love me. When you love someone, you're curious about everything he does, everything he is.

I knew because that's how I felt about Quinn.

17

Merry

I managed to avoid Quinn's calls for a week and two days, until it was time to go to New York. Lulu folded my laundry as she watched me pack.

"What's your plan, Merry? You intend to be his good girl forever?" Lulu smoothed out the wrinkles in my black jeans with angry, determined hands.

I shoved a book into my backpack as I worked on the right response. Tomorrow I'd take my biweekly Greyhound ride to see Dad, riding the bus to Port Authority, and then the ferry to the prison. Each time, Lulu came over the night before to berate me in advance for going. Then, when I got back home, she'd be waiting for me, wringing the visit out of me like water from a sponge.

"Dad's good girl?" I was too tired to argue. Avoiding Quinn's phone calls had left me limp. I'd begun the day in sleep deficit. "Is that who you mean?"

I picked up a sweaty bottle of Michelob. Lulu knew that I'd slept with

Quinn again. She'd read the signs, and when she asked and I answered, she'd simply shaken her head. Her reaction depressed me, as though my transgressions were now so unsurprising they rated no more than a gesture.

"Right. Daddy's good girl," Lulu said. "I can't imagine Quinn thinks of you as a good girl."

"It's not like our father has anybody else." Our conversation had the exhaustion of repetition as we laid out our tired arguments without hope. Each of us was years into waiting for change from the other.

Lulu grabbed my backpack. She arranged and wedged things far better than I ever could. "So what?" She rolled a cotton sweater around my copy of *Ms. Magazine.* "He doesn't deserve anyone."

"Like it or not, he's family," I said.

"You and Drew are my only family." Lulu refolded a shirt.

"Do we have to do this?" I tried changing the subject. "How's work?"

"Work is a constant state of terror. I thought being a resident might bring relief, but now I have the fear of an intern killing someone while they're under my supervision."

"At least you love what you do."

"Maybe that's because I like who I am," she said.

"Screw you." I turned away so she couldn't see me pinch my forearm hard and fast to keep from touching my chest. Lulu believed sharing her brute opinions would help me, and nothing convinced her otherwise. "I'll find the right job. Not everything is about my being whatever loser you think I am."

Lulu zipped up the backpack and leaned on the headboard, pushing my pillows behind her. At least I'd made my bed before she came over. "I don't think you're a loser," she said, "but you give it all away. Look at Quinn. You don't believe he really has anything to offer, do you?"

"What should he be offering?"

"Security? Marriage? A life? A family?"

"Maybe none of that interests me. Maybe I want a different life."

"Fine. What kind do you want?" She clasped her hands on top of her head and looked up to the heavens for help in saving my slut-worn soul. "Going to bars and sleeping with other women's husbands isn't a life."

"It must be a life, because I'm living it." I finished my beer, watching Lulu watch me. I lit a cigarette, and Lulu coughed.

"We just want you to be safe. And happy."

"We?" I searched the room. "Is Drew hiding in the closet? Christ, Lu, you're not even married yet. What, are you and he so joined at the hip you can't even say you want something without bringing him in? He didn't hang the moon, Lulu. Maybe what you wish isn't what I wish. For instance, I wish you'd see Dad. Just once. For me."

Lulu's face tightened. Closed for repairs, closed for the winter, closed for the season. Lulu shut down at will.

"Not going to happen, Merry," Lulu said. "Never going to be. Find a new wish."

I took the 5:45 morning bus and planned to take the 8:00 back that night. I leaned my head against the Greyhound seat's headrest, feeling the familiar tug in my chest as the bus pulled into Port Authority. I dreaded getting off and seeing the crumpled newspapers and food wrappers covering the bus station, watching the bums panhandling, and smelling stale coffee and urine. No matter how many quarters and dollars I gave away, I knew it made no difference.

Port Authority had become a den of hungry families, thieves, and legless men on wooden platforms. A woman layered in sweaters despite the September heat held out dirty-nailed fingers, clawing for the money I was about to offer.

I caught a subway downtown. Shoppers filled the Saturday morning train. I shifted my backpack so the straps could dig into different spots.

Thick graffiti obscured the subway windows, making it impossible to see out. My feet rested on some sticky, dried-down puddle of what looked like blood, which I prayed was soda.

The woman seated across the aisle took a mirror from her purse and turned from left to right, examining herself. She appeared to be in her mid-forties. As my mother would be now. Like Mama, she had dark hair, though not as thick and lustrous. I touched my own dark waves. This woman's hair seemed thin, despite her sad efforts to make it puffy. I could see where she'd teased it, the empty spots between the stiffly sprayed strands.

I tried to imagine what my mother would look like, but, as usual, I only saw photographs. Mama had frozen at her death age. Lulu was now a year older than Mama had been when she died, but at twenty-eight, Lulu seemed far younger than my memories of Mama. My mother's death added years to her memory; she was ever the adult and I would always be the child.

The woman across from me twisted her wedding and engagement rings in circles. Perhaps she felt my eyes, because she looked up at me with the "What? What?" expression New Yorkers perfect.

I arrived at the ferry exhausted from trying not to stare at people. Every female on the train became my mother or Aunt Cilla. I wished I'd slept while traveling from Boston. Quinn's last phone message played in my head.

Come on, Merry! Meet me at Burke's tonight.

I'd listened after Lulu left. The thought of a night in his arms had pulled at me so hard I'd had to take a pill just to avoid the *See him* screaming in my head. I'd gone into my dwindling stash of Valium, first spilling them on the bed to count, and then cutting one in half. My complaints of back pain brought only so many pills from my doctor. After swallowing the half tablet, I'd watered down a glass of Chablis by half and then half again, and sipped at it as I watched television, increasing the volume each time the phone rang.

I pulled my shirt away from my chest, trying to shake in cooler air as I waited, next in line. My top had a high neck to hide my scars and long sleeves so I'd attract as little attention for being a woman as possible.

Officer McNulty's grin showed his age. Blinding white dentures had replaced his familiar tobacco-stained teeth.

"Merry, how are you?" He gave me the briefest of examinations for contraband. "I hear from your father you've a position in a court."

I nodded. "I work with the victims."

He nodded. "Good, good for you."

155

He said this as though working in criminal justice was my karmic re-ordering.

"Have a good visit," he said. "It's your father's highlight. You're a good girl."

Everyone knew that, even if Lulu said it as a curse.

I walked across the never-changing floor. The spotted linoleum forever reminded me of blood splatter and bits of brain, a path to my father.

A grin split my father's face, the same damn smile each time. *Love me! Make me happy! Let me be a father for an hour!*

I leaned in and felt his arms around me. Despite the rules, he snuck a hug in with the sanctioned kiss on the cheek. *One of these days, Dad,* I always warned him. One of these days, he wouldn't get the benefit of the doubt and some new guard would pull him out and klop him right across the back.

Dad smelled smoky and a little stale. Metallic odors clung to him. From the bars on his cell? From the shop where he made glasses for the inmates? We still barely spoke of anything that went on inside Richmond, locking the prison away like the knowledge of a mad aunt.

"How about some circus peanuts," Dad." I put my hand down low and grabbed his, squeezing tight for a second, then pulling away from his iron grip. "I left a package for you. Hope it still tastes good after being X-rayed."

"You look good, sugar." We sat, and he peered across the table at me. "But tired. You're not burning the candle at both ends again, are you?"

"Again? When did I ever burn them the first time?"

"Don't kid a kidder." He seemed concerned, trying to be a real father right in the middle of the visiting room.

Gray showed in the stubble of his beard. Poor Dad never got a close shave. His razors had to last a long time. How long had he been using the too-used blade that scraped his face?

"Do you need a refill in your account, Dad?"

He pushed my words away with his hands. "I'm fine. I'm working, aren't I?"

"Right." I'd get him some money as soon as I got home. I tried to re-

156

member how much I had in my checking account. Three hundred? I'd send twenty dollars.

"So who's the guy?"

"What guy?"

"The guy who put those black rings under your eyes."

I touched the thin skin beneath my eyes.

"Look, Tootsie, whoever he is, he isn't right for you. You're not back with that ballplayer, are you?"

"He's not a ballplayer, Dad; he used to be. He owns a gym."

"Gym, schmim. He owns a wife and kids. He's a bum. Get rid of him." He tapped the edge of the table for emphasis. "No one but a bum cheats. Say what you will, I never cheated on your mother."

Jesus, take me now. "I didn't say I'd gone back to him."

"And you never said you didn't."

"It's immaterial. I'm not seeing him anymore."

"Cheaters cheat, that's what they do. You need a man you can trust. Someone to lean on."

"Right. You're right, Dad." Telling him about Quinn had been crazy, a desperate reach out for help, for closeness.

"I worry, Sugar Pop."

"I know you do." I rummaged in every corner of my brain for a conversation I could have with my father where I wouldn't want to drive a knife into my own heart.

"So," he said. "Your sister, how was her birthday?"

"It was two months ago."

"Right. I knew that." He ran a hand over his chin. "Jesus, these razors. I go around like a bum. I know when your sister's birthday is, Merry. What I meant to say is, what did you do?"

"We went out to eat. With Drew."

"Drew, huh? Seems like he's always around. Think he'll be my son-in-law?"

I nodded. "Sure do, Dad. He's one of the good ones, like you want for me."

"Not a cheater, right?"

"No. Not a cheater." Not a cheater, not a beater.

My father's crime had another name now. My job forced me to name him more than a killer; now I knew to call it domestic violence. My father was a specialized killer. Now I had something else I couldn't bear to think about.

Lulu said *domestic violence* sounded too clean for what our father did. She didn't want to talk about it. *Murderer* was enough of a name for her. She said nothing else mattered.

But I knew she was wrong.

"Does Lulu ever ask about me?" My father wore his puppy eyes.

"She usually wants to know how the visit was."

She wants to know if you finally dropped to your knees to ask forgiveness. She wonders if you finally howled to the winds and admitted that you ruined our lives.

"She asks if everything's okay." I crossed my fingers at the lie, knowing how angry Lulu would be if she heard me.

"It'll never be okay. I'm stuck here forever." He smacked one hand into the other, and I jumped at the sound. "Jesus Christ, what am I supposed to do to get her to come here? She's as stubborn as your mother ever was."

I sat tight and straight, crossing my ankles and pressing them together.

"It would help a hell of a lot if she wrote to the parole board, you know."

I let his voice trail off. "I'll ask again."

He made thumbs-up signs with both hands. "Hey, that's all I can ask, right? Thanks, Tootsie."

18

Merry

June 1990

Lulu's June wedding day dawned pure with promise. Helping her dress, I worked hard to keep the atmosphere as clean and beautiful as the North Carolina sky that filtered in through the French paned window. The sky was southern-spring blue, and we had a view of Asheville spread out before us. The hotel room's elegance reflected my sister's regal bearing. "You look beautiful."

Lulu gazed at herself in the mirror. "I should have eloped."

"Mama would like that dress," I said. Satin slipped over Lulu's hips like thick cream. "You have such a great body. Like Mama."

"You're the one who looks like her, not me."

"But you have her body."

"How would you know?"

"I know."

Lulu shook her head. "No. Mama was curvy. Like you. You think that I'm built like her because she was tall, tall compared to you, but you have her shape. You're her in miniature."

Looking in the mirror, I studied the reflected contrast between my dark hair and my shell pink dress. Mrs. Winterson, Drew's mother—*Call me Peg, hon*—would be horrified by the high neckline, just as she'd been by the scar-hiding dress I'd worn to the rehearsal dinner last night. Next to Peg, I'd looked like a nun. Her tight-fitting yellow silk dress with four-inch heels dyed to match had showed off a set of breasts she treated like a favorite accessory.

"Honey, look at that beautiful bosom and that tiny little waist." Peg had eyed me up and down with triple-mascaraed eyes. "You have to wear something cut down low, honey."

Drew had intervened before his mother went any further. Drunk as she was, I wouldn't have been surprised if she'd taken out a pair of nail scissors and cut my cocktail dress down to the cleavage.

"Mom, between you and Daphne, we'll have enough to go around," Drew had said, lifting his chin toward his sister's overflowing breasts.

"Drew!" Daphne had scolded, leaning against her plastered husband.

Peg Winterson had tinkled her deep-cigarette laugh. "Well, don't blame me if you get the heat vapors, Merry. Really, high neck and sleeves in June!"

Lulu must have been thinking my thoughts as she continued looking in the mirror. Cupping her hands under her breasts and pushing them up to make small mounds, she asked, "Bosomy enough for Peg, do you think?"

Lulu's light brown hair curled in a loose knot gathered low. She'd suffered the hairdresser's machinations insisted upon by Peg gracefully. "I look like a milkmaid, right?" Lulu asked, touching her unadorned white dress.

"You look ethereal," I said. "You can leave the hootchy-kootchy to Daphne and Peg."

"Grandma." Lulu smacked her lips to set her lipstick. "Remember how she told me not to wear miniskirts?"

"Because you'd look like a hootchy-kootchy dancer," I said. "I wish she were here. How old would Grandma be?"

"I don't know. What's the difference?"

"I'm just curious. Don't you wish Mom were here?"

Lulu crossed her arms over her breasts. "She'd show enough cleavage for the entire wedding."

"And look better than anyone in the Heritage Ballroom."

"Anyone in the entire Grove Park Inn," Lulu added.

"Anyone in the state of North Carolina." I turned my head from side to side. "Do you really think I look like her?"

"Don't fish. You know you do."

"Dad says you look like his side of the family."

"Grandma would be eighty-seven, I think," Lulu said. "And Mimi Rubee would be sixty-six, or maybe sixty-five. God, she was young when Mama was born."

"Dad asked me to give you and Drew a present from him." The moment I said the words, I wanted to wind them back in.

"What? A tin cup?"

"Don't be mean, Lulu. Not today."

"Just don't say his name, okay? Don't give me any presents from him." My sister shook her head. "It's my wedding day. Stand up for me—Drew's drunken relatives are about to eat me alive. I just want it to be perfect, just for today."

"And for tomorrow?"

"Calm. Good. Sweet and nice. Is that too much to expect?"

"No." I took Lulu's hand, her white-gloved-all-the-way-to-the-elbow hand, and we walked out to her marriage.

Lulu and Drew spent their honeymoon in Iceland, where the average June temperature was fifty-four degrees and the record for heat was something like seventy. Drew's summers with his family in North Carolina had given him an allergy to hot weather. While visiting his parents the previous August, he'd broken out in rashes, which he'd ascribed to the weather. Lulu thought he was allergic to his voluble drunk mother, but Lulu kept her counsel, and passed the calamine lotion.

Besides, Lulu had said, she liked the idea of going to Iceland. She couldn't go much farther and still be in this world. In Iceland, she could let go of deception. She wouldn't have to remember her made-up past. If they had books to read and Drew could find an occasional poker game in the hotel, they'd always be happy. As long as they had each other.

161

In a moment of prewedding vulnerability, Lulu had said letting go of our father's name was her best wedding present of all. I knew how she felt—I wished I could take Drew's name. Not that I'd ever break my father's heart like that.

I packed up my apartment during the weeks I waited for Lulu and Drew to return from their honeymoon. I was getting ready to move into the huge, rambling Cambridge house they'd bought before the wedding. We weren't going to live in the same space, of course; I'd have my own apartment with my own entrance. Long ago, a previous owner had divided the house into two apartments. The Victorian home sat on a big corner lot. My entrance would be on one street, while theirs would be on the other.

I supposed it seemed pathetic, me living next door to my sister and brother-in-law, but it felt safe for Lulu and me, and Drew didn't seem to mind.

When I'd met Drew, I couldn't miss how he and Lulu came together like magnetized dolls. Drew's life didn't have the drama of Lulu's, but he'd grown up with elements of craziness. Drew's father blamed Drew's mother's southern roots for her drinking, her affairs, and her overlarge personality. Drew's mother blamed the state of Nebraska for her husband's frozen personality. Their ice and heat created a house of storms.

Lulu and Drew both worshiped peace.

When I moved into the new house next week, I'd walk up one short flight of steps to enter my three medium-size rooms. I suspected my apartment had once been the servants' quarters, but that seemed fair, as Drew's money had financed the entire deal.

Drew and Lulu entered their much larger apartment off an outsize deck built in the back. The house had modern touches, especially the updated kitchen and master bath, to suit Lulu, while retaining the period details, like the ornate crown molding and ceiling medallions that drove Drew crazy with architectural love. I'd heard enough poetic waxing about the antique amber doorknobs to be satisfied with that particular topic for the rest of my life.

Lulu and Drew had tons of room on their side. They could have kids, and offices, entertainment centers, and even a massage parlor if they so wished. It was all fine with me; three rooms suited me. I had no intention of procreating. Motherhood made you a prisoner. I remember Mrs. Cohen always watching out for her granddaughter, Rachel, practically tying herself to the little girl for fear she'd fall out a window or something. Each time Rachel visited, Mrs. Cohen locked up anything the little girl might swallow, eat, or be smothered by, choke on, or use as poison.

When I babysat Rachel, I didn't dare blink because that meant I spent a moment blind to her imminent death. I didn't want children, and though I never said a word, I hoped Lulu and Drew wouldn't have them either. The three of us would do just fine as our own pack of refugees from family dysfunction living in Cambridge.

My emptying apartment seemed smaller and dirtier the more I packed. Each poster had covered some sordid detail I'd forgotten, such as the hole Quinn had punched in the wall the last time I'd told him to leave, when I'd threatened to call his wife if he ever contacted me again. Like the area where I'd thrown up Manischewitz wine after some half-assed Passover seder Lulu, Drew, and I had attempted; I'd covered the pink blotch on the gray carpet with a hooked rug.

Whitney Houston came on the radio with a song that reminded me too much of Quinn, and I snapped it off, replacing her with a properly bitchy CD from Janet Jackson. Yeah, what have you done for me lately?

My cigarette pack was almost flat. Just one left. One would never get me through the night, and besides, I'd sweated right through the roots of my hair. I needed air-conditioning to go with my cigarette.

I woke up the next morning in Gary's apartment. Gary, whose last name was lost to me, gave a gurgling snore. Gary had been crushing on me for quite a while. I knew that. His girlfriend, Sheila, a nurse, had been at work the previous night while Gary hung out at the bar shooting pool. I remembered leaning over as he lit my cigarette, showing my breasts along with my scar, not caring, hungry for admiration like a whore for hundred-dollar bills.

We'd gone to his apartment because mine was such a mess. That we'd gone to any apartment at all was the problem. I lifted the bedcover as quietly as possible. My head pounded. I swung one leg, then the other over the mattress. A pilled blanket topped nasty gray-white sheets.

Gary had air-conditioning, however.

Hadn't I promised myself never to show up at Burke's on a Saturday?

What had I been thinking? Why hadn't I bought my cigarettes from the gas station on the corner?

I tiptoed toward the bathroom, crossing the gritty wooden floor of the triple-decker apartment. Nothing new to me. Slept in one of them, slept in all of them.

"Hey, don't sneak away."

I turned and offered Gary a sick smile.

"I better go," I said. "What if Sheila comes?"

"She doesn't have a key." He rolled on his side, pulling up the sheet like a girl, maybe to cover his beer belly. "It's not like we're engaged or anything."

Soft blond hair fell over his balding forehead. I'd only seen Gary in a baseball jersey and Red Sox cap, which covered all his vulnerable spots.

My nudity felt like an advertisement. I picked my clothes off the floor and clutched them as best I could to cover my naked breasts and front. "I have to get home and pack."

"I can help. I'm a terrific packer," he said with a boy's smile.

"That's okay. My place is a wreck."

Gary swept a hand around his apartment. "This isn't exactly the Taj Mahal. Let me at least make you breakfast."

"Coffee. Coffee would be great." I rushed into the bathroom and pulled on my clothes fast enough to make Superman envious. I covered my index finger with toothpaste and spread it around my teeth and tongue, trying to scrape off the taste of beer and Gary. The mirror reflected clownish black mascara stains under my eyes. I opened Gary's medicine cabinet, feeling only a little funny about it, wondering what he might have that I could substitute for eye makeup remover. Vaseline? Finally, I found a grungy looking tube of Jergens lotion, which probably belonged to Sheila-without-a-key.

I dabbed some under my eyes and succeeded in smearing the black in larger, oilier circles. My sunglasses were in my car. I would have dived out the bathroom window for them, but we were on the second floor.

When I entered the kitchen, Gary gave me an appreciative look. "You look cute in the morning."

He walked over and put an arm around my waist. I backed away from his unbrushed breath. Didn't the man need to pee, for Christ's sake? "Thanks. Bathroom's free."

"Coffee is almost ready. Be right back. Don't go anywhere."

I could have cried from the frustration of wanting to be home, wanting to be out of Gary's apartment and away from Gary's love-hungry, sex-hungry, romance-hungry eyes eating me up like a roaming Irish bear. I watched the coffee drip down with caffeine-starved eyes. When finally the last bit of liquid spit out of the coffee funnel, I rinsed two cups, one yellow with a long brown crack inside, the other a relatively intact World's Best Boyfriend mug. Given the lousy options, I chose the crack.

"Ah, it's done." Gary picked up his now clean mug and tipped it toward me. "Sorry."

Not knowing if the apology was for the dirt or the message, I shrugged. "No problem."

He came over and tugged at the corner of last night's T-shirt. The wide-open V-neck made it too easy for him to find a shoulder to kiss, though I wore a camisole underneath. I wriggled away. He pulled me back. "You taste good."

"I have to go."

"Not yet." He traced my collarbone with his tongue, then a callused finger. "I want you."

I let him lead me to a kitchen chair. He tugged his shorts down and sat. He grabbed me and pulled everything below my waist off in a quick, easy motion. He brought me on top of him and grunted. I buried my face in the hollow of his neck and waited for him to come.

Hot water beat at me. I soaped my arms, my feet, scrubbed Gary from between my legs until the Ivory soap stung. I washed my hair twice. I covered myself with talcum powder, Cashmere Bouquet like Grandma used to sprinkle on us. Lulu said that Mama used it also. When the

165

weather was hot, Mama cooled us with alcohol, then the powder, so we wouldn't sweat while we slept.

I put on the lightest T-shirt I had and slipped into a pair of scrub pants Lulu had given me. I poured myself a third cup of coffee, toasted an English muffin, and spread it thick with butter and slices of cheddar cheese. I grabbed the stack of mail I'd been avoiding and made piles.

To be paid.

To be thrown away.

Dad's letter.

When I finished the English muffin, I slit open Dad's letter and read:

Dear Merry,

    How was the wedding of the century? I can't wait to hear about it. Most of all, I can't wait to see some pictures. You'll make sure you bring them, right? Make sure they are the size that I can keep—you know it, right? Otherwise, call and they will tell you.

As though I hadn't known since childhood exactly what possessions Richmond County permitted.

Once again, I find myself wishing you could convince your sister to come and visit me. I think if I saw her face-to-face, I could explain everything. Do you think she ever reads my letters?

Last time I asked, Lulu told me to mind my own business. Later, probably after she spoke to Drew, she said she read them once in a while, but usually she just shredded them into confetti. *"You'd tell me if anything important happens, right?"* I suppose she meant if our father got cancer or leprosy. Would she visit him then?

Big news here—they want me to take on a larger role in the optical shop. We're serving three more facilities now. Your father will be managing the biggest shop in the system.

Facilities. System. They. Our communication was a series of careful codes.

I think this will help next time I'm up for parole, but you know what will make the real difference. Please. Work on your sister. I am getting to be an old man in here.

Not able to resist any longer, I rubbed and rubbed my chest, moving my hand from smooth skin to puckered ridges.

In three years, I'll be fifty. You should see the old men in here—they look like death warmed over. I don't want to be like that. I want to hold grandchildren someday. Please. You're my only hope, Tootsie. Love and Kisses, Daddy

Part 3

19

Lulu

July 2002

I woke before the alarm on Monday morning, my mouth dry from the air conditioner. My older daughter, ten-year-old Cassandra, stood over me, arms on her hips, eyes narrowed, looking angry but not injured. My initial shot of adrenaline backed down, and I readied myself for today's tale of disparity in the Winterson home. Early on, Cassandra had solidified her role as our family monitor. Daily she decreed what was fair, mean, or righteous. Being a budding actress added to her histrionic family performances. Sometimes I regretted having enrolled her in the drama classes she'd taken to as though she were a young Meryl Streep.

"Ruby gets whatever she wants, just because she's younger," Cassandra said, allowing no time for me to adjust to waking. "You and Daddy treat her like a baby, and I don't get away with anything."

"What's wrong?"

"Ruby wanted pancakes and I wanted waffles, and Daddy said he'd flip a coin. But she cried, so of course, the big baby got her choice."

I knew the story ran deeper, and the prospect of digging it out wearied me. "Get in, sweetheart." I held up the sheet and blanket.

Cassandra slipped under the sky blue comforter and took a deep breath, readying herself to list off her grievances. My daughter smelled like my expensive soap, which she believed should belong to all of us, especially her.

I didn't have to be at work until ten, though soon the girls would leave for whatever summer vacation activity Drew had planned for them. *Beach today,* I thought. Drew worked from home; we'd transformed the attic rooms on the top floor into his studio.

Cassandra snuggled close. My bedroom gave off a clean, cool feel. The white cottage furniture reminded me of Martha's Vineyard. White shutters on the windows, my collection of porcelain vases, and the translucent bowls on the bookcase and dresser all soothed me. Drew had painted the walls a snowy white and hung the painting he'd done that I loved most, blue irises against a sun so intense it burned from the canvas.

"Daddy always gives in to Ruby," Cassandra complained.

"I'm sure he'll make you waffles tomorrow."

"But I wanted them today. She's just a crybaby. I don't think the cut even hurt."

"What cut?" I sat up.

"It's nothing, Mom." Cassandra drew away, shifting to her back and crossing her leg over her bent knee. "It's stupid that Daddy even let her cut strawberries. Anyway, it wasn't anything. She just cried and pretended so she could get her pancakes."

"I'd better check on her."

Cassandra tugged at my nightgown, trying to pull me back down. "She didn't even bleed except maybe one little drop. Everyone does everything for Ruby."

"Enough, Cassandra." My impatience grew. I needed to see Ruby before taking my shower.

"You're not being fair," Cassandra complained. "No one is."

"What do you want?" I struggled to keep my voice even, knowing I'd already failed, my irritation already spilling over the nice white and blue room.

Motherhood had never been my dream. I'd never thought I'd be very good at the job. *See, Drew. This is why you're the mommy and I go to work.* Not that he'd argued with me about our division of labor. Drew had worked hard in his campaign to sell me on motherhood. In the end, his strong want had won me over, though the thought of being a mother had terrified me. It still did; it had turned out to be worse than I'd ever imagined. I hadn't known how much they'd own me, how every fall they took would raise bumps on me.

"Why can't you take us to the beach today?" Cassandra asked.

Why are you so hard to please when we give you so much? "Daddy's taking a friend for each of you, right?" I said. "You don't need me."

Maybe we gave them too much.

Cassandra got up on her knees, pleading with me to understand. Her lank brown hair falling over her shoulders reminded me of my own. "Yes, I do need you," she said. "You never come. You haven't even seen how good I swim the crawl now."

"We'll all go this weekend. I promise."

"Sure," Cassandra said. "I bet."

She sounded as though I broke promises every day. Was that how she viewed me? "And we'll go to the bookstore and get a new batch of summer books."

Every way I turned as a mother, I disappointed someone. Ruby and Cassandra were warring nations, always needing different things, never satisfied at the same time. At any moment, I faced disappointment, failure, or terror. At some point, all these were certain to occur, right?

See, Drew? I knew it. Having children ensured enduring life's worst crap. By hounding and bribing me into pregnancy, Drew had forced me to become a hostage to terror. You give birth, and then worry becomes your lifelong caul.

Had my mother felt that way? Had thoughts of danger threatening Merry and me kept her up at night? Trying to catch memories of Mama felt like trying to hold rain. I didn't remember sensing her worry, but she was my mother, she must have worried. I gave myself comfort with those thoughts.

Ruby ran through the door. Drew walked behind balancing a mug.

"Did you wake her up?" Ruby asked Cassandra. She turned to her father. "She's in trouble, right?"

"No, she's not in trouble," I said. "Don't be an instigator."

"What's that?" Ruby asked.

"*Instigator* means someone who starts something, but not in a good way," I said.

"Someone who acts like a baby," Cassandra said. "And who cries all the time."

"You pooped in your pants!" These were eight-year-old Ruby's final words in most fights.

"Ruby! How many times do we have to tell you not to say that?" Drew said. He placed the coffee in my hand. Ever since Cassandra had had a horrible bout of food poisoning on the way home from the Cape and couldn't hold out for a bathroom, this had been Ruby's favorite taunt. "You know Cassandra was sick."

"You shouldn't be rude and mean," I added.

Cassandra stuck her tongue out at Ruby, and then turned accusing eyes on Drew. "I told Mommy you made Ruby her pancakes, even though I won."

Looking for ways to knock out my daughters' bad traits—Cassandra's need for hair-splitting fairness and the mantle of victimhood, Ruby's attempts to push her way to the top—appeared to be a Sisyphean task. My girls had so many wearying qualities. Civilizing them overwhelmed me. How much easier it would be to simply throw them gobs of goodies as though they were rabid dogs. *Candy! Toys! Hot dogs! Come get them, girls! Ruff! Love me!*

"But I got hurt," Ruby said. She held up her hand, showing me a Sleeping Beauty bandage on her tiny palm. "See?"

"Cassandra, Ruby did get hurt. We talked about this," Drew said. "Tomorrow you'll get waffles."

Cassandra collapsed in on herself, leaning back against me. I stroked her fine, light hair, wanting to run far from all of them. Cassandra sighed out her loss. She turned to me and took my face in her hands, staring as though I were the blood running through her veins.

"Please stay home with me, Mommy," Cassandra begged. "Let Ruby stay with Daddy, and you stay with me today. Don't go to work. Please!"

"*Lulu?*" Merry's scream cut through the drama. "*Drew?* I'm grabbing some coffee, okay?"

"Fine," I yelled back down.

Drew squeezed Cassandra's knee. "Come on, honey. You know Mommy has to go to work. Plus, we have to pick up your friends."

I grabbed Cassandra for a hug around her dejected shoulders before she left. "It will be fine," I told her.

Fine was my word of the morning. Fine for me not to see Cassandra for a single full day this summer and fine for Merry to pour a cup of coffee. It was fine about four workdays out of five, when Drew's already brewed coffee usually trumped the prospect of Merry making her own.

I didn't worry about Merry walking out her front door wearing slippers and pajamas, running around the corner from her apartment to my and Drew's entrance. The unusual was the usual in Cambridgeport. Walking in nightwear didn't come close to earning us a place in the neighborhood freaky line, not in the part of Cambridge where Drew, Merry, and I lived.

The marionette lady, who carried wooden puppets to speak for her, lived on one side of us, and a platinum blond drag queen who stood six foot, five inches without his stiletto heels owned the house on the right. Even more amazing, right here in the heart of Cambridge, we had a Republican. He covered his house with American flags and played Taps each night on his front porch.

Following September 11 the previous year, our ultraliberal neighborhood had declared a brief détente with the neighborhood Republican. For a few weeks, everyone gathered by his house at dusk, listening as he played. Now, almost a year later, the neighbors again treated him as a crazy outcast.

Sometimes I was startled to wake up in the role of mother with daughters, wife with husband, no longer a virtual orphan trying to keep herself to one drawer or one room, but able to spread out from a starkly lovely bedroom to a well-ordered basement. Even after years of living in this house, in this identity, I still didn't know how to stretch out to live in all the corners of my world.

Despite my trappings, I suspected that it was only Merry's presence next door that kept me stabilized. Sometimes, even though I didn't tell anyone, the realities of my daughters and my secret father locked away in a New York State penitentiary collided inside me like a clap of thunder. Mama still lived inside me as the beautiful-angry mother of my earliest years. I'd always have to hide the reality of my relationship with Mama from my girls. Sadder, when I searched for ways to be a mother, what motherhood meant, my memories of Mama were of no use.

I drove up the final ramp to the top floor of the garage attached to the Cabot Medical Health Care Building. Staff parking was first come, first served in Cabot's survival-of-the-first-to-arrive plan. By 9:50, time forced us into the Siberia of parking real estate, the outermost corners, where our cars were vulnerable to rain, snow, or the beating sun.

Cabot Medical thrived on malice and discomfort, from the vicious parking battles to our careful tracking of Red Sox wins and losses. Working this close to Fenway Park, we prayed for them to lose, caring only about shortening the season of insane traffic. Screw the pennant.

I'd gone straight through from Cabot Medical School to the Cabot Medical Health Care group practice. They offered a job, and I accepted.

I hurried to the staircase, ran down to street level, and crossed the hot courtyard to the glass-and-bronze entry. Running stairs was my only form of exercise.

"Morning, Doctor Winterson." Jerry the coffee guy had the lobby concession. A paraplegic with massive arms, he'd designed the operation to his reach and comfort, daring anyone to complain about having to crouch down for their sugar or creamer. I admired his skill in using his disability to blackmail his way into extra income. No one dared not to buy something, not with Jerry's hints that turning down his muffin, tea, or ready-made sandwich reflected on your generosity toward the handicapped.

"Jerry probably has a mansion by now," the receptionist, Maria, had muttered last week. Even so, she said it while clutching a chocolate chip cookie baked by Jerry's wife.

"I've had my coffee, and I brought my lunch," I said as I passed Jerry's

cart. I held up my L.L.Bean lunch bag as proof. "I'll pick up a dozen cookies for the staff meeting later."

"If we have any left," Jerry said darkly, as though if he sold out it would
be a bad thing, and probably my fault.

"I'll take my chances." I opened the door to the inside staircase and ran
up three flights to Internal Medicine, coming out in a large open hall car-
peted in industrial gray and leading to pods labeled A, B, and C. As I entered the B pod, Maria waved from the circular reception area, nodding
as she spoke into her headset. Patients leaned toward my white coat like
drooping weeds seeking sun.

Sticky notes fluttered from my computer screen. Area secretaries
stuffed our mail slots so full with administrative memos and junk mail
from drug companies that we of B pod communicated by stickies and bits
of paper taped to chairs.

Cabot Medical had become a hatred-inducing practice, hounding us
daily with reminders about money: *Bottom line! Remember capitation! More
patients in less time! Accrete or burn!* I waited for the day the Medicrats told us
to troll through bingo parlors for new patients.

My patient roster had gradually changed into a solid block of women
whom I considered the almost old; doctors seemed to have less patience for
these transitional women. I felt for them. I'd be one someday soon, and, unlike many acquaintances, I didn't pretend otherwise; I didn't want to be
one of those females who were surprised by their swift fall, women who
barely had time to wave good-bye at being beautiful, being needed, or being wooed as they slid toward retirement and the gray world of invisibility.

I made time for the almost old; in return, they clucked and fussed over
me as if I were their personal miracle worker. *So clever, this one.*

I peeled notes from my chair and computer. A larger-size hot pink Post-
it screamed from my desk lamp.

*Where are you? I had to drink coffee alone with the master of boredom. Doctor
Denton kept me prisoner for twenty minutes of soul-killing tales of gardening.
Please, come cleanse my aura and hear about my DATE. What are you planning
for your birthday tomorrow? Can I take you to lunch? Check schedule for upcoming
patient crush. Sorry. Kisses, Sophie*

Sophie, the nurse with whom I teamed, had become my closest friend since Marta had left Boston for a rich husband. Patients came to Cabot as much for Sophie as they did for me. She knew how to comfort and give hugs when they cried for their lost wombs, their vanished sex lives, and the alopecia that horrified them each time they looked in the mirror. They, in turn, kept an eye out for a suitable husband and father for Sophie and her three nightmarish boys.

"Sounds great," I'd said when Sophie told me about yet another patient's eligible nephew. "Remind Mrs. Doherty that her son should bring his whip and lion-taming chair when he picks you up."

Sophie stuck her head in the door. "Your ten-twenty is waiting, and your ten-forty is checking in. In addition, I had to squeeze in Audra Connelly. She found a job and she needs a full physical before starting."

I studied my schedule laid out on the computer, color-coded courtesy of the Medicrats upstairs. "And just how do I manage this? Magic?"

"You're the doctor. Figure it out."

I nodded. Audra's husband had recently died from pancreatic cancer, the once-massive and cheerful cop becoming skeletal and yellow as he suffered the pain by folding in on himself. I'd figure it out. "What time?" I asked. "Oh, wait—I see."

She'd squeezed Audra's appointment into 4:10. I massaged the back of my neck.

"How about a birthday lunch tomorrow?" Sophie asked.

Birthday tomorrow.

Anniversary of my mother's death today.

Merry and I dreaded memorializing the event, but if we didn't recognize the day in some way, we'd wait all year for the inevitable punishment, so we always marked it together. Some years we'd snuck to her grave, bringing red roses. My mother had become Snow White in my smoky memories, with lips the color of fresh blood, hair blacker than lacquered china, and skin white as a geisha's.

Most years we watched sad movies to honor Mama. Repeatedly, we'd heard Mimi Rubee say, *My Celeste was beautiful enough to be a movie star.* When we'd lived at Duffy, we'd saved the quarters Grandma

Zelda slipped us and snuck off to the Loews theater on Mama's death day. After we had moved to the Cohens', we'd continued the practice. Asking them to take us to Mama's grave site never seemed a possibility.

Each year we picked the saddest movie with the most tragic actress, moving through the decades from the Loews in Brooklyn to videos to DVDs, choking with sobs as we watched *Sophie's Choice* or *Terms of Endearment*, wondering how devoted our mother would have been had she lived. I couldn't imagine her letting gray roots grow in, as the mother had during her daughter's illness in *Terms of Endearment*. The thought made me ill with guilt. Merry was supposed to rent tonight's movie. We'd watch. She'd drink. We'd cry. Then we'd go to sleep. Happy anniversary, Mama.

By four o'clock, seeing a patient familiar enough for me to sit and chat for a moment offered more comfort than I'd had all day. Screw the Medicrats. My feet were killing me. Hunger pains growled. Extra patients had cost me lunch.

"Audra," I said as I walked in. "How are you?"

"I'm fine, dear. I think I have a job."

"Are you sure you're ready?" It had been only four months since Audra's husband died.

"More than. A few more nights watching television, and I'll bash the poor screen. I've been going over to help at Ocean View, you know, the nursing home where my mother and Hal's father are, but I think even they're getting tired of me." Audra smiled, her mouth covered with what little lipstick she hadn't worried away. She looked thinner than the last time I had seen her, which she couldn't afford, being one of those spare Irish women without flesh to lose. "The kids are visiting too much. They need to live their lives."

"Let's make this about you. What's the job?" I asked as I skimmed through Audra's vital signs.

"A library assistant in the Brookline schools. I think it could be perfect for me."

"They'll be the lucky ones," I said. "Blood pressure, good. Weight, too low. Are you feeling okay?"

"It's all fine except for too many nights eating a bowl of cereal for dinner."

"You have to treat yourself as well as you did him." I warmed the stethoscope in my hands. "Take a breath."

"When have you ever known a woman to do that?" Audra asked, gasping out the held air. "We only do it for others."

"Any complaints?"

"Just the usual—I hear all the same things from the girls in my bridge club. We ache. Our feet hurt. Our faces don't look so good." Audra smiled. "Lucky this job doesn't require beauty."

I touched her shoulder. "You'll always look lovely. You have the classic looks every woman wants. Like Katharine Hepburn."

Merry had left a message earlier that she'd rented *Doctor Zhivago*. I liked Geraldine Chaplin—the wife—more than Julie Christie. Chaplin's dark eyes and mild face offered more comfort than Christie's beauty.

I panicked. What color had my mother's eyes been? Were they blue? Had they been deep brown, like Merry's? We had only black-and-white photographs of Mama. Who would know? Whom could I ask?

"Well, I have Hepburn's crinkled neck. But who cares anymore?" Audra clapped her hands together, bringing me out of my reverie. "Will you listen to me? Goodness. I've had a wonderful life, and now I'm getting ready for a new adventure."

"A new adventure, yes. You never know what life holds, right? Now, if you slip open your gown and lie down so I can examine your breasts, we'll be just about done."

Audra's freckled breasts exhibited her pregnancies. Her thin, papery skin showed wear and tear; her nipples revealed signs of suckling infants.

"Could you lift your arms, Audra?" I came closer, pushing my glasses tighter to the bridge of my nose. "Hands behind your head, okay?"

Exam-table paper crinkled as Audra settled back. Bright fluorescence highlighted by the white steel cabinets and chrome fixtures emphasized every mole and age spot on Audra's flesh. I placed the pads of my fingers on Audra's small breasts, using the new approach I'd learned, covering each spot with three different levels of pressure. Instead of moving in a circle around Audra's breast, I went from top to bottom across the chest area to include the breast tissue that reached from the collarbone to the bra line and into the armpits.

Nothing seemed wrong, except for a roughness at Audra's nipple. I adjusted the lamp, pulling it a bit closer, and leaned in, seeing redness and scaling around the right one. I ran a finger over it, then squeezed, looking for discharge. The left nipple seemed free from any skin changes. I went back to the right breast, tracing the scaling with my finger, then moving around the areola.

"Have you had any problems with your right nipple?"

"No. Is something wrong?" Audra turned her face to look at me. Until now, she'd kept the usual demeanor of a woman having an intimate exam, studying the ceiling with the stillness of a mannequin. Concern now animated her face.

I glanced at the breast and back at Audra. "I notice a bit of a rash. Have you noticed it?"

"It's been a bit itchy, now that you mention it. Should I be worried?"

"You can leave the worrying to me," I said, meaning it. My co-workers accused me of continually searching for zebras in horse corrals. My terror of missing a diagnosis sent me down testing roads the Medicrats argued against repeatedly. "It's just a small rash. Have you changed detergent? Soap? Bought a new brand of bras?"

"I've been swimming at the Brighton Y. Could chlorine cause it?"

"Certainly possible," I said. "Chlorine's a strong irritant. But since you're due for a mammogram anyway, I'll add a few tests."

"Should I be worried?" she asked again.

We should always be worried. Every second of every day.

"You've had a history of eczema in the past, and you've been under nothing but stress, so it's likely you have eczema on your nipple."

"Oh, Lord, please don't let the eczema be coming back," Audra said.

Please let the eczema be coming back.

*

The popcorn bowl was almost empty. Merry and I took turns reaching in and scrabbling for popped kernels among the unopened, hard pellets. Why did some kernels have to be so obstinate?

"You worry about everything," Merry said. "One scratchy nipple and you have her dead and buried." I'd told her about Audra's exam and my fears.

"As though you don't do the death watch," I replied. Merry and I spent our lives waiting for loved ones to disappear or die. I couldn't imagine what I'd do when Cassandra and Ruby were old enough to leave the house without Drew or me.

"That's why I know you're nuts." She hit the remote button to open the DVD player and retrieve *Doctor Zhivago*. "Mama would have liked this movie. She'd think Geraldine Chaplin's character was too good to be true, though. She'd like Julie Christie."

I didn't know where my sister got this baloney from, being she wasn't even six when Mama died. Merry had built a Mama from memory shreds, from pictures, and from what I had told her over the years.

"Who'd you like?" I wondered.

"I hated the way Geraldine Chaplin was good, good, good, and went around taking care of everyone. And what did she end up with?"

"She got away from it all."

"But Julie Christie got Omar Sharif." Merry refilled her wineglass and put her feet up on the coffee table. It seemed impossible Merry would be thirty-seven in December. She still acted like a kid waiting for life to begin. Insubstantial, like her furniture, a cast-off desk from Drew, board-and-brick bookcases, and a coffee table made from a giant wire spool, which she probably got from a phone repairman she'd slept with.

"Omar Sharif never made anyone happy," I argued.

"Don't you think he made them happy for a little while?"

"Why did they want him anyway?" I asked. "He was so dismal."

"I thought he was romantic. He believed in everyone." She folded her legs under her and brushed her fingers over her chest. "I think Daddy believed in Mama for a long time. Too much."

"And that's why he did it? Is this his newest theory or yours?" I grabbed the empty pizza box, holding it so none of the crumbs fell out. "That's a horrible thing to say. Especially today."

"I'm just wondering. Why do you get so mad if I even just wonder and try to figure things out?" Merry picked up the greasy paper plates.

"Because Mama deserves this night from us, and she'd want us to leave him out of it."

20

Lulu

I crushed the unopened birthday card my father had sent. My fingers cramped up as I tried to obliterate the thick paper from my house, from my life. My daughters, Drew, and Merry waited in the dining room. Fifteen minutes earlier I'd left them, going noisily and with much ado to my study, giving them time to put out my "secret" birthday cake.

I threw down the rough prison-stock envelope and halfheartedly sorted the mound of mail on my desk. The correspondence lent an unwanted note of disorder to the room. The chaos gave me the jitters, but I felt too headachy to deal with bills. My urge to go upstairs, take a cool shower, and fall asleep chewed away at my responsibility to be celebration-happy, especially in front of the girls.

I grabbed the balled-up prison envelope and smoothed the paper, not wanting to let my father get the best of me. After slitting open the envelope, I pulled out the hand-drawn card covered with bright red and blue balloons.

Dear Lulu,

Holy moly—if you've turned forty-one, then I'm almost sixty! I'm getting
to be an old man in here—and trust me, cookie, this is not the place to get old.
(Not that I ever expect you to end up in a place like this.) From what Merry
tells me, you just get more successful each year. Pretty good, Cocoa Puff.

If I ever did write to my father, the reason would be to say, *Never call me*
Cocoa Puff again. I could still hear him saying the words, throwing them
through the bit of space where I'd cracked open the door.

"Don't worry, Cocoa Puff. Mama won't get mad. I promise."

Mama didn't get mad. Mama died.

I closed my eyes for a moment, gathering strength to read the rest of
the letter.

Your mother would be amazed. I can just hear her now: Where did Lulu get
those brains? I think it must have been your grandpa on her side—I can't
think of anyone else in our family with enough smarts to go to medical school.

I closed the card, thinking I might have a fury-induced stroke if I read
any more. How did he manage to throw in that breezy reference to my
mother, as though she were in Boca Raton rather than moldering in a coffin? Here's a news flash, Dad—we have no "our family."

Adults should be able to offer themselves up for adoption. I'd find a
family who gathered at every holiday ever invented—quick, get out the
Columbus Day tree!—offering ourselves immeasurable occasions to use
our in-family jokes and us-only references. A family that celebrated birthdays in some way other than sending homemade birthday cards from
prison.

I ached to say things like *Oh, Jesus, I haven't called Aunt Mary in ages!* I
wanted to walk into a warm house and have worried people grab my arms
and ask, "How bad were the roads, Lulu?" as I shook the snow out of my
hair.

Adopting adults should be as desirable as rescuing beautiful little Chinese girls.

Maybe this would be the year I'd tell the prison to forbid him to send me mail. My daughters were both getting old enough to notice "Inmate Correspondence Program, Joseph Zachariah, 79-X-876" on the envelope flap and "Richmond County Prison" as part of the return address. He'd been banned from telephoning me ever since I had my first phone.

Our shredder groaned as it made confetti from my father's card, then the envelope.

I rotated my head to the right and the left, stretching away tension. I imagined my family secretly placing candles on my birthday cake. The girls had barely contained their excitement about the hush-hush dessert. Cake! Ice cream! Sugar, sugar, sugar!

Drew realized I hated this day, and like a good husband, he sympathized, but only to a point, the point when my neuroses poked into our daughters' need for normal family interaction. Given my druthers, I'd eschew all festivities, and until I became a parent, I had. However, decent motherhood demands everything in the world from you, including pretending happiness about your own birthday, and letting your children own a piece of that supposed joy.

I closed my eyes and tried to wish away the stress backache wrapping itself around my spine. I pushed my fingers deep into my lower back and rubbed. I grabbed two Excedrin and washed them down with cold coffee. Then I took a breath and opened the door to the impatient sounds of my daughters waiting for my gasp of delight at the pink—Ruby's choice—and purple—Cassandra's—helium-filled balloons floating around the ceiling like lost clouds, dangerously close to the fan blades spinning over the table.

"Mama!" Ruby barreled into my arms, shrieking. "Guess what we have, Mama!"

I hugged her hard, loving the feel of her perfect little body, the silk of her dark hair under my cheek. Ruby looked like my sister and husband more than she resembled me—as though Drew and Merry had mated and then snuck their embryo into my womb. Merry's eyes stared out from Ruby's face, miniature little chocolate Tootsie Pops, under Drew's sharply arched eyebrows and over his snubbed nose.

"Happy birthday, Mama." Cassandra's prim tone acknowledged the importance of the occasion.

Drew bent me backward for a Hollywood-style kiss to the shrieking delight of the girls, who loved watching him loosen me up. Merry pulled me to the table and seated me before a stack of presents. I shut my eyes for a moment and invoked the gods of false gaiety.

"First things first," Merry said. She sat across from me and lifted Ruby on her lap, the two of them looking like mother and daughter. If Mama were here, the picture would be complete, three generations of beauties. Ruby leaned against my sister's chest, the strands of their hair a perfect color match.

Cassandra stood at my side, her thin hand on my knee. She rested her head briefly on my shoulder, and I kissed her cool cheek. She presented pale, ethereal, and Lutheran-pretty, like Drew's mother, both with green eyes smudged with gold.

Just as in my childhood, I felt like the plain one, Drew's constant assurances meaningless as I stared at my sister. Maybe I'd choose a homely family to adopt me—I'd like to try being the pretty one for a change. On the other hand, my no-nonsense looks offered approachability. My patients presented their secrets with the predictability of the tides. *I drink at night, but no one knows,* the bus driver told me. *I cheated on my wife. Please, test me for everything,* begged the history professor. *I hide Dove chocolate bars in the bottom of the hamper,* confessed the depressed nurse with uncontrolled diabetes.

Merry pressed a present into my hands, and I tugged at the opulence of curled ribbons circling the box. Finally, I took the scissors Drew offered and snipped them open. The girls watched with a hush.

"It's special!" Ruby said. "We got it from—"

"Shh!" Merry held a finger to Ruby's lips.

"Let Mommy be surprised," Drew said. He moved to sit next to me, pulling Cassandra onto his lap.

I ripped off the wrapping from the heavy-for-its-size package and lifted the top of a stiff silver box, the sort of box given by expensive stores. Merry saved boxes like this forever. Bright tissue paper—hot pink, neon blue, parakeet green—layers of it needed to be unpacked before I reached the present. "I can tell who wrapped this."

"Daddy made the package beautiful for you," Ruby declared. "But Aunt Merry—"

Again, Merry shushed Ruby. I pushed away the wrapping. Under the tissue, a glossy hexagon box shone. I recognized the object immediately. It had come from what my mother had deemed *Grandpa's collection*. Mama had decorated our living room with these exotic treasures. Mother-of-pearl triangles ornamented the polished surface, meeting at a circle of glittering green stone. It had been many years since I'd seen this box. The last time had been during my final visit to Aunt Cilla's house, when I'd realized my mother's sister had taken all my mother's belongings.

Mrs. Cohen had thought it important to put some sort of closure on our relationship with my aunt and uncle. She drove Merry and me over to Aunt Cilla's house in Brooklyn, leaving us alone there for a horrible half hour so we could "talk."

"What, what are you looking at?" Aunt Cilla had said when she saw me staring at the amethyst ring on her right hand. "Am I not supposed to have a memory of my sister?"

When she got no response from me, she'd turned to Merry. "And you, who's taking you to see the monster now?"

"How did you get this?" I asked Merry.

She grinned as though she'd pulled off quite a coup, too damn excited to notice the warning in my voice.

Cassandra answered. "She got it from Aunt Cilla."

"Aunt Cilla had it in New York!" Ruby said. "Aunt Cilla!" Ruby repeated the words *Aunt Cilla* with relish, though she'd never met her. The girls had never met a soul from my side of the family except, of course, Merry. Ruby, our athletic girl, who played in the family-rich Cambridge Little League, came home with stories of teammates' grandparents, cousins, and uncles on a regular basis.

"She gave it to Aunt Merry. For *you*," Ruby made clear. "Aunt Cilla."

For me. Indeed. That would break tradition. My mother's sister hadn't done anything for us since she'd banished us from her house and sent us to the orphanage.

"I remembered how much you loved it," Merry said. "It was your favorite."

I started to remind Merry that she couldn't possibly remember anything from before Mama died, then stopped. "Thank you." I ran my fingers over the top, smooth and cold as I remembered.

Once a month, when Mama took them down from the shelf, Merry and I had made little worlds with the boxes. Mama had placed them carefully on the carpet and let us dust and shine them. Seven black onyx boxes in all different shapes and sizes, some inlaid with green and red stones along with the mother-of-pearl.

"It was your mother's," Cassandra said in whispery wonder. My mother, by her absence, by her rare mentioning, had been elevated, along with my father, to the status of a hovering saint. My children lived to the fullest our myth that a fatal car crash had taken both our parents. Only Drew, Merry, and I, and my tiny bit of family left back in New York—family we never saw, and never should—knew the truth.

"Right, it was my mother's." I ran my fingers through Cassandra's hair. I wanted to shove the box away, before my past tainted my daughters'. "I see another present. Is it for me?"

"Don't you miss your mother?" Cassandra asked for the millionth time. "Isn't it sad that she's dead? She died when you were little, right?" She bound her hands together as though showing respect.

"Not so very, very little," I assured her. "I was your age, and you're not so very little, are you?" I playfully clipped her chin.

Ruby clasped her hands together, imitating Cassandra's prayerful position. "Who took care of you?"

My daughters took every opportunity to pepper me with their questions.

"You remember, honey, Aunt Merry and I went to the special sleepover school."

"Why didn't you go live with Aunt Cilla?" Cassandra asked as though for the first time.

I repacked the box, covering it with the vibrant tissue. "You know the story already."

"Okay, girls, let Mommy open her other present." Drew reached for a small box and handed it to Cassandra. "You can give this to Mommy."

Cassandra took the box but didn't offer it to me. "But why?" she asked again. "Why didn't she take you? She's your aunt. You were all alone!"

Merry wrapped her arms tighter around Ruby. "She wasn't an aunt like me, sweetie. I'll always take care of you, no matter what. But Aunt Cilla had too many other responsibilities."

189

"And she was too sad from everyone dying, right?" Ruby said, repeating the family litany. "So she was too pressed. About the accident."

Drew took over. "*De*-pressed. Right, Aunt Cilla was depressed. Now give Mommy the present, Cassie."

I took the present Cassandra held out. Her ecologically correct wrapping, the *Boston Sunday Globe*'s comic pages, covered a small velvet jewel box. Inside, sitting on a fluffy mound of cotton balls sprinkled with tiny ribbon shavings, were a pair of macaroni shells dipped in gold glitter. A shaky pink glitter *L* decorated each one.

"*L* for Lulu," Ruby explained.

"She knows," Cassandra said. "Do you like them?"

"We made them." Ruby's eyes sparkled. "They're earrings!"

I touched them carefully. Drew had applied some magic artist substance to render the macaroni jewels buttery-slippery-smooth. "They look like real gold."

"I made the letters." Ruby picked the earrings up and handed them to me. "Aren't they pretty?"

"Do you like them?" Cassandra asked again.

"I love them." I unscrewed the plain gold studs I wore most days and put in the shells.

"Oh, you look so beautiful, Mama!" Ruby gasped.

I went to the mirror hanging above our oak buffet and turned my head from one side to the other. Layers of glitter trapped in the hard resin shimmered.

"We made them together, Daddy and Cassandra and me." Ruby ran a small hand down my arm, then grabbed my hand and kissed it. "Because we love you. We'll always take care of you."

I covered Ruby with her pink and white fairy princess comforter, kissing her in the pattern she'd long ago established: right cheek, left cheek, and chin. When I got to Cassandra's room, she'd already cocooned herself in her patchwork quilt. After one more glass of water for Ruby, one more kiss for Cassandra, I slipped out and into the kitchen, where I leaned over the sink and took deep breaths, letting my anger beat back before joining Drew and Merry in the living room.

I tried to imagine what it had been like for Merry, seeing Aunt Cilla. My sharpest memory of her would always be the hours following Mimi Rubee's funeral, when everyone went back to Aunt Cilla's house after leaving the cemetery. I'd been what, eleven?

I won't have Joey's girls living here. Not in my house. They're black marks on my sister's memory, a dark shadow on my mother's name. Having them here is ripping out my kishkes.

I'd swallowed Aunt Cilla's words in silence, nodding, as though agreeing with my aunt that, yes, Merry and I were exactly what she said: dark shadows, black marks, *kishke* rippers.

I went to find my sister.

"What in the name of God were you thinking, Merry?" I sat close to Drew on the couch, seeking his body heat. Drew preferred the air-conditioning at a cool sixty-seven degrees. Even in July, I pulled on cotton cardigans.

"I worked my behind off to get the box for you," Merry said. "For one thing, I actually saw Aunt Cilla."

Itchy curiosity about Aunt Cilla's fate fought with my need to scream no. No boxes from the past. No Aunt Cilla. No bringing any of it into my house.

No more passing information about me to our father.

My present glowed poison green from the table. Sticky tentacles crept at me from the onyx box. I scratched x after x on my arm.

"I don't want it." I crossed my arms against my chest. "I don't want anything from that time in my house."

Merry came forward in the bentwood rocker and pointed at me. "You need *something* from back then or you'll never deal with it."

"News flash: I don't plan to deal with it. Is that what you're doing during those visits to prison? Dealing with it? Hah!"

"Are you planning to let the kids think their grandparents died in a car accident forever?"

"Just what do you suggest?" I couldn't admit that I kept hoping our father would die before I had to face some ultimate decision. I brought my knees close to my chest, protecting myself from the box's vibes. "Should I let you take them to prison with you next time you visit him?"

"It would be better than trying to hide him forever. Doesn't anyone but you get a vote?" Merry turned to Drew. "Aren't you concerned about this giant lie you're feeding the girls?"

"Don't ask him, ask me!" I almost yelled, holding back only because of the girls.

"Watch it," Drew said. "I'm not a lamp, for Christ's sake."

I slid away from Drew and picked up Merry's wine, taking a giant gulp, knowing it drove him crazy. Put together a woman drinking and a woman getting emotional and you'd see my husband harden like concrete.

"Great idea, Lulu. Add fuel to the fire," Drew said.

"It's my fire," I said. "And you, Merry, don't bring me any more remembrances."

"You know it's just going to blow up in the girls' faces, don't you? You can't live in denial forever." Merry never gave up.

"At least I'm not rolling around in it every day," I said. "Unlike you, I don't need to have criminals be my entire life."

"Screw you," Merry said. "Being a probation officer isn't because of Dad. Here's something for you to consider—I thought you'd like the box!"

Drew untangled himself from me and took away my wineglass. "Time to go home. Time to go to sleep. This is over."

Merry ignored Drew and came over to the couch. She lay down, placing her head in my lap. I rubbed her back, feeling her tears stain my pants. After a time, she rolled over and gave me a toothy, wet-eyed smile. "I'm sorry," she said. "I just wanted to make you happy."

"I know." Merry had an expensive smile, with expensive teeth, teeth that had rotted courtesy of the New York City orphanage system and the terrible genes she'd inherited from who knows which side of the family. I had helped her fix those teeth by spending thousands of dollars ten years before. My marriage, which came with Drew's good-size nest egg, had enabled me to pay for this. Thank God I didn't know how good size it was when we dated, tempted as I might have been to marry him solely for the money. However, I married for love, for Drew's ease in the world, for his caretaking, for accepting Merry as part of our bargain.

For asking less of me than others had.

For keeping watch over us.

For his willingness to join me in ignoring my father's existence.

I could afford to forgive his need to shut us down when we boiled over, and his chafing under the bubbling quicksand Merry and I kept at the edge of our lives.

"I love you, Drew," I said from where I sat with Merry.

"I know."

"And I apologize," I said.

"Right." He gathered up the birthday garbage from around the room, avoiding my gaze.

"And I love you, Merry," I said.

"I know, too," she answered. "But someday you're going to have to tell them."

Not necessarily, I thought, but I let it go, imagining our father having a heart attack, being stabbed in a prison argument, too tired to argue.

Merry and I stayed on the couch, wrapped together in our wine-rendered love-hate until Drew pulled us apart. He walked Merry out the door. I heard the key turn in her lock, heard her door open. I listened as she entered her apartment, heard the sound of her footsteps over my head as she walked across her wooden floor.

The past trapped us. Even now, at forty-one and thirty-six, we remained prisoners of our parents' long-ended war, still ensnared in a prison of bad memories, exchanging furtive glances, secrets known and secrets buried flashing between us.

"Coming to bed, Lulu?" Drew stood in the doorway of the living room. His expression of sympathy seemed curdled by my and Merry's tired repetition.

"Soon," I said. "I'll get there soon."

21

Merry

I hugged my rigid brother-in-law good night and walked into my apartment, snapping on lights as I headed to the bedroom. I ripped off my clothes, threw on an old basketball T-shirt I'd once plucked from Drew's Goodwill pile, and turned on the TV as I went past the set.

Despite the effects of alcohol buzzing through my head, I forced myself into the bathroom, where I smeared on an expensive cream guaranteeing me an eternal wrinkle-free, moisture-rich existence. Even in death, I'd be pretty.

Creamed, I collapsed on my unmade bed, falling back on my pile of pillows. Crimes in the hood topped the TV news. I listened closely, tuned for which of my probationers had been arrested on some new charge of rape or murder. Please God, if it was one of my clients, let it be for a simple assault. Being a probation officer, I was accountable for hundreds of thugs and gangbangers, and each time one of them committed another crime, I felt responsible for some family's pain.

In Dorchester tonight, police are looking for the assailant of—

I listened for the name of the murdered and the murderer.

Julius Trager, who was gunned down leaving his Rutherford Street home. The Roxbury Community College graduate recently began training as a veterinary assistant.

I couldn't think of any of my probationers who dreamed of working with animals. Having such a client might be nice, although if he were in a vet program, it would probably be so he could stage matches of dogs fighting to the death.

Vague jealousy gnawed at me as the smugly pregnant anchorwoman commented on Boston's ever-rising homicide rate, she picture-perfect, even pregnant; I absently tracing my scar and wearing my brother-in-law's castoff. Running my fingers along the raised line I knew so well had become so automatic, I couldn't imagine breaking the habit. Touching it only when alone, that was my victory.

I tapped the middle of my chest, away from the scar, three times. What had the massage therapist said, the one my friend Valerie sent me to last Christmas? That it would clear my chi? Release my chi? Cook my chi?

Was it realistic to expect a chi change when I couldn't even remember its place or function? Valerie was always trying to right my life, from finding me a man to changing how I related to clients. She was a juvenile probation officer—we worked in the same court but different areas. Her life was as messy as mine, filled with bars and bad boyfriends, but because she didn't worry aloud, she mythologized hers as being superior.

Perhaps I'd made a mistake getting the box, forcing the past down my sister's throat. Still, someday Ruby and Cassandra would most likely find out they had an actual, living grandfather rotting in jail. *How can you not worry about Judgment Day?* I wanted to scream at Lulu.

Poor Drew; I knew why he'd seethed. Drew had been in on Operation Box. Lulu's rejection hurt him. Drew lived for appreciation, recognition—everything he'd never gotten from his mother or father. Unappreciated or ignored, Drew turned a bit mean.

In truth, my own throat ached from not shouting my deepest truth. *Stop leaving me alone with him.* My dim-witted hope of someday sharing the burden with Lulu never left, no matter how many times I trudged off by myself to Richmond Prison.

Visiting the evil Aunt Cilla the previous weekend had provided a relief simply for the pleasure of not having to lie about my past for one moment in time. Not that my aunt had asked squat regarding my father; Aunt Cilla hadn't even whispered his name during the two hours she'd allotted me.

I'd knocked, and then waited on the hot enclosed porch until Aunt Cilla opened the door a crack. Aunt Cilla, seven years my mother's senior, at sixty-five, looked like a fun-house mirror of how I imagined Mama would appear if a computer morphing program aged her photo image. My washed-out aunt was never pretty like Mama, but she resembled Mama—the cheekbones, the lush mouth—enough to give me the chills.

Aunt Cilla still lived in Brooklyn, though in a house I'd never visited. Times had been good to her and Uncle Hal, disproving any moral theorists claiming the meek shall inherit the earth. Aunt Cilla's spacious home, when she grudgingly let me in, shone from the ministrations and shopping habits of a house-proud woman.

She showed me into the living room, her lips tightly sealed. I saw Uncle Hal and Cousin Arnie framed in gleaming silver, pictures of all the family events no one invited me to—my cousin's bar mitzvah, the wedding of a couple I'd never known. My cousin had kept his frail appearance. My aunt still had her mean spirit.

"Here," she'd said. "It's wrapped. Do you want to check it?"

"For what?" I'd asked, confused.

She'd shrugged. "I thought maybe you'd want to make sure I didn't cheat you."

Cheat me how? By passing off Corning Ware as onyx?

"That's okay," I'd answered.

"I assure you, I'm completely trustworthy."

"Aren't you curious how I am? How Lulu is? Your great-nieces?"

"Why? No one keeps in touch with me. The first time you call, it's because you want something." She'd folded her arms across her chest. "Did you ever think I might wonder how you were?"

"Why didn't you ..." I'd paused, trying to imagine what to say.

"I had no idea where you were. You disappeared, your sister and you."

She'd put a hand on top of the box. "I had to go digging in the attic for this. Who knew I still had it? I would have wrapped them all for you, but you only asked for one."

"I'd like anything you have of my mother's. I mean, anything you're not using," I'd added, seeing her clutch at the neck of her white blouse.

"The few things your mother left are all the memories I have."

"We don't have anything, Aunt Cilla. Just the few pictures Grandma Zelda had."

"Zelda. Ptoi." Aunt Cilla had made a spitting sound.

I'd pulled back as though she'd smacked me. "That's my grandmother."

"She raised a monster."

Scabs had flown off my festering hate of Aunt Cilla. "She loved us. You abandoned us. Who's the monster?"

The visit hadn't gone very well.

The pregnant anchorwoman said good night, and I snapped off the television, grateful for another night without seeing a single one of my probationers starring on TV. By way of a lullaby, I scrunched my pillows into shape and previewed the upcoming day.

Tomorrow morning I'd meet with the newly formed Community for Peace group. Colin, my muscle-gone-fat, ideals-gone-political boss, the chief probation officer, had gotten into the habit of appointing me liaison to any groups he considered soft ones. His expression, *the soft ones*, always said in a scoffing tone. Colin deemed soft anything with the word *strategy*: strategies for peace, for less murder, for more jobs, for less police brutality, for more child care in court, what Colin called we-are-the-world groups. When only white people were around, he called them diversity groups, a sneer encasing his words.

I wrapped the comforter tighter and listed the next afternoon's clients. Jesse Turner, near murderer. Shaundra Ellis, pickpocket. Victor Dennehy, coke dealer and batterer. Oliver Peterson, rapist. In order, they were depressed, easy, asshole, and suck-up scum. Sleepy, Dopey, Grumpy, and Sleazy.

After work, I had yet another blind date courtesy of Drew. Trying to get me married off seemed to be his hobby. The guy was a doctor who worked in the same place as Lulu but played handball with Drew, and I think was also in his poker group. He was a specialist with an *o*. Orthopedist? Ophthalmologist? Ornithologist?

The next morning I returned from the community meeting energized from being with people whose pants weren't hanging off their asses and who didn't have packs of Marlboros tucked in their T-shirt sleeves.

"How was the meeting?" Colin yelled from his office as I walked by.

I turned and went to his doorway. "Do you really care?"

He swung his squatty legs up on his desk. "Nah. Community for Peace." He snorted. "Why not just call it what it is: White Liberals of Dorchester Loving the Sounds of Their Own Voices." Colin laughed; he cracked himself up on a regular basis. His eyes were puffy, as though he never slept, or always drank.

"Surprise, Colin, it was mainly African-American women."

He swatted a hand toward me. "Big deal. Same bullshit."

"Right, the bullshit of women not wanting their sons shooting or being shot. I see your point."

"Don't give me that crap. What do these saints plan to do besides complain to us as though it's our fault?" Colin tapped a pencil against his knee. "Maybe they'd do better giving their sons a swat on their asses."

I sat in the guest chair across from Colin's desk. "Don't you get tired of being you?"

Colin smiled wide and generous. "Even Bill Cosby agrees with me."

"Screw you, and screw Bill Cosby," I said. "You love using him as a convenient place to hang your racism."

"I'm a racist for thinking parents should control their kids?"

I lifted myself out of the chair, not bothering to answer his tired question. "The women want to meet once a month, and they need someplace safe. I told them they could meet here. Get me money for coffee and donuts."

Probation world ran on coffee and donuts.

In my office, I dialed the phone as I crammed a brownie in my mouth. Early lunch.

"Was Lulu really mad at me?" I asked when I heard Drew's voice.

"She was pissed, but it's not terminal."

"What'd she do with the box?"

I heard him taking his measured Nebraska breaths.

"Come on, I can take it. Did she slam it? Throw it? Hide it under the bed?"

"She took it to work."

"Took it to work?" I tried to imagine this, my sister putting the box in her briefcase and carrying it to the car. Why? To hold her stethoscope?

"I think she just wanted it out of the house and didn't know what else to do. You know Lulu, out of sight, et cetera. Got to go. I have a project I need to finish before the girls come home."

"Wait," I said. "Are you still mad at Lulu?"

"I guess maybe that's none of your business. Do you want to know if I'm still mad at you?"

"What did I do?"

"Talked me into trying once more," he said.

I picked up yesterday's coffee, which looked okay enough to drink, and took a sip of the cold, bitter stuff. "It's not like I held a gun to your head. It's about your kids, right?"

"No. I think it's about you two. You just keep convincing me otherwise. Let me know how the date goes. Act nice."

"What kind of doctor is he? I forgot."

His sigh was loud enough to cover the midwestern plains. "An ophthalmologist. I told you."

"I forgot. Sue me."

I hung up thinking I'd take the damn box back and put it right in the middle of my damn coffee table, forcing my sister to see it every damn time she came up the damn stairs. Then I'd give Drew and Lulu a trip to a therapist for their anniversary. A headache sprouted up, and I popped two Advil, washing them down with the dregs of yesterday's coffee.

"Ms. Zach?" Jesse poked his head in the door, tapping the oversize gold watch on his scrawny wrist to indicate how on time he was. "Surprised?"

He dropped into the chair in front of my desk. At five nine, wiry thin with square black glasses and a child star grin, Jesse wasn't a young man you pictured leaving someone beaten half to death. In this case, the victim had slept with Jesse's girlfriend, and Jesse, smack in the middle of a vodka-aided rage, saw no way out other than obliterating the competition.

"Yo, aren't you going to give me a big pat on the back?" His eyebrows went up in a gesture of *huh, huh, ya love me, huh?*

"Yo? Have I entered the realm of homeboy for you?" I asked. "Kudos on being on time."

"Kudos?"

I picked up his folder, hmming and umming as I read a sheaf of pages. "Looks like you missed an entire week of AA."

"My moms was sick."

I frowned over the folder. "Your mother was sick last month."

"So she's sick again."

I picked up the report from his anger management counselor.

"How come you're not participating in classes?" I asked. "Your reports from DanGerUs No More"—God, I hated that name—"look not so good."

"Aw, they don't know nothing."

"Little participation. Late. Seems uninvested," I read. "What's up?"

"I'm supposed to be invested in some assholes making us act out skits? Damn, Ms. Zach, how can I talk to a bunch of white guys pretending to be my boys?"

"It's called role-playing. It's meant to help you learn how to gain control over situations."

"I know that. You think I don't? Anyway, I have control over the situation, oh, yes I do." Jesse placed his hand on his hip as though to signify a gun.

"What? Are you trying to intimidate me, Jesse?" I put the folder down and laid my hands flat on the desk. "We've put in a lot of time. If you want to throw it all out, just say the word."

Jesse leaned back and stuck his legs out, pouting now like Ruby or Cassandra. "I hate them. They're always making us talk stupid shit."

"What kind of stupid *stuff*?"

"Our mothers. Our fathers. Come at me correct. You think those people know what the hell they're doing?"

"Hell?" I asked.

"You think they know what the *heck* they're doing?"

He took a pen off my desk and clicked it on and off. I grabbed it from him. "Jesse, you're ordered to the program—what I do or don't think about them doesn't mean anything. What matters is the judge seeing you do what you're supposed to do. What matters is staying sober. What matters most of all is getting your GED. None of which I see happening, do I?"

Jesse scuffed his untied sneakers on the floor.

"Tie your sneakers. When you come here, you look respectful. New probation rule—sneakers tied at all time. I see you walking anywhere around here with untied sneakers, you're going in front of Judge Jackson."

I breathed out my frustration while waiting for my next client. Frigging jerky kid, smart, funny, talented. His written work, the homework DanGerUs No More had sent, showed brilliant raw writing. He could go to college after he finished his GED, and then God knows what.

Most of all, I'd like to thank my probation officer, Ms. Zachariah. Without her, I'd be rotting in jail. This Oscar for best screenplay is as much for her as it is for me.

Finally home, getting ready for my date, I outlined my eyes with thick blue liner. Maybe it wasn't the most subtle choice, but I felt hot seeing cobalt rimming my dark eyes. I loved looking in the mirror. I could kiss myself when I looked this good.

Women aren't supposed to do that. We're supposed to be all *oh, I'm too fat* and *no, really, look, my eyes are much too close together,* but my looks were my only reliable source of comfort. I worried I'd already held on to them way past their sell-by date, worrying at my skin, my hair, my profile, poking at them like a kid with a half-shredded teddy bear. I'd end up one of those raddled old women walking around with licorice-colored hair and strawberry blush caked in my wrinkled cheeks.

The bell rang. The ophthalmologist. I picked up the glass of wine I'd balanced on the bathroom sink and finished the last sip. I shrugged a silky tank top over my head, carefully checked the neckline, and then pulled on my jeans. I turned sideways, looking to see if I could still get away without a bra.

Screw it. Why not let the ophthalmologist get a good look?

*

Between my house and the restaurant he'd chosen, I learned that Michael Epstein, Eye Doc, had an American flag plastered on the bumper of his car, wore what appeared to be a ten-thousand-dollar suit, and probably believed invading anywhere would be justified in the name of protecting America and providing oil for his gas-guzzling Mercedes. Maybe he spoke to Drew's latent red-state values.

"After you," he said, holding the door open.

I gave a closemouthed smile, and he led me by the arm into the restaurant. A steak house; it seemed Michael was a Capital Grille man, Chestnut Hill branch—not even Newbury Street. God forbid you didn't eat your steak in a suburb. If I ever wrote *The Dating Habits of American Men,* I'd warn women that men who brought you to opulent steak houses on the first date had small penises, voted Republican, or both.

I enjoyed looking across the table and seeing Michael, however. Sometimes I craved a compact, tight body like his, although, being really a male version of mine, it made me slightly suspicious of myself when it turned me on. I preferred to think I liked that it was the opposite of Quinn's type. Opposite was a good thing; it would keep me from thinking about him. God willing, I'd be less likely to allow him those periodic visits, which began with exhilaration and ended with depression. Our last date, less a date than a double screw, had been months ago.

"So," Michael said, after the waiter had taken our order, "tell me about Merry Zachariah."

"Quick overview? I like walks on the beach, running with the wolves, and singing soprano at church suppers."

"That's funny, since your sister is Jewish." He looked me straight in the eye, and I noticed his were a kind brown. "Decided against me already?"

"Sorry." I lifted my shoulders in what I hoped was a cute gesture. I didn't want him going back and telling Drew and Lulu I'd been a bitch. I could hear my sister now. *You don't even try.* "My work makes me too sure of myself."

"Are you ever wrong?"

"Ask if I'm ever right." The waiter interrupted with our drinks, a martini for the doctor and wine for me. "Thanks." I picked up the glass and twirled the delicate stem, watching the burgundy liquid slosh. Then I saw my bitten-to-the-nub fingernails contrasted against the sparkling crystal and folded my fingers inward.

"The wine has nice legs." Michael nodded at my glass with a chuckle, though I didn't get the joke.

"Wine legs are funny?"

He took a sip of his martini and let out a long sigh of appreciation. "Ah. Perfect. So dry you could fold it."

I knew he thought the line clever and had used it before. A dating line. I had my own.

"Legs," he said. "The supposed mythical indicator of wine quality. You can tell someone is a wannabe when they try to evaluate wine that way, but it's just physics, the wine's surface tension and alcohol content. It's called the Marangoni effect, the fact that alcohol evaporates faster than water, but it's not about quality because…"

Because I don't give a fuck.

"I'm going on and on, right?"

I lifted my eyebrows.

He reached across the table and put a hand on my wrist. "Drew didn't tell me how lovely you are. You and Lulu don't even look like sisters. Not that your sister isn't attractive, it's just, well, you're so, you're sure both parents are the same, right? Oh, God, I'm so sorry."

He got a stricken look on his face, telling me Drew had told him the sad story of our car-wrecked parents. Poor little orphans. Men hardened just thinking about how they could rescue us.

"My sister is beautiful."

"Oh, she is, she is."

Liar, you don't think that at all.

"It's just that you're so, um, well, you're a knockout. Lulu's more PTA pretty."

I shook my head. Why did men think they'd impress me by making me a winner of some competition they'd just announced? "Tell me about you," I said.

*

I woke with the Eye Doc's scent on my skin, a sweetened musk. I turned to the right to see the clock. Three A.M. He snored softly, lying on his back with his arms open to the world. Apparently, he didn't need to curl up in a fetal ball to sleep.

I put a soft finger on his shoulder. No response. I pressed in and wiggled back and forth.

"Mmm?" he mumbled.

"Michael?"

"Mmm?"

"Time to go."

He turned his head and looked at me, blinking, maybe trying to discover in whose bed he slept. Ah, yes, Drew Winterson's easy sister-in-law. The one he's probably trying to pawn off so she'll move out. Right. "You want me to leave?"

"Sort of."

"Are you kidding?"

Sure, I woke you up in the middle of the night to tell you to leave as a joke. "I can't sleep with someone I don't know."

"But you can have sex with him?" He rolled onto his side, leaning his head in his left hand. He ran a finger down my bare arm and lifted the camisole strap, which had slipped off my shoulder. "I like you."

"You don't even know me." I sat up, tucking the sheet under my arms.

He reached out and touched the top of my scar, peeking out from my lacy top. I pulled away.

"How'd you get the mark?"

How many ways could you get a scar circling halfway around your breast? A scar that looked like someone had tried to lop your breast off.

"Knife fight as a kid."

"No kidding? Poor baby."

"The residential home we stayed in was pretty rough." *Listen,* Lulu had said when she invented this story for me, *it could have happened. Think of what did happen to us in Duffy-Parkman.* Yes, I could easily have gotten into a knife fight at Duffy.

"Why were you in a residential home?"

How much had Drew told him? Men didn't trade secrets between handball volleys. Especially silent Drew. Lulu? Probably not much. They were just co-workers. Doctors. They didn't share life stories between giving Pap smears and checking for macular degeneration.

"After our grandmother died, no one was left to care for us." I had it down to one cold, juiceless sentence.

"Wow. That must have been awful." He ran a hand over my hip, drawn hot and ready to my tragedy. If Lulu ever let me give out the real story, I'd have men lined up for blocks.

"It wasn't so bad. We only lived at Duffy a few years before we got foster parents. Our foster father was a doctor."

"Wow. That was lucky."

"Right. We were lucky."

He tugged at my hip, trying to draw me to him. "Come here. Let me make you feel lucky again."

Despite my misgivings, I followed his command. Once more, then I'd send him home. Michael was one of those great Republican lovers who try to rock you as though they were cowboys.

No big deal, I told myself. I'd let him make me feel lucky.

22

Merry

September 2002

I woke up needing a strong cup of morning coffee but lacking the energy to make it. Valerie and I had closed the Parish Lounge the previous night, though I commended myself for rotating a plain Coke for each one spiked with Jim Beam. Bonus points for not bringing home the too handsome, too young, too interested man.

I walked around the corner from my apartment entrance to Lulu's, scuffing fallen maple leaves with my slippers and trying to taste autumn's promise of change. I needed it.

During the summer, when I'd had five or six dates with Michael Epstein, I'd hoped the Eye Doc might be my passage into a changed life. By Labor Day, I'd pushed him away almost as fast as I'd welcomed him to my bed. Eye Doc didn't turn out to be the type of man with whom I could carry off the split personality required by my orphan story. He turned out to be too earnest, not someone I liked lying to. Nor did he have whatever magical quality Lulu said I would recognize, something letting me know in an instant that I'd be safe sharing secrets.

Sometimes it seemed Drew might be the only man alive deserving of that honor, and Lulu had him.

"Mommy's still asleep," Ruby announced as I walked into the kitchen.

"Did Daddy make coffee?" I bent to kiss her.

"You smell," Ruby said. "Didn't you take a shower?"

"Not yet," I said. "Why don't you pour me a cup of coffee, Miss Bad Manners?"

"You know I'm not allowed to touch hot stuff," Ruby said. "You're testing me. Right?"

"Right." Lulu and Drew made rules, and I tested them. I grabbed a mug from the cabinet.

Drew walked in toweling his hair. "Out of coffee at your house?"

"Forgot to shop."

He handed me a sweating silver pitcher from the refrigerator. I added the heavy cream Drew from Nebraska loved, watching the rich swirls lighten the black, steaming liquid in a way my skim milk never did.

"It's a new blend," Drew said. "How do you like it?"

Drew had a coffee obsession. I took a small sip, then another. "Great. Perfect." If I married, my husband would probably have a horrible obsession bringing only shame to both of us, porn or cheese fries.

Drew shook his head. "You're a terrible judge. You like everything."

"Then why ask me?"

"Well, not everything. Michael still asks about you."

"Give it a rest, Drew."

He handed me a saucer for my cup. "He's a good man, Merry."

I plopped down at the table. "Ruby, bring me a bowl, okay?"

Ruby looked up from the book splayed open in front of her. "I'm reading."

"And I need help from my niece because I'm so tired that I have to finish my coffee before I can find the strength to pour my Cheerios. Now be a good girl and get me a bowl."

Ruby made some disparaging sound to show what she thought of me, but she got up. "You know, Aunt Merry, I'm sleeping over my friend Jessica's house on Saturday. Her father is taking us to swim lessons. I won't be here to wait on you." She dragged a little white step stool to the counter and reached for a bowl. She was small for her age, as I had been.

"Good for you." I yawned and leaned my head back.

"You're awfully tired," Drew said.

"I read until one in the morning."

"Must have been pretty interesting, that book." Apparently, he had heard me come in last night.

"Thanks, hon." I took the bowl from Ruby. "It was," I answered Drew. I finished the coffee and held my cup out for more, my hand shaky.

Drew poured me a refill. "I worry how often you read late."

I spooned up a small portion of cereal and milk, trying not to show my distaste. My stomach measured right at that delicate balance between throwing up and a manageable nausea. Food sometimes held the worst at bay—I prayed this was one of those times.

"Morning." Lulu walked in, yawning and holding *The Boston Globe* still rolled up and bound by a red rubber band. "Here's a surprise, I can't wake Cassandra up." She took the mug Drew held out. "Get dressed for school, Ruby."

Ruby squeezed Lulu around the waist. "Cassandra didn't even hug you yet, right?"

"Come on, you, let's get dressed." Drew swung Ruby on his shoulders and gave me a significant look before he left the room. What was he trying to convey? What a significant slut I was? *Sorry we can't all be as pure as Lulu.*

Lulu shook her head. "If Cassandra ends up needing medicine for acne, Ruby will complain, *It's not fair, why can't I have pimples?* Then Cassandra will say, *I had them first. She shouldn't get any.*"

I felt an overwhelming surge of love for my sister, sitting with her feet up on the chair, sloppy-cute in an old white T-shirt and boxer shorts. Her hair fell over her forehead in a manner I missed when she tied it back. Without lipstick, Lulu looked younger than usual, and she always looked young. She complained that, without makeup, she looked anemic, but I thought she looked wholesome and endearing.

"We never did that, did we?" I said.

"Did what?"

"Complained over who got what constantly." I ate another spoonful of cereal.

"Who would we complain to? What would we ever fight over? Our three books?"

I heard the stop sign in Lulu's voice, but caffeine and food had lifted away my headache and nausea, and the sheer absence of pain gave me an unnatural feeling of well-being. I wanted to milk a moment of sentiment and share some sisterly bonhomie.

"True, but still, we didn't," I insisted. "We didn't fight over stuff. We always looked out for each other."

Lulu took her legs off the chair. "I'm happy when Ruby and Cassandra act feisty. I worship their being brats. We didn't get five spoiled minutes our entire childhood."

"Maybe we did before everything happened. Isn't that possible?"

Lulu carried Ruby's cereal bowl to the sink. "Could we not have a breakfast trip down memory lane?" Her back was to me.

I put my elbows on the table and held my face in my hands. "Don't you think we must have had a few good times? Before? Dad says we had some decent stuff. Do you think he makes it all up?"

Lulu whirled around. "Quit it, okay? We had no good times. Everything about our childhood is depressing. Every single effing thing."

"Including me?" I felt the tug of tears and pinched my arm hard.

"Yes. Including you, when you're like this."

By the time I got to work, I'd put the conversation in perspective and tucked away my hurt feelings. Lulu hated waking up. Morning was the absolute stupidest time to try to talk to her. Anyway, my sister could read the signs of a hangover, and the knowledge made her mean. Lulu probably knew exactly how many drinks I'd had, how close I'd come to sleeping with the inappropriate guy, and even how many tablespoons of Pepto-Bismol I'd swallowed since breakfast.

I threw my bag on my desk, thankful for having avoided Colin on the way in. He also seemed to sense when I was feeling lousy, then how to dig in and torture me.

Running through my phone messages, I heard the usual crap from one whining client after another, telling me why they weren't showing up: Grandmother dead. Uncle dead. Cousin in coma. Car ran over sister. Uncle murdered brother. Over the years, my clients had killed off half the population of Boston to avoid coming to our probation meetings. I thumbed through my schedule as I listened, highlighter in hand.

"You okay?"

I looked up. A bleary-eyed Valerie stood in the doorway. "Tell me, did we get especially trashed last night, or are we getting too old to drink?" she asked.

Valerie hadn't bothered straightening her hair this morning, just pinned her curls into a halfhearted bun. I envied her ability to flip back and forth between ordinary and beautiful. If she woke up tired, she didn't give a shit. She only painted and sprayed herself on days she felt ambitious. "You got a problem with me, it's your problem" was Valerie's motto.

What was my motto? It wasn't "*In vino veritas,*" because I drank with Valerie at least twice a week, and still, as close to the truth as I ever came was my fake confession to her that I had an uncle in a New York jail. My motto had become "Prevaricate for peace."

I held up a finger, telling Valerie to wait a moment, and backed up to hear the last phone message again.

Michael Epstein calling. Again. Are you willing to give us another chance? Assuming yes, I'd like to invite you to join me in New York City, where I have a conference to attend. We'll stay at the Waldorf. How about it? Ready to see how the other half lives? Call me. I'll buy you a fancy New York outfit. Just kidding. Well, not really. I'd love to be the one to spoil you. Again, call me.

I replayed the message on speaker for Valerie.

"Should I be insulted?" I asked. "Do you think Drew put him up to it?"

"Maybe. After seeing you this morning, I bet he made a 911 call to Eye Doc. 'Take my sister-in-law and I'll pay you!' But you should go anyway."

I drew a highlighted line through the last canceling client. "Why?"

"You never gave him enough of a chance. That scuzzy kid you almost took home last night wouldn't be taking you to the Waldorf." Valerie reached over and picked up my coffee cup, taking a long slurp.

"Scuzzy? He was gorgeous." I grabbed the cup from Valerie. "Look, you put lipstick all over it."

"It's lipstick, not liquid herpes. Gorgeous face, scuzzy soul. Anyway, gorgeous gets you nothing. He was an overage student hanging out in a cheap bar."

"We were two overage women hanging out in a cheap bar. What does that make us?"

"Gruesomely desperate. The doctor was great in bed, right?" Valerie swung her legs up and placed her scuffed loafers on my desk.

"Jack the Ripper was probably good in bed," I said. "The worst men always are."

"Plenty of crappy men make crappy lovers. Trust me, I know better than you."

"You think so?" I shuffled the papers on my desk, moving the must-do pile closer to the phone.

"You want a match-off for who screwed the greatest number of crappy men?"

My headache knocked. I rested my forehead on the cool metal desktop. "No. I don't want that written in my permanent record as the only contest I ever won."

Thirty minutes later, Valerie's stinging honesty echoing, I left a message for Michael accepting his offer. Then I took enough Advil to face Victor Dennehy. He strutted in as though he expected me to lie down, spread my legs, and moan. His pants hung down so low, I glimpsed his pale white lower back.

"Hey, *Mizzz* Zachariah. I'm on time, huh?"

Another one for whom being on time was the zenith of success. Victor gave me a self-satisfied smile, slumped in the chair across from my desk, and splayed his legs.

"Sit up straight, Victor."

"You my probation officer or my manners teacher?"

"As far as you're concerned, both. You go for a job interview and sit like that, no one's hiring you."

"No one's hiring a guy with a record anyway."

"Not if he acts like you, he won't."

Victor glared at me, but sat up nevertheless, closing his legs on his prized package. I opened his thick file and looked through the reports. "Looks like you're still giving them attitude at the batterer program. Plus, you owe them money."

"That's all they care about. Money, money, money. Like it's their religion or something." He took a letter opener from my desk, tapping it against the edge. "They should do it for free."

I leaned over and took the letter opener from him. My clients were like six-year-olds, the way they grabbed things off my desk. "Would *you* work with you for free?"

Same questions, same complaints. Every week I felt more poisoned. By the time Jesse, my last client of the morning, came into my office, I was ready to give him a hard time simply because I was hungry and tired.

"You okay, Ms. Zachariah?" Jesse asked as he walked in. "You don't look so good."

I gave a little huff of a laugh. "Thanks a million."

"No, I mean it."

Tears stung my eyes. I hated that. I hated when any bit of niceness made my body react as though I'd received a million dollars. "I'm fine." I sat up straight. "Just allergic."

"To us?" Jesse swept his hand in a large arc to encompass all the lost men wandering through the halls of justice.

"Pollen."

"No can be," he said. "Pollen is a summer allergy; the fall is ragweed."

"Fine," I said, picking up his file. "Ragweed then."

"You're not in such a good mood, huh?" He cocked his head to the side. "I'll bring a smile to your face."

"How?"

He reached around to his back pocket and pulled out a folded paper. "Look at this." He handed it to me.

I opened and read it. "You passed! You got your GED."

He smiled big. "Yeah. You were right. It wasn't so hard. I knew more than I thought." He rolled back his shoulders, grabbing back his cool after letting it slip for a second.

"And?"

"And?" he mimicked. "Yeah. I registered for some classes. And not at Roxbury Community College—I know I have to stay away from what's his name."

I didn't appreciate Jesse calling the man he'd almost murdered what's his name, but I'd pick my battles.

Michael was excited about whisking me away. He didn't know I'd traveled to New York City about a million times since leaving the Cohens', visiting my father at least once a month.

Flying to New York City turned out to be more trouble than renting a car and driving, the way I usually did. Flying now meant you were guilty until proven not quite so guilty. Security agents at Logan Airport were cautious, even suspicious. Did my clients face this every day? If they treated Michael and me as potential terrorists, my tough-looking clients must have had to crawl to planes on their bellies, hands clasped behind their backs.

"Safety before courtesy these days," Michael said complacently when I complained.

Our taxi stopped in front of the Waldorf Astoria. I waited as Michael paid the driver, taking note that he gave a decent tip. At least I didn't have to make cheapness a point against him, along with what now seemed like an ever more Republican attitude. A blue-suited doorman opened the taxi and offered his gloved hand as though I were minor royalty.

I refrained from gasping as we entered the vast lobby. Overwhelmed by the marble, the brass fittings, the frigging shininess of everything, espe-cially measured against my Valerie-borrowed shoes and discount clothes, I snorted instead. "Couldn't feed too many orphans with the money spent here, could you?"

Michael put an arm around my shoulders. "If it makes you feel better, we can eat in the Bowery. Maybe bring a few bums back to share the room."

I smiled. "When in Rome."

"Am I Rome, or is Rome the hotel?" He guided me toward the check-in desk.

Michael seemed smarter than I'd originally judged, which made me uncomfortable. Before I could think of a clever quip, we were in front of the desk clerk. Her makeup was more artful than mine would be on the fanciest of occasions.

"Doctor Epstein, welcome." She nodded at him; again, with the Waldorf the royalty treatment. "Room 445 is ready."

Captured light sparkled in the chandeliers.

Watered silk lined the hallway.

Carved plaster ceilings boasted angels and cherubs.

Then I saw the room! Oh, the room. A bed bigger than my living room. More pillows, softer pillows, than I'd ever had—pillows for a princess's head. The armoire—etched with what, gold?—curved out generously, waiting for any amount of clothes I could offer.

After the bellhop left with Michael's money tucked into his hand, Michael gave me an old-school movie scene hug. I expected a director to yell "Cut" at any time.

"What first? Drinks? Food? Shopping?" he asked, murmuring in my ear, nuzzling me.

"Yes, yes, and yes, but first, drinks. Definitely drinks." I didn't care if it was afternoon. Despite the opulent surroundings, I was in prison town. Blurring the edges was first on my list.

We got back from the bar with reality nicely hazy. I stepped into the shower, already in love with the creamy tiles, dulled silver appointments, the thick terry robe waiting for me. In love with the *fancy-pants* toiletries, as Grandma Zelda would have said. In a bathroom like this, you could wash away your entire life.

Michael stepped in behind me as I lifted my face to the steaming spray. "Mind?"

I leaned back, feeling his chest hair tickle my back. "Don't mind."

"Wash your hair?"

"Please. And thank you."

I closed my eyes and felt him rub in shampoo. The sweet scent of almonds surrounded us. His fingers dug hard.

"Am I ruining your hair?" he asked. "Is this too rough?"

"It recovers. Rough away."

Ghosts called as I stepped on the Staten Island Ferry the next afternoon. I hadn't been on the boat for years, but without a car, ferries and cabs were my only option. Michael had a morning of conference business. I'd told him I'd be shopping for presents for Lulu's girls, which brought back memories of lying to school friends about the Saturdays when Doctor Cohen took me to see Daddy.

When I sighted the Statue of Liberty, a sharp ache for Grandma twisted through me. Looking at the hole where the World Trade Center had been, I tapped my chest so many times I feared my fellow passengers would think I was suffering a coronary. Things drop away, and you wonder if they ever existed.

When the cab dropped me in front of Richmond's barbed-wire fence, I already felt drained. Officer McNulty had retired, and I found myself missing him far more than the daughter of a prisoner should miss a guard. Susannah and Coriander were long gone, and fat Annette didn't visit Pete anymore. My father said Annette lost a hundred pounds. *A hundred pounds, can you believe it? That's like losing you!* After the weight loss, Annette divorced Pete. Now Pete had a new wife he'd found online, also fat.

As usual, the sour smell of too many anxious bodies filled the visiting room. My father sat at our table, the old wood a little more nicked with each passing visit, notches marking time. His hair had turned salt-and-pepper gray, but, he'd kept his jailhouse muscles.

He stood. His smile broadened as I got closer.

"Look at you, Sugar Pop! A million bucks. No, wait, I got to adjust for inflation, right? A billion bucks—that's how gorgeous you look."

He said some form of this every time, but I still grinned, always starving for the words.

"So, how's tricks?"

"Good, good. Guess what. I came to New York with a date." I raised my eyebrows up and down like Groucho Marx. "A doctor, no less."

"Your sister's here?" My father straightened on the bench. "Where is she?"

Oh, sweet Jesus, I could slit my throat. "No. No. Sorry, Dad. I didn't mean to get you excited. I really meant a date. He's an ophthalmologist. An eye doctor. Hey, you'd like that, right?"

He slapped a hand against his forehead. "What's wrong with me? Of course, if she were here, she'd have come in with you."

"Sorry, Dad." I watched him shake off his disappointment. "Anyway, an eye doctor. Not bad, huh?"

"How long you two been together?"

"A few months." I stretched the relationship to make it sound better.

"And you never told me?"

"I wanted to make sure he'd stick."

"And?"

I put out my hands to indicate *who knows?* "Maybe. What do you think?" "You know what I think. No one is good enough for my little girl."

My father laced his fingers. "But I worry about some guy who takes you to shack up in Manhattan. What does he want from you? I know how guys are, and they don't buy the cow if you give the milk away. At the end of the day, a guy likes an old-fashioned girl. Otherwise, it's just a good time to them."

I sat on my hands to keep them from crawling up my chest.

"Did you bring pictures?" My father rubbed his hands in anticipation.

I reached into my pocket and brought out pictures from Ruby and Cassandra's first day of school. They wore brand-new Gap outfits and held hands, grinning, as they stood against the living room window.

My father smiled down at the photos. "Jeez, such gorgeous girls. The little one looks like your mother. Like you. And you have new pictures of Lulu?"

I handed over a shot of Lulu and Drew taken when they'd grilled hamburgers on Labor Day.

He shook his head, smiling at the image.

"Lulu doesn't want you to write any more letters to her. The girls are getting older," I said in a burst of words.

Years ago, I'd confessed to my father about our deceptions, how we'd

216

killed him off. Since then he and I referred to the deceit in the same side-ways manner my family did everything.

"Just what are you girls planning to do when I get out of here?" he asked. "Hide me?"

When he got out.

"Your sentence isn't over for eight years. We'll worry about it then," I said.

"Here's the good news. I've been saving it. My lawyer thinks I have a shot at the next parole hearing."

How many times had I heard those words? "Right, Dad."

"You just may be surprised, missy."

Lulu swore that my relationship with our father had hardened like glue at age five and a half, when he went to jail, with no growth since. I told Lulu one rotation in psychiatry did not a psychiatrist make, but still, her observation popped into my head on a regular basis. Too bad that it made no impact on my behavior.

"I know, I know, you think I'm the boy who cries wolf," he said. "But this might be my chance. All my good time, it's adding up. I've been the model prisoner, Tootsie."

I shivered as though the devil had walked over my grave. My father's dream of getting out was our nightmare. "The hearing is in December, right? How soon could you be out?"

My father grinned huge, as though he'd never stabbed me, never killed Mama. "If they vote yes, and the vote could happen soon, I might be out by spring."

I wouldn't worry. Lulu said he'd never get out on parole.

"So, tell me more about this doctor," my father said. "Any chance I'll finally get a grandchild from you?"

"Michael got a suite at the Waldorf Astoria for us. He has a medical conference. Yesterday, we went to Saks." I ran my hands along my whisper-thin cashmere sweater. "You like?"

"You always looked good in red." He studied me without his usual admiring smile. "So, he took you shopping. Who does he think you are? He's treating you like a high-priced hooker. You're not some tramp. What kind of jerk is this guy?"

I opened the hotel room door. Michael lay on the bed with an arm behind his head, his shoes off, and a baseball game playing on the flat-screen television built into the armoire.

"Where were you?" he asked. "You had me worried."

"Sorry." I sat on a tufted silk chair and kicked my expensive new shoes across the room. The chair drove me crazy, uncomfortable and so tiny I didn't know whose ass would actually fit on it.

"You okay?" he asked, lifting his head.

I shrugged. "Just tired."

He pointed the remote at the television, clicked the set off, and came to me. "Poor baby, schlepping through New York City alone all day. Did you take cabs as I told you?"

For which he had given me money. Was he trying to remind me? I stiffened as he placed his thumbs on the knots in my neck and dug in deep. Was he waiting for his payoff?

"You're so tense. Where did you go?" He looked around the room. "No packages? Are they bringing them up from downstairs?" He reached for his wallet, as though getting ready for another New York tip job.

"Stop quizzing me." I shrugged him away, shaking off the hand he still had on my neck. "No presents, no packages, no nothing, okay?"

"Whoa! Calm down. I was just curious where you went. Did you go to a museum? The Met has a Renoir exhibit. I meant to tell you."

He looked so goddamned educated and serious, so clean and ironed. I wanted to drink beer and blast music until he screamed.

"Yeah, Michael. I went on a museum tour. Then I went for a ride on the Staten Island Ferry." I flopped down on the bed.

His face fell. "I'd planned the ferry for tomorrow morning. Oh, well. We'll just have to stay in bed a little longer."

He joined me on the bed, tracing the lines of my body, reaching to unbutton my jacket. "Want a massage?"

A massage, code for "Let's screw." Merry, Merry, source of his instant pleasure, right? I pushed his arms off and jumped up. "Would you please stop pawing at me? Jesus, this trip was a mistake."

He pulled away, his face blank, and turned the game back on. "Tell me when you're hungry. We can get room service." He paused and stared at me with an unreadable expression. "Or go out. Or, if you want, if you're afraid I'll keep pawing at you, we can just eat separately."

I crossed my arms. "Whatever."

23

Lulu

Drew walked into the bedroom, his face concerned and needy. *Get in line,* I thought. "Lulu, we need to talk."

I motioned him away and covered my nonphone ear with my hand.

"This is important," he insisted.

I finished talking to Sophie, hung up, and swung my legs out from under the sleep-warm comforter. "It's like you're one of the kids when you interrupt me that way."

"Did I disturb some holy doctor conversation?"

"Don't be sarcastic. Sophie just gave me bad news. I need to go in earlier than I thought." Drew's attitude should have warned me of looming trouble, but my preoccupation with the test results Sophie had just given me had put my patient front and center. The tests revealed awful news for Audra Connelly, and she was one of my favorites.

Poor Audra; first her eczema had turned out to be Paget's disease. Then she'd found she had underlying breast cancer, like most Paget's patients developed. Now the cancer had spread to her lymph nodes. Sophie said Audra wanted, needed to talk to me. Audra trusted Doctor Denton medically, but he overwhelmed her. Doctors such as Denton, caught in their statistics and tests, weren't capable of managing an older woman's emotional concerns and needs.

I pulled underwear from my drawer and forced my still-wet hair into a bun.

"Lulu, wait." Drew grabbed me, taking me from my neatly arranged rows of beige and black bras.

"I have to go." I tried to pull away, and he spun me around.

"Stop and listen, Lulu," he barked. I clenched my shoulders and iced up. Drew knew how I hated displays of anger. One of the traits I loved was his unusually long fuse. "We need to meet with Cassandra's teacher."

"What's wrong?" I held my underwear to my chest.

"She's going through another fear stage. I know, I know that's common at her age. The teacher agreed, of course, but apparently, she's free-falling. I would have told you last night, but you were asleep before I came in."

"I was exhausted." I dug my fingers into my upper arms, making little Cs with my short nails. "What's wrong, what's Cassandra doing?"

"Telling kids stories about how they might be adopted and not know it, or how they should watch out for kidnappers. That someone might be following them." Drew took off his glasses and rubbed the bridge of his nose. "One mother finally called the school because Cassandra was talking so much about kidnappers murdering children."

"Oh, God." I sank down on the bed. "Do you think my sister said something to the girls? She's been acting crazy since she came back from New York."

"This isn't about Merry." Drew fell beside me. "I think kids pick stuff up by osmosis."

Osmosis. I thought how Mama forgot to buy us food, leaving our nutrition to Harry's Coffee Shop or to freezer-burned chicken potpies. By eight, I was throwing them in the oven. I knew Mama had been unhappy with us, with Dad, with our life. She didn't have to say anything. The potpies spoke for her.

However, we had a good life here.

Drew and I sat stupidly for a moment, staring at our honeymoon photos of milky icebergs floating in white-blue lagoons.

"I bet Merry told her something," I said. "I just bet. I'll kill her."

"This isn't about Merry," Drew repeated. "She'd never do that. Not without your permission."

I laughed. "My permission? Merry thinks everything is community property. I'm surprised she hasn't taken you as her husband. Made us into Mormons."

"Christ, Lulu, she loves the girls," Drew insisted, ignoring my jab. "Why the hell would she do that?" He picked up the shirt and pants he'd thrown on the chair the previous night, after coming home sweaty and exhausted from playing handball with Michael.

"That doesn't mean she's smart in how she shows her love." I headed toward the bathroom.

"This isn't about Merry and you." Drew threw down his belt when I said nothing. "Oh, wait. What am I saying? Of course it's about you and Merry. It's about your whole damn family."

"Maybe it's Cassandra's drama classes. She never stops acting," I said. "I have to get to work. We'll talk about this later."

"Do you even listen?" Drew asked. "You can't just ignore the problem and leave."

"I'm not ignoring anything. Make an appointment with the teacher. I'll be there. Leave me a message."

"It's not just about the teacher meeting. It's about everything."

When I didn't respond, Drew looked like he was counting to ten. I recognized the signs. He touched my shoulder. "It's time they knew."

I moved away. "Dead topic. You knew that from the minute we met."

"You heard what your sister said when she got back from New York. They might release your father. It could be as soon as this spring."

"My father's been saying that crap forever. He's not going anywhere."

"And if he does?" Drew followed me into the bathroom. "What then, Lulu?"

"Then nothing. He's still dead to us."

"He's not dead to Merry."

"Fine." I reached over and turned on the shower. "She can have him."

Drew stepped in front of me as I tried to push back the shower curtain. "What about the girls? You can't ignore that he's their grandfather."

I pushed past him and got into the tub. "Their grandfather is as gone as my father." I turned the showerhead to pulsate. "He died along with my mother. Drop it."

Drew pulled the shower curtain aside. "You can't wish someone dead. You have to deal with this." Water soaked into the sleeve of his cotton sweater.

"No. I don't." I felt as though I were on the top of a roller coaster about to drop. "If you can't accept it, then maybe you have to leave."

"You'd choose me leaving over dealing with your father? Is that what you're saying?"

God, what had I said? I'd die if Drew ever left me. I stepped out of the shower. "Don't ever leave. Promise. I'm sorry. I just can't do it. I'm sorry. I'm sorry." I grabbed him. "Please, Drew. Don't go away."

"It's okay, Lu. Shh. It's okay." Drew threw a towel around my shoulders. "I'd never leave."

"I bring so much trouble."

"It's all part of being a family. Calm down. Cassandra will be all right; I'll talk to her teacher. I'll make the appointment."

Audra looked pale and too thin. Five pounds less than she'd appeared three weeks before, when she'd already been a wraith. I took her hand and gently squeezed. "How are you?"

"Not so good."

"I can imagine."

She shrank into herself. "I know it's growing and things look bad. I want your help in making decisions."

I placed a light hand on her arm. "You should bring your children in to help with the decision making."

"Doctor Denton thinks we should do another round of chemo," she said, ignoring my suggestion. "What do you think, Doctor Winterson?"

"I can help you go over the options." This wouldn't get me recommended for Cabot's employee of the month. Sophie had already reminded me twice that I hadn't yet responded to the medical director's memo regarding *clarifying your frequent visits with Audra Connelly. Aren't they duplicating visits with Doctor Denton? What is the reason for these appointments?* "Maybe he'll check into clinical trials for you."

Audra nodded, too ready to plunk her life into my hands.

"In the end," I reminded her, "it's always your choice."

"What would you do if I were your mother?" The paper lining the table rustled. Audra sat up straighter. "That's what my daughter told me to ask you."

A good daughter would do anything to save her mother, I thought. "I need to know which path you want to take. How aggressive you want to be."

"I want to see my grandchildren grow up."

Articles, I scratched on my arm. *Clinical trials.* I'd cancel my lunch with Sophie, get a sandwich from Jerry, and eat it while I read articles online.

Fortunately, the rest of my morning patients were easy—a cold, followed by a strep throat, anxiety, gastritis, sprained toe, Pap smear, and a pulled back muscle. I got to Jerry's cart at eleven-thirty, which in Jerry's view was too late to expect much of a lunch selection.

"I'm almost sold out." He steered his wheelchair closer. "You should have gotten here earlier."

"When? At breakfast?" I bent down and studied the sandwiches.

"Most people buy when they get here. If you didn't bring your lunch so often, you'd know that. What you got left is tuna or egg salad, Doc. Which will it be?" From the impatience in his voice, you'd think a line for Jerry's food snaked out to the parking lot. "People will be here any minute."

"What kind of bread is this?" I pointed to egg salad on yellowish bread.

"Anadama."

"What's that?"

"My wife bakes it." He wheeled over to the sandwich area and plucked up a sandwich. "It's cornmeal; you get corn muffins. You'll like it."

Before hearing my opinion, he placed the sandwich in the thinnest bag known to humankind. Actually, I remembered a thinner one.

"Coffee, right?" Jerry poured it without waiting for my answer.

"Fine." I'd been planning to have a Coke, but I didn't want another argument. I handed Jerry a ten-dollar bill and waited for the tiny bit of change I'd get. Which I would, of course, put in the glass jar marked "Paraplegic Veterans" in Jerry's slashing scrawl. No one had the guts to ask him who, what, or where the paraplegic veterans were. Most of us assumed it was Jerry and a couple of his drinking buddies.

"Louise."

Damn. I gave a phony smile to the medical director. Peter Eldon was born to be petty. When he was a child, I'd have bet he was the tattletale, the class monitor, the one who stuck his arm straight up in the air each time the teacher called for a volunteer. Now he was an overbearing Medicrat in love with his own authority and all things English. Today he wore what looked to be a hunting jacket.

"Peter. How are you?" I asked.

"Not so good. Some of my staff have been ignoring my e-mails." He loomed over Jerry. "Coffee. Black. Bran muffin." He turned back to me. "I'm compiling my monthlies, and I need to wrap up your department. You, Louise, are my squeaking wheel." I'd swear he'd developed a British accent since our last encounter.

After pouring the coffee, Jerry stretched his arm to the back of the rows and grabbed the smallest bran muffin, placed it on top of the covered coffee without using a bag or waxed paper, and handed it to Eldon. The muffin absorbed moisture as we spoke. Good job, Jerry.

"Two fifty," Jerry said.

Eldon wordlessly gave Jerry three dollars, keeping his hand out for change. "When can I expect them, Louise? And what exactly are you doing with that patient requiring you to double up on Denton's work?"

"The patient requires extra."

"Extra what?"

"Her husband died of cancer not a month before her diagnosis. She needs comfort. Help."

225

"Refer her to a social worker." He juggled his coffee and muffin.

I took cleansing breaths. I didn't grab his hot coffee and spill it on his balls. "I'm not sure Denton has the time to deal with all her needs. He's a man, and when he examines her she feels ugly."

"Personality isn't our stock-in-trade. Stick to the internal medicine patients and leave oncology to Denton."

Jerry interrupted. "Hey, wait, Doctor Winterson. I forgot this." He reached for a chocolate chip cookie, slipped it in a bag, and handed it to me.

"Send in your monthlies, Louise," Eldon said. "I'll be flagging this."

When he entered the elevator, Jerry snorted.

"Thanks for the cookie, Jerry."

He waved *it's nothing.* "The guy's a solid asshole." With those words, Jerry capped off our bonding and wheeled over to serve the now-growing lunch crowd.

I headed to the stairwell. I'd stay as late as I needed to finish. Having him, having anyone, question my work, think I'd made mistakes—that didn't happen to me.

24

Lulu

All I wanted to do when I arrived home after hours of writing reports was collapse in bed, but my sister's fragrance greeted me as I entered the living room. Merry's scent usually trailed beside her, a lemony rose—a delicate perfume that had turned tart when I'd tried it. Smoky sweetness from the fireplace drifted through the house.

Drew and Merry seemed uncomfortable when they saw me. Merry, curled on the couch, managed to look both sexy and innocently vulnerable dressed in baggy blue sweats. Drew, slumped in the rocking chair, looked exhausted after his day working at home and then being with the girls. Kids drained everything but blood from you, their maturation feeding off molecules siphoned directly from the nearest adult in charge.

"The fire smells great. What a treat." Instead of heading straight for bed, I went to Drew, kissing the top of his head, breathing in his musk of straightforward drugstore shampoo, cooking odors from supper, and a faint memory of the sunny cologne he slapped on each morning.

He stiffened. "It's eight-thirty. Where were you?"

I pulled away, confused. "I had to work late. It was an emergency. Didn't you get my message?"

"Did you get mine?" He crossed his arms over his chest. "Did you forget you were supposed to meet me at the girls' school for our meeting with Cassandra's teacher?"

I slapped my head. How could I forget Cassandra? What in the world was wrong with me lately? "I'm so, so sorry."

"Sorry?" Drew's voice rose on the word. "I canceled a client meeting I'd scheduled three weeks ago. A new client. A series I want very much."

Merry stirred. "Maybe I'd better go."

"Please, yes," I said, turning from Drew to Merry.

Drew shook his head. "Stay," he ordered.

Merry leaned forward, then back, settling on remaining locked upright and seated.

"What was the big emergency?" Drew asked.

I took a breath and thought before speaking, wanting to compress my mistake into as few words as possible. "Eldon's after me. Either it was finish reports or he'd pull the plug on what he considers unnecessary visits with one of my patients. Breast cancer. Incredibly fast-growing."

"Unnecessary visits?" Drew banged his hand on the wooden rocker arm.

I jumped as though he'd smacked me and backed away.

"Where's your head, Lulu? Just once could we take precedence over your job?"

I grabbed the mantel edge and squeezed. "Okay, I forgot the appointment. But you don't need to act as though I hung Cassandra over a cliff."

"How would you even know?"

Don't be mad at me; don't be mad at me. "So she's talking about being adopted. Every kid has that fantasy. Nightmares. I had an entire pretend family."

"Comparing anything to your fucked-up childhood doesn't offer me

228

comfort. It's not like you have a bit of experience upon which to draw for stellar, hell, even halfway-decent mothering."

"Stop," Merry said. "The kids will hear you. Being mean to Lulu won't help Cassandra. Don't say stuff you'll regret."

"Thanks. I forgot what a relationship expert you are." Despite his words, Drew stopped.

Merry came over and put an arm on my back. "Sit down, Lu."

I let her guide me to the couch, where I sank down, pulling a pale yellow cushion over my stomach, kneading the cotton-covered down in both hands. "I just forgot, Drew," I said. "I didn't mean for you to have to handle it alone."

"I know, I know." He fidgeted with his watch. "Still. How could you forget your daughter because of a patient?"

I wondered the same thing. Weren't children the most important thing in a mother's life? Weren't they supposed to rent most of the space in your brain? Didn't children make you so acutely aware of others that everyone became in some way your child? Could Hitler have been Hitler if he'd been a father?

Stupid reasoning. My father was a father.

"Everything piled on top of me," I said.

"Your daughter needs you. This isn't a case of having little adoption fantasies." He handed me a manila envelope from the coffee table. "Cassandra's family pictures."

I shuffled through the sheaf of scratchy drawing paper. Cassandra drew all of us, including Merry, in the bottom right corner of the paper. Everyone was underlined. A wavy half circle surrounded us. Ghostly men and women, drawn larger than life, floated above our family.

"Want to hear how the school shrink interpreted them?"

"They sent her to a shrink?"

Drew waved my question away. "She's the guidance counselor. Just listen. Children who perceive their families as insecure underline the family figures."

"You mean Cassandra's insecure, or she thinks we are?" I didn't want to hear this.

"The whole family system," Merry said. "She thinks our family is insecure."

"Have you become a shrink, too?" I curled my toes up and down, trying to get control of my mouth.

"The guidance counselor didn't have a clue about our family, about our mother and father," Merry replied. "And yet, look what she said."

"Now this is all about them?"

"Just let Drew finish before you go off into the world of denial."

I closed my mouth. Acid bubbled in my chest.

"See the floating figures in balloons?" Drew said. "The counselor thought they could be secrets. She asked if we were having problems, if maybe Cassandra was worried we were going to get divorced. She hinted that I was having an affair, for God's sake."

I stared at the picture, trying to recognize Cassandra's watery circles as balloons.

"Okay," I said. "I understand. But is this really so off the charts?"

Apparently, Merry could contain herself no longer. "Her teacher is suggesting she go to a private shrink. For counseling. Are you listening? Are you blind, deaf, and dumb?"

"You listen. You're acting as though the teacher said Cassandra needs to be locked up in an insane asylum." How dare they? How dare she, this teacher, make my child into some sort of deranged child at risk? "I know something about psychology, also."

"You had a rotation for what, a month?" Drew said. "A hundred years ago?"

"And her teacher had what? One course, five hundred years ago?"

Drew grabbed the pictures from the coffee table and stuffed them back in the envelope. "We need these for the meeting with the child psychologist. I made an appointment for next week. Shall I enter it in your PalmPilot? Will that help you remember?"

I threw my hands up. "How could you make an appointment without letting me check this doctor out first?"

Drew's face looked hard enough to crack wood. "She's connected to the school."

"All the more reason to distrust her."

"Do you even hear yourself?" Merry slapped the arm of her chair. "Cassandra is having family issues. She thinks someone might kill her. She's afraid of being kidnapped. She worries about being abandoned. Does any of this sound familiar? Does it sound like something maybe a daughter *and* mother need to deal with?"

"Did I ask for your opinion?"

"When did I start needing your permission to talk? Aren't I part of this family? Isn't that what you're always saying—*It's all about us, we only have us, Merry? The five of us have to stick together, Merry?*" Merry plunked herself down next to me on the couch. "There are *six* of us, and you have to face it."

"Face it? Have you figured out just how I present a grandfather who murdered their grandmother? Don't you think I've thought about it a thousand times since they were born? What? You're so high and mighty? Special Merry, who faces her father?"

Merry looked like I'd smacked her. I fought the instinct to comfort her, make her all better, and swallow my rage.

"Cassandra might be reacting to us having lost our parents at practically the same ages as she and Ruby are now," I said. "She's overidentifying with our being orphaned by a car crash." *She's okay. Cassandra is fine. Just fine.*

Merry opened her mouth in disbelief. "But that's not what happened."

"It's what she thinks happened, so it's what happened. Leave this alone, okay? I'd rather Cassandra and Ruby worry about Drew and me getting in a car crash than have them know I've spent my life trying to forget seeing Mama dying in front of me."

What? Nothing to say now?

"What do you think I see at night when I close my eyes?" I asked. "You and Daddy bleeding out on Mama's bed. For my entire life, ever since then, I've had to be responsible for everyone and everything, including you."

Merry shook her head slowly, as though I were a stranger. "This isn't about us, not like that. We have to take care of Cassandra now."

I threw the pillow I'd been clutching to the floor and stood. My arm trembled as I pointed a finger toward Merry. "I care for my daughter. I make the rules. This is my family, and if you don't like my mothering, then maybe it's time for you to go. Get your own husband. Get your own children. Stop sucking on my life."

I marched out of the room and into the bedroom, slamming the door behind me. I kicked the dresser and etched deep lines up and down my arm, wondering what I was supposed to do. After dropping to the floor, I placed my head on my knees. I wrapped my arms around my legs and prayed for one person, one grown-up, somewhere in the world who I could call.

Sickened by my weak posture, I tore off my clothes, dropped them in a heap on the corner chair, pulled on a soft, billowy nightgown, and collapsed on the bed.

The door creaked open. I waited for Drew to come and kiss away my tears.

"Mommy? Are you okay? Are you mad at me?" Cassandra walked in on little tiptoes, as though the sound of her footsteps might anger me.

I wiped my face dry and patted the bed next to me. "I'm not mad at you, honey."

The bed barely registered her weight as she fell on it, spilling into my arms, folding her long, thin body as small as possible, so I could wrap her up into a package I could hold. "I'm in trouble, right?" She pressed her lips together.

"You're not in trouble. You're feeling troubled. That's a world of difference."

"But Daddy had to go and talk to my teacher." Cassandra pushed her face deep into my shoulder, muffling her voice, hiding her face.

"Because she wants us to know that you're scared."

Cassandra didn't move. I felt her stiffen.

"Do you want to talk about it?" I asked. "The kidnapping? Being adopted?"

I felt her shake her head.

"You know that you're not adopted, right?" She shook her head again. "When I was a little girl, right around your age, I thought maybe I was adopted. I think every ten-year-old girl in the world wonders that at some point."

"But you had to be. Fostered. After."

232

"After my parents"—I hesitated—"died. Right. But I had thought about it before, honey." I held her tighter. "Maybe you think about it because you're afraid you'll lose me and Daddy like I lost my parents."

"What if I do?"

I leaned my cheek on top of her head. "You won't."

"You can't be sure." She backed away from me, crossing her legs. "You and Daddy drive together all the time. You could die like they did."

As I started to reassure her that she'd always have Aunt Merry, I imagined my sister introducing them to our father. Fatigue pressed down, pulling me toward the unconscious world. "Don't worry, honey. It could never happen twice to the same family."

Cassandra's eyes thinned with mistrust. "You don't know."

"I do know. Because of statistics. Something you learn in college. It's a kind of math."

"Math?" She clasped her hands, lacing her fingers into a steeple, with which she covered her mouth. "How does it tell you that?" she asked, her words muffled.

"Statistics are about chances, the likeliness something is going to occur. When you get older, you learn this formula sort of math for figuring out chances of things happening. And statistically, chances of you losing me are infinitesimal." I smiled. "Which means it won't happen."

Her body relaxed, slumping toward me. "You're sure?"

I nodded. "I'm sure." I pulled the covers back, kicking my way in. "Let's both go to sleep."

Cassandra pressed in close until we matched up like notched dolls. Slowly her body relaxed, her breathing became even, and she slept.

I loved this child. She was my breath and my body. More than anything, I needed to keep her safe. Nothing else mattered.

Silent tears slipped from under my closed lids, tears of fear, fear I'd never be able to comfort anyone so easily again.

25

Merry

The next morning I woke before the alarm, grateful to be free from my shallow and unsatisfying sleep. I stared out the window with gritty eyes, drinking coffee, watching and waiting until I saw Drew walk to the car with Cassandra and Ruby. My nieces held his hands as they made their way through the drizzling rain.

Ruby's determined little steps kept up. Cassandra strode wearing the crown of the elder, then and always, the powerful child. Both walked under Drew's protection. How did that feel?

The moment Drew's car pulled away, I went to Lulu's door. "Did you mean it?" I blurted the moment she answered my frantic knocking.

"Did I mean what?" Her truthful eyes belied her question.

"Any of it; did you mean any of it?" I asked.

Lulu reluctantly opened the door wider and let me in. "Let's not do drama this early, okay? I have to leave for work by nine." She headed down the hall with me trotting behind her.

We entered the kitchen, and I grabbed a mug. Lulu sat on a stool at the counter and resumed spooning up bran flakes from a bowl I'd bought her, white with cornflowers.

"I have to get to work, too." I poured cream in my coffee. "I just want to talk for a minute."

Lulu gave a much too obvious look at the wall clock, then her watch. Did my oh-so-important sister need to synchronize? I clenched the warm mug to keep my hands from shaking. My right foot pumped like a metronome.

"We both went overboard last night," Lulu said. "Let it go."

How exactly had I gone overboard? I twined my leg around the chair. "I just wanted to help. Aren't you worried about Cassandra?"

Lulu slammed her spoon into the bowl. "What exactly did you not understand about let it go?"

"How am I supposed to let go of the things you said? *Get your own life, Merry; get your own husband, Merry; get your own children, Merry.* Is that what you really want?" Ancient cigarette cravings overwhelmed me. I grabbed the family-size Cheerios box and began stuffing my mouth with handfuls of dry cereal.

Lulu closed her eyes. "This is why I didn't want to start."

I finished chewing a mound of mush and asked, "Don't you think I'd like to have a Drew of my own?"

"You've certainly auditioned enough candidates."

Lulu smiled, and I decided she was trying to be funny, not mean, at least not deliberately. "I haven't exactly had a terrific pot from which to draw," I said.

"Bars aren't the best places for finding husbands."

"You were drunk when you met Drew," I pointed out, reaching in for another handful of cereal.

"But we weren't at a bar. And he wasn't drunk." Saint Lulu rinsed her bowl before putting it in the dishwasher. "What about Michael? Didn't he like you?"

"I blew that one." I hadn't told her what a bitch I'd been to Michael during our weekend in New York. He must have had some self-respect, because he never called again.

"Maybe you should call him. Apologize for whatever you did."

"It's too complicated." What possible reason could I give him for my Jekyll-Hyde routine? Besides, Michael was too nice for me.

Lulu sprayed organic cleanser over the countertop. She hated dirt in the house. She hated having chemicals near the children. She'd wrap her girls in plastic if she could. No, she'd have Drew do the wrapping. Lulu worried me. Not being able to control everything around the kids' environment could drive her crazy someday.

"You have to let the Dad thing go." Lulu had her back to me when she said this. Then she wiped her hands on a blue checked towel and turned around. "He's going to tear us apart. And I don't want to hear it from Drew either, so do me a favor and stop talking to him about it."

"Do you think I should call Michael?" I asked Valerie at lunch. She and I rotated our lunches out between the least horrible courthouse-accessible restaurants. Today was Dumpy's Sandwich Shoppe. A slight sheen of grease coated the plastic tables; nevertheless, the place represented the best of bad choices.

"Do you *want* to call him?" she asked, picking at the crust on her un-eaten roll. Valerie was in overdrive. I'd have bet anything a diet pill rattled around her empty stomach. She'd blown her hair straight despite the October rain ready to frizz it back up again. Yesterday she'd worn a pilled sweater and crumpled khakis; today she'd ironed knife-sharp pleats into her skirt.

"Who are you, my shrink?"

"Do you need a shrink?"

"Very funny." I picked up my egg salad sandwich and took a huge bite. Overmayonnaised egg spilled on my chin.

I wiped my mouth with a scratchy brown napkin and watched Valerie make little fork roads though her bright orange macaroni and cheese.

"Do you like him? Want him?" Valerie asked.

I held my palms up, indicating my total lack of opinion.

"How can you not know what you want?"

"I think I usually want whoever wants me."

"Jesus, how pitiful. No wonder you work with losers."

"You work with the same losers."

"Uh-uh." She shook her hair, obviously enjoying feeling it fly around. "Only juveniles for me. They still have a chance."

"Right. You're the goddamned Mother Teresa of the courthouse, and I'm neurotic. So, do you think I should call him?"

"I think you should call him."

Before I could ask why, my client Jesse walked in. I'd be seeing him after lunch, but now he only raised two fingers in greeting, cool, barely acknowledging me.

"Who's that?" Valerie asked.

"Jesse. The one who got his GED. Now he's enrolled in Bunker Hill Community College." I lifted my chin as a hello to Jesse. "So I guess it's not only the juveniles who can change."

"We'll see." She crumpled her napkin and threw it on her plate, despite having taken perhaps two bites. I shoved the last of my rapidly eaten sandwich in my mouth.

"Call Michael," Valerie ordered as we left Dumpy's.

Jesse was waiting for me when we got back to the courthouse, following me from the lobby to my office, shuffling his sneakers as a coming attraction to his nasty scowl.

"Listen, Ms. Zachariah, I have other things on my mind than studying shit like the history of Ronald Reagan." Jesse caught my glare from where he slumped in the chair. "Stuff, I mean."

We weren't having our best meeting. He was irritable and in a make-fun-of-the-white-lady mood. Reading him was easy, but out of kindness, I let him think he was getting something over on me.

"Jesse, the thing about school is you don't get to pick and choose what you study. College is not a Chinese restaurant."

"Bunker Hill is a place for retards to go to college."

"That can't be true because you're enrolled, and you're pretty darn smart when you're not being an idiot."

"Says you." Jesse scowled at his feet. His sneakers gleamed white. I didn't want to think where he had gotten the money to buy them.

"Says me, and I'm your PO. It's not like I'm your mother."

Jesse sank down farther and gave a mean little chuckle. "I guess not, since you ain't drunk or offering to blow every guy who walks by."

"Sit up straight," I said, sick of his self-pity. "Grow up. No one's going to give you a break because your mother drinks or your father's dead. Just because someone hands you a ration of garbage doesn't mean you have to keep hold. You have to be the one to let go, Jesse. No one else will do it for you."

I'm not sure if my little tough-luck speech did any good; Jesse shuffled out as nasty-faced as he'd walked in.

Beer, wine, bourbon; thoughts of alcohol suffused me as I rode the train home. I got off the Green Line at Boston University, then trudged across the bridge connecting Boston to Cambridge. The coat I'd needed that morning now just served to hold my sweat-dampened blouse closer to my body.

I went to the nearby Whole Foods and grabbed a chicken salad sandwich, thick with mayo, a near-copy of my lunch. Anything healthier meant going to the counter, and talking to anyone was more effort than I could afford. I chose the cheapest bottle of wine Whole Foods carried and checked out.

Drew's and the girls' shrieks traveled around the corner as I reached my front door, their shouts indicating the fun, games, and all that other wonderful family shit they had next door. I quietly searched the pit of my overstuffed purse for my keys, not interested in saying hello.

After throwing the sandwich in the refrigerator, I uncorked the wine and poured myself a generous glass. I looked in the mirror and toasted my supper companion.

"Happy loser day." I leaned in closer to see how much I'd aged since the morning. Dry skin flakes collected in the edges of my nose. Mean little lines grew before my eyes until my face resembled crazed porcelain. My humid-wild curls appeared too young and long for my old, wrinkled face. I made nasty eyes at the crumpled-wrinkled-dry-faced loser in the mirror. I didn't even own a fricking car.

No wonder Michael had rejected me.

I hadn't found the guts to call him. Instead, I'd sent an e-mail, which I'd written and rewritten until I captured what I'd hoped was a breezy, off-the-cuff tone.

Michael,

(No "Dear." The salutation seemed too formal, too desperate.)

Too late to apologize for being an absolute horror in NYC? Can I offer an act of contrition dinner? I'll cook and provide the wine, with or without legs. All best, Merry

Michael had responded twenty minutes later:

Dear Merry,
    Thanks for your kind invitation, but best we leave things where they are. You're lovely, but at this point in my life, I don't want emotional swings, nor can I build up the interpretation skills a relationship with you seems to require. Warm regards, Michael

Warm regards, indeed. Desperately seeking comfort, however cold, I parsed "lovely." Beautiful or sweet? I supposed he meant beautiful, if not beautiful enough to override an "emotional swing." Sweet, I hadn't been.

Screw him.

I poured a third wine and picked at my sandwich, putting it down between bites to grab the remote. I drained my glass and got the phone. I knew what I needed.

The last time I'd slept with Quinn had been many months ago, when we'd gone to a motel so far up the coast we could have walked to Canada if we so desired. He'd made the trip sound romantic, but when we arrived, I saw the only atmosphere offered was anonymity. We stayed two nights, screwing repeatedly in the frantic way we pretended meant passion.

239

Now here he was, back in my bed. I supposed I should feel proud of myself; I had my married man thing down to maybe three times a year.

Quinn climbed on top of me, pulling down the straps of my black camisole. My breasts touched his chest as he banged into me. I wound my legs around him, barely feeling him through my wine-induced numbness. He ground down to a finish, coming in a hot pulse. Air washed against my cheek as he let loose with an almost inaudible groan. Emotional cripples. Both of us.

"Need anything?" he asked a few moments later, burying the words in my neck.

He meant had I come. "I'm fine."

Quinn took me at face value. He'd never worry about my so-called emotional swings. He lifted himself on his arms and fell off me so he could stare at the ceiling. He placed an arm over his eyes in his after-sex-ostrich manner. If he couldn't see me, he hadn't wronged his wife. Quinn's modus operandi.

"Not bad for an old man, eh?" he asked.

"If you need compliments afterward, perhaps you should work harder." I leaned over him and took my glass from the night table.

"If you want orgasms, perhaps you shouldn't drink so much."

I drank the few remaining sips of wine. "That never used to be a barrier. Perhaps you're getting too old."

"Perhaps you are. Turn to me, let me see." He pulled me over on my side. Quinn still had his football strength. He ran a rough thumb in the hollows under my eyes. "Is this thinning skin? Are these lines?"

I pushed him away. "Is this softening?" I poked at his stomach. "Can you feel the approach of Viagra in your future?"

"And Botox in yours?" He leaned back and put his arm out for me, waiting for me to conform to his body. "Am I the only one who knows the bitch you really are under those Kewpie doll looks?"

"Kewpie doll? Old man, old man," not wanting him to see how his words hurt.

"Face it, Merry. They say when you get older you have the face you deserve. Maybe that's not true. Look at us, still beautiful, still handsome. Maybe in the end, you have the person you deserve."

26

Merry

A week later, certain I'd let Quinn into my bed for the last time, I cleansed my apartment of even the slight traces he'd left in my life. The few photos of us, I shredded. The cheap locket he'd given me, I tossed. The glass vase in which I'd placed the flowers he'd brought, I recycled to Goodwill.

I gave up men. Married men, fat men, thin men, men of muscle, men of steel, sensitive, smart, fools, and fops; I'd finished with them all. I furthered my purification journey by cutting out alcohol and M&M's. I joined a women-only gym, ready to become physically strong and emotionally sound. I left for work looking forward to saving souls and returned high on the wise advice I'd dispensed all day.

Before heading upstairs, I checked my mail. A letter marked with the familiar words "Richmond County Prison" glowed toxic from among my cable and Visa bills. I allowed my automatic response, pouring a Jack Daniel's, to wash through me without acting on it and marched up to my refrigerator for a V8, reminding myself how much better my skin seemed since I'd replaced alcohol with vegetable juice. I considered smearing the blood-red liquid on my skin until I'd look twenty.

I crouched in front of the fridge, holding off on the letter until I had some food as a shield. On the bottom shelf, I found a bowl of tomatoes shrinking in a pool of oil, vinegar, and wilted cilantro leaves. After sniffing the sad mixture, I took a forkful, hoping vinegar acted as a natural enemy of food-borne bacteria.

Then I opened my father's letter.

Dear Merry,

Too busy to visit your old man these days? Got a new boyfriend? Not only have I not seen you since you visited in October, I've only gotten that one card from you. Not even a letter, just a store-bought card. I haven't seen a picture of the girls in ages, and at their age, they grow like weeds.

My father, the expert on the stages of childhood.

Well, never mind. Here's some good news. It won't be long before I can see those girls in person. Guess what? I'm getting out in March!!!!

I know you thought it would never happen, but my years of good behavior are finally paying off. The prisons are getting too crowded, so they're moving out the old guys like me (ha ha!) to make more room for gangbangers and drug dealers. This place is crawling with scum. These young kids have no respect. Well, too bad for them. Their loss, my gain, right?

I gulped another glass of V8.

So, even though my sentence isn't up for eight years, I'm getting out. I need you to come up right away. I've called you plenty of times (even though I have to wait in a line of idiots for an hour to make the calls), but you're never home and I didn't want to leave this news on your answering machine.

We need to make plans, Tootsie. I don't even know how big your apartment is. And I got to make things right with Lulu. You have to make her come up here. You come here this weekend so we can start talking about all this. *Also, find out about optician places in Boston, because I need to have them transfer my parole to Massachusetts (you can help, right?) and I need a list of where I can look for a job. Plus other stuff.*

this. Also, find out about optician places in Boston, because I need to have them transfer my parole to Massachusetts (you can help, right?) and I need a list of where I can look for a job. Plus other stuff.

With your connections, this should go easy.

Fear overtook my body one inch at a time, moving like Novocain through my veins, paralyzing me in some merciful way.

I had no one to call and no one to tell. Lulu would need managing, and Drew, the only other person in the entire world I could tell—his loyalty had to be to Lulu. Drew would be my partner in taking care of Lulu; he couldn't help me.

I raked my finger up and down my chest. I stumbled into the bathroom and opened the medicine cabinet, looking for rescue. Finally, behind the aspirin and Pepto-Bismol, I found half a bottle of Vicodin left from a root canal the previous year. I carried the bottle into the kitchen and swallowed two tablets with V8.

What in the name of God could I do?

I went to my bedroom and fell on my neatly quilted bed. I lay face-down and thought of my mother. Spectral pictures wrapped my memories. Each year, Mama's image morphed into the Virgin Mary a little more, until now my recollections of her resembled the Holy Mother oil paintings lining Duffy's hall.

Memories of my childhood rushed past the Vicodin and V8. I imagined the white pills eroding in my stomach as they soaked in the red liquid. I prayed for the drugs to decompose and numb me fast.

Mama had screamed and screamed while I'd lain frozen on her bed. I'd ripped pieces of my mother's chenille bedspread as my father tore my skin. Wetness followed searing pain. Daddy tried to hold me with his blood-soaked hands. Then darkness came and I had no other memories until Lulu came to the huge hospital where I'd lain alone forever, and gave me a tiny doll.

Lulu.

How could I tell her?

*

I took her to eat at Delfino restaurant on Friday, just the two of us having a sisters' night out.

Lulu tipped her head toward my wineglass. "What happened to purification?"

"Anything can become extreme, even temperance. Ready to order?"

"You're so jumpy. What's wrong? You've been like this for days." Candlelight cast shadows on Lulu's wine-softened features. She bit off the end of a breadstick.

I brought my menu closer. "I'm just hungry. Let's order, then we can talk."

Lulu smirked with knowing. "See. I knew we had something to talk about." She put on her reading glasses, smiling with the pleasure of having uncovered the truth.

I caught the waiter's eye and raised a finger toward my empty wineglass. Lulu, she of the still-half-full glass, noticed and widened her eyes. "Two drinks before dinner?"

"Just figure out what you want, okay?"

"Fine, fine. You're a big girl." Lulu picked up her menu, looked for a moment, and then placed it down. "But it's been wonderful seeing you so healthy."

I almost slammed my hand on the glass table, imagining the shattering, the blood running. Instead, I smiled. "The manicotti here is great."

The small restaurant invited intimacy. I'd brought my sister here as a man might bring a date, jumpy with wanting her love. I'd hoped the candles, the red walls, and the glass tables covered with sheer lace clothes would make Lulu yearn for our twoness. Lulu and Merry against the world; no one came between us. Please, God.

"Okay, then. I'll have the manicotti," Lulu said. "How'd you find this place, anyway? Who knew his neighborhood existed?"

Quinn had introduced me to Delfino. Being far from his South Boston home made it perfect for us. "You didn't know Roslindale existed?" I said.

"Of course I knew it existed. I just didn't know it had things like excellent restaurants. You've taught me something." She tipped her wineglass to me. "To you."

Clinking my glass against hers, I said, "To us."

"To us," she agreed and sipped. "Oh, this is nice. No children. No paperwork. Once in a while, it's good to have just us."

"I told you."

We talked of everything and nothing through the main course and dessert. Then I wanted cognac, sambuca, anything, and I hoped Lulu would also have a strong after-dinner drink.

"Come back to my apartment," I said. "I need to show you something. I bought a bottle of B&B." The rich liqueur softened Lulu.

"I feel like I'm on some sort of perverted date. Are you trying to get me drunk?"

"I love you, Lulu."

"I love you, too." She laughed, uncomfortable as always with emotion served straight up.

"Remember when you came to the hospital? Right after?"

"I walked about a hundred blocks." Lulu pinched dripping wax from the candle between us. "And I think it was a hundred degrees."

"You saved my life."

"Hardly. I bought you a cheap doll or something."

"I'd been alone for so long. Mimi Rubee only came once."

"I still can't believe no one came to see you." She frowned at the memory and twisted her napkin into a rope.

"I guess everyone was too freaked out to remember me. Grandma probably sat outside the front door of the jail night and day, waiting for them to let her see Daddy. And Mimi Rubee must have been a basket case."

"Still," Lulu said. "Someone should have come."

"Maybe everyone thought someone else was taking care of it." I swept chocolate cake crumbs into a pile and brushed them into my hand, shaking the sticky bits on my dessert plate.

"I don't think *anyone* even thought about us long enough to wonder if anyone took care of anything."

"You were the one who took care of me, of us," I said. "I don't even know if I ever thanked you."

Lulu shook off my words. "We only had each other."

"Except Anne Cohen. Don't you think she cared?"

Lulu rested her chin on fisted hands. "No," she said after a long silence. "If she had, someone would have taken care of us after she died. She would have made sure of it. That's what you do for your kids. Anne wanted to love us the same as her own kids, but she couldn't, and that probably made her feel awful."

"Maybe that's why she was always buying me those expensive clothes." I remembered my short period of feeling rich. "You wouldn't let her get you a thing outside of the basics."

"I didn't want to get used to anything I couldn't keep up." Lulu's loosened hair reminded me of her as a teenager, flannel shirts and overalls masking how skinny she was, big black hiking boots announcing her anger each time she stomped into a room.

"Have you ever felt safe?"

Lulu hugged herself, gripping her upper arms. "What do you mean?"

"You know, safe. Because I don't think I ever have."

Lulu didn't answer, her softness leaving as we moved closer to unsaid words. That Day. Then. Him. Her.

"Because I simply never have felt that way," I continued, despite her silence, "and I wonder about you. I wonder if it's possible for either of us to wake up happy in the morning. Maybe you can, because of Drew and the girls."

"Haven't you ever been happy?" she asked.

"I don't know."

Lulu gathered her hair into a pile at the back of her head. "I don't know either. I don't know how normal people feel. Ever since that day, I've watched everyone, waiting for clues for the right ways to act. What do happy people look like?"

"What do safe people do? How do they make decisions?" I picked up my credit card receipt. "Come on. Time for that B&B."

"Sounds perfect," Lulu said. "And thanks for dinner."

"Thanks for my life."

Lulu's hands shook as she read our father's letter. I studied her face for clues to my future. Spots of red mottled her pale complexion. She scratched circles or squares, I couldn't tell which, with her right foot. Long after she should have finished reading the few paragraphs Dad had written, she continued staring at the letter.

"Do you want something to drink? Some water?" I asked to fill my need to speak, to keep from pouncing on her. *Will you help me? What should I do? What's going to happen?*

"I could kill him." Her face turned blank. Here was the Lulu who'd lived at Duffy, at the Cohens'. "Who the hell does he think he is?"

"Calm down," I said. "We can figure this out."

Lulu didn't look at me. "There's nothing to figure out, Merry."

"What about everything he said? What he asked for? What am I going to do?"

She crumpled the letter and threw it on the floor. "This is what you do."

I folded my knees in as close to my chest as possible.

"Nothing. You're not taking care of him." She emphasized each word by shaking a finger at me. "Got it?"

I shrank from her, desperate for words to make it better. Make us safe. Make her not angry. "It'll be okay, Lu."

"It'll be okay?" Her ragged laugh made me tap my chest. "Look at you. You're already a wreck. Jesus. For God's sake, Merry, don't tell me you're even considering having him come here." Before I could say another word, Lulu went on. "That man's not coming within ten thousand miles of me or my family."

"I thought I was part of your family," I whispered.

"Of course you are. Give me a minute to digest this." She bent down and retrieved the crumpled letter, shaking it at me. "When did you get this, anyway?"

"A few days ago."

"Why didn't you tell me right away?"

"You know how you are about him."

"How I am about him?" She laughed. "What did you expect? How should I be about him? Tell me, exactly how should I be?"

"Don't yell," I pleaded. "It's not my fault."

"So, are you happy now? Isn't this what you were always begging for? *Write a letter to him, Lulu. Call him, Lulu. See him, Lulu. Write the parole board.*"

247

"I never asked you to write letters to the parole board."

"But you wrote letters, didn't you?"

"I didn't know what else to do," I said. "I didn't know how to say no."

"Well, now you're both getting your wish, aren't you?" She threw the paper back down in disgust, wiping her hand on her shirt as though she'd touched filth.

"Don't." I moved to the edge of the couch, clutching a small pillow, concentrating on familiar objects to still myself. Thick unread books. Un-opened magazines slick with promise. TiVo blinking.

"Don't what?" Lulu asked. "See? This is why I stayed away from him, so I wouldn't get caught in this shit."

I flung the pillow away. "You could stay away because I was there."

"Bullshit," Lulu said. "What's that supposed to mean?"

"Right from the beginning, I had to take care of him. I had to be his family while you did whatever you wanted. Grandma didn't drag you to the prison week after week. Oh, no! Lulu was special. So smart. So sure of everything. No one could make you do anything."

"I was so special? Jesus, Merry. Who was the little princess? Who was so beautiful that Anne dressed you like you were her personal Barbie doll?"

"You think that's what I wanted? To be a pet? I was drowning. I was smothered in everyone's needs while you became a doctor. Got married. Had kids. You got the future, Lulu."

"You could have let go of him anytime you wanted. I begged you to let go."

"And I begged you to help me." I went to Lulu and took her hands, run-ning my thumbs over her knuckles, her skin rough from constant scrub-bing with medical soap. I pressed her hand to my chest. "Help me, Lu. I can't manage this by myself. What should I do? Help me."

27

Lulu

D rew?" I laid a gentle hand on his back, not wanting to wake him and desperate to wake him. Our bedroom was dark except for the flicker of the eleven o'clock news.

"Hmm." He rolled over to face me, his expression less closed than it had been for the past few weeks since we'd fought. Because he was half-asleep or because he was ready to let it all go?

We'd been living in a wary détente since agreeing to send Cassandra to a therapist, walking on the eggshells of agreeing to disagree. First, I gave in to the idea of sending her to a therapist, despite my misgivings. Then, after finally convincing me to send her, Drew began harping on his fear. He'd become convinced that by not telling the therapist the true family story we'd end up confusing and hurting Cassandra more than helping her. In the end, he'd given in to my frantic arguments for keeping things as they were.

"Are you awake?" I asked.

"I am now." He smiled. He touched my shoulder and pushed gently.

"You look like Nixon with your shoulders up around your neck like that. What's wrong?"

I clasped my fingers into a temple and brought them to my lips. Drew reached up and brought them down. "What is it, sweetheart?"

"He's getting out." I didn't have to explain any further. There was only one *he* in our family. "Merry just told me."

"Christ. So that's what the dinner was about." Drew sat up and rubbed a circle on my back. I loved that he struggled up through his sleepiness rather than trying to draw me down to him. "What do you need right now?"

"A hit man?" I crossed my arms. "Merry wants me to help her with this."

"With what exactly?"

"With him wanting to set up house here." My arm hurt. Physician, heal thyself. I recognized the signs of an anxiety attack. I scratched NO, NO on my arm.

Drew tipped my face to him. He looked straight into my eyes. He took both my hands in his. "You're not alone. You're not a little girl. We'll get through this. Together. I promise."

My breath came in short, stabbing pants as I rocked in an ancient pattern of self-comfort.

"No one's going to hurt you, Lulu. No one's hurting anyone." He came closer. "You're not alone; I'll never let you be alone."

Cabot Medical Health Care Building swarmed with patients anxious for diagnoses before the holiday. Thanksgiving closed in with three days to go. At home, Cassandra spun in circles. Sparks of therapy flew off her. My father's imminent release bore down like a sick joke. Merry sagged with his weight, her eyes begging me for help even though she'd dropped the subject. Drew and I were regaining our closeness, but his constant monitoring of Cassandra reminded me how precariously we all rested on my lies.

I was glad to be at work.

Outside Audra's exam room, I skimmed her chart as I put off the inevitable. The experimental drugs had halted the spread of her cancer while simultaneously causing damage to her heart tissue.

Sophie tapped my arm with a patient's chart as she passed by. "I stopped in and said hello to Audra. She's ready and anxious."

"I know." I heard my own testiness.

"I know you know," Sophie said. "But do you know you're not holding her every breath in your hands? Your doctor-as-God complex is getting out of control. Please, relax a little. You look like hell."

I frowned, studying the chart for miracles. "I like Audra."

"I like her also. I want her to live. I want all our patients to live, but you're giving away too many pounds of flesh for this one. What's wrong?"

Scenes from childhood kept bubbling up since I'd learned about my father's release. Even as I held Audra's chart, I heard my father knocking at the door. I smelled the metallic odor of blood mixed with beer.

"It's nothing," I said. "Just Audra's husband dying so recently, her kids, everything.... It's nothing."

Sophie didn't even pretend to listen to my babbled reasoning. "Do something fun this weekend, okay? You'll have four entire days."

"Sure, with one day cooking and three days cleaning."

She snorted. "At least you don't live with monsters. Imagine Thanksgiving with my boys."

"Right." I knocked softly on the exam door before entering. "Sometimes I forget how lucky I am."

Audra's cheekbones were skeletal ridges. Scalp freckles showed through her brittle red hair. Excess pigment had produced the dark spots marking her chest. None of these temporary side effects of Audra's treatment overly bothered me, though I wasn't so confident about her drug-weakened heart muscle.

I placed a light hand on her arm. "How are you feeling?"

She shrugged. "They say the cancer growth is slowed way down. That's positive, right?" I reached for my stethoscope and she lowered her gown enough for me to see the knobby points of her shoulders.

"Yes. That's excellent news." I warmed my stethoscope, then placed it on her back. "Breathe. Hold." Her labored breathing and slowed heartbeat sounded similar to her exam the previous week.

She waited until I finished listening to her vital signs before saying, "But my heart is getting worse?"

"So far I didn't notice any changes from last week. Though you've lost another pound."

She shrugged. "I can barely eat, and when I do I either throw up or it goes out the other end."

I pressed on her ankle, checking for edema, which would indicate a worsening heart problem. "You're not swollen. Good."

"Traci, my youngest, is really angry. She thinks the cure is killing me. Can she call you?" Audra grabbed my arm when I didn't answer immediately, her hand so fine-boned and narrow it had become a claw. "Please? I need you to talk to her. She wants reassurance, but I'm so scared I don't know how to tell her not to worry. And Doctor Denton, God bless him, this isn't his cup of tea."

"I can't tell your daughter not to worry," I said. "But it's certainly not hopeless."

Audra's smile took up most of her face. "So, that's what you'll say."

"What did you and Aunt Merry used to do for Thanksgiving when you were orphans?" Cassandra asked. My girls stared at me big-eyed, once again confusing me with Anne of Green Gables.

Merry topped off her glass of wine and then gestured with the bottle to Drew, who nodded. I opened my eyes wide like my daughters'. *Wine here, please.*

"When we lived with the Cohens," I said, "we had big meals like this."

"Who came?" Cassandra watched me with laser eyes, hungry for knowledge of my childhood. Since Cassandra had started seeing the therapist, it had become worse and worse. *Who, why, when, where.* No detail seemed too small for my daughter to dissect.

"Let's see. There were the Cohens, of course."

"Anne and Paul, right? Doctor Cohen?" Cassandra asked.

I tried to look relaxed. Just walking down memory lane, folks. "That's right. And their children. They were already grown-ups." Cassandra listened as though a nugget of gold might surface. "And Anne and Paul's grandchildren. I think. Right, Merry?"

"Right." Merry buttered a roll and shoved half of it in her mouth.

"God, Mom, you don't remember?" Ruby shook her head and frowned, my judgmental little beauty queen.

Cassandra looked at Ruby as though she were an uninvited guest. "Mom was traumatized." Cassandra drew out the word. "From being an orphan."

"Did Doctor Johanna teach you the word *traumatized*?" Drew asked.

Cassandra bobbed her head yes. "She said maybe I picked up on Mommy's trauma." She turned and looked at me with great sympathy. "Not because of anything you did, Mommy. It's all on an unconscious level. That means without knowing you did it."

"I think you mean *subconscious*, honey," Drew said. "*Unconscious* means being sort of asleep. *Subconscious* means doing something without realizing it."

"See, Cassandra?" Ruby smirked. "You're not so smart."

"Why don't we all say what we're thankful for?" Merry said. "I'm grateful for having particularly brilliant nieces."

"And pretty. Right, Aunt Merry?" Ruby preened in the soft velvet dress she'd insisted on wearing, despite the casual clothes the rest of us wore. She matched the opalescent china with which Drew had set the table. Red wine for adults and cranberry juice for the girls shimmered in Irish cut crystal glasses, wedding gifts from Drew's relatives.

"Pretty is as pretty does," I reminded Ruby. I worried that my younger daughter thought she could skate through life on prettiness and winning swim meets. "How you treat people is more important than how you look."

Ruby swept back her silky hair, looking not at all convinced. "What are you grateful for, Mommy?"

Not being dead.

I sipped my wine, troubled by my thoughts. "I'm grateful for having a wonderful husband, two wonderful daughters, and a wonderful sister."

"You sound like Aunt Merry," Ruby complained. "You can't copy. Everyone has to come up with something different."

"Who said?" Cassandra asked.

"It's the rule. The new rule." Ruby stuck her chin out. "Otherwise it's not real."

"Okay," Drew said. "I'm grateful the turkey is delicious, Mommy's stuffing is perfect as ever, and Aunt Merry made cherry pie just so I don't have to eat pumpkin."

"No, Daddy." Ruby looked like she might cry. "We need to do this serious! Like at school."

"What did you say at school?" I steered the conversation from family and Thanksgiving at the Cohens', which could lead to Thanksgiving at Duffy. Duffy, where canned cranberry sauce sat upright in chipped bowls, the can markings visible on the red towers. The only girls who ever ate the tinny-tart stuff were the girls so fat, so desperately trying to fill themselves, they'd lick the can if allowed. Scraping our plates clean of the thin servings of turkey and watery mashed potatoes, we looked only at our food, as though ashamed to be seen celebrating in such poor company.

Ruby puffed up with importance. "I said I was thankful for my family, of course, because they love me so much. And I was thankful no one I knew died at the 9/11 World Center. And that Osama Laden didn't come to Cambridge."

Maybe Cassandra's fears had nothing to do with me or my subconsciously poisoning her mind. Maybe 9/11 was our problem. All children waited for disaster now. It didn't have to be born of our front yard.

"That's lovely, Ruby," Merry said.

"What are you grateful for, Daddy? And don't say food," Cassandra warned.

Drew put down his knife and sat back. "Everything I'm grateful for is right in this room. Copying good things is okay, Ruby."

"Daddy got it perfect. Now, let's eat this meal we're all so grateful for," I declared. *I love you, Drew. You rescue me.*

Cassandra forked up a small mound of stuffing. Her quivery look presaged sentimental tears. "Do you still feel like an orphan, Mommy? Do you think about your mother and father all the time?"

Jesus, Mary, and Joseph, rescue me from my past. Give us this day our daily future. Make me know what to say, God. Grant me a peaceful past. I want to rest.

"I think about them sometimes," I managed to say. "Not always."

Cassandra tilted her head to the side, her eyes alive with some understanding that thrilled her, more of the Doctor Johanna wisdom coloring our lives, no doubt. "Does it hurt to talk about them? They live in your heart, though, so you always have them with you. Right? So you're okay. Right?"

I drank half a glass of water to pass words from my dry lips. "Of course I am."

"So, we're all okay, right?" Cassandra pressed.

Ruby bit down on a roll in slow motion, crumbs falling to the table-cloth as she waited for my answer. Despite any fights they might have, the girls lived in the world of emotional primogeniture, and Cassandra's judgment ruled.

Drew pressed his hands flat, keeping his fingers splayed and firm. "We're okay. We're all sad Mommy and Aunt Merry's parents died, but that was a once-in-a-lifetime tragedy. We're fine."

Drew's last words came out with more firmness than he probably intended. The girls jumped like twitchy kittens.

Drew grinned to offset his dour message and heaped stuffing on his already full plate. "We'll celebrate Christmas soon, and you'll get a million presents from Grandma and Grandpa Winterson. No more past. Let's concentrate on what *will* happen, okay?"

I'd take Drew's words to heart. Live for today, be in the present. Who cared if it sounded like New Age hoo-ha; I needed to stop passing on fear and horror, unknowingly or not. Maybe I'd been subconsciously feeding the girls Zachariah grim fairy tales. I would retrain myself. No more watching for bogeymen at the door.

For two weeks, I managed to keep my vow. I whistled a happy tune. I woke before Drew, bringing him coffee, then waking the children with newborn lighthearted mother vibes. I ran in circles to avoid being alone with Merry, not able to face the knowledge that I shouldn't leave her by herself, not caring, so great was my need to be away from the nightmare of my father getting out.

Merry had respected my warnings to let me tell Drew in my own time, but I hadn't yet told her that I'd told him. That would have made it too real.

I pushed my father out of my mind and lived in a land of cookies and milk.

On the third Monday morning in December, I crumbled. Everyone woke in the throes of anxiety. Ruby had a book report due, and she hadn't yet colored in the back or front cover, or stapled it together. Cassandra needed a birthday present for a party she'd be attending the next day and feared we wouldn't remember. Drew had a client meeting, a possible chance to illustrate a new series by a semifamous children's book author. He'd spent the entire weekend sketching versions of some magical tribe of environmental warrior chipmunks. I thought they looked terrific, but he repeatedly added and subtracted one more blade of grass, one more acorn.

As for me, Audra had suffered a heart incident and spent the weekend in and out of intensive care. Her children had besieged me with calls, hounding me for predictions on which they could count, wanting me to be doctor and soothsayer. Denton had been out of town, and no oncologist on call would make the decision to stop the cancer drug, a decision that could simultaneously save and kill her. *You know her best,* the last oncologist had said.

"Did you hear me, Lu?"

"What?"

"Don't forget you're picking up the kids today." Drew looked nervous. "I'll call and remind you."

"Do you really think I'd forget to pick them up?" I watched the girls slurp up their cereal. Ruby's expression said she believed anything bad was possible, while Cassandra maintained her Doctor-Johanna-says-it's-all-fine face.

"I need to finish my report cover," Ruby said.

"I'll set my watch to give you a reminder call, Lu," Drew said.

"You'll be in the middle of a presentation, for goodness' sake," I said. "Girls, hurry. It's almost time to leave."

"I can put the watch on vibrate. It's not a formal presentation."

"I haven't finished my cover," Ruby shouted. *"No one is listening to me!"*

"No one can help but hear you. Now listen to me. Everyone." I pointed at Cassandra, who'd opened her mouth—no doubt wanting to make sure her needs were on the list. "Quiet. Drew, I'll pick up the children. Concentrate on selling yourself. Ruby, march into the living room right now and finish; Daddy will be in to help you in a minute. And Cassandra, we'll stop at the CambridgeSide Galleria on the way home from school."

"Me, too?" Ruby asked. "Can I get a toy?"

"Anything you want, sweetheart." Buying happiness for my children sounded like an excellent choice today.

Audra's youngest daughter, Traci, smelled of stale cigarette smoke. She clutched my arm as I tried to back away from her mother's bed. Audra's vital signs had plummeted in the last few hours. The family waited for the on-call oncologist, a man they'd met only once before.

"Please, Doctor." Traci pinned her light blue eyes to mine. "Stay until he comes. He's so difficult to speak with; he intimidates everyone. You're the only one Mom trusts."

"Stop, Traci," Audra's reedy voice broke in. "You're being rude."

"I'm not being rude, Ma." She wrapped her hands around the steel bed railing. "You tell her, Owen," she said to her brother.

Audra's children visited in rotation. She had so many I hardly remembered their names, but I remembered Traci, the intense one.

Owen rose from the molded plastic chair he claimed on each visit. Owen resembled his father as I imagined he'd been before the cancer. Ruddy. Widely built.

"Calm down, Trace." He put an arm around his sister. "Doctor Winterson, it would mean the world to us if you saw your way clear to help us speak to this new oncologist."

He looked at Audra with a sad smile. "You give my mother hope and will."

I waited for Audra to tell Owen to stop, let the busy doctor go. Instead, her watery blue eyes pleaded as life leaked from her.

I bent close to her. "Audra, what is it you want?"

Audra's papery palm slipped against mine. With tremendous effort, she pulled herself up, bringing us closer to eye level. "You're my lifeline."

I'd see if Merry could pick up the girls.

28

Merry

I watched Ruby and Cassandra through the window of the courtroom's child-care center. Cassandra read a Bugs Bunny book to a toddler, giving the girl little kisses on the top of her head as she turned the pages. Ruby rolled a green speckled ball back and forth between twin toddler boys, clapping each time one caught it.

These girls owned me.

After picking them up an hour ago, I'd had an unavoidable meeting. To head off my nieces' complaint that they weren't babies who needed a playroom, I'd asked them to help the child-care counselors, leaving a box of cheap, sugary donuts, the kind Drew and Lulu never allowed in the house, as incentive.

The drop-in center had opened only a few months before. Plastic push toys still gleamed, and the jigsaw puzzles were still complete. Community for Peace had fought for the playroom, tired of seeing children watch their mothers and fathers stand, sometimes defiantly, sometimes shamefully, in front of the judges.

Colin, in a rare display of humanity, hadn't blocked the playroom once the community cleared the necessary bureaucratic hurdles. Even he hated watching the kids standing still and stiff in their tiny pressed shirts and dresses, as if keeping their clothes neat would help Mama or Daddy. On the other hand, maybe he just hated seeing kids, period. Having the child-care center kept them out of sight. Either way, we got the place.

I blew kisses through the playroom glass before going in to get my nieces. "Time to leave." I carefully shut the door behind me after entering. Having children loose in the court wouldn't earn me any brownie points.

"Two more minutes?" Ruby pleaded.

Cassandra glanced up from the book she was reading, giving me a quite-grown-girl expression, which I interpreted as meaning, only a few pages to go.

I perched on a child-size wood chair and watched the girls, who looked so serious, so lovely, that I wondered if I'd been wrong in nagging Lulu to tell them the truth. Perhaps you could bury the past and live with it. Look at my nieces, so sweet and helpful.

The girls enjoyed playing miniature grown-ups, but, unlike Lulu and me, they'd never have to face actually living out the roles. Maybe if I stopped worshiping the truth, they could remain innocent. Maybe I hadn't been thinking of Ruby and Cassandra all these years. Maybe I just hadn't wanted to be alone with Dad.

I should take a lesson from Lulu. Compartmentalize. Lock my father in a box. I still hadn't responded to his letter. Next week I'd go to Richmond County Prison. I'd take care of him, but keep him away from the girls. I'd protect them from the ugliness. I could control my father if I had to. If he wanted my help, he was going to need to give up all this "my granddaughters" crap.

Cassandra closed her book and lifted the little girl off her lap. "Come on," she called to Ruby. "Aunt Merry's waiting."

"Just because you're done doesn't mean I am." Ruby shook her head. Her unraveling braids flew around. "I promised we'd play ten rounds."

I sent a pleading look to Asia, the center director.

"Don't worry, Ruby," Asia said. "Now's quiet time anyway."

I didn't want my sister finding us here. Not that I'd make the girls lie. I just didn't want Lulu having to search for us.

Ruby handed Asia the ball. "It's Kenny's turn," she said. She picked up her book bag and turned to me. "Can we come here again? Could I get a job here? Not for money, just like a helper."

Cassandra rolled her eyes. "Sure, Mom will let you work here."

"It's nice that you want to help, honey, but you're a little young," I said. I steered the girls toward the probation department. "Regulations wouldn't permit it."

"Or Mom," Cassandra said.

"Speaking of Mom," I said. "Let's get back to my office before Mom comes. She promised she'd be here before my next meeting." I had to appear before the judge with an out-of-compliance client, and I couldn't worry about the girls during that time. I glanced at my watch, praying Lulu wouldn't be late. This particular judge was a stickler, and this particular client was a pain in the butt.

"Will she be mad if we're not waiting for her?" Ruby asked.

"Not mad," I said. "But possibly a little worried."

When we got to my cubicle, I cleared a space at the edge of the desk opposite from where I sat. "Read or do your homework." I checked my watch. "Mom should be here in ten minutes."

"I'm going to draw a picture of Kenny and Sean," Ruby announced, referring to the twin boys she'd been playing with. "After I finish my homework."

I pushed a half-eaten box of ginger snaps toward the girls. "Do me a favor. Wait until the ride home before telling Mom about the playroom."

"Weren't we allowed to be there?" Cassandra asked.

"She might worry because it's in a court."

"Is it dangerous?" Ruby asked. "Criminals are everywhere, right?"

"Yes," I said. "But policemen are everywhere also."

"Do killers come here?" Excitement laced Ruby's question, as though I worked with the glitterati: Murderers! Rapists! Thieves!

"Poor Mom's always worried. Probably because your parents' dying makes her scared," Cassandra told me in a confidential tone.

"Maybe we shouldn't tell her about the playroom, then." Ruby knelt on the wooden office chair, leaning over her homework sheet.

"It's okay not to tell her," I said. "But you can't lie." Explaining sins of omission versus sins of commission seemed a little sophisticated, but I hoped they got the point.

"Aunt Merry, how much is twelve times twelve?" Ruby asked.

"Isn't that supposed to be your homework?" I shuffled through papers until I found the report I needed.

"I did it. I just want to see if I'm right."

I took the paper from Ruby. "You got it, honey."

"Hey. *Mizz* Zachariah."

My client, Victor Dennehy, stood in the doorway. "Who are the kids?"

"What are you doing here, Victor?" I rose to head him off. His date with the judge was in an hour. "You're supposed to meet me in the court-room."

The moment I got close, I smelled the alcohol. His hooded eyes belied his casual stance. I'd seen Victor earlier in the week, and we'd gone over his awful recent record. He'd missed every session I'd put as a condition of his probation: AA, batterers' intervention, NA, a parenting course. He'd had two dirty urines. Then I'd received a call from his frightened girl-friend telling me he'd started smacking her around again. *Get him cleaned up*, she'd begged. *For the baby.*

"Why you got to disrespect me?" Victor spoke in his Boston brand of white-kid-speaking-tough-black. A traditional Irish scally cap covered his rusty brown hair. The guards would have made him take the hat off when he came in. He'd probably shoved it in his pocket, putting it back on the moment he was out of their sight. Last week I'd had to ask him to remove it twice.

"I have to be to court"—he whacked his right hand into his left—"because of you."

"Calm down, Victor. We can talk in just three minutes." I pointed to-ward the hall. "Wait in the lobby, okay? Three minutes."

"Fuck that."

I prayed someone had heard him swear and would call security.

"Victor, I have children here. Three minutes."

"They yours?" Before I could answer, Victor laughed. "Pretty stupid, bringing your kids here. And you say I'm stupid."

"I never said you were stupid, Victor."

"Yeah, you did." Victor looked as though he might cry.

His mood was swinging from one end of the spectrum to the other. Drunk, high, or both? I chose my words carefully. "I said not going to your programs was a stupid thing to do. Not you. You're anything but stupid. You're a smart kid. That's how I know you'll go wait for me."

"Why you wanna send me to jail? I can't go back."

Victor, though wide, was short. I grabbed his eyes with mine. "Of course not. We'll talk about it. Soon. Like I said."

"You should talk to me now." Victor marked each word by hitting the wall. "Not be babysitting."

"I hear you." I moved left, blocking my office entrance as much as I could.

He rolled his shoulders and filled his chest. "Did you know I got a court date in an hour?"

"I know that." I turned for a moment and saw Cassandra and Ruby standing statue-still. I should have left them in the playroom. "I'll be with you."

"Can't you make it go away?" he pleaded. "Can't you make them cancel it?"

I nodded and made my voice sympathetic. "Okay, I'll tell the judge you're doing better."

"Do you promise?"

"Of course I promise."

"And I won't go to jail. For sure?" Victor's voice shook. His chubby cheeks made him appear younger than his twenty-two years.

"For sure."

"My girlfriend's always worried about the baby. Who'll support her? Support the kids. And my mother will kill me if I go away again."

"I hear you." I couldn't help but have some compassion for this screwed-up kid thinking his mother would be angry with him. I imagined her, tough, with thinning hair and a widening middle, her looks murdered by pregnancies, booze, and worry.

"You got to promise," Victor begged in a loud voice. *Good, be loud,* I thought.

The office door next to mine opened. Paul Lunden came out. Bald, three hundred pounds, and fond of pink Brooks Brothers shirts. No one missed Paul or ignored him. "You okay, son?" he asked Victor as he lumbered over.

"I'm not your son, spook," Victor said, stumbling a bit as he spoke. "Now you really fucked it up, Ms. Zachariah, calling over your boy."

Victor was drunker than I'd thought. Coked up, also, I'd bet.

Paul put his hands up, taking the one-down position. "We can talk this over. Don't want to say things you'll regret, do you?"

"Faggot," Victor said and spit. He slammed me out of the way and pushed his way into my office. Grabbing Ruby by the arm, he swung her in front of him. "You going to talk to me, Ms. Zachariah? Do I have to wait now?"

Ruby screeched as his hand closed around her little arm.

"Aunt Merry!" Cassandra screamed. "Help her."

"You're hurting me," Ruby cried.

"Shut up." The warning seemed meant for all of us. Victor held Ruby with his left hand and circled her throat with his right. "Otherwise I'll snap her neck."

I took a step. "Victor, let her go. We'll see the judge. I promise."

"Sure. I bet. The minute I let go, that fat asshole will be all over me." He pointed his chin at Paul. "You get the judge down here now with something guaranteeing I won't be in jail. In writing. And I want my lawyer. Otherwise you'll be taking home one dead kid."

Paul backed away from the door. "I'll get her. Right now."

"And I don't want the bitch judge. Get me a man. A white man."

Ruby whimpered. Cassandra sat straight and still on her chair, except for sneaking out her foot to touch her sister's.

I ripped the skin of my palms with my nails. I ordered myself calm.

"I understand, Victor."

"You don't understand shit."

"I do. You're angry. You think no one does anything for you and everyone's out to get you."

"It's true. This shit ain't my doing."

29

Lulu

One more red light and I'd start screaming.

Audra's family had kept me at the hospital so long that I was going to be horribly late picking up the kids. Poor Merry would be going crazy waiting for me. Hadn't she said she had a meeting? A hearing? A court something?

Merry had saved me that morning. I'd been too hard on her lately. I steered around a double-parked car on Washington Street, finally only a few blocks from the court.

Persuading her to pick up the kids had been pitifully easy. Within moments of my call, she'd changed clients' appointments and borrowed Valerie's car to get the girls. Maybe Merry thought coming to my aid would help knit us back together.

"Don't worry," she had said. "The girls will be fine."

They'd probably be more than fine. Merry's patience with them outstripped mine by miles, I hoped because being an aunt is an easier job than being the mother, and not because she was nicer.

All these years I'd hounded her about seeing Dad, was she in fact the better person for visiting him while I'd hidden him like a dirty rag? Had I let Dad's actions determine mine for my entire life? Perhaps I'd been his prisoner.

Traffic slowed. Another red light. Christ. I drummed my fingers on the dash, a habit Drew hated.

Audra had decided not to take more cancer drugs. She'd wanted me with her because she couldn't fight her children and the oncologist. Audra needed someone to give her permission to stop fighting.

The light changed. I managed one more block before traffic stopped again. I stepped on the brakes, impatient, bored with my thoughts and my own company. Police cars clogged the street, driving me wild, since the courthouse was practically in sight. An ambulance screeched up from behind. Shootings, murder; this poor neighborhood had every crappy thing. I turned on NPR, but the news depressed me so I switched to an oldies station. Chuck Berry sang "no particular place to go."

I looked at my watch. I had somewhere to go. Merry must be going insane. I'd made her late for her court date, I bet. She probably thought it was my way of saying my job was more important than hers. Did Merry think I spent my life finding ways to put her down?

A crowd grew on the sidewalk and spilled into the street. They had the excited look people get when they're at the fringe of disaster, involved yet safe. Strangers ask each other what's happening, becoming temporary best friends.

I put the car in park and opened my door. I craned my neck, trying to see beyond the Jeep Cherokee in front of me. Horns honked. Stuck drivers screamed, "What the hell? What's going on?"

I peered around, figuring out my options. Fog cast a pall over the already ugly street. To my right an auto repair shop had a full lot. Iron grates that seemed permanently rusted covered the windows of a grocery store. Gawkers appeared to be settling in.

"What's happening?" I yelled repeatedly, trying to catch someone's eye. Finally, a middle-aged woman wearing a bright turban took pity on me.

"Some crazy is holding hostages." She shook her head. "The world's gone mad."

People say that as though the craziness started just today, as though yesterday was all peach pie. I leaned back against the headrest. Christmas music played. Holiday songs drove me nuts, but at least this was one of the less offensive tunes. "Have Yourself a Merry Little Christmas." Pathos at Christmas seemed like the right emotion. Just keep me from the happy jolly holly.

I made tonight's supper in my mind. Turkey meat loaf. Fast, but with the shine of homemade. Drew would appreciate it. How often did he get to have home-cooked food made by someone other than himself? Thank God, Drew had handball and poker, or I'd have driven him crazy by now.

This is 103.3 news on the hour. Reports, still sketchy, on the courthouse hostage situation indicate that a child is being held in the probation department of Dorchester Court—

I turned off the car and got out, running down the street.

"Lady, they're going to tow your car," Turban Woman yelled.

I ignored the warning, ignored everything except checking to make sure my purse hung from my shoulder. I'd grabbed the bag automatically. Medical training. Emergency plans. I might need my license to get in. Doctors get privileges.

Elbows bumped, and people cursed as I thrust my way through the mob.

"Who the hell you think you are, woman?"

"Watch yourself!"

"Hey, you pushed me."

"My kids!" I yelled as the thickening crowd closed off my path. "My kids are in the courthouse."

"We all got people in there, lady." A heavy woman pressed me back with an extra-hard shove.

"My children are being held." My voice hoarsened as I screamed. Just feeling my words might be true gave me the strength to keep pressing forward. "I need to get to them."

No one gave an inch.

"Move, damn it." I pounded on any shoulder or back within reach. "The police are waiting for me." My fist became a battering ram as I bellowed, *"Let me through!"*

Finally, some man, tall, tall as God in the moment, took pity and parted the sea of men and women. "Let her through, people. She needs to get through."

Miracles come from an authoritative tone such as he possessed. I took in his height, a sense of a worn army jacket, an earring glinting in olive skin. A beard?

A gaunt older cop blocked my path when I finally arrived at the courthouse steps, his expression blank and uninterested. "You can't come in, lady."

I huffed, trying to regain my breath. "My kids. My children. In the courthouse."

His face became human. "Girls or boys? How old?"

"Eight and ten," I puffed out. "Girls. With my sister. Probation officer. Meredith Zachariah."

He put an arm out and drew me toward him. "Come with me."

He guided me to a large square room that fed into smaller offices. Another police officer, Hispanic and portly, with guns and hardware hanging from his belt, put his hand on my elbow.

He motioned me to a chair at the far end of the room, when all I wanted to do was kick it over and rescue my girls. Another officer gave me the rundown on what was happening. I shivered as he described the scene, the crackhead holding my babies. I'd kill him. Take one of their guns and kill him.

When they finally moved me farther into the room, in case they needed me for negotiations, I had a sight line to what they pointed out as Merry's office. It was so close I recognized my sister's back. The man came into view. So young. Young, probably high, and thinking that only this moment mattered. Believing he was the center of the entire world.

I saw Ruby and gasped. The young man held her.

"Quiet," the detective in charge said. She'd introduced herself that way, the detective in charge. Dark hair hung in a bob around her face. She seemed too pretty to hold my daughter's life in her hands. "Don't say anything until we instruct you. Remain quiet. See what's on the floor?"

I craned forward, narrowing my eyes until I saw a brass letter opener under the toe of Victor's shoe.

"He held that at her neck earlier," the detective in charge said. "Stay calm or we can't have you here."

I peered harder, concentrating on the open office door. Merry stood at the entrance; Cassandra sat ramrod straight on a chair on the outside of the desk. Ruby, my poor Ruby, he pressed close to his body, one hand around her neck. The silent room allowed me to hear their words.

"I thought these were your kids," the man, really a kid, said.

"My nieces, they're my nieces." Merry's firm tone sounded unfamiliar.

"You lied to me?"

"I never lied to you, Victor."

Did Merry know what she was doing?

"What then? You playing with words?"

Had he tugged Ruby tighter to him?

"You willing to fuck with her life?" he said.

The police officer, not the detective in charge, placed a hand on my shoulder.

"Victor." Merry sounded sincere, calm.

"My mother will kill me." Tears clogged his voice. I listened for hysteria.

"I'll talk to your mother," Merry said. "I'll explain."

"You're just shining me on. You don't give a shit about me."

He toyed with Ruby's braid. Nervous, unspent energy. I stopped breathing.

"No one cares about me. Maybe my baby will. But you're locking me up, so it don't matter. You think I'm just another fuckup. Everyone does."

"No, Victor." Merry knelt lower, squatting next to Victor. "Do you mind? My legs hurt. You want to rest? We can both sit." My sister lowered herself to the floor and crossed her legs. I held my breath.

The man sank down with Ruby between his legs, placing his hands on my baby's shoulders, no longer grabbing her neck. Ruby winced. He must have been pressing deep into the little bones on either side.

I crossed my arms and dug my fingers into the soft flesh under my sweater. I wondered if the police had reached Drew. I wondered if I'd ever hold Ruby again. Cassandra strained to see me, her eyes wide and terrified.

"You'll get out of this okay, Victor," Merry said. "I can help."

"Fuck it. Game's over." This man, this boy, he rested his head on top of my baby's head, even as he squeezed her bones. "I might as well take myself out."

"Tell everyone to stand down," the detective told the man at her side. "No suicide by cop."

"Don't talk like that, Victor," Merry said. "You have hope. Listen to me. I do this work because I care about you guys."

He snorted. "Sure you do."

Merry leaned forward, as though the two of them were cozying up for a long chat. "Why do you think I ride you so hard? Because I don't want you becoming a hopeless man."

Now my sister sounded teary. Play or real?

"What do you mean?"

"I mean I want you to be okay. I want all my guys to be okay." Merry clasped her hands together in a prayerful position. "I understand you. I came up worse than you."

"Yeah. Sure." He crossed his arms over Ruby, as though hugging her, as though she were his. "I'll back out of here. I'll use the kid as a shield. That'll work, right?"

"No, Victor." Merry leaned her elbows on her knees. "You're gonna hurt yourself."

"Nah. I'll make it." He moved his hands around Ruby's waist, readying himself to pick her up.

"Get him," I said to the detective. "Go get him."

She turned to me and whispered, "His rap sheet includes choking, assault with a gun butt, smacking his girlfriend's head into concrete. Stabbing. We want this to go peacefully. Your sister's doing well."

"Your baby needs a daddy," Merry said.

"Who'd want a piece a shit like me for their father?"

I couldn't take my eyes off the brass letter opener. Was his hand moving? Were his fingers twitching? Was Merry watching?

"Children love their daddy. No matter what."

Victor ignored her, running his hands over Ruby's arms, shaking his head. He started to cry.

"My father's in jail, Victor," Merry said. "And I love him."

He looked up. "Your father's in prison?" He put Ruby in a loose headlock and stretched forward. "Fuck that. You're lying."

"It's true. My father killed my mother. Then he tried to kill me. It ruined

271

my life." Merry sounded as serious and honest as I'd ever heard her. "Here. I'll show you."

Merry moved her hand to the neck of her sweater and tugged down, revealing her ugly scars. "Do you want to ruin your baby's life?"

He didn't say anything, just kept staring at the angry ridges marking Merry's chest. She released her sweater and once again hid her scars.

"I see my sister out there. Their mother." Merry nodded at Ruby and Cassandra.

For a moment, his bloodshot eyes looked out, searching for me.

"She never told these girls what happened, because of her shame and anger. She said her father was dead. They're just finding this out right now, this very minute. Right, girls?"

Ruby and Cassandra nodded. Shock covered their pale faces. Even a monster could see they weren't lying. Victor's hands lay limp on Ruby's shoulders as he stared at my sister.

Merry started to get up, stopping and leaning on one knee. "I stuck with him because someone had to. I visit him in prison. Even though I hate going," she confessed. "I work with you so your baby doesn't end up visiting you in jail. My father became an old man in prison." Merry looked him in the eye. "Don't ruin your daughter's life, Victor."

Victor collapsed on top of Ruby, imprisoning my baby in his arms. Merry reached out and gently pulled the letter opener from under his foot. She rose to her knees and pulled his arms from around Ruby.

"Ruby," I called. "I'm here."

The detective and police officer held me back as I tried to run to my children. I strained against their arms, pulling at their hands, raking them with my nails.

"Wait," they commanded as officers headed toward my girls.

"Ruby," Cassandra yelled. She flew off her chair, knocking it to the floor as she raced to her sister.

Merry took Victor in her arms, rubbing her hand along his back as tears ran down her face.

Cassandra reached Ruby before the police. Ruby leapt into her sister's arms. My daughters wrapped themselves together so tight the officers could only stand before them.

They handcuffed Victor.

They released me.

I entered Merry's office and fell to my knees before my children.

A tow truck had taken my car. Drew had come. Now we were home. The girls were safe. I didn't know if they could ever feel protected again, but at least Drew and I could hold them, watch them, and kiss them as we huddled in the living room.

Chinese food sat on the counter, congealed and cold in greasy white cartons. Sophie had brought the food over. We'd called Cassandra's therapist; she thought watching the news was the right thing. *Let the television lead to discussion,* she'd said. After dinner, we turned on the set and saw Ruby on the screen, clutched in my arms as police led a crying Victor Dennehy away in handcuffs.

"What are they going to do to him, Aunt Merry?" Ruby curled in Drew's arms, touching the edge of her mouth with her thumb, an old habit.

"Put him in jail," Merry answered.

"Will he be locked up forever?" Ruby slipped her thumb into her mouth.

Merry frowned, wondering what the right answer was, I supposed. Where was her honesty now?

"He'll be in jail until he goes in front of the judge." Merry curled herself into a tighter ball on the easy chair. "Then they'll decide. He'll likely be in jail for a long time, but not forever." She looked at me. I was on the couch with Drew. The back of Ruby's head grazed my shoulder as she lay in Drew's lap. Cassandra pressed close on my other side.

"Is our grandfather in jail forever?" Cassandra asked.

Drew snapped off the TV. Ruby's thumb sucking echoed in the silence. "No," he said. "Your grandfather won't be in jail forever."

Cassandra opened her mouth, then closed it, as though not sure what to say. She changed her position from leaning on me to leaning against the sofa arm.

"Why didn't you tell us about him?"

I rested my head against the couch, scratching tiny hearts on Ruby's back. "I wanted to protect you." It was the truest answer I knew.

273

"From what?" Cassandra asked. "From him?"

"No. Not from him. He's in jail."

"Then what?" Cassandra moved to the wooden rocker.

"I didn't want you to know you had such a bad man for a grandfather."

"Is he?" Ruby asked. "Is he a bad man?"

"Of course he is." Cassandra's huff made her sound awful and old. She sounded like Aunt Cilla had sounded so long ago. "He killed Mommy's mother."

"But didn't you ever miss him, Mommy? Don't you ever want to see him?" Ruby looked at Drew and then sat up so she could stare right into my eyes. "Maybe he wanted to say he was sorry."

Sorry doesn't bring back the dead, Ruby my love. I held the words on my tongue, and then swallowed them down.

I came back from putting the girls to sleep in our bed. Drew and I'd spent an hour upstairs with them, and then he'd stayed after they fell asleep. We'd take turns with them until we all went to bed, together, so they wouldn't wake up alone.

I fell on the couch. It looked as though Merry hadn't moved from the chair where I'd left her. I reached over to the coffee table, picked up her glass, and took a long sip of brandy.

"How are you?" Merry asked.

"Numb. How are you?"

"Trying to get numb." Merry placed a hand on her stomach. "I still feel like I might throw up."

"Getting drunk won't help." Even as I spoke, I regretted my words. The last thing I wanted to do right now was criticize my sister. "Sorry. I didn't mean that the way it sounded. You must be a wreck. Maybe more than I am."

"Watching might have been worse than being in the middle of it," Merry said.

I nodded. "Watching was bad."

"Are you angry?"

"At you? It wasn't your fault. I never should have suggested you take them to the courthouse. About saying what you said? It worked, right? But still..." I let the words trail off, not sure how to go on.

Merry squeezed in next to me and put a hand on my leg. "It hurt me. Saying it. Having the girls hear it—especially like that."

"But they're my girls," I said. "I don't know if you can really ever understand."

"They're my nieces. My family. I love them. Ruby's life was in my hands."

"I'm grateful for what you did. But now they know everything." I finished Merry's brandy. "Were you waiting for an opportunity like this?"

"Lulu." Merry pressed a hand to her forehead. "I wasn't revealing your secrets. I had to save Ruby's life. I knew what I was doing. Don't you ever think maybe sometimes I'm right?"

Merry cut me off when I tried to speak.

"Sometimes someone other than you has an answer." She crossed her legs and took my hand. "Sometimes we need to work together. Decide things together. Seeing what happened today, did you learn anything? Did you learn that hiding doesn't work?"

I wanted to go to bed, lie next to Drew, breathe him in, and breathe me out. "I learned what I already knew."

"What?"

"The world isn't safe for us."

30

Merry

The overheated train to Dorchester stopped and started as it left Park Street Station. I unwound my choking scarf and stuffed the fabric in my pocket. I considered skipping the next step in my commute to the court-house—the crowded bus—and walking the twenty blocks. Wet wool smells mixed with the overpowering lime cologne worn by the man pressed close to me. I thought I might throw up from the combination and prayed to hold myself together until the crowd thinned out at U Mass, when I'd travel against the rush-hour tide.

Reading my book was impossible without a seat, so I didn't even try. To occupy my mind, I played little games, memorizing the ads above my head and anagramming the words describing language schools and health careers until I couldn't pretend anymore. The only thing on my mind was how much I didn't want to go back to the courthouse.

I'd been home for a week; we all had. Except for Drew making forays for food and DVDs, we'd not ventured out. The weather had cooperated by providing steady sodden snowflakes. We'd wrapped the girls in blankets on the couch, snuggled close to each other, and lived life movie to movie.

Even Lulu had skipped work, leaving the couch only to take calls from Sophie. I'd spoken to no one, letting voice mail take my calls, letting Colin sort through the messages. I sent Valerie a short e-mail: "Tell everyone thanks for the cards, and let them all know I'm okay."

I wasn't okay.

Day after day, I had held Ruby close and pressed my cheek to her soft hair. Cassandra and Ruby, after a lifetime of poking for every shred of family history they could unearth, spoke not a word about our father. They'd mentioned nothing of consequence for such a long time that we became frightened. Then, suddenly, Lulu had pressed for sharing and unburdening of the soul.

"Cassandra," she'd said, "can you guess what my favorite books were when I lived with Mimi Rubee, when I was your age?"

Cassandra had shrugged. "Not now, I'm reading."

"Ruby," Lulu had tried later, in the middle of a Monopoly game. "Do you want to know the games Aunt Merry and I invented when we lived at Duffy?"

Ruby hadn't even looked up as she grabbed another handful of kettle corn from the bowl. "Can't we just play?"

Lulu and I became partners trying to untangle the mess of deceit while the girls worked to staple all the lies back up. They rejected everything we offered. Having a mysterious imprisoned grandfather who'd murdered a grandmother long assumed car-crashed was apparently less interesting than reading Harry Potter. Everyone—Drew, the girls' therapist, as well as their pediatrician—assured Lulu that Ruby and Cassandra could ingest only teaspoons of the trauma. Lulu wanted to feed them the story whole, wanted them to digest it and move on. And this didn't even touch incorporating Victor into the equation.

Moreover, Dad still waited out there.

"You okay, Ms. Zachariah?" Jesse walked into my office as though the very air was fragile and he had to move carefully to keep the molecules from colliding and causing a catastrophic event.

"Fine, just fine." I leafed through papers on my desk searching for something to distract me from wanting to run away.

"I brought you something."

I looked up, expecting another piece of paper indicating that Jesse had achieved some milestone and needed my celebratory excitement to seal his happiness. He held a thick sheaf of catalogs and offered them to me. Curious, I placed the pile on my desk, reading the title of each one in turn:

New England School of Law

Boston University School of Social Work

Cummings School of Veterinary Medicine at Tufts University

I shuffled the books top to bottom and back again. "You're considering all these fields, Jesse? Terrific." I feared my voice sounded devoid of terrific. I hoped I wouldn't depress poor Jesse back into a life of crime.

"I got them for you, Ms. Zachariah."

"For me?" I turned over the veterinary school catalog, expecting puppies with giant, begging eyes, and saw students who looked about fifteen wearing white coats.

"You need to get out of here, Ms. Zach." He clapped his hands together and pointed them at me. "Not that you can't handle us—look how you did Victor, who's nothing but a mama-boy pussy. Sorry," he added.

"I appreciate your concern, but this isn't about me. Your probation ends in a few weeks. We have plenty of work to do."

"You're right. My probation's ending. I'll probably be the last client who takes your advice for a long time, huh? Why not quit while you're ahead?" He reached into his pocket and brought out a crumpled sheet of paper. "I had to write this for English class. At Bunker Hill. Anyway, the professor said I should show you."

I smoothed out the paper, laid it flat on my desk, and began to read.

MY LIFE-CHANGING EVENT

This is about my probation officer. It's less than the 500 words we had to do (not by much) but I think it should be okay.

Since I was twelve this is what I've done: Did every drug except crack (cause the crackheads around me look like walking scabs.) Banged every girl I could by telling any story they want. Smacked them if they didn't listen. Forced one to get rid of a baby—because I didn't want to be nobody's baby daddy, because I knew I'd be a shitty one just like mine. Pulled my mother off the streets, when it looked like she might die. Let her stay there when I couldn't care enough for both of us anymore. Stole pocketbooks, even off old ladies. Dropped out of school. Almost killed a guy.

Since I got arrested and got put on probation (for almost killing that guy) this is what I've done: Gotten a GED, because my PO made it part of my probation. Stayed straight because my PO made me take urines every week. And made me pay for the damn tests. Got a job, because my PO made it part of my probation. Read books, because my PO made a reading list part of my probation. Ended up here, in Bunker Hill Community College, because it's part of my probation.

Now my probation is ending and I'm leaving Bunker Hill. It's over. I'm done. Now I'm going to Northeastern. Because my probation officer got me the application. She said I made her proud.

In the beginning, my probation officer wrote this on top of my probation plan: "Many persons have a wrong idea of what constitutes true happiness. It is not attained through self-gratification, but through fidelity to a worthy purpose. Helen Keller"

The bitch of it was that I didn't even know who Helen Keller was, and I was too embarrassed to say so, or to let her know I cared that I didn't know. But I made sure to find out—even though I started learning by watching the movie about her. After that, I read her book. Even though it wasn't on the list. That was the first time in my life I ever read anything that I didn't have to. I found out maybe I like reading.

Maybe the quote was my life-changing event. Maybe it was being arrested. Maybe it was being put in a cell long enough to realize I didn't like sleeping on sour-stinking jailhouse cots. I don't ever want to ride that iron horse again.

I don't know if my probation officer done the quote thing for every guy she has, or if she saw something in me. It didn't matter. What mattered is she made me see something in me. She made me ready to find my worthy purpose. So, I guess meeting Ms. Zachariah and having her as my probation officer was my life-changing event.

I looked up. Jesse met my eyes.

"Ms. Zach, you never seem happy," he said. "I don't think this place is your worthy purpose."

Preparing for Quinn to arrive that evening was an angry mix of beauty chores. I sliced open my right leg while shaving. I stabbed myself in the eye with my eyeliner brush. I tugged on sweater after shirt after sweater looking for something that didn't say, *I have absolutely nothing except other people's lives, other people's families, and other people's husbands, so fuck me right here, then go home.* Giving up on men, and most especially giving up Quinn, had once again failed.

The moment he arrived, Quinn asked, "Are you okay?" He held me at arm's length, checking me as though to assess the damage. "I read the article in the paper. You handled the whole thing like a trouper."

"Is that why you called?" I offered him a beer. "To congratulate me?"

"Don't you believe I could worry about you?"

I didn't want to answer. I just wanted to go to bed, and so we did.

As Quinn pounded into me, it became clearer and clearer that whatever my worthy purpose might be, it wasn't Quinn. My excitement dissipated until Quinn must have felt as though he were screwing sawdust. It sure seemed that way to me. My breasts squashed under him as he pressed closer. Quinn's method of forcing out an orgasm, whether I wanted one or not, wasn't working.

Tonight it felt like he banged me out of meanness.

Knowing Quinn's remarkable control, and what he probably saw as dedication to my pleasure, I was aware that, unless I did something, he'd keep at it until I came. We weren't about anything except the sex, so he always wanted to tie that one thing up in sparkling ribbons. I suppose in that way he was loyal.

"Jesus, you fill me up, Quinn," I said, feeling the shudder of excitement in him that my lie brought. I dug my heels into his back and bucked up toward him, drawing him in deeper. I ripped my nails down Quinn's flesh, acting out his whorish fantasies.

Baby, baby, baby.

Oh. Do me.

Quinn wrenched from me a sad orgasm born of friction and time, and then he came.

Did Quinn worry about me? I wondered as he collapsed on top of me. If I died, would Quinn come to my funeral? Could I go to his? Would I dare?

How could I sleep with a man I wasn't sure would attend my funeral? A man whose funeral I had no right to attend? How did I kiss a man I couldn't see buried? "What am I doing here?" I whispered to his shoulder.

"Please, no, Merry. Not again." He struggled up and rolled off me. "I must have told you a million times, we have what we have. If you don't want it, fine, I'll go. I don't do scenes."

True. Quinn had never done scenes, and he'd never lied to me. He'd been the most constant man in my entire life, the most constant one not locked up, though Quinn might as well have been in jail for how much he shared my life.

And I'd picked exactly this man.

31

Lulu

I inched toward Cabot Hospital at three miles per hour, barely able to see through the snow and afraid of ending up in a ditch. A nor'easter was clobbering Boston. The only joy in my life was that Christmas, when we'd had to pretend we were okay for twenty-four hours, was over.

Thirty minutes into my commute, a red light blessed me by allowing me to release my cramped fingers from clutching the wheel. Normally, in thirty minutes I could have driven to the hospital three times. Dense flakes swirled thicker and faster with each passing moment.

The light changed, but the stalled traffic remained unmoving. After sitting trapped in my car for another ten minutes and getting no farther than half a block, I pulled into a near-deserted McDonald's parking lot. I didn't think anybody would bother with my car on a day like this, but just in case, I placed my CABOT MEDICAL DOCTOR ON CALL placard in the rear window and bundled up to walk the final ten blocks to the hospital.

I hoped my electric yellow hat provided enough visibility to stop truckers from mowing me down in the slick, storm-obscured streets. My mother-in-law, a big proponent of "brightening up your face with a little color, honey!" had sent the hat for Christmas. At the time, I didn't imagine ever using it; now I was glad I'd thrown it in the car. I caught a glimpse of myself in the rearview mirror. My face matched the snow, but the hat stood out like a beacon.

A biting wind tugged at my hat as I trudged toward the hospital, my face tucked down. Within moments, the shell of my knee-length down parka turned dark as the coat worked overtime to repel moisture. Fellow travelers wrapped in layers passed me, wet, red faces pressed into chins, all looking like overstuffed moles.

The dank smell of snow-soaked clothes rose from me as I entered Cabot's warm lobby. I nodded at the man selling papers, unwound my scarf, and buried my hat in my purse.

"Happy New Year, Doctor Winterson," the paper man said.

"Same to you, Kelly." I never knew if Kelly was his first name or his last.

"Your girls okay?"

"Doing better, thanks."

Being on the news had made my family public property. That which I'd dreaded my entire life had come true; the newspapers had ripped away my privacy. After their initial traumatized silence, the girls had peppered me with questions about their grandfather and grandmother. They hadn't asked to meet my father, but the day would arrive; which day remained the only mystery.

I tried not to be angry at Merry. Truly, I didn't think I was, but nothing felt the same. Merry had forced my life out of alignment.

The hospice unit of Cabot Hospital, despite signaling impending death, offered more comfort to me than the rest of the hospital. Without machines blinking and hissing and with fewer tubes tangled around beds, a sense of humanity seeped in. Frail and weak as Audra appeared, she looked like a person again, not an experiment in medical carnage.

Audra seemed to be napping, but the moment I walked into the room, her eyes opened. "Doctor," she whispered. She seemed thinned to transparency. "Thank you for coming."

"You don't have to thank me, Audra."

"You've had a rough time." She coughed, then worked to catch her breath. "Your poor daughters."

"Don't worry about the girls. They're fine." I gave her ankle a whisper of a tap.

"And yourself?" Audra reached for my hand, and I offered it to her, careful of her easily bruised skin. "Children bring us closer to God, but sometimes so close we get burned. All my hardest moments, where I truly believed I might die from fright, were around my children."

Seeing that man's hand around Ruby's throat had frightened me more than Teenie's apron soaking up Mama's blood. More than Merry almost dying by my father's hand, and that had almost destroyed me. Without Ruby or Cassandra, I couldn't envision living. People did, but how? What kind of strength did they tap?

How had my father put a knife to his child?

Merry always said she didn't remember anything. I found it hard to believe. Had she screamed and screamed while I got Teenie? Did she see my father kill my mother? Had she watched? Was that why my father tried to kill Merry and himself, to take away the pain of knowing, to erase that picture?

I needed to know.

A washcloth rested in an ice bath. "It's snowing like crazy outside," I said, wringing out the cloth and wiping Audra's lips.

"Open the blinds. I want to see." Audra turned toward the window. After letting in the light, I tucked extra pillows behind her back. The bank of windows revealed the whirling storm. We sat quietly, watching.

"It's so lovely," Audra said. "God's work."

I envied Audra's comfort of faith. "It's lovely when you're not walking in it. I wouldn't mind if God skipped the snowstorms."

"Everything has a place in the universe."

"War? Children dying?" I watched snow melt from the heat of contact and slide down the window.

"Maybe that's what I hope death brings, putting all the pieces of all the puzzles together. Perhaps these things are meant to test us. To separate the wheat from the chaff."

"But why?"

"You know what I've learned?" Audra said. "Dying is easier than watching your children in pain." She looked away from the hypnotic storm and faced me. She placed a delicate finger on my forehead and swept away the stray hairs moisture had unraveled from the rest. "Maybe when we recognize the trivial for what it is, we can concentrate on what we love most, what we most treasure."

Staten Island seemed so ordinary. I guess I'd expected fire and brimstone lining the road to Richmond Prison.

Drew steered the car down a road lined with AutoZone, T.J.Maxx, and gas stations. I tried to picture Merry traveling these roads as a child, as a teenager, as a woman.

Merry hadn't seen our father since he sent the letter announcing his upcoming release. Despite his pleading Christmas card, Merry remained implacable. She wasn't ready to see him and couldn't predict when she would be again. Never, I hoped. After a lifetime of burying her anger in service to our father, seeing the letter opener held at Ruby's neck had broken his hold on Merry, broken it so wide open she wouldn't even write him to explain why she wouldn't go see him.

For me, seeing Ruby in danger had made it imperative to see him.

So here I was.

Drew parked the car in a lot adjacent to the prison. Black wire fencing all around seemed held together by tetanus and rust. Our simple car shone among the scabrous clunkers filling the lot.

"Are you sure you don't want me to come in with you?" Drew turned off the engine.

"I need to do this alone."

He gripped my knee hard. "There's no reward in that. We're a team, Lu."

I laced my fingers to calm my shaking hands and held them to my mouth. Lavender-scented hand lotion couldn't cover the bitter smell of my dread. I had made poor Drew stop at every McDonald's and Burger King on the way to Staten Island, needing constant bathroom breaks for my contracting bladder and tepid ginger ale to calm my roiling stomach.

"If I don't confront this alone, I won't go deep enough. I'm not sure

285

what I'll say, but if you're with me, it might end up being easier just to let you handle the hard parts."

"Would that be so awful?" Drew put a hand on my shoulder. The weight pulled at me with the promise of deliverance. "You've done it alone your whole life, with your father."

I shook my head. "I'm not even sure why I'm here." I'd told myself I'd planned this visit for Merry, to help make up for the years I'd built barriers and left my sister to slam into the walls.

"To face your ghosts?"

"I don't know." I worried the edge of my worn leather pocketbook. I wiped my sweaty hands on my plain black wool pants. Black winter boots suffocated my feet in the hot car. I wore a simple gray sweater. Mourning clothes, it seemed. What did you wear to meet the father who murdered your mother almost thirty-two years before?

What did you talk about?

I had asked Merry.

Anything and nothing. My job. Ruby and Cassandra. You.

My skin iced over knowing she'd brought my girls into the prison. Brought me.

"Talk to me, Lu. Let me help you." Drew placed a warm hand on my leg.

I loosened my grip on myself. "You help me every day." I wove my fingers into my husband's strong ones. "Knowing you'll be here when I come out is all I need."

I started to open the car door, stopping halfway and blurting out the words that had been choking me since 1971. "I always thought Mama dying was my fault."

"Why?" By not rushing to say *oh, no* or tell me *that's impossible,* but instead asking *why?* Drew gave me a present, one more reason to love him.

"When Mama said 'He's going to kill me. Get Teenie....'" I stopped and brought my hand to my mouth.

"Whatever you say is fine. You're fine." Drew rubbed a small circle on my back. "We're fine."

"I waited, Drew. I froze."

"It felt like a long time," Drew said. "But it wasn't."

"How could you know?"

"Because I don't care how old you were, I know you."

"Maybe if I was faster she would have lived."

"No. You couldn't have stopped your father. You were a little kid." Drew hugged me. I felt as frozen as I had that July day when Teenie and I found my mother's body. I barely felt my husband's arms.

I left the car.

Stinging wind hit my face as I walked toward the sign marked VISI-TORS in chipped enamel paint, a faded red on the black metal door. Merry had told me what to expect, yet nothing but seeing this place for myself could make it exist, could make me realize how hard coming here must have been for my sister.

I carried only my license and a small pack of tissues, both tucked in my pocket, as Merry had instructed. She'd warned me about toilet paper running out in the visitors' bathroom. I stood in line behind a skeletal old woman. All fat beneath her flesh had disappeared, leaving her desiccated as a dried apple doll. She clutched a lilac cardigan around her shoulders. Sad, droopy curls covered her head.

She turned to me. "Husband or father?"

"Excuse me?" I asked, shocked by her voice. I'd imagined this scene as a close-up of my father and me. Other characters had never entered the picture.

"Who are you visiting?" She sounded impatient. Perhaps her question was standard procedure. Merry hadn't told me people talked while wait-ing. If anything, I'd imagined invisible walls of shame separating visitors. "Your husband?" she asked. "I've never seen you before."

"My father." People prefer talking about themselves to hearing about others, so I asked a question, presuming she wanted to confess something. "Who brings you here?"

She snorted. "My son. The bane of my existence."

Why was she here for her bane of a son? What had her son done? I had no knowledge of the prison protocols, what the visiting women traded, and it was mainly women here. Coinage mattered in every society, and one had to be aware of the proper trading materials. I nodded as if I un-derstood, while praying the line would move quickly.

"He promised he'd never be back in," she said. My sympathetic nods offered encouragement. "The drugs, they can't shake it once they get hold, am I right?"

"That's certainly true," I agreed.

"You seem like an educated woman. Am I right?"

"I went to college."

"I could tell. So maybe you know what's wrong with this world. Is it just evil?" She patted a curl, seeming reassured by the little roll. "My boy, he sold my rings." She held up her bare hands as evidence. "And yet, here I am. Do we ever learn our lessons?"

I thought of Grandma's eternal loyalty to my father. Would I travel that far down the road for Ruby or Cassandra? "Being a mother demands our whole life, I suppose."

"Oh, it's my turn." Her cherry lipstick smile revealed bright, even false teeth. She patted my hand. "Good luck, dear. Our cross, right?"

Our cross. I touched a gold-glittered macaroni earring, the childhood project made long lasting by Drew. The banes of our existences these men? The word *bane* came from Old English: slayer, murderer.

The guard frowned at me, despite my easy-to-search clothes—no pockets, no cuffs—not acknowledging my good manners or decent clothes, as though no one passing through the prison gates deserved his respect.

He passed me on, and now the only obstacle I faced was seeing my father. I walked forward.

The visiting room reeked of ammonia, reminding me of my month in the morgue, when the odor of formaldehyde had crept into everything I owned. Tables and benches bolted to the floor lined the room. No glass barriers protected me. Merry had warned me that there would be no shield between us and that people hugged, however briefly. A torturous image.

Merry had told me he'd recognize me, he'd seen pictures. I didn't think I'd know him, but I knew him immediately. Though thinner, with his black hair silvered, wearing glasses I supposed he'd made, this man carried the ghost of my young father superimposed over his orange prison clothes. His eyes were too eager, too wide, too starving for the sight of me. I shrank back, wishing for Drew.

288

I walked over resolutely, not giving myself time to stop and think. I crossed my arms over my chest. *Don't come close,* my arms warned.

"Lulu. Oh, Jesus, it's really you. When they told me you were coming, I couldn't believe it." He dabbed his eyes, swiping at them with his prison orange arm. He reached out. I didn't pull away fast enough; he drew me to him and kissed me. His bristly cheek touched mine. He smelled of sanitizer, like the liquid gel we pumped over our hands at the hospital. Had he rubbed this stuff on for me?

"Hands!" a guard called.

My father pulled away. "Not allowed more than a second for a hug here." He smiled. Christ. His eyes, those eyes were eating me up.

Stop looking at me.

"But it won't be long now. Your sister told you, right? That I'm getting out?"

I nodded.

"Cat got your tongue?" He laughed. "It's okay, sweetheart. It's been a long time. I understand."

Sure has been a long time since you killed Mama.

He sat and indicated I should sit across from him. "Right there, honey."

I sat up straight on the backless bench, folding my hands in my lap.

"You didn't come here just to stare at me, did you?" He poked his head forward as he had when I was a child and he was about to tell jokes.

"Knock, knock!" My father tapped his forehead, trying to get me started in our game.

Knock, knock!

Who's there?

Police.

Police who?

Police let us in; it's cold out here!

"You're supposed to say 'Who's there?' remember?" His smile faded a bit.

Knock, knock!

Who's there?

Doris.

Doris who?

Doris locked, that's why I had to knock!

"Is Merry okay? She hasn't called or written. I'm worried." My father drummed his fingers on the wooden table in a nervous, rapid beat. "Jesus, Lu, did you come to give me bad news?"

Knock, knock!

Who's there?

I love.

I love who?

I don't know, you tell me!

"It's time to leave Merry alone," I said.

My father shook his head as though my words didn't compute.

"It's time for her to have her life," I said. "You tried to take it away one way. You failed. Then you managed to do it another way."

"This is why you came?" He appeared ready to cry any moment. I snuck a look at the guard closest to us. He was young, African-American, and had so little expression in his face he could pass for dead. I prayed it was against the rules for prisoners to cry.

"You came to torment me?"

"I came to tell you you're not moving to Boston."

My father's face changed from wounded to challenging. "And you're in charge of where I live now?"

Back in Brooklyn, he'd switch moods that way. *Your father could turn in a New York second,* Mimi Rubee used to say as she massaged white balm into her face, flower-sweetened cream promising smooth skin forever. Merry would already be asleep.

After Mimi Rubee and I finished watching TV, we'd get ready for bed, I brushing my teeth, she chasing away wrinkles. Then we'd talk, feeling safe enough to explore for a few minutes because soon sleep would take us away from the nightmare in which we lived.

Watch out for him.

But he's in jail, Mimi Rubee.

Never mind jail. Until he's dead, his hand will reach out. Underneath it all, your father is a weak man, Lulu. He's a failure who even botched killing himself. Weak men are the most dangerous, and failure makes them worse. Stay away from him. I warned your mother, but she never listened.

"I'm not in charge of anything about you," I said. "But since you're getting out early, you'll be on parole. I'm making it my business to learn all the conditions of that parole. Remember the letters you wanted me to write? You move to Boston, and I'll write letters like you wouldn't believe."

"This makes me very sad," he said. "Forgiveness is the most important quality you can have, did you know that? I've taken seminars in here. Forgiving helps you heal, Lulu."

"Are you even partially serious, Dad?" The word slipped out before I could bite it away. The strange flavor from the past tasted harsh on my tongue.

He clasped the edge of the table, leaning in, straining toward me. "Don't mock me. Look at you. You haven't seen me since your grandmother's funeral, and the first thing you say is to stay away from your sister? Your sister is an angel. I know it helps her, the love she gives me. Listen. I memorized this for you."

Dad held his hand up, warding off my protest. He cleared his throat, exactly as he had when he sang to me back in Brooklyn, and began quoting some parable of prison lore. "'Withholding forgiveness is like being in a prison. The person who will not forgive is the one locked inside the four walls.' Maybe that's not exact, but it's pretty darn close."

The shape of my father's eyes resembled that of Merry's, as did his long lashes. Feminine on him. On Ruby, these same lashes were yet another perfect brushstroke.

The eyes weren't the windows of the soul. I stared into my father's wanting to rip into the backs of them and see what remained. Would it be horrible? Would it look like Merry's doll had when the glass eye fell out, leaving nothing but a terrifying, dark void?

"How do I forgive what you did?" I asked. "How did you forgive yourself?"

"I try not to think about it anymore. It's a closed chapter. I was drunk. I was a kid. I had no clue what I was doing. I've paid for it with my entire life."

"No. Mama paid."

"Your mother is gone. I can't bring her back."

"Where's your remorse, Dad? Where is your sorrow?"

"Don't presume to know me, Lulu."

"How could I? You ripped yourself away. You tore up our lives."

"It doesn't make anything right, but damn it, your mother was no saint," he said. "You haven't come to see me once, Lulu. Not once. You're my daughter."

"Not anymore," I hissed. "Beg God for forgiveness, not me. It's not mine to give. It never was. It never will be."

"Don't you think if I could I'd turn back the clock? Don't you know your mother haunts me? I loved her, I loved her so." He slumped. "Sorry? The word *sorry* doesn't cover what I am."

Feeling pity for my father hurt too much, so I held on to my anger. Moreover, for whom was his sorrow? Was he remorseful that he'd killed my mother or was he regretful for himself?

"I want my family. We have so few years left." My father offered his open hands. "Okay. I have no rights, Lulu. I won't move to Boston, not if you don't want me."

Biting my lip until it became numb, I scratched NO, NO, NO into the soft flesh inside my arm. Swallowing, I finally spoke. "I've put fifteen thousand dollars into an account for you. For when you get out. To start your life. I'll make sure you get it."

For you, Grandma. I promised I'd take care of things, and now I have.

"Can I write to you?" he asked.

"Have I ever been able to stop you?" I rose to leave, my stomach hollow.

He folded his hands. My father. A penitent. My curse.

I walked away, then stopped and turned to face my father. "What color were Mama's eyes?"

"The same as yours, Lulu. Just look in the mirror."

32

Merry

April 2003

I'd stopped visiting my father. After years of being his faithful daughter, his good daughter, the daughter on whom he relied, when I received the letter notifying me of his release, I'd stopped cold.

His letter had turned me to stone. Everything that followed—Victor, my troubles with Lulu—had sent me deep into a place from which I'd had to struggle to come back.

Now, here I was. Back in Brooklyn, looking for my father's house.

Forsythia bloomed along the dense bushes lining the street. Bensonhurst, a Brooklyn neighborhood I'd never visited, seemed made of different brick than the Brooklyn of my childhood. I'd grown up surrounded by the dingy pink buildings of Flatbush. Here the bricks looked redder.

I checked the house numbers as I walked. Slowly. Putting off the moment. Twice I reached for my phone. I wanted to hear Lulu say everything would be okay, not to worry, but I pushed away temptation. I had to comfort myself. Lulu didn't know that I'd come to visit, or even that I'd left Boston at six that morning. If she'd known, she'd have convinced me not to make the trip.

My father killed my mother.

It would be thirty-two years in July.

I'd been five and a half.

Lulu had never visited him.

I always had.

Everything would be okay.

Halfway down the block I spotted my father holding on to a chain-link fence. Seeing him free stunned me. No guard-enforced rules were in place to prevent his hugs or kisses. To-the-minute visiting hours wouldn't limit our time together. I tapped my chest repeatedly, giving myself full freedom to trace my scars through my soft spring sweater. No one plucked my fingers from my father's mark.

His smile grew wider. He dipped his head a few times, motioning *come on, come on*. I dragged myself forward, my steps punctuated by shaky breaths. If my father hadn't been outside waiting for me, I'd have turned and gone back to my rented car.

Finally, appearing impatient, my father unlatched the gate and walked toward me. I looked for signs of prison clinging to him, his gait—did he walk like a man being watched? Did he look nervous, as though too much space was around? All I saw was a graying man with a still-muscular build walking with the stride of a handsome man. Rectangular wire-rim glasses had replaced the Clark Kent frames he'd worn in prison, appearing oddly fashionable, as did the white Gap-looking shirt he'd tucked into a pair of beige chinos.

Grandma Zelda always said my father had been a hoo-ha fashion plate.

"Baby doll," Dad said softly. "Tootsie." He pulled me in for a long, hard bear hug. *Hug back, hug,* I prodded myself. I put an arm around him, forcing him to embrace the lifeless column I'd become. He pressed my rigid arms into my ribs.

"So," he said. "Look at this. Here you are." He kept a hand clasped on my elbow even as he gave up the hug.

"Nice house." I pointed at the ordinary two-family, giving my arm something to do besides not hug him.

He beamed. "I did okay, huh? Come on." He chucked his chin at the bushes. "Forsythia. Brooklyn's official flower."

"I didn't know that." My words felt clumsy, too big for my tongue.

"The apartment I got, it's not bad. Well, you'll see it, of course. It's small. In the basement. An in-law. But, hey, got to start somewhere." He led me down the driveway to a side entrance, opened the screen door, gesturing for me to enter first. "Take the stairs to the left."

A thin carpet runner covered the worn wooden steps leading down.

"Go ahead," he said. "Go in."

I opened the unlocked door to a painfully clean kitchen.

"I rented it furnished, but it's not bad stuff. For now."

"I'm sure everything's fine, Dad." My jaw needed oiling. I'd rusted like the Tin Man.

Black place mats were aligned straight and perfect on a gray-veined Formica tabletop. A chair was tucked underneath the exact middle of each side of the table. Round brass studs held red leather seats to the chairs' metal frames. White enameled cabinets hung over a cracked porcelain sink. The refrigerator and stove looked as though they'd have blocks of ice inside. I'd fallen into a hole in time.

"Here's the rest." He pointed through a doorway, proud, motioning for me to follow. Low-pile rugs covered most of the scuffed wooden floor in the combination living room–bedroom. He'd positioned a tweed daybed and chair at perfect right angles. In the corner, a desk and dresser stood straight with an old trunk between them. Van Gogh's *Sunflowers* hung framed in yellow plastic.

"It came furnished," he reminded me. "But I bought the picture and the trunk."

"You keep it neat."

"Habit. One thing out of place in my cell drove me nuts." He cleared his throat and changed the subject. "Soon I'm going to refinish the floors."

He showed me the small bathroom, which had a faded pink tub and sink and the same linoleum stamped with cabbage roses that covered the kitchen floor. Soap, toothpaste, and a green plastic glass lined the immaculate sink edge.

I made a show of admiring the small pantry holding Lipton soup mix, Froot Loops, and cans of tuna until we went back to the kitchen.

"Sit," he said. "We have lunch."

I touched the place mat lightly with a fingertip, feeling the newness, feeling positive that I was the first to use it, and that I was my father's first guest. He placed two Corelle plates down, white with a thin blue band, and matching cups and saucers. "Do you drink coffee? I can't have anything stronger in the house. Regulations."

I nodded, as though home regulations were the most normal thing in the world. "Coffee's fine. Great."

"How do you take it?" The glass creamer and sugar bowl looked out of place in his rough hands, yet he held them with a shy delicacy.

"Just milk." I tried not to cry at realizing my father didn't know how I drank my coffee.

"This is half-and-half; I'll get the milk."

"No, Dad, don't. Half-and-half would be a treat."

"See? That's what I thought." He beamed as he placed the creamer in front of me. "Look at you, not an extra ounce. Perfect as ever." He swung his arm around to indicate the framed gallery on his wall. An assault of photos hung in collages and individual frames. Every picture I'd given my father, he'd enshrined in wood. Tape marks still showed from where he'd hung them on his cell walls.

I saw my nieces as babies, as toddlers, as six- and ten-year-olds. Ruby in a pink tutu, Cassandra graduating from nursery school. My college graduation. Lulu's wedding. Some looked as though he'd enlarged them. Hours of work were evident on the wall.

"I made the frames myself," he said. "I set up a little shop in the cellar. I'm only half done. My landlady tells me I have the prettiest family in Brooklyn."

"Except we don't live in Brooklyn, Dad."

"But I do, and didn't you all start with me?" He put down a plate of bagels, enough for us to have half a dozen each. "I didn't know what kind you'd want, so I picked some of each. Look, I bought garlic, plain, poppy, and something called 'everything.' That one I don't remember. I don't think they had it before. You pick first," he insisted, as though we might face a shortage.

He went back to the refrigerator and returned with a platter heaped with lox and a pink tub of TempTee whipped cream cheese.

"I haven't had TempTee since Grandma was alive."

"I still feel like I should pick up the phone and call her," my father said. "She never let me down. God knows I disappointed her."

What was he expecting from me? *No, Dad. You were a good son.* "She was good to all of us," I said. "I never relaxed with another adult my entire childhood." I reached for an everything bagel. "Only Grandma."

"Not even me?" he asked.

I held the bagel and knife still. "Are you kidding, Dad?"

"Honey, we saw each other all the time. How could you not be relaxed with me?" My father's eyes begged me to lie. *Please, give me this bit of peace,* he pleaded in silence.

Appetite gone, I put the uncut bagel on my plate. "Dad, why do you think I haven't seen you since December, or was it November?"

"Because of Lulu," he said. "I thought maybe she told you not to come."

Overwhelmed by the desire to rip the framed pictures off the wall and smash each one, I tore the bagel in half, then in half again. "How can you tell yourself these fairy tales?"

"Will we have to cover the same ground over and over now that I'm out?" My father picked up the knife and sawed a plain bagel in half, slowly, millimeter by millimeter until it fell apart, then went for his butter knife.

I reached out and stopped him, placing my hand on his. "Do you have scars?" I asked. "On your wrists?"

My father pulled his arms away, as though he thought I'd grab him and hold him down so I could see for myself. "Why do you have to do this? It happened so long ago."

I stood and undid the top two buttons of my baby blue sweater, which I now realized was all fluffy angora and little-girl cute. I pulled the left side off my shoulder. "Do your scars look like this?"

"Stop. Please." He came toward me. I backed away.

"You've never even seen my scars," I said. "You've never seen what you did, Daddy."

"I don't have to see them, baby. I live with what I did every single day."

"No. I do." I closed my eyes, determined that I'd scrape the skin off my arms before I let myself cry. "I felt as though I were locked up in jail with you. When I wasn't visiting, I was thinking about you being in there or dreading the visits because they terrified me, or feeling so guilty about dreading them, I'd write you a letter. And in all that time, only once did you tell me you were sorry."

"Didn't you know? I'm always sorry. Baby, I was just a kid when it happened."

"No. You were twenty-eight. I was the kid."

"What do you girls want from me? How can I make it up? How can I get you to understand how much I need you both, how much I love you? I want my family," he begged. "Please, sweetheart, you've always been there for me. Don't do this to me now."

"When were you there for me?" I pulled up the shoulder of my sweater and leaned forward. Every beat of my pulse thudded in my ears.

"Didn't I at least try?" he asked. "I kept up with your schoolwork, your boyfriends, your career—I cared about everything you did; it all interested me. Every report you wrote and all the drawings you sent, the cards, the poems; I have your entire life in there." He pointed through the doorway.

My father made fists of his trembling hands and rested his head on them. I wondered if trying mattered, knowing, whether it did or not, his pain splintered my soul.

My father was right; he did have my entire life. He owned it.

"Okay, Dad," I said. "It's okay. I'm just suggesting you think about it, understand why it's not something we can put away as easily as you'd like."

I picked up my mangled bagel and spread TempTee on top, not knowing what I could do for him at this point, except eat the bagel.

"It's all there," he said. "In my desk. Every single thing you wrote. Do you want to see?"

"Really. It's okay, Dad." I choked a piece of bagel past my dry throat and into my clenched stomach. "Never mind." *Please stop talking, please stop, please stop.*

"You think I'm a monster, but I'm not. Do you understand? It's late, but, please, I can still help you."

His eyes were mine.

My father was a limited man. He'd never grow. I could only hope to learn how not to hate him immoderately or love him too much. I needed to make my father life-size.

I pressed my fingers against my mouth. My father had robbed me of so much. My mother. My family. A life I wanted hovered in the distance of my imagination, but being in his home, staring at his eyes, my eyes, I had neither the cowardice nor the courage to leave. And someday Lulu's daughters might ask to meet their grandfather, and even if my sister managed to take them, she'd only have room for her rage.

"It's a good bagel, Dad, the everything. I like it."

He gave a shaky smile. "You never had it before?"

I shook my head. "It's new to me." One more fib. One more lie. One more present for my father. Lulu would probably think I was weak, but doing it felt right for me.

He reached out and took one. "Then I'll try it. On your recommendation, Sugar Pop."

A few months later, I'd moved to New York. Park Slope, where I'd found an apartment, felt like Manhattan with elbow room.

Brooklyn? Lulu had said. *You're moving to Brooklyn!* She'd said this as though we'd escaped the pogroms of Russia only to have me move back to the rubble-strewn town we'd left behind. Perhaps she spoke the truth, but at least I'd moved to a much-improved area of Brooklyn, many steps up from where we'd lived. I'd escaped the hovels.

I carried groceries, enjoying scuffing through the October leaves as I walked home. Sycamores lined my street, broad-trunked and protective. Traditional Brooklyn brownstones were everywhere, looking like prosperous men, proud of their portliness. Past owners had sliced most of the old buildings into apartments and co-ops, though occasionally you could peek through a lit window and see an original home, grand in its massive rooms and luminous wood panels struck gold by crystal chandelier light.

I climbed the stairs of the brownstone where I'd bought a second-floor co-op with Drew and Lulu's help. My four rooms embraced me. Deep mahogany shutters kept out the wind. Other times, open, they let the sun outline the intricate parquet floor patterns. One piece at a time, I'd discovered secondhand furniture that fit perfectly. The couch I'd bought new, covering the deep jewel red with sapphire blue cushions.

My father had found a burled-wood bookcase put out for trash and managed to see the beauty under its layers of filth. Three weeks ago, he'd lugged over the finished project using the van from the optical shop where he worked, presenting me with a redone piece so shiny with polyurethane he'd most likely ruined its value as an antique.

I unpacked my groceries and lined them on the open shelves my father had painstakingly painted to match the couch cushions. We had dinner together once a week. Sometimes we went to restaurants. My choices, tiny ethnic finds; his, Brooklyn steak joints. We'd always finish the night with a movie. My choices, weepy dramas; his, musicals. More often he cooked, another of his growing list of avocations: Northern Italian cooking, refinishing trash, twisting wire into intricate miniature figures, anything in this world he could do to make me happy, except talking about the past. That he wouldn't do, though occasionally, when he wasn't aware of it, he'd lapse into a memory of the four of us and feed me a story scrap on which I'd dine for weeks.

I placed take-out sushi on a pebbled glass plate and poured cranberry juice into a tall tumbler. Grabbing a textbook and a highlighter, I sat at the small wooden table I'd found in an antiques store on Atlantic Avenue.

I lived my life working, studying, and seeing the new friends I'd made. My visits to Cambridge were infrequent, though not so much that I felt a stranger when I did go. I needed time to build barriers between Lulu's beliefs about me and the growing newer me. She needed time to remake a family that didn't include me always half in and half out. I needed to become an aunt, a sister, a sister-in-law, not a hungry child pressed up against the glass of Lulu's world.

I had planned to come to New York to work with victimized children or women. So many dream clients had been available: children of torture, rape victims, and hopelessly battered women. When I found an agency of last hope specializing in milieu therapeutic visits for surviving sons and daughters of murdered parents, I thought I'd arrived home. I'd read their literature as though I were Madame Curie discovering radium. In the process, I learned I'd grown tired of feeding on my own guts and decided I didn't have to pay for the sins of my father anymore.

Now I worked in a cool, quiet art gallery. They required only a pretty face and a steady hand to give out brochures, leaving me plenty of time to study as I sat at the reception desk wearing the approved black sheath or suit. Along with a surplus of damaged people, I discovered that New York City had fast-track programs for career changers. Within a year, I'd have my certification to teach in an elementary school.

I turned the page of a text on child psychology as I dipped a California roll in ginger and soy. My father insisted on giving me almost half his paycheck each week, for tuition, joking that it was about time he paid for his kid's college. Each time he made the joke, I thought of my mother. I wondered if Mama could see me. What would she think of the arrangement my father and I had built? Would Mama want me to take the money?

Before leaving Boston, before making my final decision, I'd spent a night trying to feel Mama, asking her to come and tell me what to do about Dad. When Mama remained silent, I'd taken her silence as consent.

Mama would want me to change.

Mama would definitely want me to take the money.

Sometimes I looked at my life and got queasy—no husband, no kids, no boyfriend, just my father and me. Was this everything Lulu had feared? At those times, I'd hop online and search dating sites. I'd twitch for a Jack Daniel's.

Then I'd calm down and remind myself for everything there is a season. This was my healing season. Eventually the leaves would all fall and new leaves would grow back.

I savored my dinner. Soft jazz surrounded me. I highlighted more passages in my book that would help me understand my future students. Afterward, I'd call Lulu just to say hello.

33

Lulu

December 2003

I parked next to an old black Cadillac Seville, then walked the half a block to Aunt Cilla's house, thinking how different old Brooklyn cars were from those in Cambridge. Instead of fifteen-year-old rusting Civics, Brooklyn had hulking Cadillacs with busted taillights. I'd rented a car at the airport. Merry would have lent me hers, but I hadn't yet told her I was coming to New York. It was a sunny December day, Merry's thirty-eighth birthday. I wanted to surprise her.

A shiny Toyota Avalon sat in Aunt Cilla's driveway. I opened the door to the glass-enclosed porch, surprised it was unlocked. The porch was empty, maybe because no one used it in the winter or maybe because no one ever used it. I announced my arrival with the hanging brass knocker, banging until I heard footsteps.

An age-spotted hand pulled aside the lace curtain on the entry window. Aunt Cilla peered at me with suspicious eyes.

"Lulu?" she asked. I recognized her immediately, even though she looked every year of her age and more. Her face had sagged into the bull-

302

dog shape at which it had always hinted. Her body had taken on the contour of so many older women, sticklike legs and too-skinny arms stuck into a fat Mrs. Potato Head middle.

"It's me, Aunt Cilla."

She opened the door and stared. "You look like your father's side. Like his father."

"Right. My grandfather."

"Merry, your sister, she looks like your mother."

"I know." I hoped my smile was sarcastic enough for her to see through her thick glasses.

"She hasn't visited me once since she moved here. Even though she lives in Brooklyn. She called Arnie."

I nodded as though Aunt Cilla had made a modicum of sense. Merry had dinner with Cousin Arnie once a month. It was difficult to picture him now a stockbroker.

"Come in," Aunt Cilla said. "Uncle Hal wanted to be here, but he's at work."

Probably still ashamed of dropping us off as though we were so much trash.

"I can't get him to retire," she said. "Tell me, who goes to a shaky-handed old dentist?" She wiped her hands on her faded, green-checked apron.

"Shaky old women with false teeth?" I offered.

Aunt Cilla clicked her tongue. "Still with the fresh mouth, even after all these years."

She held out her arms for a hug. I held my breath, leaned in, and gave her my Oprah hug. *God, Lu, I can always tell when you don't want someone touching you*, Merry said. *You give the same hug Oprah does when the guests are too starstruck and she needs to keep her distance.*

"So, can you have lunch? Or are you just going to grab everything and go?" Aunt Cilla steered me inside. "Hal brought the boxes from the attic."

We walked into her kitchen. The high-gloss appliances and expensive-looking walnut cabinets were an uncomfortable contrast to Aunt Cilla's aged face. Her old kitchen, the one I remembered from childhood, had been the blond wood that was then the height of fashion. I remembered my mother snarling at my father the entire weekend after she'd seen Uncle Hal's remodeling job.

The table was set with Mimi Rubee's china. That I also remembered. Mimi Rubee had given the service to Aunt Cilla soon after my grandfather died. Mimi Rubee didn't want the old-fashioned Haviland, festooned with pictures of dancing maidens, garlanded with green and gold. My mother had hated the dishes, as attached to modern as Mimi Rubee, both of them buying white melamine stamped with turquoise starbursts.

"Arnie keeps hocking me for these." Aunt Cilla shook her head. "A grown man who collects plates. I should give the whole service to you. If you don't like it, you can put it away for your daughters."

I started to protest, worried Arnie would feel sidelined. Merry had told me he hid being gay from Aunt Cilla. Instead, I looked at my aunt and said, "I'd love them."

She seemed taken aback. Clearly, it had been a hollow offer.

"In fact, I can come back tomorrow and wrap them."

"I better wait, I need to ask Arnie." Her words trailed off as she took a platter from the refrigerator.

I could have rescued her, but I didn't. "I'll tell the girls. They'll be so excited. Why don't you box the dishes up and ship them to us? On the other hand, perhaps I should have Merry come and pick them up. How would that be?" Would it be pushing it if I offered my father's services in carrying the dishes out?

"Your mother's boxes are in the living room." Aunt Cilla slammed a plate of chopped liver and egg salad on the table. "You can look through them after we eat. See what you want. Make your decisions."

"I don't have to decide. I'm taking everything."

Aunt Cilla placed her hands on her hips and pulled herself up to her full shrunken height. Like so many women of her generation—didn't I treat them, didn't I know?—she showed the signs of osteoporosis and someday would be pocket-size. "If you take it all, what will I have to remember my sister?"

"You've had years to memorize everything, Aunt Cilla. Anyway, how do I know what you put in the cartons and what you kept?"

"Are you accusing me of stealing? Of lying?" She held a hand to her chest. Diamond rings cut into her plump fingers. "How dare you? See, this is what comes of trying to be nice. I wanted to start fresh, like Arnie said I should. Why would I steal from you?"

I took a giant scoop of chopped liver and smeared it on a piece of rye bread, licking the excess from my fork. "Mmm. Good." I covered the chopped liver with a piece of lettuce and folded the bread into half a sandwich. "Why would you do that to me? I don't know, Aunt Cilla. Why would you abandon me to an orphanage?"

I packed up the car as soon as I'd choked down the thick half sandwich, Aunt Cilla watching with pursed lips as I chewed. We had stayed silent as I carried six cartons to the car. I waited for some milk of human kindness to overtake me after carrying the last box out. Uncle Hal had labeled it "personal items," inking the words over the prestamped DAWSON DENTAL SUPPLIES.

I stood by my rented car, looking back at Aunt Cilla. She pulled her sweater tighter with one hand as she held open the front door, waiting. I walked to the driver's side, opened the car door, and inserted the key, feeling Aunt Cilla watching and waiting, maybe expecting me to come back and hug her. Kiss her.

Two sad little girls had once waited and waited for someone to take care of them.

The engine caught, roared, and I drove away.

Driving to Park Slope from Mill Basin took about thirty minutes. Block by block things changed. My aunt's suburban-looking street turned to the busier Avenue N. When I hit Flatbush Avenue, I saw the Brooklyn of my childhood. The area grew shabbier and darker. Storefronts were crowded with piles of cheap offerings, discount giant bottles of strangely named shampoos, rayon shirts in wild colors, dresses stiff with sizing, made to last until the first washing.

My children would like this—seeing my childhood—but it was too close to my father. I needed more miles between him and here to feel safe.

The girls asked to see their grandfather once in a while. Now, I no longer told lies. I simply said no. Someday perhaps they'd visit him anyway, but while they were under our watch, Drew's and mine, we'd keep them away from him.

That was my plan. On occasion, Drew broached the subject, and, when he did, I tried to explain myself to him. I listened as he spoke. I forced out words for him as my heart banged away. I loved my husband. I couldn't afford to love my father. I'd never give up what little peace I'd gained.

As I approached Prospect Park, life spread out, the architecture allowing breathing space around people. The Park Slope streets looked green with trees and new money.

Merry's street had no driveways. I crammed into a parking spot between a Matrix and a Prius. I reached into my bag and took out my cell, pressing her speed dial number, the first in my phone.

Merry came out and ran across the street.

We hugged and kissed. She seemed as though she'd known for weeks that I'd arrive, rather than the fifteen-minute warning I'd given. She wore lipstick and velvet.

It took us three trips to get the cartons up to her second-floor apartment, both of us sweaty afterward despite the December chill. A pot of chili simmered on the stove, lending warmth and spice to the air. Perfectly glazed challah sat on a brick red earthenware plate.

"Look at the miracle," I said. "You finally learned to cook."

"No. Dad did."

I studied my sister's face. Was she waiting for a reaction? However, she simply looked Merry. Piquant. Rock-star pretty. She seemed sweet, like she had when she was little. She'd lost her clenched edge.

"Good that he's finally useful," I said. I'd never told Merry I'd given him the fifteen thousand. She'd told me about the tuition he paid and the furniture he made, but none of it made me want to see him, not even a little. The only difference was, I finally didn't care that Merry did. "Let's see what we have in here."

I sat on the floor next to the pile of boxes, looking for the one I'd asked Uncle Hal to label especially for me. "Here. This one's for you. Happy birthday."

I watched as Merry slit open the tape Uncle Hal had aligned so carefully. After removing a layer of crumpled newspaper, she uncovered a black onyx box inlaid with mother-of-pearl. She looked up, the box clutched in her hands, tears filling her eyes.

"Don't start crying yet," I said. "You have more to unwrap."

"Help me."

I scooted over and reached into the box, pulling out another newspaper-wrapped object, surprised at the weight I'd forgotten. Under the paper, I stroked the stone, as smooth and cold as it had always been. "I have the one you gave me on my dresser," I said. "I thought we'd divide the rest of these."

"Remember how we played with them?" Merry opened another and held the box to her cheek. This one had a vein of intricate silver running in a circle.

"Mama called it playing. Actually, we were cleaning them for her."

"Still, it was nice." Merry looked dreamy, remembering things I didn't think possible. "Especially in the summer, when they felt so good. Remember how we rubbed them up and down our arms and said they were our cooling stones?"

"Afterward we'd be filthy. All that dust." Little gritty dirt balls had covered our bodies, even between our toes.

"Mama always made us take a bath right after." Merry stretched her legs, keeping a hand on a box.

"Then she'd wipe our arms and chests with the alcohol."

"No, she did that before we went to bed," Merry said.

"No, she did it after our bath, when we'd be all hot from the water."

"After the bath she'd put on powder."

I shook my head. "You're so wrong."

Merry got up on her knees and dusted off her hands. "Actually, I might be right."

"Maybe," I said. "But I doubt it."

Merry laughed and reached for another cardboard box. "Do you know what's in here?"

"The rest is all a surprise," I said. "I told Aunt Cilla we wanted everything of Mama's; that I was taking her things home. For you and for me. I think we're ready and I think it's time."

Acknowledgments

Before offering thanks to those who helped with this book, let me say this: I wish this story were science fiction instead of realism. For ten years I worked with men who, like Merry and Lulu's father, destroyed their families—men who weren't monsters, but who did monstrous deeds. This book is for their children, the ones who suffer unnoticed, and for all amazing men and women who dedicate their lives to helping these children. You may never know whose life you've saved. Thank you Federation of Jewish Philanthropies, Doris Bedell, and Camp Mikan for the gift of childhood.

Thank you Stéphanie Abou, golden agent extraordinaire, who provided everything I needed, including joy, wisdom, and friendship, and thank you Foundry Literary + Media for making me feel cared for and special. Thank you everyone at St. Martin's Press for being supportive and kind, and for gifting me Hilary Rubin Teeman, the extra-insightful, smart-as-a-whole-college editor, whose judgment I treasure. For the design and production team, and especially for copy editor Susan M. S. Brown, all I can say is wow! To Steve Snider and the art department, thank you for drawing my imagination. And thank you Sphere Publishing, in the United Kingdom, for welcoming me so thoroughly, especially my brilliant and warm editor, Jo Dickinson.

Merci, Editions Calmann-Levy in France, *danke* Diana Verlag in Germany, *bedankt,* Uitgeverij Artemis in Holland, and תורה, Kinneret in Israel; thank you all for taking Merry and Lulu worldwide.

One million hugs to Jenna Blum, my lucky star, wonderful friend and teacher, and to all the beloved council, now and before: Amin Ahmad, Christiane Alsop, Nicole Bernier, Edmond Caldwell, Cecile Corona, Kathy Crowley, Elizabeth de Veer, Stephanie Ebbert Devlin, Elizabeth Gallagher, Chuck Garavak, Leslie Greffenius, Iris Gomez, Javed Jahngir, Ann Killough, Henriette Lazaridis Power, Elizabeth Moore, Necee Regis, Dell Smith, and Becky Tuch. It would be impossible to find a better group of writers and critiquers. May we always keep forming and reforming.

One million kisses to the group: Ginny DeLuca (who read and critiqued every version of this book,) Susan Knight, and Diane Butkus, BFF, you are as much family as friends, and to Nina Lev for listening to me talk about my imaginary friends as we walked the pond year after year.

To the superb writers of The Splinters: RJ Bardsley, Chuck Leddy, Leslie Talbot, Len Sparks, Kate Wilkinson, Jill Rubenstein, and Paul Parcellin, who gave me courage and shared their wisdom.

Thank you Grub Street! What would any of us do without you—fearless leaders and brilliant writers Chris Castellani, Whitney Scharer, Sonya Larson, and Whitney Ochoas. You make a home for us!

And to my family: Becca Wolfson, Sara, Jason, and Nora Hoots, Jill Meyers, Nicole Todini, Jeff, Morris, Jeanne, Bruce and Jean Rand: I hold you all in my heart. And, in memory of my mother, Joyce Cherlin, this book is yours as well as mine.